Not a Mourning Person

Potions and Passions
Book 2

CATHERINE STEIN

ISBN: 978-1-949862-06-5

Book cover and interior design by E. McAuley:
www.impluviumstudios.com

To my parents,
for instilling in me an abiding love of books and words.
You were my first and best teachers. I love you.

I

The Book of Love

London
May, 1884

$\mathcal{R}$ACHAEL HAD NO INTENTION of dressing like a tiresome, old crone simply because she was in mourning. To be honest, she had mourned the loss of her situation for the first few months, but since then she hadn't been able to bring herself to feel the slightest bit glum. She'd never mourned the man himself. He'd gotten what he deserved. It was nearing two years since he had died, and she was quite ready to be done with the entire thing.

If her late husband had had the sense to die in public, she would be almost out of blacks by now. But, no. He'd been unceremoniously dumped in the Thames, never to be seen again.

Things would have been simpler if she'd been able to tell the police exactly who had rid the world of the odious man and how. She would never breathe a word of that story. Her friends had the decency to have entrusted Rachael with the truth, and she wouldn't repay them with disloyalty.

In the end, she had struggled through months of paperwork

before Fasching was declared dead. Thank God for good lawyers—and possibly fabricated evidence—or she might still be waiting.

Rachael made a circuit of the ballroom, nodding to acquaintances, giving the assembled crowd a good, long look at her newest dress. Her feet moved in time to the floating melody of a waltz, though she wouldn't dance tonight. She had come to see and be seen. The sensational widow appearing in society for the first time in months. An exhibition of beauty and fashion, bathed in the warm glow of top-quality potion lamps.

She found herself an unoccupied corner and lounged against a spindly-legged side table, flaunting her bare arms, an expression of disinterest masking her thoughts. She didn't need to look to know eyes had followed her. Her dress was scandalous. It was black, naturally, but in a fine silk that shimmered in the light and fell to the floor in an elegant drape. Its plunging neckline showed her ample bosom to great advantage, while the stiff whalebone frame kept everything in place and emphasized her narrow waist. It also rendered the tiny jeweled straps superfluous.

Rachael adored everything about the dress, and knew she looked stunning. She did not, however, look respectable. The whispers had already begun. Excellent. People were certain to talk about her the next day. Tonight, though, few dared approach her.

"Rachael! Lovely to see you."

Her head swiveled toward the familiar voice. Well. She hadn't expected to see *him*, of all people.

"Mr. Ainsworth." She gave him a perfunctory nod, belied by her genuine smile.

Henry strode directly to her, blue eyes twinkling with mischief, drawing too close for propriety, as their friendly game dictated. He even had the temerity to pull up the strap that had slipped off her shoulder. "You don't happen to know where

I might procure a decent cup of tea, do you?" he whispered seductively in her ear.

"You'd like that, wouldn't you?" Rachael replied aloud.

"Very much so." He gave her a roguish smile.

"Upon whom are you spying tonight?" she inquired, using their proximity to speak privately.

"I'm not at liberty to say."

His usual response.

"You must be working. You and Elle don't attend high society parties. Where is your charming mistress, by the way? I can't imagine you would go out without her."

"My *wife* is in the kitchen, checking that the food isn't poisoned."

"Oh, have you married her, then?"

He gave her a hard look. No, of course he hadn't. They seemed to enjoy flouting convention. Rachael could respect that.

"You suspect tainted food this evening?" she asked. She had thought such repugnant scenarios were behind her, since her husband had died.

"Not at all. Elle is taking precautions. We don't wish our children to grow up without a father."

Rachael's brows rose. "Children? Gad, Henry, have you gotten her with child again? You breed like rabbits. I can't understand it."

"Elle spent most of her life missing her beloved family. If she wants to build one of her own, I'm not going to deny her that."

"Ha! You are simply eager to surround yourself with a horde of willful females."

His grin transformed his face from ordinary to handsome, and Rachael was struck with a pang of regret. She ought to have married him eight years ago.

"Willful females are my favorite sort," Henry chuckled. "Which is no doubt why we are friends. And now, I'm afraid I shall have to take my leave of you. If I linger too long, everyone will begin to wonder who the devil I am. But I will say, before I go, that your dress is smashing, and you must tell Elle who made it for you. I want to see her in something similar."

His cheeks went pink, and his grin turned bashful. Probably embarrassed by his own lurid imagination. Ridiculous man.

Rachael offered him her hand, and he bowed and kissed it.

"Good evening to you, Mrs. Fasching."

He vanished into the crowd, and she took up her pose once again, though now she scanned the room, watching and thinking. His formal departure irked her. Every time someone spoke her married name, her ears burned and her muscles clenched. She could never fully be rid of the loathsome man until she shed that name.

Unfortunately, her father had involved himself in the same criminal scheme as her husband. His disgrace meant she couldn't use her maiden name, either. She was stuck until she remarried. Perhaps it was time she did just that.

Her eyes sought Henry, thinking again about what might have been.

No, she chided herself. *We are best suited as friends.*

They would have been tolerably happy, she was certain, but not violently so. Tolerably was no longer good enough. She'd seen too much these past years. She knew, now, the depths love could reach, the things it could drive a person to. She wouldn't settle for ordinary affection, or a mere infatuation. She wanted mad, passionate love, of the sort that inspired all the worst poetry, and some of the best.

There was the small matter of how she would attain such passion when her own heart was hard as iron, but Rachael pushed the thought aside. Hard hearts went hand-in-hand with stubborn temperaments. She would put her willful disposition to good use.

Rachael abandoned her table and strode into the center of the room with all the confidence and hauteur of royalty. She was decided. She would find herself the man with the deepest, most passionate heart in all of London and woo him until he fell at her feet in adoration.

Unfortunately, no such men were in attendance tonight.

After an hour of meaningless flirtations, Rachael insinuated herself into a conversation with several women who were discussing the current fads in poetry. Isobel, her cousin and confidant, was a great devotee of the poetic arts. Rachael had tagged along to lectures and readings during the months they had lived together, and had been pleasantly surprised to find she enjoyed it.

"I have my own copy at last," sighed a pink-clad young thing who had been introduced as Miss Meredith Helmsley. The girl clutched a slim volume to her chest. "Have you read it, Mrs. Fasching? It is shocking, but, oh, so delightful."

"You refer to the book of supposed Anglo-Saxon love poems? I have not, though I hear it is all the rage."

"And rightly so! I cannot believe you haven't read it. I very near swooned the first time I did."

"I'm not one for swooning, Miss Helmsley. I'm more easily swayed by scholarly reviews than general clamor, and the consensus among the scientific-minded is that the book is no more than an elaborate hoax."

"It can't be. The passion in these words runs so wild, it can only be the product of an ancient, untamed warrior." She shoved the book at Rachael. "Here, you must read it for yourself. I will return, but first I am due to have a dance with Lord... um... oh, someone or other. The handsome one they say seduced Lady Ellerby's parlormaid. Ta!"

"Well."

Rachael glanced down at the book, running her fingers over the gilded lettering. *Love in the Age of the Warrior: An Anonymous Translation into Modern English of Newly Discovered Romantic Anglo-Saxon Verse.* Ridiculous. She flipped it open and scanned the first few pages.

The conversation continued, but Rachael couldn't have said what they were discussing. Her world dwindled to the verses in her hand. They were mesmerizing, seductive, and profoundly, breathtakingly emotional. Rachael's skin grew hot, and her palms began to sweat.

Miss Helmsley was wrong. These words weren't the product of an ancient barbarian. They were something infinitely better.

· · · ❦ · · ·

The bell above the door jingled as Rachael stepped inside her favorite potions shop. She waved at Marie, the petite French spitfire behind the counter, and hurried to the back room, rapping firmly on the closed door. Elle answered promptly.

"Special request?" she wondered.

"Something of the sort. Is your husband here? I stopped by your house, but was told he is out."

"He is mapping some new serum sources just outside town. I assume he will be back in time for tea."

"Might I ask a favor of the two of you?"

Elle gave a crooked smile. "You may always ask. We might not comply."

Rachael scowled at the sass. For a former barmaid, the woman certainly thought highly of herself.

"It's in regards to this." Rachael held out her new book.

Elle's brows raised at the loopy script that spelled out the title. "I've heard of this," she stated. "I thought it was a hoax."

"I don't doubt that. Do you think your Henry can prove it?"

She shrugged. "He likes a challenge."

"Good. Find me the man who wrote it."

II

In Want of a Wife

June, 1884

*A*VERY COUNTED AT LEAST FIFTEEN THINGS he would rather be doing at the moment. It was an unpleasantly high number, given he was doing his damnedest to keep his mind on the ball. He wouldn't be here had he a choice in the matter. He had important work to do. But his blasted Aunt Eugenie…

He trod on his dancing partner's foot, and she let out a yelp. She was a pretty thing, with plenty of money, and from a good family. If she had smacked him with her fan, as his carelessness deserved, he may have offered for her. As it was, she didn't even demand an apology, and he was left to mumble something insincere.

When the music ended, he excused himself with the smallest bow courtesy would allow. His partner rushed off to join a gaggle of other young ladies, who pressed their heads together and chattered, probably about his ill breeding. He wouldn't bother himself to consider any of the rest of them.

Damn the old biddy anyway.

Desperate for a break from dancing, Avery scanned the

room for any gentlemen he might speak to without experiencing crushing boredom. He hated small talk. It was one of the many things he shunted into the category of "waste of time."

What he really wanted just now was a stiff drink. His eyes drifted toward the refreshments table, surrounded by smiling faces and piled with glasses of champagne and punch. He jerked his head away with a muffled growl. Looking at the libations would only intensify his torture.

He surveyed the room, considering his chances of ducking out for a few minutes. Even a man of his known eccentricity wouldn't be so uncouth as to take a swig from his personal flask in front of everyone, but perhaps he could escape to the library for a moment's peace.

"Cantrell! I hadn't expected to find you here."

Avery turned toward the voice. "Sizemore." He gave the other man a nod. They had been acquaintances for a dozen years now, with too little in common to breach the walls of friendship. One of many such relationships in Avery's life.

"I thought you detested parties and only cared for work."

"I'm in the market for a wife. Therefore..." He gestured at the party around them. "I hope to accomplish the whole thing as quickly and with as little pain as possible."

Sizemore gave a snort. "I was under the impression that marriage is only the beginning of an entire lifetime of pain."

"Hopefully not. I don't intend to marry an annoying woman."

In truth, Avery didn't wish to marry at all. He'd been putting it off for years, thinking he'd get around to it someday. His goal had been to undo the curse before he had any children. Then Aunt Eugenie had up and died.

"A rich woman, though, eh?" Sizemore chuckled. "Going to fancy up the estate and move out to the country?"

"I doubt it," Avery muttered. To be honest, he wanted nothing to do with the crumbling estate, neglected first by his father, and then by himself. "In this day and age, I don't see why a man even needs to own land out in the country. I'm content with my London townhouse, and my investment income is sufficient to maintain a gentlemanly lifestyle."

"Why marry, then?"

"It was my aunt's dying wish."

Or, rather, her will had stipulated that her money would pass to him upon his marriage. Avery had planned for his inheritance to fund the restoration of the estate, after which he would sell it for a fair price. He could contest the will in the courts, and probably win, being her only kin, but the hassle and the legal fees were off-putting. A quick marriage seemed a simpler solution, and he did need a wife eventually.

Sizemore snickered. "Good luck," he said, then hustled off to request a dance with a vapid-looking girl in a horrid, pink, frilly dress. She couldn't have been more than sixteen.

Avery's preference was for a woman closer to his own age, which would push his search into the realm of spinsters and widows. There weren't many of either to be found here, and those he had met were plain and—far worse—frightfully dull. With a sigh, he squared his shoulders and steeled himself to rejoin the ranks of the dancers.

"Professor Avery Cantrell?"

The sultry voice gave him pause, and he turned slowly. "Yes?"

The woman standing before him wore a dress of black velvet, with a neck cut so low she was in danger of spilling out. He wouldn't complain if it happened. Her wry smile told him she was neither surprised nor displeased he had taken some time before looking up at her face. A silk top hat sat upon her coiffure, tilted at a rakish angle. He thought the masculine adjective suited her, given her boldness. A tiny scrap of a veil hung from the brim—a ridiculous nod to widowhood that he found amusing nonetheless.

He wondered briefly if she might be a courtesan and what the price might be for her services. He wouldn't be averse to a romp.

She thrust her hand at him, holding it so they might shake hands rather than giving him the opportunity to bow.

"Rachael Fasching," she introduced herself. "It's a pleasure to make your acquaintance."

He shook her hand. He had heard of her, despite his tendency to shun social events and gossip. She was the widow of an American who had up and died in some enigmatic fashion. She had a great deal of money and was not afraid to show it—or herself—off. Even at the University talk was circulating about a dress she had worn to an event weeks before. "Half-bare," someone had described her.

Avery had no notion how she knew who he was or why she had approached him, so he said the first thing that came to mind. "Would you care for a dance, Mrs. Fasching?"

"Yes, I would, thank you."

They took to the floor and joined the other couples. She moved with grace, her steps keeping perfect time with the music. Avery found her to be an interesting enough partner that he displayed his own dancing skill to its full advantage for the first time that evening. Together they glided across the floor in perfect natural unison.

No longer flustered by her audacious dress, Avery took the opportunity to consider her further. She was beautiful—unblemished skin, bright eyes, a shapely nose, and full red lips he would love to taste. Still, something deeper tugged at him. She had a deliberate way of surveying the room and of looking into his face. A keen curiosity. She was searching, thinking. He wanted to know what ideas rattled around in her head.

"So," she said, leaving him waiting for some time before she continued on. "I understand you are a historian."

"I am. It's not so much a profession as a calling. I don't need the income from my lectures. It is, rather, a passion of mine I enjoy sharing."

She looked amused by his automatic defense of his

gentlemanly status. Hadn't her late husband been in trade? Damn. Avery expected she found him pretentious.

"You study the old Anglo-Saxon days, in particular?"

"Yes."

"That sounds fascinating. Do you dig up graves, looking for bronze swords and ancient ships?"

"The swords from the period are of iron, and my colleague, Professor Purcell, runs the majority of the excavations. My specialty is research, analysis of document fragments, and translations of important texts. I assemble what disparate clues we have and piece them together to give us insight into the lives and minds of our ancestors."

Pretentious again. *Cantrell, you bloody fool.*

"Of course." She nodded, her perfect lips pinched in thought. "You, then, must have an opinion on this new book of love poems?"

The mention of his failed scheme induced a burst of rage. "It's a bl—" He nearly forgot himself and cursed in front of her. "A hoax," he finished. "It's ridiculous, melodramatic nonsense."

She met his scowl with an unflappable smile. "I found the verses quite moving, irrespective of their authenticity."

"They are rubbish," he growled. "I wish it had never been published."

"Well." He half expected her to stop dancing and put her hands on her hips. "We are all entitled to our own opinions."

Avery reined in his temper. "Very true. I disapprove, however, of some anonymous scoundrel playing on feminine sensibilities to sell books."

A part of him was proud of just how eager the ladies were to read his poems. Those feelings were most often quashed beneath the frustration that all his hard work had been for nothing. The book had generated plenty of talk, but no increase in donations or funding from the University.

Mrs. Fasching surveyed him from beneath narrowed brows. She had long, thick eyelashes that shaded her golden-brown eyes. "I should like to think that sincere verse could be appreciated by anyone, regardless of gender."

Avery winced. There was nothing sincere about the dratted book. He'd written it by imagining the sorts of things a hopelessly besotted fellow might say to his lady love. He'd never been besotted in his life. He couldn't afford that sort of distraction.

"I imagine that is true," he said, by way of reconciliation. Anything to change the subject.

"I'm glad we are agreed. Have you any favorite verse, Mr. Cantrell?"

"*Nunc est bibendum*," he grumbled.

She laughed. "Horace. The Cleopatra ode. A suitable choice for a scholar. And I quite agree, 'Now is the time for drinking.' Shall we abandon this dance in favor of some refreshment?"

Avery nearly replied in the affirmative. She was a student of the classics? Who was this woman? She possessed the body of Calypso and the mind of Odysseus.

"Ah... No, thank you," he managed. "I'm afraid I'm actually *not* drinking tonight."

"But you do drink at other times, clearly. What's special about tonight?"

"It's a fasting day in the old Anglo-Saxon tradition. Saint Aethelwulf."

One dark eyebrow twitched. "You don't say. Well, I must tell you that it's quite ill-considered of him to have his day of temperance during our party."

"I couldn't agree more." He gave her a deep bow. "It has been a pleasure, Mrs. Fasching. You are a superior dancer and a compelling conversationalist. I hope you enjoy your refreshments and the remainder of your evening."

"Thank you, Mr. Cantrell. I, too, have enjoyed our time together. It has been most illuminating."

With that peculiar comment, she whisked herself away

with the bearing of a queen, and soon disappeared into a gaggle of admirers.

"It has, indeed, been illuminating," Avery commented to himself. He gave a despondent shake of his head. Forget parties. He would put out a matrimonial advert. His list of requirements was short.

Dull scholar seeks wife. Only beautiful, sharp-witted, enigmatic widows need apply.

III

An Offer

*D*EAR *ISOBEL,*

Last night's ball, I'm afraid to say, was tedious for the most part. My dress did draw some amount of attention, but nothing like the uproar still lingering from Lady Chesterfield's ball in May. I can't quite understand it, as I don't think the amount of bare skin was much different from one outfit to the other.

Perhaps some of the lack of interest may be due to the talk about Miss Meredith Helmsley. She wore a ridiculous pink puffy thing that made her look like a French pastry. Many gentlemen in attendance imagined her quite delicious, I don't doubt. She is a horrendous flirt. She is but sixteen, but leers at men like a professional. Her father had better marry her off soon, or she is certain to ruin herself.

But to the more interesting part of the evening: my husband search. I was, indeed, able to find the time to speak with Mr. Cantrell. We shared a dance, where he showed himself a capable and well-bred gentleman. He is scholarly and shrewd, and just enough a misanthrope to scare off gently-reared females. I, of course, conversed with him amiably.

He became most defensive when I brought up the subject of his book. I think, perhaps, he is embarrassed by it. He is by no means a dandy, and refined professors do not go about putting their sensitive souls on display for the world.

All in all, I think he will do nicely.

I know what you are thinking. "Rachael, you can't pick a husband this way!" Truly, though, I see no other way to do it. People put on such false faces in public. Professor Cantrell's book shows his hidden, inner thoughts, and I find that more reliable than any words spoken at a party.

I must say, however, that he has decidedly eccentric tendencies. He did not partake of any food or drink the entire evening, explaining it away with a jest. Odder still, when the ball came to a close, he rode off on a horse! In his evening clothes! What sort of gentleman doesn't use a steam car? His suit was new and smartly tailored, so he doesn't appear to lack for funds. I intend to pay a visit to his office this afternoon, so perhaps I will unravel some of these secrets.

Beyond that, there is not much to tell. The musicians were adequate, the food was average, and the champagne, I suspect, was not authentic. I do wish so many hosts would stop cutting corners in that respect. I have taken to buying all my wine from Ainsworth Imports. I know my friend Mr. Ainsworth thinks his family cheats everyone, but the Faradays, who run the operation, consistently have the best product.

I hope you are well, and I will write again soon.

Your cousin,
Rachael

The door to Mr. Cantrell's office had been left ajar. Rachael peeked in without knocking. The room was unpleasantly crowded. It wasn't untidy—Cantrell was an organized scholar, not an absent-minded one—but it lacked space enough to contain all his books and papers. The shelves overflowed, books were stacked on the floor, and the desk was all but hidden beneath piles of papers, held down with colorful glass weights.

Mr. Cantrell sat behind the desk, tapping his pen against the paper in front of him. His coat was off, and his tie loosened. A pair of spectacles perched on the end of his nose. Striking. Handsome, though he would never be called pretty. His cheekbones were too protruding, and his jaw severe, but there was a rugged virility to his face that appealed to her. He had an eye for fashion. His waistcoat was sleek and well-fitted, civilizing his broad-shouldered physique. She liked his smart attire, but thought he would look even better in a dirt-stained, half-unbuttoned shirt and sporting a day's growth of beard. Perhaps she had lived too long in America.

Rachael rapped on the door, and he called out for her to come in without looking up. She swished into the room, her scarlet dress taking up all the available space.

"Good afternoon, Mr. Cantrell."

His head snapped up, and his jaw dropped. He hurried to compose himself, removing the spectacles and straightening his tie. When he rose to greet her, however, his words were less than genteel.

"Are you stalking me, Mrs. Fasching?"

"Don't be ridiculous."

"You approached me at the ball, and now you have come to my office uninvited. I must conclude that there is something you want of me. Would you be so good as to tell me what it is?"

"I enjoyed our conversation last night. I should like to continue to have such discourse in the future."

He frowned down at her. He was an excellent height. She needed a tall man to match her own imposing stature.

"That seems a feeble excuse for your presence here. How, may I ask, did you even know where this office is? For that matter, how do you know who I am? I'm not often out in society."

Rachael couldn't conceal a grin. She knew even more about him than he suspected.

"I have friends who are adept at finding things out."

"Is that so?"

"You sound a bit cross, Mr. Cantrell. Didn't you enjoy our time together last night?"

"I did, in fact. You were a worthy dance partner, and an interesting conversationalist. Today, however, I have important work to do, and I have no time for idle chatter. If you could tell me without further delay what I can do for you, it would be most appreciated."

"I should like you to explain why you faked a book of ancient poetry, and now insist on disparaging your own work."

His dark green eyes hardened. "I don't know what you're talking about."

"You needn't fear that I will expose your secret. I have no desire to endanger your career. This is for my own curiosity only. I know you are the author of that book. I should like to know what you were thinking when you wrote it, and why you decided to pass it off as a historical text instead of claiming the work as your own."

"Mrs. Fasching," he ground out through gritted teeth. "I'm not going to discuss this, no matter how you pester me. I'm thoroughly tired of the subject, and I must beg you to drop it."

"Very well. I will say only that I found the poems to be both well-written and heartfelt, and I think they speak highly of your intellect, your tender heart, and your passionate nature."

The irritability subsided, leaving a bemused frown in its place. "My dear lady, I have neither a tender heart nor a passionate nature. I'm well noted for being dull and unemotional."

"I can't believe that."

"It's true nonetheless."

"I suppose if you don't wish to talk today I shall simply have to come back at another time when you are in better spirits."

Further argument wouldn't serve her purposes. The man possessed a certain stubbornness that would make sensible discussion difficult, and she wished to keep their relationship cordial. She could take her time uncovering the mystery of the book—and the myriad other puzzles Mr. Avery Cantrell presented. He intrigued her, and she looked forward to observing and analyzing his eccentricities.

"I'm in fine spirits," he sighed. "It's only that I am quite busy."

Her eyes skimmed over the stacks of papers. "Yes. You look to have mountains of work before you. You must be very devoted to your research."

"I am."

Rachael had never been devoted to anything in her life, except, perhaps, her wardrobe. It was a shame, really. She was surrounded by friends with passions, yet she never seemed able to drum up any of her own. Henry had advised her once to "do something" with her life. That was two years ago, and thus far she hadn't found anything that suited her.

"I should like to have an occupation," she mused. "Not as a means of income, you understand, but a hobby that I might pursue. I seem to have reached my limit for reading books and studying the arts. I fear I have become boring."

His dark eyebrows rose in disbelief, and he chuckled. "You? Boring? I should think not. You are a fascinating woman, Mrs. Fasching."

She beamed. "Thank you. Of late I haven't lacked for things to do. I have been concentrating on my upcoming marriage."

The humor in his expression faded. Rachael felt a rush of triumph. He preferred her unattached.

"You intend to remarry soon?" His tone was bland, though

his eyes fell to her dress. "I notice you have thrown off your widow's weeds."

Rachael spun in a circle to allow him to admire her from all sides. "Do you like it? I only just had it made."

"It becomes you."

"Thank you."

He nodded to her and dropped his gaze to his papers. "If there is nothing further, I must return to my work. Allow me to congratulate you on your engagement."

"It's not official yet. I don't know that the gentleman in question will think to make me an offer, though I know he is seeking a wife. I may have to do the thing myself, I'm afraid."

His eyes rose to meet hers once again. "A woman making an offer of marriage? That would be a fine story for the gossip columns. Perhaps someone ought to warn the poor man."

Rachael steeled herself for the moment of truth. The enormity of the risk caused her skin to prickle. She knew so little about him, and he was reluctant to share. Clearly, he was a man accustomed to holding his passions in check. Would she truly be able to release them?

It was now or never. He sought a wife and she didn't think he would waste time finding one. Everything she had seen proclaimed him to be the right sort of man. This was her chance to snare him before some young, flighty thing did.

She gifted him with her most captivating smile. "I just did."

IV

Taking the Plunge

AVERY PACED THE HALL. His office was too bloody small. How was a man supposed to gather his thoughts when he could hardly move?

Bellamy, Avery's personal secretary, emerged from the office, arms loaded with documents. The young man looked harmless, with his mousey brown hair and his suits that were perpetually three years out-of-style, but his mind was sharp, and he never wasted time on frivolities. Avery appreciated that. "I'll take these down to the library, then?"

Avery waved a hand at him. "Yes, yes."

It irked him that Bellamy had no place of his own. Once, Avery's office had been big enough for a secretary's desk, but since that blasted gold belt buckle had been unearthed, all the funding had gone into digging. He was left with one tiny room and whatever schoolboys he could recruit as unpaid research assistants.

He couldn't blame Purcell. Museums wanted gold more than crumbling bits of paper. Damn people for minimizing the value of stories and documents.

Avery stopped pacing and looked at his secretary. "On

second thought, why don't you use my office? I'll collect a few things and take them home. Perhaps I can concentrate better in private with a good drink."

Bellamy frowned down his hawkish nose. "Is something troubling you, sir? You seem distracted. I thought this latest collection of legends showed promise?"

"It does. I may need to travel out to the coast and hear some of the stories firsthand. It's all too easy to miss important information when transcribing, especially after hearing multiple versions of the same tale."

"Certainly. I can make arrangements as soon as you would like."

Avery continued to pace. "I've made progress. That's the important thing. There's a chance I can reverse this curse."

"I hope that to be the case. Might I say, however, that you don't have the look of a man who is excited by these developments?"

Avery bit back a rebuke. Bellamy's impertinence was that of a friend, not an employee. Avery shooed him back into the office. He could use a confidant.

"I will have to tell my future wife, Sebastian."

"Ah. The marriage business is troubling you? Perhaps you might put off your search until you find your cure."

Avery shifted nervously. The room was too damned small. "No, no. It could be years yet, and I'm not getting any younger. May as well get it over with. But I can't expect to live under the same roof as anyone without some explanation of the reasons behind my eccentricities." He suppressed a shudder. His father had learned that lesson only too well. "Can I risk telling her beforehand? I might scare her off and be left without a bride. I could wait until the deed was safely done, but that feels duplicitous. Do you agree? Or do you think it depends on the woman?"

"I'm no expert on matrimony, sir, but it's difficult to go wrong with honesty. Am I right in thinking you have a particular woman in mind?"

"No." He stilled. "Perhaps. There is one woman who has caught my attention. I can as yet think of no reason not to marry her."

"Are there reasons you *should* marry her?"

"Oh, plenty. She is beautiful—always a positive. She is wealthy, so I needn't worry that she might tax my income purchasing her marvelous dresses. She is a widow, so I won't have the hassle of bedding a timid virgin."

She is bold, witty, peculiar, fascinating.

"She wants to marry me." Lord knew why.

"Solid reasons."

"She's an unusual sort of woman, but as I am an unusual man, I can't find fault with her for that." He walked over to his desk, shoved some papers aside, and took up a fresh sheet and a pen. "I should research the matter. I will invite her to the opera."

"A fine idea. Shall I procure tickets in your usual box?"

"Please."

Avery scrawled a brief letter. When he reviewed it, it sounded overly formal, but he signed and sealed without any changes. He didn't wish to be too affectionate or friendly yet. He would spend an evening in her company, and see how he felt about an alliance afterward.

It was a step in the right direction. His jitteriness began to ebb. Bellamy scurried away with the note, leaving Avery to dive into his research with renewed enthusiasm.

The door to Mrs. Fasching's townhouse swung open, and she whisked out to greet him, dressed once again in red and looking as regal as any queen. Avery was entranced. Her body and face were pleasant to look on, but much of her beauty stemmed from her air of supreme confidence. Her every movement said, "I am someone to be looked at and admired."

He took her hand and helped her down the stairs and into

his waiting carriage. He took a seat beside her, and gave the signal to his man to drive off.

"Well," she said. "I'm pleased to see you have a steam car, after all. I did feel some apprehension, after seeing you depart from the ball on a horse the other night. It was shocking, I must tell you."

"Ah, yes. I don't drive, you see, and I find it's often a greater hassle to be shuttled about than to travel myself on the back of a serviceable animal."

She peered at him from beneath raised brows. "You don't drive? Peculiar."

He nodded, but said nothing more. The explanation needed to happen soon, before she changed her mind about him. The more he thought about it, the more he realized how off-putting his unusual habits would be to a lady of good breeding. The problem nagged at him throughout the first act. How to tell her. When to tell her. He had no good answer.

"I should like to go for a walk," she declared at intermission, standing up and striding from her seat without waiting for an escort. "Will you accompany me, or do you prefer to remain brooding in your seat?"

"Brooding?" He hurried to follow her.

"Indeed. It's your poetic sensibilities, I'm certain. Has the pathos of the tragic story affected you, or are you still swamped with work?"

"Neither."

"Hmm." Mrs. Fasching raised her eyebrows at him, but let the matter drop. "This is a fine opera house, don't you think? I'm not a fan of the Baroque style, personally, but the frescoed ceilings are tastefully done, and these halls are open enough to soften some of the flamboyance of the decor."

"An astute observation."

One of many, it happened. As they walked the halls, she expounded on the singing and the costumes in great detail. Savvy comparisons to other plays, performers, and composers displayed her broad knowledge. Her remarks on their fellow attendees showed her social acumen. She was, without a doubt, a woman who knew what she was about. Her cheeks were rosy, her eyes shining. Avery did little more than nod, content to watch her enjoying herself.

"Lovely dress," slurred a man deep in his cups, lurching toward her. She dodged his hands and ignored his leers, but Avery gave him a harsh stare.

All throughout their stroll, men gave her suggestive looks, of varying degrees of subtlety. She met them all with casual disdain. Avery found it impossible to be similarly unaffected. When a haughty man offered her a seat in his box, Avery took a firm grip on her arm.

"She's with me."

The man sniffed and stalked off. The moment he was out of hearing distance, Mrs. Fasching began to laugh.

"You might have at least tacked a 'Your Grace' onto your tongue-lashing."

"Was that man a duke?"

"He is. You don't leave your university often, do you?"

"I see no reason to mingle in society. Particularly when the highest among us cannot comport themselves any better than a drunken lecher."

She patted his hand. Even through the gloves, the affectionate gesture sent a rush of heat down his body. "Your defense of me is charming. Unnecessary, but charming." The potion-lit lanterns flickered from yellow to red. "Come. The show is about to resume."

Avery absorbed even less of the second act than the first. He couldn't keep his eyes off Mrs. Fasching. His charming, self-possessed companion would make him an ideal wife, if only she could accept the truth of his curse. It was a risk he had to take. There was no sense in waiting.

The moment the carriage paused outside her door, he asked, "May I have a word with you in private?"

She gave him a knowing smile and nodded.

When the drawing room door closed behind them, he took up her hand, as he believed was the done thing, pressed a kiss to the back of her glove, and looked into her eyes.

"I have spent much time thinking on it, my dear—all evening, in fact—and I have concluded that I would be most honored if you would agree to marry me."

Her smile was wide, and adorable little crinkles appeared at the corners of her sparkling eyes. "I accept, of course. You won't regret it, Avery, I promise."

Her use of his given name carried a delicious intimacy. His body stirred in response. He dropped her hand and took her in his arms. She gazed up at him with eyes full of desire, cheeks flushing. Those lips that had spoken so fondly were plump, red, and luscious. He yearned for a kiss, but when she leaned in he had no choice but to pull away.

"Do you use cosmetics enhanced by potions?"

The question made her frown. "Of course. They're the best. You can't think I would paint myself up like some streetwalker?"

"Certainly not. But I'm afraid I can't kiss you just now."

"Whyever not?"

"If I ingest any potion, of any sort, it will kill me. Even to get some on my skin would prove fatal. The serum that gives them their potency is to me a deadly poison."

She stared at him in horror. Time slowed to a crawl. The entire world fell silent, but for the heavy thumping of his heart in his chest. His muscles tensed, braced for rejection.

If the truth was repugnant to her, she had only to rescind her acceptance of his proposal. He wouldn't think ill of her if she did. No one could be expected to take on so problematic a man.

She didn't retreat. She was too stalwart to run.

Avery opened his mouth to tell her she was free to leave him, but before he could get the words out, her arms wrapped about his waist.

"You poor, dear man! I can't even imagine it! With potions everywhere? It must be dreadful." Her golden-brown eyes glittered with resolve. "I shall take special precautions to keep any potions far away from you."

Avery exhaled slowly. His arms tightened around her, and his pounding heart at last began to slow. This was the woman for him. This was his bride. He would wed her and never look back.

V

Together Triumphant

Dearest Cousin,

You must prepare yourself for some shocking news in regards to Mr. Cantrell. I discovered last evening that he has a terrible allergy to potions. Can you imagine? With more potions developed each day, it must be most trying for him. It explains all the odd things I have noticed. He can't have a drink at a party because the glassware may have been washed with one of those new cleaning agents. He doesn't drive his own steam car because he can't refuel it, maintain it, or even check the potion level before a drive. He must instead employ a servant to drive him around. I don't know if you know this, living in the country, but such an affectation is seen as pretentious, unless you are traveling somewhere without adequate space to leave the vehicle. Gentlemen take great pride in the care of their cars, and it must irk him to be unable to do so.

I have consented to marry him, despite this discovery. I'm more certain than ever that he possesses a deeply romantic soul. His daily difficulties don't allow for him to be anything but serious and sober, but you have read the poems, so you will understand.

I have nothing else to report just now, and I need to begin thinking on my wedding plans, so I will bid you adieu until the next letter.

Yours,
Rachael

Rachael perched on the edge of a chair in Avery's small office, as she had done every day this week. She was curious by nature, and she couldn't keep herself from delving into his everyday life. Oddly enough, he didn't seem to mind her hovering while he worked. Not once had he asked her to leave or suggested that her time would be better spent elsewhere. She would take full advantage.

Avery's dedication to his work fascinated her. He spent hours at a time in the office, and she didn't doubt he had read every single page in the cramped room. Reading was a safe pastime for someone who needed to avoid potions, but that alone couldn't account for his commitment to the research. She meant to discover his other motives.

Rachael had spent much of her first few visits perusing the books on his shelves and reading selections from some of them. Thankfully, he hadn't asked her opinion of them, because she would have been forced to admit they were quite boring. Where she had hoped for riveting verses like his fraudulent love poems, she had found dry historical analysis.

Her biggest fear was that he might ask what she thought of the books he had written. She'd slogged through several dozen pages of two of them. It was impossible to dredge up much interest in the tales of long-dead, ancient peasants. Wasn't there some Anglo-Saxon epic about warriors and monsters? Where was *that* book?

Today, she had brought her own reading material. She had a newspaper, to scan the latest gossip columns, and her fiancé's book of faked ancient poems, because it would give her an excuse for being here, if anyone commented on her presence. Despite her freedom as an independently wealthy widow, she had called on him alone so many times in rapid succession there was bound to be talk eventually, and she hadn't yet officially announced their engagement.

Rachael liked flirting with scandal, but no more. Draw attention, get people talking, yet maintain an aura of respectability. She wielded superiority and nonchalance like finely honed blades. Some people thought her of questionable virtue, but she had never taken a lover during or since her marriage, she shunned gambling and tobacco, and she never drank to excess. Her clothes were extravagant, and she loved to cause chatter at any social gathering, but she knew well the rules of decorum. She had mastered the art of bending those rules, but she never broke them. No one could ever say they had caught her at something truly disgraceful.

Today's paper contained no interesting gossip, and she soon put it aside to reread her favorite poems. Avery looked up at her now and again, so she deliberately turned her chair so he could see the cover of the book. When he noticed it, he sighed and rolled his eyes heavenward.

She gave him an amused smile. "Don't you approve of my choice of reading material, Mr. Cantrell?"

"You know I don't."

"I must admit, it's an obvious forgery. This one, here, is a lovely little verse. A warrior's sort of love poem. 'Struggling singly. We join, we fight. Together triumphant.' I like it very much, but any fool knows that 'triumphant' is a Latin word and not an Anglo-Saxon one."

"It's not a word-for-word translation. Some of those differ from the original Anglo-Saxon text in order to maintain the poetic feel and convey the proper emotions."

"Original text? Did you write every poem in Old English? Truly?"

"The book could hardly make a claim to legitimacy without

showing itself to be a translation of *something*. There is an original document. I have a copy of it here somewhere."

He poked through his shelves for a time, while she waited in silence. She wouldn't chance saying anything lest he realize he was now engaged in a discussion of the book he claimed to despise.

"Ah, here we are."

He placed a stack of papers on the desk in front of her. She scooted the chair closer and looked them over, frowning at the unrecognizable words and strange letters.

"It appears no more than gibberish to me, I'm afraid."

"Here is the one you mentioned," he said. "Shall I read it to you?"

"That would be delightful, thank you."

He adjusted his spectacles and cleared his throat. "*Lýpig, lífbysig,*" he began. "*Wit áfégap, wit áfiehtap. Sigefæstu samwist.*"

The guttural words rolled easily off his tongue, the alliterative lines lending them a musicality that surprised her.

"That was lovely."

"Thank you. If I were to give it a literal translation, the first line means solitary, struggling for life. The second is much the same as the modern text. The last line, however speaks of togetherness in terms of living together, or matrimony."

"Oh, ho! So they are triumphantly married! You didn't convey that in your translation."

"No, I didn't. I couldn't find a good modern equivalent. I think the translation carries a similar emotion, however."

She leaned across the desk, drawing almost close enough to kiss him. "And I have caught you out at last. You have admitted to writing the thing."

"Yes, yes," he grumbled. "Don't tell anyone. I have enough to worry about as it is."

"I promise."

"Thank you."

Their eyes locked. His were the beautiful, dark green of

a murky pool. They held mysteries in their depths, and she savored the chance to uncover all that they hid.

"Did you use any potions today?" His question was a whisper, and a soft breath against her lips.

"No."

He kissed her, a gentle, lingering press of the lips. When she leaned in for more, he grew bolder, his tongue gliding across her lips in a silken caress. She opened for him, inviting him to explore further, ready to give him as thorough a taste as he desired.

A loud knock startled her, and she sprang away. She had forgotten the door was standing wide open. Thank heavens she was engaged to the man she had been kissing.

A teenaged boy stood in the doorway, holding a slip of paper, his face a heated crimson. He coughed awkwardly and held the paper out to Avery.

"I'm sorry to interrupt, sir, but a telegram has arrived for you marked as urgent. I thought you would want it as soon as possible."

"Yes, thank you, David. Please, allow me to introduce my fiancée, Mrs. Rachael Fasching. Rachael, dear, this is Mr. David Beech, one of my assistants."

"I'm pleased to meet you, Mr. Beech," Rachael greeted him, as calmly as if she hadn't only moments ago been kissing a man across his office desk.

"A pleasure," the young man replied. His embarrassment lingered, and he scurried off the moment the paper was safely in Avery's hands.

Avery unfolded the missive and adjusted his spectacles again. "Let's see what this is all about."

His frown deepened as he read the note, and when he looked back up, his eyes held both sadness and worry.

A chill ran down Rachael's spine. "Is the news very bad?"

"A worker has died at the site of our current dig."

"Oh! How dreadful."

"That's not the half of it. The authorities suspect foul play. They think he was poisoned."

Most women would have swooned or cried at such unpleasantness. Rachael swore.

VI

An Unusual Request

"I'M SORRY, MAY YOU… WHAT?" Avery asked. He must have misheard her.

She retreated immediately. "I'm sorry. I shouldn't have asked." Her eyes were downcast, her shoulders slumped, a posture of submission from a woman who usually held full command of any room she entered. Her fingers clenched, and a hint of anger crept into her voice. "I know it's not my place."

What the devil? Avery's lips pinched into a tight frown.

"As we are not yet married, it's not *my* place to tell you what you may and may not do. I'm also not the sort of man who desires to control his wife's every movement. If you are looking for such a man, I suggest we break off the engagement."

Her eyes rose to look at him, an expression of bafflement on her face.

"Now, would you be so kind as to repeat your question?" he asked. "I don't think I heard aright."

"I only wondered if, perhaps, I might accompany you on your journey." Her words lacked their usual assurance, her voice soft, uncertain.

"That's what I thought you said. I didn't realize you had

any interest in the matter. Certainly, you are free to travel wherever you wish."

"I…" Her mouth remained fixed in a puzzled frown. "I don't know whether I have any interest in the matter. I have interest in learning more, and in seeing what goes on at one of your digs."

He nodded. "I would be happy to show you around the dig site. Are you sure you wish to go now, however? There may be unpleasantness while we try to learn what happened to that poor chap."

"I shouldn't wish to interfere."

Avery crossed his arms and swallowed a grunt of frustration. At this rate, they would remain standing in his office doorway for hours and never accomplish anything at all. What the devil was wrong with her? Where was that poise he so admired?

"I'm not worried about interference. I'm worried about causing you grief. Please answer me honestly, so that I may understand: do you wish to accompany me *now*, or do you only wish to go to the site at some time in the future?"

"Now. I thought I might be some comfort to you? If this incident is upsetting?"

Her hesitation was a step up from her former docility, but only just. At least now he knew her true thoughts, and could move forward.

"That's very kind of you," he told her. "I will see to the purchase of train tickets and reserve two rooms in a hotel for the duration of our stay." His gaze fell to her lips, still rosy from their kiss. That brief taste had only whet his appetite. "Unless you prefer to cause a stir before our marriage?"

The puzzlement gave way to wonder, leaving her eyes large and round. Her voice regained its customary authority. "Not a stir of that magnitude. Traveling together will be quite enough."

Avery couldn't contain a smile. "I believe the wait will

make you all the sweeter. We can arrive in time for the evening meal, if we catch the right train. If I send a carriage for you in an hour, can you be ready?"

"Name your time, sir, and I will await you then."

"Excellent." He kissed her cheek and walked her to the front of the building. He had no need to hail a cab. Her bright dress drew eyes from all over, and several tried to zip to the curb the moment she stepped outside. He let her choose one and handed her up into it. "I will see you again shortly."

"Thank you. I will make arrangements to have announcements of our engagement sent out. Do you have a list of friends and acquaintances who should receive a formal note?"

"Uh…" Avery thought for a moment. He did so little social maneuvering that he'd never even considered wedding guests. "My secretary should have that information," he decided.

The poor, overworked man. Bellamy would be left to handle everything for at least the next few days. Avery bloody well needed another assistant. With a criminal investigation and a potential scandal looming, funding would only be harder to come by. As head of the minute "Department of Anglo-Saxon History and Literature," any troubles would land in his lap.

The moment Avery entered the library, Bellamy hopped up from among his pile of books, his blue eyes peering out from behind his long nose, his expression more serious than usual.

"You look upset."

Always to the point. Avery liked that about him.

"One of the workers at the site turned up dead. It looks like poison, and could be a homicide."

"Gad! What do you need me to do?"

Avery ticked off the list on his fingers. "A pair of train tickets to Ipswich, first class, of course, two rooms at my usual hotel, the services of a steam car for the duration of my visit…"

"A car? I don't think I'll be able to find you a driver via telegram."

"I'll handle that problem once we arrive. I will have a lady with me, and will need a proper carriage for her."

"You are taking your affianced bride? A singular notion."

"It was her notion. I simply agreed to it. I can't deny that it will be pleasant to have some company."

"I suppose you wouldn't wish to marry her were she an ordinary woman. You'll have to tell me more of her. She dresses well, and she's quite the beauty."

"I don't recall introducing the two of you."

Bellamy grinned. "Sir, she visits your office every day. People have noticed. We've all seen her."

"Yes. I suppose that can't be helped, can it? On that note, please send a list to her home of anyone who needs a formal announcement of our engagement. That can be done after the details of our journey are settled, of course."

The secretary snatched up his notebook and scribbled several incomprehensible lines of shorthand. "Anything else before you leave?"

"No, unless you think of something I've missed. In that case, have it done at once. I must return home and have my trunks packed. While I'm gone, I'm afraid you will have to deal with any questions, keep track of the young assistants, and handle any new materials that arrive for my perusal. My current notes are sitting atop my desk. Please review them and read the relevant documents for anything I may have missed. Also, do sort through the books and send some of them off to the library. I don't need them all, and I'm tired of tripping over them."

Bellamy nodded and scribbled.

"And Sebastian?"

The secretary looked up. "Yes?"

"Thank you."

"You're welcome, sir."

"I don't say it enough, but you are invaluable. You have free use of the office. Enjoy it. I hate how you are always left here in the library."

"I'm very fond of the library. I don't mind."

"Good. Oh, and please refrain from using that silly color-changing ink that you like so. I don't want any potions spilled on my desk."

"Of course. It's a shame you can't enjoy it yourself, sir. It lends a festive quality to the research, I find. It's also very popular with ladies, I'm told. Good for personal messages. I will see to your travel arrangements. I hope your journey may be as pleasant as possible, despite the unfortunate happenings."

Avery left him to gather up his books and papers, knowing Bellamy would handle everything in his usual proper and efficient manner.

Avery was in remarkably good spirits, given the circumstances. He couldn't comprehend why Rachael wanted to accompany him on this journey. Their travels weren't likely to be pleasant, considering what lay in wait at the dig site. It wasn't the sort of thing a gentleman ought to expose a lady to.

A wry smile touched his lips. Rachael was no ordinary lady, and he was selfishly pleased to indulge her. Her presence would make the trip both more interesting and more endurable. This marriage business was turning out better than he had anticipated.

VII

Infernal Contraption

*D*ARLING ISOBEL,

Well. The tea service on the train to Ipswich was appalling. First class passengers should not be made to suffer so. The tea itself was of inferior quality, served lukewarm, and there was almost no food to speak of. Some tiny sandwiches on soggy bread, and nothing further. I shall lodge a complaint with the company.

Happily, the city itself is a prettyish sort of place, and the hotel is of an acceptable standard. They have provided me with a maid for the duration, since I am traveling alone, and she seems competent. She didn't fumble with the buttons when I changed for dinner, and the room looks well-kept.

My room is next door to Avery's (it's becoming increasingly difficult to think of him as "Mr. Cantrell"), which suits me very well. We are close enough to inspire plenty of talk, especially as regards our purpose in traveling together, but since we are engaged, there can't be too much fuss made. We could share a room and not be ruined socially—I _am_ a widow, after all—but I prefer to maintain my reputation. Still, being so close to him generates a sort of flutter in my belly that I'm quite enjoying.

Dinner at the hotel was better than expected. The roast was tender, and the vegetables only mildly overcooked. They were glazed with a nice red wine sauce, which made up for the deficiency.

I believe it may take a bit of time to become accustomed to Avery's peculiar habits. He carries his own silver, can you imagine? It's a lovely matched set that he keeps tied with a bit of ribbon and carries in his coat pocket. He tells me the dishes in public establishments are almost always safe, as soap and water is much simpler when washing so many dishes. It's also easy—so he says—to check into the method of washing before having a meal. Almost all silver is polished with potions, however, even the settings which are not real silver. Avery says he can never trust the silver, and will only ever use his own fork, etc.

I pretended it was entirely normal for a man to have his own personal table setting, despite the stares. Really. Some people are just intolerably rude. He shouldn't be forced to take his meals in his room like some invalid because he suffers an unusual condition.

We are to travel to the dig site tomorrow. I wonder if Mr. Cantrell will be expected to view the body? That would be most gruesome. I hope that part of things has already been handled, but it would be quite sensational, wouldn't it? When we discover who the poor man is and how he died, I will write to let you know. Until then, it will have to be a mystery to us both.

Affectionately,
Your Cousin Rachael

Rachael walked a circle around the rented steam car, nodding her approval. It was an open-topped two-seater, well-appointed and relatively new. Precisely the sort of vehicle a gentleman ought to be driving. It would go very well with her red carriage dress and her custom-made driving goggles, which were wrapped in red ribbon with a silk rose above her left ear. The goggles were far more fashionable than anything one could find in a shop.

Avery paced beside her, flexing his fingers inside thick leather gloves. "It seems serviceable," he grunted. He paused by the front of the vehicle and gingerly lifted the protective cover that concealed the engine.

"Drive the thing myself," he mumbled. "Damned stupid, arrogant…"

She couldn't catch any more, but she thought he was scolding himself. She knew his surly mood stemmed from nervousness about handling the vehicle. He'd done this for her. He was too much the gentleman to subject a lady to an improper mode of transport. An unwanted and all-too-familiar sense of guilt washed over her.

Always too curious, Rachael. Never content with your place. The echo of her father's constant berating sparked a rush of hot anger. Shut out because she was a woman. Her questions never answered. Her opinions never valued.

Until now.

Why had Avery agreed to let her come along? She had expected a refusal, and—since he was a polite man—an assurance he would keep her informed of his well-being. Such a response would have been better than what she'd ever gotten from Fasching, who had merely sneered at any interest she took in "men's affairs." That was life. That was the way men behaved.

No, she corrected herself. Her friend Henry Ainsworth would take his wife anywhere she asked. He was content to let her run her own shop, and use her income to cover most of their expenses. He was wildly eccentric, though, and she was everything to him. Rachael couldn't expect them to behave like a normal couple. She wouldn't expect a man to treat *her* in so irregular a fashion. Not outside her wildest dreams, at least.

Those dreams were why she had persisted in asking, despite years of refusals—the hope, however small, that she might be considered special enough to have her whims indulged. That someone might listen and care what she had to say.

Now Avery had, and she was at a loss for how to react. Happy as she was to be included, she feared he already regretted the decision.

"Do you know how to tell if this infernal contraption is properly fueled?"

Rachael came up beside him and examined the engine and fuel tank. Everything looked clean and in good working order. As a rental, she expected it to come fully fueled.

Avery gestured at the tank. "There are markings, but I can't read them without my spectacles, and I don't dare lean closer. I don't want to inhale any fumes."

He held his hands out and stared at the gloves, twisting them back and forth, looking for signs of potions. Rachael brushed him aside. She checked the fuel and the water, tightly closed both tanks, looked over the starting mechanism, and ran a finger over a few spots to test that moving parts had been oiled. Her own gloves might never recover, but she had brought extra pairs.

Confident the carriage was ready for the journey, she adjusted her goggles and checked that her hat was well secured. "All is as it should be," she told him. "We can depart whenever you desire."

He gaped at her. "You *do* know cars!"

"Well, of course. I know it's considered uncouth here, but in America women drive the steam cars fully as much as the men."

"Do they? You know how to drive, then, from your time there?"

"Indeed."

The tension eased from his shoulders. "Splendid! You shall drive us. I will navigate."

Rachael opened her mouth to reply, but nothing came out. She saw no reason not to drive. She nodded her assent, shaking off her amazement that he had suggested it. This would have to go into her next letter to Isobel.

Rachael gripped the hand crank and gave it a firm tug. A few rotations and the engine roared to life. Avery walked her to the driver's seat, helping her into the car as if it were perfectly ordinary for a gentleman to let his lady drive him about. She adjusted her skirts. The new traveling dress was comfortable and didn't restrict her movements. She hadn't anticipated driving while wearing it, but she found it well-suited to that purpose.

Avery circled around to the back of the car, pausing to strip off the gloves in such a way as to leave them turned fully inside-out. He shoved them beneath their day-bags with a look of disgust that suggested he'd just as soon see them burnt. He donned an ordinary pair, pulled his goggles down, and took his place beside her.

"Let's be off, then," he said, sounding much more himself.

Rachael opened the throttle and steered the car down the road. It was a fine machine, a smooth ride with a quiet engine. Nicer than the carriage she'd driven around the New York countryside. Improvements had been made in these new models.

"Infernal contraption!" She laughed. "This is a beautiful vehicle, sir. You have slandered her."

"My apologies for the ungentlemanly outburst. I was— uncomfortable, to say the least. Thank you for driving. It would have been mortifying had I driven us into a tree."

"Driving isn't difficult. The modern steering wheels are very responsive. Working the throttle takes a bit more practice, as you need to get a feel for how much to open it to achieve the acceleration and speed you desire. You are a very learned man. You would take to it quickly, I have no doubt."

"Perhaps we can find a time in a quiet location where you could give me lessons. For today, I find this arrangement very pleasant. You handle the carriage deftly."

"Thank you. I hope I shall not cause too much of a scene when we arrive."

He laughed. "Do you, now? Be honest, my dear, you love to make a scene."

She pinched her lips together. "Yes. The attention can be a great deal of fun. I take my scandal in moderation, however. I am 'sensational,' not 'outrageous.' What I meant, however, was that I don't wish to cause you embarrassment when you are seen being driven by a woman. I may enjoy generating talk, but I would never assume you felt the same."

"You're right. I don't like to be the center of attention. At every party I find myself looking for the nearest exit. My work suits me better than any social gathering. As for today, don't fret. The men at the site will be far more shocked I brought a woman at all than by the fact that you are driving."

"You could have asked me to remain home," she pointed out, hoping he might give some hint of why he'd granted her request.

"We are betrothed," he replied. "Everyone might as well become accustomed to seeing us together."

"Do you mean to say you expect me to accompany you on all your travels?" A little burst of excitement fluttered inside of her, and she tried to keep it from creeping into her voice. She was glad her gaze was fixed on the road, and her eyes hidden by goggles.

"I couldn't say. I've found you regularly defy my expectations. As I'm still puzzling out the mystery, I won't make a comment on what you might do, lest I give offense. I *will* say, however, that I'm enjoying your company thus far, and I hope we may travel together again often."

Rachael's fingers tightened on the wheel. Her pulse quickened, and she felt a flush spreading across her skin. She'd been right. She'd been so right to want to marry this man. He wouldn't disappoint her. His heart was primed for wild, unquenchable love. She *would* win him over.

She forced herself to concentrate on the road and not the man beside her. His proximity made her tingle. They were almost shoulder-to-shoulder, and she could smell the tangy scent of his shaving soap.

"It's a fine day for a drive, is it not?" she remarked.

"Yes, very pleasant."

He didn't appear to notice her discomfort, and after several minutes' conversation about the weather, she relaxed. They spent the remainder of the drive in an ordinary manner, speaking of ordinary things, as would any two people getting to know one another. It was enjoyable, but no different than outings she'd had with friends and acquaintances in the past.

Why, then, was her skin so sensitive? Why did her ears prick up at the sound of his voice? Why couldn't she shake the feeling that beneath every polite word they exchanged lay the merest sizzle of passion, just waiting for the right moment to burst into flame?

VIII

Worth One Thousand Words

"*T*HEY DON'T..." Rachael could hardly contemplate the idea, "...*live* here, do they?"

She stared at the canvas tents. They were arranged in a neat row and were in good repair—so far as her untrained eye could tell—but the thought of using such a thing was nothing short of abhorrent. Why, they were fully as small as the water closets in her townhouse! It was so... barbarian.

Avery chuckled. "Now you see why I chose the hotel at Ipswich," he replied. "Here on the site, things are rather more primitive. I don't stay here, myself, and it's certainly no sort of place for a lady."

"I should think not!" Rachael exclaimed. "I doubt I could fit my trunk and a bed together into one of those tents!"

The little shelters did have an uncouth fascination, however. She walked down the row, examining them, even peeking inside one which had the flap tied back—a breach of propriety just as scandalous as she liked. Inside were two cots, covered with plain wool blankets. A box sat at the end of each cot. Nothing more could fit within the tiny space.

"Two men per tent? It's worse than I thought."

"They don't seem to mind, my dear. Don't trouble yourself.

In fact, Purcell claims the rustic living to be restorative for one's health and mental state."

"If I should have to live in such a place, I assure you, it would *not* improve my mental state."

She glanced around the area. "Do they cook over a fire? And is there nowhere to sit but these tiny stools? How do they have a civilized meal?"

"We shall see at luncheon, I suspect. Think of it like a picnic."

Rachael hated picnics. Sitting on the ground was nothing but a hassle and a good way to get dirty.

"That wouldn't be so bad," she temporized, "if it weren't every meal of every day."

"True. All I know is that some men seem to like it. Personally, I always lodge in town and ride in. I overnighted once in a tent and it was… Let me just say that I am surly in the mornings as it is. That next morning I was in such a state that even our stoutest diggers kept their distance."

"Surly, you say? Not you, sir. I can't imagine such a thing. I'm sure you are always agreeable."

"I know you are teasing me, madam, and you will not get a rise out of me." He gave her a frown that was supposed to be stern, but looked more like he might be suffering from indigestion.

"Of course not," she answered, gracing him with her best innocent smile. "You are always agreeable!"

"Always agreeable?" queried an affable tenor voice from behind them. "Cantrell, I hope you aren't telling lies to the ladies to win them over."

Rachael turned around to see a man of a bit more than average height, with light-brown hair and wide brown eyes. He had one of those faces everyone found pleasant and desirable in a friend. She wouldn't have called him handsome—not as Avery was—but he looked nice. His suit was of much better quality than she would have expected anyone living in these tents to wear.

"Hello, Robert," Avery greeted him. "Allow me to introduce my fiancée, Mrs. Rachael Fasching. Rachael, this is my colleague, Professor Robert Purcell. He leads all the excavations."

Purcell bowed over her hand. "A pleasure to meet you, dear lady."

"The pleasure is mine, sir. I've heard much about your work here. I'm looking forward to learning what goes on at a scholarly dig. I'm sorry it has to be under unfortunate circumstances."

"Thank you. We are handling it as well as can be expected. Please, allow me to show you around."

He offered his arm and led her away from the tents, to where the men were working. She caught a glimpse of Avery's face as she turned. He wore a real frown, now, almost a scowl. She wondered if he would accustom himself to other men taking an interest in her, or if he would simply glare at everyone for the remainder of his life. For some reason, the thought made her laugh.

"You seem a very pleasant lady," Purcell remarked. "How did Cantrell snare you?"

"I told him I intended to marry him, and he agreed it was a fine idea."

The professor's eyebrows rose in surprise. "Perhaps I should have asked how *you* came to know *him*. He doesn't often leave the office."

"I'm a fan of his writing," Rachael answered, pleased to have a perfectly honest answer that didn't in any way reveal the truth.

"Ah. A lady scholar. Excellent. You will enjoy your glimpse into our work."

She did enjoy it, for perhaps a quarter of an hour. The excavation itself was tightly controlled. Digging took place in small, roped-off areas, with small tools, and the process was recorded and photographed. It was the most modern of digs, she was told—scientific in the extreme. It didn't appear that they were finding anything.

Avery and Purcell stepped aside for a private discussion, leaving Rachael to wander alone. Unfortunately, one part of the dig looked much like any other, and she was forced to feign enthusiasm as the workers chatted at her.

Many of the men gaped like she was a foreign creature they had never seen. They attempted polite discourse, but they stared, they didn't know how to bow, and they used common slang. Rachael nodded and smiled and tried to keep near enough to Avery to eavesdrop on his conversation.

"...Can't believe you found a wife," the professor was saying.

"I told you I intended to marry."

"I didn't think you were serious. Or, at least not so serious as to have done the thing so quickly."

"Mrs. Fasching took me by surprise. She made the decision a simple one."

Rachael beamed at the praise. The odd, little man pointing at some hole in the ground mistook it for interest in his babbling, and blushed.

"Why on earth did you bring her with you?"

"She asked to accompany me."

"But the investigation! If she should be exposed to any of the gruesome details…"

Rachael took two steps toward Avery, forcing herself not to turn and stare. *Yes, let me hear the details. Who died? How? Where?*

Whatever else Purcell said was too quiet to hear, but Avery replied, "Not to worry. She isn't one of your young ladies in distress. Now, tell me what happened. Where and when was he found?"

Purcell motioned for Avery to follow him. "This way. We discovered him first thing in the morning. The body lay face down, only steps from the privy. We summoned the police at once, and every man here has given a preliminary statement."

Rachael missed the next portion of the conversation, but soon maneuvered herself back within hearing distance by introducing herself to the group's photographer. Lord Hunstable was a terribly pretty man of about twenty years, with dark, curling hair, a cleft chin, and the most fashionable of moustaches. She would have been content to stand and admire him, the way one might do with a piece of fine art, but he offered to show off his photographs, and that provided her the perfect opportunity for spying. He flipped through images of the dig site, the trenches, and some bits of iron that supposedly came from ancient, Viking-like ships. Rachael nodded at the photos and listened to Purcell.

"I've tried to keep to the routine," Purcell said, "but the men are justifiably nervous. Your presence will help them feel we are doing all we can, I hope. Sacrifices must be made, however. I've had to rescind my invitation to Professor Dashell."

"Dashell." Avery spat the name as if it left a bad taste in his mouth. "He would never have deigned to visit in any event."

"He will come around eventually, I'm certain of it. We only need to keep trying. I will reach out to him again once the police investigation is finished."

"You're too optimistic, Robert. He'll probably raise a toast to our misfortune if he learns of our current troubles. Best we resolve this as quickly and quietly as possible. What did that police inspector have to say thus far?"

"...Fascinating, don't you think?" Hunstable asked, disrupting her eavesdropping.

Rachael blinked. "Oh, yes, very much so. I'd love to see more."

Her false excitement kept Hunstable flipping through photos as Purcell rattled off an exhaustive description of the previous day's police investigation. She couldn't decide which was more boring. Apparently real life murder mysteries involved far more tedious note-taking than sensation novels led one to believe. She was about to give up on her eavesdropping and request that Hunstable put away the photos, when he came to a much different image.

There, before her eyes, in stark black and white, was the body of the dead man, face down in the dirt. Somewhat to her own surprise, she felt only curiosity, and no revulsion. She leaned in for a closer look. Something about the scene was odd. Her mind churned, sifting through memories and making connections.

"Oh!" she gasped.

"Dear me!" the young man exclaimed. "Mrs. Fasching, I'm so very sorry. The police, you see, they wanted evidence. To help them investigate. So I took this photo. And others. I hadn't meant to show you. I forgot I hadn't separated them out. Have I greatly upset you? Oh, dear. I'm so sorry. What can I do to help?"

"You could stop babbling and turn back to the earlier photo with the wide view of the site."

He goggled at her. "Pardon?"

"Allow me, Lord Hunstable."

She took the stack of photos and found the one she wanted. Holding it side-by-side with the image of the dead man, she studied the two, trying to determine whether her initial impression had been correct.

Avery and Purcell, who had heard the photographer's cries of dismay, came jogging over. Rachael turned to her fiancé and held out the evidence.

"Avery, look at this. Someone has been digging well outside the boundaries of the pits." She pointed to an irregularity in the dirt at the furthest edge of the photo of the body. The marks on the ground resembled those she'd seen in other photos of digging in progress. "Possibly only since the night of the murder."

IX

A Clue Unearthed

ALL OF THE MEN STARED AT RACHAEL, and for once it had nothing to do with the neckline of her dress. Hunstable, looking pale as a ghost, tried to snatch the photos away, but Rachael's long arms easily held the images out of his reach. The boy was too gentlemanly to move inappropriately close. His eyes flicked imploringly to Avery.

"I didn't mean to show her. I would never have intentionally given those photos to a lady!"

"The lady is not of a frail constitution," Avery replied. "She isn't going to faint at the sight."

And thank the Lord for that. A delicate, fainting woman would be a nuisance. He had enough troubles without worrying about a wife who needed to be looked after. He thought again how great a favor Rachael had done him by deciding to marry him. Perhaps those damned poems had done some good after all.

Rachael thrust the photos under Avery's nose, but all he could do was to squint at them. They were little more than a blur without his spectacles. He'd packed a pair in his day bag, which was still strapped to the back of the steam car. If only it weren't so damned unfashionable to wear spectacles as an ordinary part of one's attire.

He took the photos from her, and held them at arm's length. When she pointed at the relevant spot, he could recognize the location, though not the detail she had indicated.

"May I see?" Purcell inquired. Avery passed both photos to him, indicating where he thought Rachael had wanted him to look.

"Heavens!" the professor exclaimed. "No, this is no photo for a lady's eyes. Mrs. Fasching, I'm dreadfully sorry to have burdened you with this. Hunstable, put these in a separate file and mark them *clearly* as police business only."

"Yes, sir." The photographer took his pictures with obvious relief and hustled off toward the tent.

Rachael glowered. It took Avery a moment to realize her angry gaze was directed at *him*.

"Didn't you see it?" she demanded.

"Not well. I need my spectacles."

"Then why didn't you say so? Now you've given up the photos, and they've been taken away so no one can see anything."

"Don't fret, Mrs. Fasching," Purcell soothed. "We will summon the police at once and deliver the photographs directly into their care. They have experts to examine evidence of this sort. They are much better at it than you or I, and they will know just what to do." His voice usually had a calming effect, but Rachael was anything but calm.

"You think I'm a fool," she sneered.

"Not at all. I can't fault you for being overwrought. Any lady of sensibility would be, after such an experience."

"I am not bloody overwrought!"

From the look on Purcell's face, Avery guessed he had never in his life heard a lady swear. Purcell didn't use foul language himself, and wouldn't stand for any of the workers speaking vulgarities. Avery always had to take care not to let a stray "damn" escape his lips when speaking to him.

"Cantrell!" Rachael shouted. She hadn't stopped glowering at him. "You, too, think I'm 'overwrought'?"

"No, as a matter of fact, I don't."

Her brown eyes softened, but her lips remained tight. "But you think I'm mistaken about the photos."

"No. I didn't get a good look at them. Perhaps you can explain what you saw and show me the real location?"

"I'll send one of the men to fetch the police," Purcell said.

Avery dismissed him with a wave of his hand. "Go ahead. But I'm not waiting. Rachael, please show me where you think this strange digging was."

All around the site, men had set down tools and abandoned their work, their whispers slowly crescendoing into a full clamor as they pressed closer. Avery couldn't blame them for taking an interest, but he also couldn't have them interfering. "The rest of you get back to your damned jobs," he snapped. The men scattered. Purcell winced. Oops.

Avery escorted Rachael to the spot by the privy where the unfortunate bloke had met his end. Scuff marks criss-crossed the dirt, but nothing to his eye looked like the sign of a murder.

"I believe this is the approximate location from the photograph," he told her. "Whatever you saw would be in that direction. Could you describe it for me?"

"Slashes in the dirt, such as a spade would make, and a roughly circular area where the ground appeared disturbed. I don't have the photograph any longer..." Anger flashed in her eyes once again. "But how it seemed to me was that someone had dug and then tried to hide it. Having been done at night, or very early in the morning, he didn't do the best job."

She had jumped to conclusions, but Avery trusted her keen intellect. Any anomaly was worth investigating. His eyes raked across the ground. His distance vision was good, thankfully. It took not even half a minute to find Rachael's mystery spot—a small circle where the dirt had been overturned. Trampling feet had obscured it, but someone had recently dug in a location where they had no purpose digging.

"You've found it." Rachael's voice held no small amount of satisfaction.

Purcell stepped up at Avery's side. He frowned down at the offending patch of dirt. "You have very sharp eyes, Mrs. Fasching. I suggest we rope off this location until the police arrive. In the meantime, can I get you anything to settle your nerves? A seat? A cool drink?"

"I have need of a spade here!" Avery called out to the diggers, ignoring Purcell. As department head, he was pulling rank and he wanted to find out just what Rachael had discovered.

Two of the men rushed over, and Avery pointed at one of them and put him to work, instructing him to dig with care, as if this were part of their excavations. For several minutes, he, Rachael, and Purcell watched and waited. Disappointment began to set in, as nothing turned up but dirt and stones. Rachael tapped her foot irritably, the toe of her boot poking from beneath her hem.

"Got something," the digger declared.

Avery had to restrain himself from kneeling to peer into the hole. He didn't wish to ruin his suit or to interfere with the man's work. The curiosity gnawed at him, and he leaned in for a better look.

He didn't have to wait long before the digger pried an object from the ground and held it aloft for examination. It was a glass vial, no bigger than his smallest finger. If they hadn't known where to look, it would have been lost forever beneath the earth.

"Here, sir."

Avery took the vial and brushed the dirt away. He had to fight the trembling in his hands. Even with gloves on, he felt he was touching death. Not only did the bottle hold a potion, it held one that was poisonous to anyone, not just the victims of an ancient curse.

"May I look?" Rachael asked.

He handed her the bottle, relief washing over him as soon as it left his grasp. It occurred to him only afterward that perhaps he shouldn't feel good about handing a murder weapon to his fiancée.

"There is a drop or two left inside," she observed, turning it about in her gloved hands. "We may be able to find out what it contained."

"I'm all astonishment," Purcell marvelled. "Mrs. Fasching, you must forgive me for doubting you." He pulled a handkerchief from his pocket. "Shall we wrap up the bottle for protection?"

"Thank you." Rachael plucked the cloth from his fingers and folded it around the vial. She passed the bundle to Avery, who tucked it inside his coat pocket. Even wrapped so carefully, he wanted nothing better than to be rid of it as soon as possible.

"I will take this to the investigator in Ipswich," he said. "Galby was his name, correct?"

Purcell nodded.

"Good. I think we will return to town promptly. I will be back tomorrow to take statements from everyone here. I'm sorry to put it off a day, but I think this needs to be in the hands of the authorities."

"Of course," Purcell assured him.

"We will be off, then. I can take Hunstable's photos into town as well, if he has them ready by the time Rachael has the carriage prepared."

They made their bows and adieus, and Avery once again gave Rachael a hand into the driver's seat. He liked the confident way she sat there, and her fancy driving goggles were silly, yet charming.

"I'm sorry for shocking your friends," Rachael said, once the car was out of sight of the excavation. "They seem to think all women fragile, delicate things."

"Purcell is drawn to delicate women. He likes nothing more than to assist a lady in need. I think your independence flustered him."

She nodded. "He should save his concern for your photographer. A very pretty boy, but much too excitable. I honestly thought he might be the one to succumb to a fit of the vapors."

Avery laughed. "Young Lord Hunstable is one of my best students. He'll grow into a decent sort of man someday."

Rachael nodded and fell silent. With nothing to say himself, he stared at the road and watched her drive, wondering what she might be thinking.

"Do you truly intend to take that vial to the police?" she asked, several minutes later.

"Yes. What else could I do with it?"

"Do you think there's a way we could extract those few droplets from the bottom, first?"

"Why?"

"I have a friend who should be able to tell us what the poison is."

Avery's lips pinched together. He shouldn't get involved. He needed to make sure the dig site was safe, check that no one working there was under suspicion, and leave it to the authorities to find the culprit. And yet...

"Your friend has familiarity with potions?" he asked.

"She is a master. Among the best in the world."

He nodded, his mind casting aside thoughts of modern poisons in favor of ancient ones. A master potion mixer could have knowledge that might help him break the curse.

"We will make certain a sample gets to her."

He would let Rachael handle it. He couldn't wait to get the damned vial out of his pocket. And then take a bath. He doubted he would ever wear this coat or these gloves again.

X

Steaming Hot

$\mathcal{D}$EAR ISOBEL,

I feel like a true detective, after my discovery today. Yes, that is correct, I found a clue that might solve the mystery of the dead man at the dig site. It began when I was chatting with the photographer, who is quite the beautiful young man. Less overtly masculine than Avery, but prettier. You would like him. He has a very pleasant shape of face, and a little notch in the center of his chin. His jaw is somewhat rugged, but he tones it down with conservative dress and a delicate manner. He would make you a good husband. Perhaps he is rather too young, but—

"To whom do you send these letters that you write so frequently?" Avery interrupted.

Rachael looked up from her letter and her coffee. She'd been too intent on her writing, and hadn't noticed him enter. The hotel dining room had all but emptied since she'd begun her letter. Apparently her plan for being productive while showing off her dress was a failure.

"I swear you've been scribbling every spare second of our journey," Avery continued, taking the chair beside her.

Rachael set down her pen. He'd certainly taken his time meeting with the police investigator. He hadn't even returned in time to take dinner with her.

At least she had made progress in his absence. He'd left her the vial of poison, and she'd bought a dropper and a clean bottle at a chemist's shop and extracted what she could. Enough, she hoped, for Elle to examine it. The original vial she had rewrapped and sent off to the police.

Rachael relished this chance to be involved in such a sensational story. Playing at detective was both challenging and fun. She supposed she ought to feel some sorrow for the dead man, but she hadn't known him, and only with great difficulty could she conjure up the slightest bit of empathy for him.

A personal failing of hers: she didn't grieve well. While etiquette had necessitated an acknowledgment of her widowhood, she'd never mourned her husband. She had no memory of her mother's death, and had never lamented growing up without her. Sadness was simply not an emotion that often took hold of her. She might be angry, irritated, or disappointed, but sad wasn't in her repertoire. A symptom of her improperly warm heart.

A shiver of doubt raced over her, causing her to question once more the wisdom of marrying Mr. Cantrell. When he fell deeply in love with her—which was inevitable, given the romantic sincerity of his poetry—he might be heartbroken if she didn't return the feelings with equal fervor. Since she lacked the capacity for ardent love, she would have to do her very best to be good to him.

Avery waited patiently for her answer. Rachael contemplated not replying because of the rudeness of his interruption, but couldn't bring herself to do something that might anger him.

"I write to my cousin, Isobel," she said. "She lives in a small country home just outside a terribly tiny village in Bedfordshire. The house is almost more of a cottage. I stayed several months with her after my husband's death, and we couldn't have any other visitors come to stay because all the bedrooms were taken. She is a sweet girl, though, despite her poverty, and I hope she marries well. We've been correspondents since childhood. I give her all the news and gossip from town, because she rarely leaves the country. When I lived in New York, I wrote her of all the odd things that Americans do. Now I have to write to her of all the odd things that *I* do after having lived there so many years."

"I see." He sounded not quite upset, but wary.

Rachael frowned at him. "Does it bother you, that I write her often?"

"Certainly not. I would never wish to deny you of your friendship or tell you what to do with your time. But have you…" His hand lifted to his face, as if to adjust his spectacles. When he realized he wasn't wearing them, the hand dropped into his lap. "Er, have you written her about me? You have given me a detailed description of her with no prompting. I must assume you would do likewise with your descriptions of myself."

"Ah. I have, in fact, told her much about you. It's difficult to become engaged to someone and then not give some description of the person to your family."

He leaned back in his chair, his head cocked to one side, his brows crinkled together. "I'm not accustomed to having anyone talk about me. It's disconcerting, I must say."

"Don't worry. Isobel is the very soul of discretion. Even were I to forget myself and mention something too personal, she would never breathe a word."

"I'm glad to hear that," he replied, but his nervous air persisted. He'd been on edge since the morning, and the day's work hadn't lessened his anxiety. He was surrounded by too many potions, she guessed. It had to be difficult, to be away from his home and his office, where he knew everything was safe. No wonder he so seldom went out.

He fidgeted a moment, then spoke again. "You have, I assume, informed her of the curse?"

Rachael gave him a blank stare. "Curse? What curse? Surely a man of learning such as yourself doesn't believe in superstitious nonsense?"

"There's nothing nonsensical about it. I refer to my condition. The difficulty with potions?"

"Ah, of course." Rachael could understand why he might think of it as a curse. It must feel that way at times. "I thought it was an allergy, like one might have to shellfish. I have a friend with that allergy, and it can be difficult to feed him. He also won't eat olives anymore, since an… incident two years ago."

Caused by my scoundrel of a husband.

She realized, with no small amount of dread, that someday she might be forced to reveal at least some of Fasching's misdeeds. Avery hadn't asked her much about her past, but he had an inquisitive mind. He must have questions.

"It's not an allergy," he insisted. "It's a curse."

"What, did an old witch put a hex on you at birth? Do you need a fairy godmother to undo it?"

Rachael regretted the sarcastic words the moment they left her mouth. She had been born with a sharp tongue, and had been increasingly free with it since moving back to London. Her shoulders tensed, braced for the inevitable scolding.

To her surprise, he rose from his seat and said, in the calmest of tones, "I wouldn't expect you to understand. No one has thus far. Good night, Mrs. Fasching."

She watched him leave, stunned by his lack of anger. He ought to have been furious with her for making so insensitive a remark. Ladies didn't speak with such blatant disregard for the feelings of others—another problem Rachael had struggled with since childhood. She was adept at insulting people and insufficiently sorry for it. She suspected she wasn't a very good sort of person.

Even now, her primary worry wasn't how her fiancé might feel, but how she might have endangered her marriage. He could still walk away and pick some genteel, compliant sort of woman. Rachael seemed to have forgotten how to be compliant since her husband's death. Not that she had ever truly mastered the art. Her modus operandi was to behave for a time, grow overconfident, slip up, and be chastised for it. In her public life, fortunately, everyone either adored her or was awed by her, making it hard to offend.

She tried to return to her letter, but for once had no enthusiasm for writing. She sipped her coffee and stared at the page. The tale of her discovery couldn't hold her interest. All she could think was that Avery would throw her over for an ordinary, modest sort of girl—someone who wouldn't mock him, even if he were being ridiculous. Someone who wouldn't ask to join him on entirely unladylike business.

Why did he bring me along?

The novelty of traveling with her must have amused him and sparked his curiosity. There was no other reason to have agreed to such an absurd scheme. Now he'd discovered it to be a complete failure. He wouldn't indulge her whims the next time. She would be best served never to ask again. Men didn't like pushy wives.

Rachael's fingers tightened on the empty coffee cup, and it took all her willpower to set it down gently. She had a whole list of things men didn't like. She could write an entire book on things that men didn't like and sell it as an advice manual for prospective brides.

Her rebellious side applauded the idea. Men probably didn't like women who wrote books.

Would Avery like it? He worked at a university, and surely knew women who wrote books. They probably didn't insult him, though.

Rachael fretted for several more minutes before determining that she would never feel better until she had apologized. She requested a pot of coffee be sent up to Mr. Cantrell's room, then went to her own room and waited by the door until she heard the knock. She pressed her ear to the door to listen.

"Coffee for you, sir."

"I didn't order any coffee."

"The lady requested it for you, sir."

"Of course. Thank you."

A moment later the door closed again. Rachael left her room and rapped on Avery's door. He responded promptly and didn't appear surprised to see her.

"You sent coffee?"

"I didn't mean to chase you away before you were able to relax with a drink. I know you've had a long day. I apologize for my insensitivity toward your allergy."

His mouth twitched at the word "allergy," but he schooled his expression into one of neutrality.

"I shall explain the matter in greater detail someday, so that you might understand. We haven't had a great deal of time to sit down and talk together."

"No, we haven't. I have some things I must tell you as well." Though particular details might be left a mystery until after they were safely married.

"Such as?"

Blast.

Rachael wracked her brain for something to tell him that wouldn't scare him off.

"My late husband was not only an American, but he was in trade. He owned an import company specializing in potions, I'm sorry to say. I have since sold the business and all my American property, and put the money into other investments."

Remind him of her money. That was a sensible strategy. Men *did* like money. Men also liked breasts, so she leaned toward him to show off hers. He didn't miss the flirtatious motion.

"Your dress this evening flatters you, as always."

"Thank you." She had returned to mourning black for dinner, and her décolletage was covered with a filmy lace in a nod to modesty. Truthfully, it was so sheer as to be useless. It did nothing to block Avery's view, though it would impede his hands if he had a mind to fondle her. She was surprised to find that she wanted him to try.

"The servant who brought the coffee supplied two cups. Would you like to join me for a drink?"

She didn't think she would sleep well if she had another cup, but she accepted the invitation nonetheless, excited by the scandalousness of being alone in a room with him. He pulled out a chair for her, then wiped down both cups with a handkerchief. He took no chances. Avery poured her drink before serving himself.

"Milk or sugar?"

"Neither, thank you."

He handed her the cup, then poured his own, stirring in a sugar cube and a bit of milk. He leaned back, settling into a relaxed position. Like that first day in his office, he had his coat off and his tie loose. Many of the same thoughts she'd had that day flittered through her mind. He would look especially nice rumpled. Shirtless. Naked.

"Now, Mrs. Fasching, tell me more about yourself."

Rachael took a dainty sip of her drink. The warm liquid only increased the heat his close proximity had sparked. "I haven't much to say."

"Nonsense. There is plenty to tell. Where did you grow up? Who is your family? How did you come to marry an American in the first place? Did you run away with him because of his independent, roguish charm?"

The reminder of Fasching quashed her lusty thoughts. "My father arranged the marriage. It was a poor choice. I'm not sorry he's dead."

Avery's brows quirked. "He didn't raise a hand to you, I hope?"

"No. He wasn't violent toward me." Her first husband had preferred to hurt with words, or worse, with neglect. The few times she had greatly upset him, he'd refused to take her out and wouldn't admit any callers. She'd been left alone for days. At the time, she had thought it her own fault.

"But you didn't love him."

"No. He was handsome and wealthy, and at the first I thought him a good husband." *And later an adequate husband. Until he proved himself a murderer.* "I learned only later that he was a villain. He eventually became involved with the wrong people and ended up dead."

There. A safe enough description of the matter. Avery still wore an expression of surprise, but he nodded at her and spoke calmly.

"I'm very sorry to hear that. I'm glad you are rid of him. It's a wonder you are willing to consider remarriage, given your experience."

"You aren't a villain."

"So you say. But you don't yet know me."

"I know you better than you think." She smirked, remembering the thick file Henry had handed her. "I know that while you research and teach at the University, you don't accept pay for your work, preferring that the department's money go to fund your studies. I know that you have an inheritance due you from your aunt, but you can't retrieve the money until you marry. And I know that you present yourself as a commoner, but in truth you are Lord Avery Cantrell, Baron Wilwood."

He looked stunned at her revelations. "Wilwood is a silly name," he griped, "and the estate is an embarrassment. I'd rather not have people know it's mine."

"We can fix that. Don't you have money enough for restorations? I have sufficient income to take care of it. I should like to be able to use your title when we are out in society. You're correct, though, that Wilwood is a very silly name. I believe I shall go by Lady Cantrell. It sounds rather elegant, and no one expects *me* to do things the usual way."

"Go by whatever you like. I, however, do not intend to go out in society any more than I have done in the past."

"Nonsense. We must be seen together. I can't have everyone constantly wondering why my husband never shows himself."

He opened his mouth to reply, but she continued on.

"You can, of course, hide out at home on occasion, to appear mysterious and eccentric, but your reputation will suffer if you do that too often. Better to attend parties and walk about silently with a sour expression on your face. I've seen men do that, and sometimes it even attracts eligible ladies."

"I won't need to attract ladies of any sort. I need only one wife, and you have already agreed to take on that role. In any event, I have no desire to be sullen and sour. I'd rather be in an agreeable mood while I concentrate on my work."

"You are quite obsessed with your work." She didn't mean for the words to come out in a petulant tone, but they did. Terribly unbecoming. And men didn't like to be scolded.

"Yes," Avery sighed, resigned and not offended as he should have been. "But it's a necessity, and I have even grown to enjoy it."

"A necessity? I will grant you that studying history is beneficial for society, but I wouldn't have termed it so."

"Not for society. For myself. I have hope that tracking down the origins of my family's... condition... will lead me to a cure."

Her mouth opened in a silent O. "You think a cure is possible?"

"I hope so. I've been studying for years, uncovering more old tales, learning the historical people better. I know something of the ancients' limited use of potions, before they Christianized and the knowledge was lost, shunned as pagan magic. I must connect that to what I have been learning of my own family history." He paused to sip at his coffee. "But I'm not in the mood to dwell on the subject tonight. I wish to relax and think of something entirely unrelated. Tell me some gossip—the sort of thing you might write to your cousin."

"We *are* the gossip, Mr. Cantrell. Sitting here, alone in

your room. Traveling together before we are married. There will be much talk. It will be assumed that ours is a love match, and that we are so enamored of one another we simply can't stay apart."

"If I recall correctly, I have told you I'm considered to be dull and without emotion. I have neither the time nor the patience for love, and I don't think anyone else will believe otherwise."

Rachael laughed at his naivety. "Oh, they will, don't doubt it. The drab scholar, pulled out of his shell by the charms of a beautiful woman. They will eat it up. We will be the talk of the town, unless Little Miss Helmsley has ruined herself during our absence."

"Who?"

"That flirt of a girl who always wears pink. Horrid color. It's as if someone took red and watered it down and decided it was a real color. You wouldn't water your wine or your tea in such a way. It would be appalling. I don't understand why anyone would do so with fashion."

She set down her coffee cup, though it was still half full. Her intent had been to give him time to relax. She couldn't continue chattering away. "I'm afraid I oughtn't drink any more coffee this evening, or I shall never sleep. Thank you for sharing your pot. I hope you are able to rest now."

She rose from the table, and he followed immediately, escorting her to her own room like a perfect gentleman. He didn't bow or bid her goodnight, lingering just outside her door in silence. His eyes traveled over her, taking her in from head to toe. Unless he leered inappropriately, she wouldn't discourage him. Perhaps not even then.

Her own eyes seized the opportunity for a leisurely perusal of him, enjoying his exposed neck. She felt a sudden urge to kiss him there, where the top of his shirt gaped open. She strove to quash the desire. Men didn't like forward women—not for wives, at least. Her husband had been a beautiful man, and she'd never been allowed to touch him unless he initiated it. The selfish bastard.

"It's a most tantalizing dress," Avery said at long last. "You look delectable, yet untouchable. Do you intentionally choose clothing meant to entice?"

"I choose clothing that makes me feel beautiful." Rachael loved to show off, that was true. She loved to draw attention to herself. But she would happily preen in front of a mirror for no one at all. Dressing up was her one great passion.

A deep, rumbling laugh escaped Avery's throat and echoed through the hall. "My dear, you could wear a grain sack tied in place with bits of twine and still look beautiful."

Gad. What a horrid image. She would look like one of those wild children, lost in the woods and raised by wolves.

"Well. That may be true, but I certainly wouldn't feel beautiful."

His laughter drew her attention to his face. Rachael admired the shape of his jaw and the even, white teeth that showed when he smiled. She wanted a taste of his generous lips. His dark green eyes sparked with desire. She reconsidered her words. She might well feel beautiful in anything at all, if he looked at her the way he was looking at her now.

His hand cupped her chin. "Then I would have to kiss you until you did."

The kiss began slowly, as it had during their previous encounter—a tender invitation for further intimacies. Rachael accepted. She wound her arms around his neck, dragging him closer, her tongue snaking across his lower lip.

Avery emitted a growl of pleasure. It was all the encouragement she needed. In an instant, the kiss morphed into a ravenous, insistent plundering. She thrust her tongue into his mouth, claiming him for herself, forgetting she wasn't supposed to be the aggressor.

Her fingers tore at his shirt buttons, hungering for the feel of his naked flesh. His skin was warm beneath the cloth, and dusted with precisely the right amount of dark, curling hairs. Her fingertips glided over him, exploring, savoring.

Every touch inflamed her. Her senses had become wild. Her breasts grew heavy, her nipples straining beneath her corset. A rush of arousal ran through her belly and between her legs.

She dragged her mouth away from his, kissing across his scratchy jaw, creeping lower until her lips found the hollow of his throat. He tasted salty-sweet and smelled of spice and soap.

"Rachael," he gasped.

She ran her tongue along his collarbone, eliciting another groan. He was intoxicating. She reeled. Had she been too long away from the marriage bed? She had never been so eager for a tumble.

He backed her into the room, kicking the door shut behind him. With one hand, he began pulling pins from her hair, spilling her curls down her back and across her shoulders. His other hand skimmed over her hip and around to the small of her back.

"My God, but you are lovely."

She withdrew from her exploration of his neck to meet his smoldering gaze. She licked her lips and saw his own lips part in response. He tugged her closer, until she could feel the hard length of his shaft pressing against her.

"What fool would want that silly, pink virgin, when he could have you?"

Rachael brushed her lips to his. Warm. Soft. Wet. Tremors shook her body. She ached for him. "Only my husband may have me," she murmured.

He toyed with a strand of hair that had fallen just between her breasts, wrapping it around a finger that he swept across the swell of her bosom. She had been mistaken. The lace did nothing to bar his touch. His light caresses seared her skin.

"I will be your husband soon."

"Yes." His mouth found her throat, and her head lolled

back with a sigh. "Oh, Avery." She didn't think she could control herself any longer. After years of chastity, it seemed she was willing to throw it away mere weeks before her wedding.

Her body stiffened as unpleasant memories intruded on her pleasure. Lectures, reminders. Her father's constant disapproval, even though she'd never gone further than a stolen kiss. She would never forget the scathing remark she'd overheard as a child: *They're all whores, deep down. Every one.*

Rachael had prided herself on proving to him that she would never be—that even though she was gifted with beauty and surrounded by admirers, she would keep herself for her husband alone. She had been a perfect, loving daughter, and he had repaid that by selling her to a murderer to further his own investments.

Conflicting desires warred in her mind. Part of her wanted to ignore everything her father had ever said. Another part still wanted to prove that she was more virtuous than he had ever believed. Her only certainty was that her body craved what her fiancé offered. And that was good, wasn't it? A mutual passion would bring them closer and make their marriage a happy one.

She allowed herself to relax in Avery's arms, surrendering to the sensation. Her fingers wormed their way beneath his collar again, and she breathed in the scent of his skin. Warm. Delicious. Electrifying. "Oh, Avery, I do want you so."

"Why?"

The question confused her. She couldn't think straight, drunk as she was on his virility.

"Why do I want you?" Lord in heaven. How could she *not* want him? He was a ball of raging, fiery passion disguised as a man.

"Yes."

"I read your poems," she breathed, her voice sounding odd and distant to her own ears.

He pressed his lips to hers in a lingering kiss. "Then I'm pleased to have written them." He took a single, deliberate step back, letting his hands fall away from her. "Shall we stop for the evening? I understand you take your scandal in moderation."

Stop? The idea sounded ludicrous. Her body was screaming at her to take him into her bed and ride him like a wanton whore.

Stop. Yes. Absolutely. No. Oh, no, please don't.

Rachael forced a nod. Her breathing was ragged. She needed to regain her senses. No man had ever addled her so. She took her own step back, blinking at him, trying to see him as anything other than an object of carnal desire.

Avery took hold of her hand and brought it to his lips. "My darling Rachael. I await our wedding night the way a starving man awaits a crust of bread. I shall dream of you every night and wake lonely every morning without you beside me. You need only ask, and I will give to you every pleasure you desire."

Her knees felt weak. His words were all but poetry. Their frenzied embrace had unlocked the bard inside him, and he was thoroughly enamored of her. Not in love yet, but that would come in time. She had watched men fall for her before, even when she ignored them. With her encouragement, the poor man stood no chance. She hoped her affection and bodily passion would be enough to satisfy him.

Avery kissed her one final time before he left her, nearly undoing her resolve to wait. They wrenched themselves apart and mumbled goodnights.

Rachael didn't ring for the maid to help her undress. It was uncomfortable and tedious, working all the buttons and laces on her own, but it gave her body time to cool down before she slipped into her nightgown. Her wedding was three weeks off. It had seemed impossibly quick when she had chosen a date— just enough time to make all the arrangements and see to it that everything was done right. Now, it seemed an eternity.

XI

Honeymoon Plans

$\mathcal{T}$HIS WAS IT. Avery raced into his office, barely making it into his chair before he tore open the envelope, his hands trembling. The culmination of his years of dedication. This letter was the answer to his prayers for a cure. He rushed through the beginning of the message, where the woman responded to his greeting and introduced herself. He already knew who she was. He'd scoured records of births, deaths, marriages, and even pages of old family Bibles, sorting out the genealogy. Miss Annie Pelham, folklore enthusiast, was his fourth cousin, a member of the only other surviving branch of the cursed Cantrells, descended from one of the only two female Cantrells on the entire family tree. The other being his grandfather's baby sister—Aunt Eugenie. Unfortunately, his family had a strong tendency to produce sons. And men carried the curse.

His excitement grew as he read on.

Included along with the local folklore I have written down are those tales in which you expressed the greatest interest: the stories told to me by my grandparents of the Cantrell curse and our ancient ancestors. I have dubbed the tale "The Warrior and the Witch: A Legend of Potions, Poisons, and Perfidy."

Avery liked the alliteration. He loved the mention of potions. If he combined Miss Pelham's knowledge with his own, perhaps he could at last determine what had been done to his ancestor all those years ago.

> *I would be delighted to host you at my family's home in Seawell. It is a small village, but a friendly place, and I'm certain we can make arrangements. My father owns the General Store and post office, so you can continue to direct your letters there and they will be sure to reach me.*
>
> *Cordially,*
> *Annie Pelham*

Avery carefully refolded the letter and placed it in a drawer, then grabbed his pen and a clean sheet of paper and began to write a reply.

> *I am thrilled to accept your offer, and will arrange to pay a visit as soon as may be possible.*

His pen scratched to a halt. Usually when he wrote such a thing, he meant within a few days, but his wedding was only two weeks away, and he was still dealing with the aftermath of the poisoned digger. No one on the excavation team seemed suspicious, thank God. Purcell's latest telegram reported things were again running smoothly. The police had no good leads. The vial Rachael had found was believed to be connected to the death, but it had done nothing to further the investigation. He wondered if Rachael's mysterious friend had been able to analyze the poison.

Here in London, the University was full of chatter about

the incident. A few people even blamed Avery for the failure to resolve the matter. With a grimace, he turned his thoughts back to his research. Best to concentrate on the important things, while he still had any funding at all.

If I find a cure, I won't need so much funding. I could scale back my research. Perhaps even retire.

Retire. What an odd concept. He'd been doing the same thing, in one capacity or another, since he was twenty. Seventeen bloody years. Good God. What would he do if he gave it up? He could move out to the country and take charge of the Wilwood lands, as he ought to be doing. Unfortunately, such a life didn't appeal to him in the slightest.

"Damn," he muttered. The matter would require more thought.

Avery consulted his calendar. He had two public lectures coming up—scheduled months ago, before his aunt had died and his life had turned upside down. Then the wedding. He wouldn't be able to get away before then. His visit to Miss Pelham would have to come after.

He tapped his pen against the calendar. Two days after the wedding would be manageable. He would have Bellamy check the train schedules.

He snapped the datebook closed.

Hell.

He couldn't do that to Rachael. She would expect a wedding trip—probably one lasting a full month. Chances were good she had something in mind already. He'd never even thought to discuss the matter with her.

He shoved his chair away from the desk and began to pace the tiny office. He could only go two or three steps at a time before turning around. His foot caught on a pile of books, scattering them.

"Damn, damn, damn."

This marriage business was a nuisance. It would be far less

troublesome if he could just take the bewitching Mrs. Fasching as a lover and continue on with everything else as he had been.

But, no, she wouldn't stand for that. She had told him, mincing no words, that she kept herself for her husband only. Was it a struggle for her, he wondered, given her clearly amorous nature? Or was it only he who inflamed her passions so? Perhaps she was in love with him. It seemed ridiculous, especially since she insisted his silly poems had attracted her. How could random words make it worth taking on a work-crazed man who couldn't even drive a steam car? There was no point trying to make sense of it. He'd never claimed to understand women.

In some respects he looked forward to marriage. Rachael was beautiful and charming, and would be a perfect partner for bedroom sport. She had a sharp mind and a curious nature. She was odd, in ways he had yet to fully comprehend. She would make his life interesting, something he hadn't even known he desired until recently.

And he did need that inheritance.

If only the whole thing weren't so damned inconvenient. He could hardly run off to visit another woman the minute the ceremony was over, nor could he drag his new bride along on such a trip...

He paused, then bent to gather up the books he had kicked. Perhaps he *could* take her along. She had wanted to accompany him to the excavation. He could give her the leisurely wedding trip she deserved, and a visit to hear Miss Pelham's stories could be incorporated into the journey. Having his wife along would make it clear he wasn't there in some foolish attempt to reunite the two branches of the family.

An idea began to form in his mind for a wedding trip. He needed Bellamy to help him with the details. He started for the library, again cursing the stupidity of having his secretary so far away. By the time he arrived, however, his plan had solidified.

They would visit Miss Pelham, then make their way along

the coast from one seaside resort to the next until they reached Dover. For the final two weeks, he would take her across the Channel for shopping and fine dining in France. He hoped the bulk of the trip would make up for any apprehension she might have about their work-related first stop. He also hoped that by the time they departed Seawell they would have something more than the wedding to celebrate.

Bellamy looked up from his scribbles when Avery walked in. "Ah, good to see you, sir. I was just considering bringing you the rest of the day's correspondence. You had an opportunity, I presume, to read the letter I sent on from Miss Pelham?"

"Yes. I plan to visit her after my wedding. I was hoping you and I could work out some details. What of these other letters?"

Bellamy picked up a hefty stack of papers and handed it to him. Avery gaped at it for a moment. He had received more calling cards, invitations, and personal messages in the past week than he had in the entire rest of the year put together. This latest stack was no different.

"Can't you do something with all of these?" he lamented. "I have no time for this nonsense. Send replies to whomever needs them and decline all the invitations, as usual."

"Before you do that, you might wish to read the note on top that only just arrived from your fiancée. She has a list of events she would like you to attend with her."

Avery scanned Rachael's message. It was short, thankfully, because by the end he was ready to spout curses that had no place in a library.

"Impossible. I can't attend a ball, a dinner party, a gallery opening, and whatever that other absurd thing was all in two weeks."

"I believe it was a charity event, sir. To raise money for a girls' school. It's a very good cause, and one a man of your standing would do well to support."

"Fine. Send her a reply. Tell her I will attend the charity event and nothing else."

Bellamy blinked at him, his brows raised in a look of incredulity. "Pardon the impertinence, but do you truly intend to begin your marriage by making all of society—not to mention your wife—believe you a complete boor?"

"I beg your pardon!"

The young man's cheeks grew red. "Mr. Cantrell, sir, I realize you are a busy man, but your lady will feel insulted if you won't appear in public with her. It will be all the worse because you won't even spare the time to write a reply of your own. It will appear as though your work is more important than she is, and while that may, indeed, be the case, you will look to the rest of the world to be an inconsiderate lout. I will, of course, do whatever you ask, but I can't do so without the certainty that you understand the consequences."

Avery scowled at Bellamy, but he had to admit his words made sense. "How many events must I attend to avoid such a fate?"

"All of them. Or else you need to write her a personal and very contrite apology with specific reasons you cannot attend."

That settled it. They were going to Seawell immediately after the wedding, whether Rachael liked it or not. He would attend her stupid parties and she would damn well show him the same courtesy, or he'd call the entire thing off.

"Can you write a reply to tell her I *will* attend? Or is that uncouth, also?"

"It would look more affectionate coming from you. The note can be short. I will have it delivered and then have all the proper dates marked in your calendar. Don't fret that your social life will continue at such a pace. Engagements and weddings draw an unusual amount of attention."

"So it seems. Weddings, as far as I can tell, are horrid, inconvenient things. I honestly can't imagine why Mrs. Fasching wishes to go through such a hassle a second time."

"She must be extremely fond of you."

Avery snorted. "She must be insane."

"The two are not mutually exclusive."

If the man wasn't a damned good secretary, Avery might have dismissed him on the spot.

"Take some notes," he instructed. "I have plans for the wedding trip, and you need to make the arrangements. I am not to be dissuaded on this matter, so don't bother to try. I will add in my note to my fiancée that I have taken care of everything, and if she has any questions regarding the details she should direct them to you."

"Very good, sir," Bellamy replied, but his expression suggested he thought Avery was walking into trouble. Avery did not entirely disagree.

XII

What Strange Sickness

$\mathcal{R}$ACHAEL STOOD IN FRONT OF THE MIRROR, trying her best not to move a muscle while the dressmaker's assistant haphazardly shoved pins into the wedding gown. The dress was coming along well. She liked the neckline—a bit higher than her usual, but daring for church—and the cut of the bodice. The drape of the skirt was elegant, and the train just long enough to flow out behind her without being cumbersome. The shimmering silk needed no lace or other adornments. Her favorite part, however, was that the fabric was beautifully, pristinely white. She would cause a sensation.

The color was for an innocent, young girl. The styling was for a voluptuous, worldly woman. She would be both things at her wedding. She was starting again, fresh and new, with a man of her own choosing. She was older, though, and wiser. She wanted her dress to reflect all of that. She also wanted to be the talk of the town.

Once the fitting was perfected, this dress would say everything she wanted it to. Rachael adored it. She would look a veritable goddess. Avery would be stunned. She could picture his eyes, wide and staring, his mouth agape in a way that made her long to kiss his lips.

She fanned herself. Such thoughts were not helpful just now.

"Gracious, where has Mrs. Ainsworth gotten herself to?" she complained, to have another topic to dwell on. "She is usually so punctual."

"She will be here soon," Isobel soothed her.

Rachael's cousin looked well in the lavender gown she would wear to the wedding. She was a plain sort of girl, but putting her in the soft-colored silk and doing up her hair properly brought her into the realm of prettyish. Rachael planned to throw her in the path of a few wealthy men during the wedding festivities. Isobel had no money to speak of, but she would be a good wife, and she deserved a quality match.

"Turn, *mademoiselle, s'il vous plait*," the dressmaker instructed, wrapping the measuring tape around Isobel once again. Her French accent was atrocious. Rachael wished she would stop pretending to be foreign to attract customers. People ought to go to her because she was the best, regardless of where she had come from.

Isobel turned and lifted her arms to be measured. The bodice would have to be taken in. The poor girl had as little bosom as she did money. Some padding might be in order.

A knock sounded at the door. It opened a second later, before anyone had a chance to respond. Typical of Elle. She didn't wait on the approval of others.

"Well," Rachael greeted her. "You are dreadfully late. That is not like you. You shall have to hurry and begin the fitting. You can't stand up with me without a proper gown, and there will be alterations necessary to hide your condition." She eyed Elle's growing belly. "If such a thing is possible."

The dressmaker looked Elle over. "We won't hide it, but she will look elegant nonetheless."

"Honestly, Elle, I don't know what you were thinking, getting yourself in such a state at so inconvenient a time. Don't you have a child already? Isn't she good enough?"

"She's wonderful," Elle replied. "That's why I wanted another."

Rachael shuddered. "I detest babies. I don't understand at all why anyone wants them. I hope Avery doesn't want many children, because I will have no more than one. You know how to make contraceptive potions, don't you?"

"I can make short-term ones that can last you anywhere from twelve hours to three days. I alter the concentration based on how long you wish it to last. I also offer a long term potion that will prevent a child for a full year. And mine, unlike some, are one-hundred percent effective."

"Good. I will let you know what I decide. Now come and try out the gown. You will look ravishing when Madame Leroy is finished with you. Your Henry will want to give you even more babies."

"I don't think I need any sort of dress to accomplish that."

"You're right. He probably wants you to be naked at all times, except then he would never stop blushing."

The assistant stopped poking at Rachael to help Elle with the dress. "Would you like to hear the reason for my tardiness?" Elle inquired. "Or shall we continue the discussion about what my husband and I do in the privacy of our own home? I'm certain your cousin is not at all embarrassed by such talk."

She was right. Poor Isobel looked dreadfully shocked. Apparently Rachael's gossipy letters weren't enough preparation for the bluntness and sarcasm she and Elle Ainsworth shared.

"Yes, do tell. You are never late. What was the trouble?"

"I was trying to finish a final analysis of that mysterious potion you left with me."

"And?" Rachael prompted. She hoped Elle's findings would give Avery some much-needed help. The police had been useless in solving the murder thus far.

"This was my third analysis. I still have no idea what it is."

"Pardon?" Rachael was surprised. Elle knew everything

possible to know about potions. "It's a potion you have never encountered before?"

"Not only that. It's a potion unlike anything I have ever seen or heard of. The serum is... different."

"I don't understand."

"Neither do I. That's precisely the trouble. However this potion was made, it wasn't in the usual way. With so little to work with, I don't think I'll be able to learn more. I'm also hampered by the nature of the potion itself."

Rachael nodded. Elle meant the potion was poisonous. She wouldn't be able to taste it, like she often did with potions. Even touching it might be dangerous. Good thing Rachael had worn gloves when she'd taken the sample.

"What do you suggest I do?" Rachael asked.

"Continue your investigation. And if you stumble upon any other strange potions, let me know."

"I will do that. That dress looks quite well on you. It doesn't seem as if it will need as much alteration as I feared."

"Thank you. It's a lovely color. I shall enjoy wearing it. I'm looking forward to your wedding festivities."

"I am as well. I'm tired of being jealous that you have the best husband. It will be much more pleasant when I have an exceptional husband of my own. And *my* nuptials, Miss Deschamps, will be official."

Elle shrugged. "I have no interest in contracts and ceremonies. His word and mine are enough."

"How terribly peculiar. I think your Henry is enough a rogue to want to sire a bevy of bastard children, but too much the gentleman to do it with more than one woman. But I'm embarrassing poor Isobel again, and I don't wish to scare her away before I have found her a proper husband."

"Do not bother yourself on my behalf, cousin. I have long since embraced my spinsterhood."

"Nonsense. You are but twenty-five years old. That is

plenty young still. You can't possibly consider yourself off the market before you have turned thirty."

Isobel blushed. "I don't know that I was ever on the market. A few young men in the village paid me some attention years ago, but nothing came of it. I have never spent time in the city, as you have. You know we don't have the resources to move in society."

Rachael shook her head. "I will ensure you meet the right sort of man. We will look for someone who likes women who read and say brainy sorts of things. Avery will know men of that type."

"Do you always call your fiancé by his given name?" Isobel sounded more scandalized by that than by Elle and Henry's sinful living arrangements.

"Often. I don't like to be formal with him. When we are in public, of course I address him in the usual manner. But you must remember, Isobel, that I enjoy shocking people by ignoring silly things such as that. As you have heard, I nearly always address Mr. Ainsworth by his given name, don't I, Elle?"

"Yes, usually. But, then, he has always called you Rachael in return."

"Are all your friends so very odd?" Isobel wondered. Her cheeks reddened once more. "I hope you didn't find that offensive, Mrs. Ainsworth. I didn't mean it as an insult."

"Certainly not. I am, indeed, extremely odd. I think odd people are the best, don't you agree?"

"Oh, they make for interesting gossip, but most people I know seem very ordinary."

"The majority of my friends are ordinary," Rachael assured her. "We attend balls and talk of fashion and the latest fads, and sometimes poetry or books. We may even play cards. It's pleasant enough."

It bored her, though. Some people may have been content with such a life, but not Rachael. She needed more than the usual occupations. That was what made a man like Avery so very attractive. His passionate nature and his thirst for knowledge would bring her new experiences aplenty. They would travel and explore. She would watch him fall in love with her. They would be scandalously affectionate in public.

"I hope you ladies will join me for tea when we are done here," Rachael said. "I will tell you the plans for the ceremony, and I can give you all the best gossip from the Hawkins's ball the other night. I have to tell you exactly what I said to Mrs. Jennings when she remarked that my fiancé was dull and disagreeable. Part of me hopes he is in an equally bad mood tonight. I enjoy defending him."

Elle and Isobel exchanged a look and laughed.

As it happened, Avery seemed perfectly content when he picked her up that evening. His dress was never out of line with the current fashions, but tonight he had put more thought into his appearance than usual. His smartly tailored suit had been freshly pressed, and his red handkerchief and silver buttons had been chosen to match her typical look. Unfortunately, she was wearing black.

Rachael greeted him with a kiss on the cheek. "You are looking handsome tonight, darling. I had thought all these social events were wearing on you."

"They are. I approve of this particular party, however. It's a worthwhile charity that you have chosen to support, and thanking the donors will hopefully increase their donations or make them eager to give to other good causes. Also, I have heard that our hostess, Lady Ellerby, is enamored of my poetry."

"Yes, she is a big fan. So are several of the ladies in attendance tonight. Do you plan to admit to writing the book at last?" Rachael gave him a hopeful smile.

"Absolutely not. I do, however, hope to invite her to my

upcoming lecture. I would like to raise awareness of *real* historical writings."

"Ah. Well, you need only be your usual, charming self, and they will rush to hear you speak. They may even donate to your research."

"That is my hope, though I don't think my 'usual self' is as charming as you believe."

She shook her head. She had given up trying to convince him.

"You must excuse me a moment," she said. "I need to make a few changes to my wardrobe before we leave."

He blinked at her in surprise. "You look beautiful. What's the trouble?"

"We don't match. I will be only a minute, I promise."

She hurried to her rooms. Her new maid, Jenny, ran to assist her. Rachael liked the girl. She was silent and dependable.

Rachael had accessorized her dress with simple black gloves and unobtrusive jewelry, letting the soft velvet and the metallic glint of the embroidered flowers be the focus. Now, she swapped her dark pearls for a silver chain with a ruby at the throat, and longer silver earrings. She added a silk red rose to her hair, changed into her favorite scarlet kid gloves, and selected a red and black oriental-style fan. The accessories would do the talking now, but she and Avery would be a matched set.

"Still beautiful," he commented when she met him in the hall, "but more eye-catching."

Rachael grinned. The contrasting colors would draw attention. It would be good to be talked about a bit more before her wedding.

They took seats opposite one another in the cab and exchanged pleasantries as it rolled through town. Rachael folded her hands in her lap and tried not to think about how much she would rather be beside him, her hip snugged up against his, his hand on her arm, or perhaps on her thigh.

She snapped her fan open and waved cool air across her face. She hadn't expected that waiting for her wedding night would be so difficult. It had never been unpleasant with her first husband, but his affections had felt perfunctory, as had her own for him. In contrast, Avery's kisses left her aching with desire. She went out of her way to touch him. She wondered if the feeling would subside once they had engaged in amorous congress.

She distracted herself from her impure thoughts by relating her afternoon visit and Elle's comments on the poison. Avery wore a thoughtful frown as he listened, and took several seconds before he replied.

"The more I discover about the man's death, the less sense it makes. It could have been nothing more than a bad mushroom he picked and ate, perhaps after he'd been drinking. Then your discovery of the poison proved it to be murder. Now we know the weapon to be an unusual, unknown poison.

"I can't come up with a motive. The man wasn't disliked for any reason I can discover. He wasn't robbed. He had no enemies. He had little family and no money to leave them, so no one has gained in any way from his death. It seems random. Why would anyone poison a man at random?"

"To test the poison?" Rachael guessed. "Could the villain have discovered or created some strange potion and given it to the man, just to see what would happen? He drinks it and falls down dead. The person who gave him the potion panics and rushes to bury the bottle before anyone sees what he did."

"An interesting theory," Avery mused. "But in this scenario, is he innocent—more or less—because he didn't know it to be poison? Or did he know it was poison and only want to learn how fast it did the deed?"

"The former would make him a fool. The latter would make him terrifying." Rachael shuddered.

Avery reached across to take her hand. "It's something to consider, and I will pass the idea on to the police in the hopes that it might aid their investigation. In the meantime, however, please don't dwell upon it. I don't wish to ruin your evening with talk of murder."

"The matter is less distressing to me than you might think," she assured him.

He nodded. "You are a woman of fortitude."

"Thank you. Now, tell me of your lecture. It will allow you to practice before you try to convince anyone to attend."

"I will be speaking on some of our findings during the last few years of excavations, explaining how we can connect them with folklore to learn about the culture and the importance of warrior-kings. Purcell will be there, as well, and Hunstable with his photographs. They will cover some of the details of the items we have found. It is part of a three-lecture series. I am giving two of the three talks. Dashell is giving the third. I hope he doesn't turn the whole thing into a treasure-hunting spectacle."

"Dashell." The name sparked a recollection in Rachael's mind. "You and Purcell mentioned him that day we visited your excavations. Who is he?"

Avery's mouth twisted in distaste. "My rival. He despises me."

She regarded him with raised brows. "A rival scholar of Anglo-Saxon lore? That sounds rather silly."

"It *is* silly! The whole thing is absurd."

"What on earth do you fight about?"

"We don't fight about anything! The man won't speak to me. He feels slighted by something I've done, but I don't even know what that might be. He will talk with Purcell, but even then only begrudgingly. It's been like this for years. It drives me mad. We should be sharing our research, not hoarding it like a dragon with a cavern full of gold. Purcell thinks we can reconcile. I suppose I should go to Dashell's lecture. He may have learned something that could contribute to my research."

"I think that a sensible plan. For tonight, I suggest you forget him. Speak of your own lectures only."

Avery nodded. "I wish I had thought to procure an invitation for Purcell tonight. He is much more personable than I, and he would do better at persuading the ladies to attend."

"You *could* be personable, if you desired. You are well-spoken, and you have a romantic soul. If you put in just a fraction of the effort you put into your work…"

"If you make one more mention of my 'romantic soul,'" he threatened.

"What? You will growl at me and pretend to be a crotchety old man?"

"I may lose my temper and storm off, leaving you without a husband while I confine myself to my office for the remainder of my days."

"I will come up with a better epithet, then," she decided. "Perhaps something alliterative, like in your Anglo-Saxon texts."

"Don't. Please. I'm not a chivalrous knight from a tale. If you fall in love with me you will only be disappointed."

"Don't be silly. I'm not a doe-eyed schoolgirl."

"That's what I'm counting on."

The conversation dwindled, and Rachael struggled for things to say until they arrived at Lady Ellerby's home. The traffic in front of the townhouse was at a standstill.

"Thank goodness you hired a carriage," she said, letting Avery help her alight. "I know personal cars are all the rage since the decrease in potion prices, but these gentlemen will be an hour arranging for places to park their vehicles. I wonder how long it will be before pre-arranged staggered arrivals become fashionable."

"Mere days, I imagine, if you make the suggestion."

Rachael beamed at the compliment. She wasn't *that* great a trend setter, but she loved that he believed her to be.

The Ellerby house was grand without pretension, and the guests of similar quality. A string ensemble treated the visitors to pleasant music, and there would be dancing, if enough gentlemen could be pried away from their cars. Lady Ellerby greeted Rachael and Avery with a smile, thanked them for their donations, and congratulated them on the upcoming wedding. Rachael liked her. She had all the decorum of her rank—her husband was an earl—without too much superiority.

"That is a splendid dress, Mrs. Fasching," Lady Ellerby said. "And I admire your bold accessories. You do have a style all your own. Few women could make your daring fashion choices with such aplomb."

"Thank you, Lady Ellerby. Your own gown is divine, and your home just what it ought to be. You are a lady of true elegance."

Rachael relished the opportunity to give praise with no need for prevarications or sarcasm. Avery, too, approved of their hosts and surroundings. He was perfectly charming with his own greetings and compliments, despite his earlier assertions.

The evening progressed in a similarly pleasing fashion. Rachael enjoyed a number of dances with her fiancé, though the time spent in his arms did have a tendency to leave her with rosy cheeks and wicked thoughts. She had to space out their dances. None of her other partners left her needing to fan herself and take a breath of fresh air.

The champagne was authentic, and she drank just enough to feel the first edge of tipsiness. She was happy and relaxed, having a fine time. Avery, of course, sampled none of the food or drink. It continued to bother her that he couldn't partake of anything, but it didn't appear to affect his mood. She imagined he had grown accustomed to the problem years ago.

Thus far, one gentleman and two ladies had expressed interest in his lecture. A few more such conversations, and Rachael suspected he would consider the evening a smashing success.

She had just steered their current discussion to his work, when a screech of horror interrupted the merriment. Rachael's gaze flew to the noise. The entire group rushed to a table bedecked with refreshments. Rachael used her height to good advantage, looking right over the shorter women to get a view of the chaos.

A gentleman had fallen to his knees, holding his stomach and retching uncontrollably. Whatever he had eaten for dinner was now all over the polished ballroom floor, and he didn't appear to be finished. It may have been the most revolting thing Rachael had ever witnessed in her life. The smell alone was enough to turn her stomach.

The woman who had shrieked continued to wail. Her shrill, undecipherable words pained Rachael's ears. A few other ladies of delicate sensibilities began to swoon. Avery jumped to catch a fainting woman, displaying his natural gallantry. Once he had hold of her, he looked at a loss for what to do. His eyes darted back and forth, trying to find a place to put her or a husband to hand her off to. Neither materialized.

Rachael's own sensibilities weren't the least delicate. When others turned and fled, she inched closer. She needed a better look at the man to see if she recognized him. Otherwise she would need to eavesdrop on nearby conversation until she learned his name. It would be important when she reported the matter to Isobel in the morning.

A second gagging sound made Rachael turn. It came from a woman stumbling across the room, both hands covering her mouth. She didn't have time to make a polite exit. She tried to steady herself against the wall, but collapsed only a moment later and began to vomit.

The room erupted in panic. People ran this way and that, shouting, crying, pushing. Half-a-dozen others fell abruptly ill. Faces all over looked sickly or scared. Ladies and gentlemen alike leaned on one another or sat themselves down on the floor, moaning. Rachael couldn't tell who suffered true sickness and who was having unnecessary hysterics. She thought she might be the only person in the room not overcome.

Avery dragged his swooning damsel to a sofa and deposited her there with as much courtesy as could be managed. Freed from the burden, he rushed to Rachael's side and took her arm.

"Are you well?"

"As well as can be, given the circumstances," she replied. "I have been too busy dancing and socializing to eat, and I drank only the champagne. I don't feel the slightest queasiness. I won't end up on the floor like the others. You?"

"I'm unaffected. You know I didn't eat or drink this evening."

Rachael scanned the scene. She now counted ten actively sick people, and perhaps twice that many fainting, looking green, or otherwise in distress. The remaining crowd consisted of weepers, those comforting the weepers, and those running for the exits.

Lady Ellerby was among the ill. Her husband held a protective cloth over her dress, and attempted to keep her hair in its coiffure as she heaved into a punch bowl—considerably more refined than her guests who continued to be sick on her floor.

"There must have been something in the food," Avery deduced.

"Yes. And something terrible, at that. I have heard of parties where people have fallen ill from bad food, but not anywhere that it happened so quickly or so violently." She pulled him toward the door. "There is something I must tell you, let's find a place to talk."

Once outside the ballroom, they turned the opposite direction from the exiting guests and ducked into the drawing room.

"You look worried," Avery observed. "What's troubling you? We will leave at once if this rash of illness has upset you."

She shook her head. "My own person is entirely unharmed.

However, I'm worried that the cause of this tragedy may be poison."

His mouth pinched into a tight frown. "I sincerely hope not. It's more likely spoiled food. All it would take is one servant with unwashed hands to contaminate a dish."

"I have some experience with poisoned food."

He blinked in surprise. "Do you?"

Rachael took a deep breath and steeled herself for the unpleasant truth. "Just before I left New York, I was a guest at a dinner party. Many of the guests fell ill that evening. The cause was poison. Administered by my husband. An innocent man died that night."

Avery stared at her in horror. "No."

"I told you Fasching wasn't a good man. That night before dinner he gave me strict and bizarre instructions about what I was to eat. Only after the poisoning was revealed did his orders make sense. I took a boat to England at once and never saw my husband again, thankfully."

"Good God. How are you not in hysterics this evening?"

"I don't become hysterical. Such strong emotions are not in my character."

"We have that in common, then. Perhaps it's why we get on so well. Still, I must get you away from here. The stress and the exposure to sickness can't be good for anyone."

She nodded. "I agree. Come. We will make our goodbyes to Lady Ellerby and be off."

Avery started. "What? She is one of those affected! Surely you don't mean to approach her!"

"I see no reason the unfortunate circumstances should prevent us behaving in a civilized manner," she insisted. She turned on her heel and started for the ballroom. He would protest, she expected, and escort her from the house.

To her surprise, he followed after her in silence. Such an odd man. She still had no explanation for why he continued to give in to her whims.

Lady Ellerby was no longer vomiting, but her face looked green, and she could hardly stand. Sick guests lay here and there, some being attended by servants. Rachael and Avery picked their way around the unpleasantness until they reached their hostess.

Rachael dipped into a curtsy. "My sincere condolences on this unfortunate happening," she said. "You have been a most gracious hostess and you have my best wishes for a speedy return to health."

Lady Ellerby croaked her thanks and nodded to them before her husband and a maid helped her from the room.

Satisfied she had taken care of all proprieties, Rachael departed. The street outside was clogged once again, now with steam cars piloted by distraught men. There was a great deal of shouting and several tearful women.

Avery escorted Rachael down the block and around the first corner. "We will walk, for a time, until we are away from this madness. If you are able?"

Rachael's dancing slippers weren't ideal for walking, but she answered in the affirmative. She double-checked the ties that kept the train of her dress from dragging. She didn't want it ruined. It hadn't gotten the display it ought to have, given the sad end to the evening. She would need to find another event at which to wear it.

Avery was silent and ill-tempered. He didn't quite stomp as he walked, but it was a near thing. His night had been ruined. No one at the party would even remember his lecture and he had learned that his wife-to-be had been married to a murderer. Rachael couldn't see any way to console him.

Her own mind busily reviewed the entire night: the food, the drink, who had partaken of which items. She felt a certainty in her gut that something had been poisoned. Thank heavens she had only drunk the champagne.

They walked for about a quarter of an hour before Avery hailed a cab and took her home. The ride, too, was conducted in silence. It wasn't often that Rachael entirely lacked something to say, but tonight was an anomaly.

Avery saw her into the house and kissed her brow. "You will be well, here, on your own?"

"Of course."

"I would hate for you to be up all night worrying about poisons. It was only bad food. Your unfortunate history and the recent death of that digger have spurred your imagination."

"That must be it," Rachael lied.

Their eyes locked. She smiled at him as best she could, given her current anxieties. His mention of the death at the excavation site had pushed her thoughts where she preferred them not to go. If she was correct about what had transpired tonight, that made it the second poisoning in as many weeks. And the only connection she could find between the two was Avery Cantrell.

XIII

Get Thee a Wife

RACHAEL HAD NEVER INQUIRED about the wedding trip. Avery paced the small chamber in the back of the church. Weeks had passed since he'd sent his note, and she'd never asked. He didn't know why that, of all things, was bothering him this morning, but he couldn't get it out of his head. Surely she had ideas about the trip. She was filled with ideas, and usually eager to express them. On the topic of their honeymoon, however, she had remained completely silent.

Avery thought back to what he had written. He remembered it as, "I have made all the arrangements for our wedding trip. Contact my secretary if you would like the details."

It was a bit blunt, perhaps, but he didn't think it sounded high-handed. Had it made her angry, even so? The idea that she would accept it without so much as asking what the plans were bothered him. Enough, apparently, that he couldn't concentrate on anything else on his wedding day.

"Is everything still running on time, Bellamy?"

The secretary turned from his place by the mirror. Avery had provided him with a brand new suit, and he looked uncomfortable in it. He kept fidgeting and examining himself.

"Yes, sir, last I checked. Your fiancée has everything well under control."

"Good. I'd like to get it over with."

"Would you like some brandy, sir, to calm your nerves?"

Avery nearly protested that his nerves weren't suffering. Then he thought about the damned wedding trip again and decided a drink was a fine idea.

Bellamy pulled a small flask from inside his coat, and they sat and shared a drink— friends for a time, rather than employer and employee.

"Thank you, Sebastian," Avery said, after several swallows of the smooth liquor. "I feel better. Thank you also for standing up with me. It's awkward when a man has no family."

"I'm honored to be chosen."

Avery didn't think it so great an honor. Whom else could he have asked? Purcell possibly. He was nearer to Avery in social class, but Avery was closer with Bellamy. Hunstable was the son of a peer, but barely out of the schoolroom. Outside of work, Avery had no close friends. He had never had time to develop more than casual relationships with anyone else.

He had invited many of his not-quite-friends to the wedding, just to fill seats. Rachael had plenty of friends to invite, and family also. Avery had briefly considered sending invitations to his mother and half-siblings, but in the end opted for a simple, informative note. He doubted anyone had read it. They acted as if he didn't exist.

When the time came at last to take his place at the altar, he was relieved to see the church was neither empty nor crowded. When the wedding was written up in the gossip columns, his lack of family and friends wouldn't be noticed.

Music swelled and the congregation rose to its feet.

Then he saw Rachael.

His heart nearly stopped. Why had he worried? Nothing would be noticed, about him or anything else. The roof could cave in, and still all attention would be on her and her alone.

She floated effortlessly down the aisle, shoulders square, head high, silent and untouchable. Her white dress clung and flowed, concealing and yet flaunting her every curve. Avery might have thought her a phantom, but for the deeply human smile of pure happiness on her perfect, red lips. She was ravishing.

The ceremony passed by in a blur. Afterward, he couldn't recall a single reading, or any of the sermon. His mind was fixated on Rachael. He held her hands, he looked into her eyes, and he made his vows to her. She made her own promise with a firm, clear voice, though she flinched at the word "obey."

A burst of fury ran through him. What had her bastard husband done to her to cause that fear? Some part of Avery wished the man were still alive so he could strangle him.

The words "man and wife" sent a surge of protective triumph through him. *He* was her husband now. He would never harm her or frighten her, and woe to anyone who might try.

Their fleeting kiss left him unsatisfied. He could do no more in the church in front of so many people. His gaze lingered on her lips—red, moist, and slightly parted. When his eyes lifted to hers, the desire he read there sent his blood racing straight to his groin. He wanted to take her to bed, not to a wedding breakfast, but there were proprieties to be observed, so they linked arms and walked together out of the church.

He stole a few more kisses in the carriage, but she couldn't arrive at breakfast looking disheveled, and their careful embraces only compounded his frustration.

Rachael had chosen to host their wedding party at her own townhouse. Avery had to admit the elegant and impeccably furnished residence was nicer than his own house. They hadn't yet discussed what to do about their two houses. Custom dictated that she should move in with him. His house had been in the family for several generations. She had been in her house for no more than a year. And yet...

He could see himself living here, in her home. The change would be welcome. He hadn't realized, before Rachael, how much he had craved change. His life had become too monotonous. Now he was married, and moving closer to a cure. A new house could be part of this better life. He would ask Rachael for her thoughts on the matter. If she hated the place, or loved his, he wouldn't make her stay.

"I was shocked, I tell you, *shocked* when she walked in wearing that white gown," one of Rachael's chatty friends said to another as Avery wandered aimlessly through the crowd of wedding guests. "But she pulled it off, of course. She always does. Now, Mr. Barnburry on the other hand…"

"I know! That waistcoat! Did you notice the little dogs on the buttons? The man is obsessed, I tell you."

Avery continued past, shaking his head. Her friends were a stunningly eclectic assortment, and Rachael conversed happily and easily with each and every one of them. He did his best to keep up.

He nodded politely to a middle-aged widow as she flirted shamelessly with him, then spent twenty minutes listening to a Miss Mary Reynolds discuss the merits of her feminist club. One woman gave him a shy smile, then looked quickly away, wielding her book of poetry like a shield. How had Rachael ever met this many people?

"Congratulations, Rachael. You look smashing, as always!" The blond man leaned in and whispered something else in her ear. The too-familiar behavior sparked a burst of jealousy, and Avery scowled at the presumptuous scoundrel. The man simply laughed, kissed Rachael's cheek, and vanished into the crowd.

Enough socializing. Rachael held the attention of the entire party. No one would miss him. Avery snuck away to explore the house.

He discovered a fine study that would suit him well. Spacious, with sturdy bookshelves, good lighting, and well-crafted furnishings, it was everything he would have chosen in a home office. Excellent. Rachael would be happier if he spent more time at home and less at the University. A second, smaller study down the hall appeared unused. If this were his permanent residence, he could give Bellamy that room. This neighborhood was closer to the secretary's residence, so he would be able to walk instead of riding his ridiculous bicycle all over the city. Avery would mention it to him. He was here, somewhere.

"The library?" Avery asked a chambermaid passing down the hall.

"There, sir. Second door."

"Thank you."

He opened the door and stepped inside, curious what Rachael's book collection would look like. He reeled in shock. In the middle of the room, sprawled on an antique fainting couch, was Rachael's pregnant bridesmaid, her cheeks flushed and her clothing askew, in the arms of the obnoxious blond man.

"Do you mind?" the man grumbled. "The lady is in a delicate condition and has need of privacy."

"A condition for which you are every bit as responsible as I," she retorted, poking him in the chest. His necktie was undone, his waistcoat unbuttoned, and his shirt well on the way to being removed.

He took hold of her hand and brought it to his lips. "I don't deny it." His blue eyes gleamed with devotion.

All the angry words Avery had meant to say flew from his mind. The way the blond man looked at Rachael was nothing compared to the besotted expression on his face as he gazed at his own wife. The man was smitten. *That* was the look of the imaginary warrior of Avery's poems.

Bloody hell. That accursed book.

Rachael would expect such behavior from him. Perhaps not now, but someday. She harbored a mad notion that he was some sort of repressed romantic. Did she think to drag it out of him? No matter how she dug, she would find nothing. He would be only a disappointment to her.

He spun away from Rachael's canoodling friends. He needed a drink. For once, he had no worries about the glassware.

In the dining room, the remaining crowd indulged themselves with tea and cake, either squeezed around the table, or standing nearby. Avery grabbed a slice for himself and downed a full glass of champagne with it.

His eyes sought Rachael, radiant as ever, still making the rounds and talking. The morning had been a rousing success for her. She had been noticed and admired, the ceremony and the breakfast had been flawless, and she was surrounded by family and friends. The only difficulty was one disappointed young officer who trailed after her, looking like a sad puppy dog. Being Rachael, she took control of that situation as well.

"Major Blakely, have you been introduced to my cousin, Miss Isobel Stillwell? She is a very fine woman. Polished. Well-read. I think you would find her a most pleasant conversationalist." Rachael scanned the room. "She is here, somewhere."

The man took the hint at last, faked looking at his watch, and made a hasty departure.

Rachael sighed in relief. She slipped up beside Avery and kissed his cheek. "Goodness. Honestly, it is nowhere near as enjoyable to have officers enamored of you when you are twenty-seven as when you are nineteen. That man needs a wife."

"You think he might suit your cousin?"

"Perhaps. I had hoped to introduce her to a few eligible men, but she can be shy in public. I don't know why, since she is plenty chatty with me."

"Talking to strangers is never so easy as talking to those you know."

"Yes, I suppose that's true. Particularly when you are plain or lack money. It's difficult to make people notice you for your own self."

"Not for you. You put your own self on display every day. You don't fear to be different. It's one of the things I admire about you."

She laid a hand on his arm and smiled at him affectionately. Avery covered her hand with his own and gazed into those pretty, brown eyes. Heat flashed through him. It was time this party ended.

"Can we send everyone away yet?" he whispered.

Rachael's fingers squeezed his upper arm. "They have already begun to leave. It won't be long."

"Not long" was a relative term, unfortunately. Little-by-little the guests paused to make their goodbyes, some lingering so long that Avery thought his face might become permanently fixed in his false smile.

"I do hope you have a relaxing wedding trip, Lady Cantrell," said one final departing guest. "Where will you be going?"

"I don't know. My husband made the arrangements."

He flinched. The tightness in her voice suggested she wasn't happy about it.

"Oh, a surprise? How romantic. Have a good time, dear." She kissed the air beside Rachael's cheek and turned to leave.

Romantic. Good Lord.

Avery wanted to kick himself. Never mind his lack of a romantic soul. This was worse. What kind of insensitive jackass dragged his new bride off to take care of a work matter the day after their wedding? She was going to hate him, and rightly so. He needed to tell her. He needed to apologize. He needed to do it in such a way that she might be willing to accept that apology.

What could he do? Champagne? Roses? Jewelry? She didn't lack for any of those things, and had enough money of her own to purchase what she wanted. No, he needed something better, and he needed to have it ready by morning.

Damn. He'd only been married for a few hours, and already he'd gotten himself in trouble.

XIV

Wedding Night Jitters

$\mathcal{R}$ACHAEL PACED ABOUT HER ROOM in her nightgown. This was ridiculous. She was a worldly woman. She knew what a wedding night entailed. Yet, here she was, acting like a terrified innocent. Where was the bold Rachael who had kissed Avery so hungrily the other day?

In hiding, that's where she was. She was waiting, hoping someone would come along and release her from her self-made prison.

The truth of the matter was that Rachael had no idea know what to do. She had no notion what Avery might like, or what he expected of her.

Her first husband had always approached her, if he were in an amorous mood. It had been easy. She went to bed when she was ready, and sometimes he came to visit her. Never once had she set foot in his bedroom. At the time she had assumed it to be normal, but now it seemed odd. Perhaps she was spending too much time with strange couples such as Henry and Elle, who didn't even *have* separate rooms.

Rachael paused, looked herself over in the mirror, then resumed her pacing. Why didn't he come? Surely he would want to consummate the marriage, even if he wasn't feeling in the mood tonight.

She was in the mood. She had been for weeks, since that first spontaneous kiss in his office. Every kiss since had only heightened her cravings. Her memories of the carriage ride that morning were vivid. She could almost taste his mouth, warm and wet against her own. Each time he began with that gentle first brush of his lips, then grew intense when she gave encouragement. He never failed to leave her eager for the next kiss.

She was eager to touch him, as well. She wanted to strip away his clothing so she could feel his skin against her own. She wanted to learn him: the breadth of his chest, the planes of his body, his size and shape. To smell that spiciness that always tinged the air when she drew close enough.

For heaven's sake, where was he? She hoped he wasn't waiting for her to come to him. The last thing she wanted was to upset him. How could she have been married for five years and still not know how to be a proper wife?

When a knock finally came at her door she jumped and nearly let out a yelp. She scampered to the door, her heart hammering. What would he say? What would he think? If all he wanted was to get it over with, she would be crushed.

He didn't say anything at all, in fact. As soon as he saw her, his mouth dropped open and he stared. Her nightgown was just shy of transparent, and she wasn't wearing anything underneath. It was clear he hadn't expected that.

Heat suffused her cheeks. Embarrassment? Arousal? She didn't know.

"Do you like the nightgown?" she asked, silly as the question was.

"Yes," he said. "It doesn't leave much to the imagination, does it?"

"You don't need to imagine any longer. You are my husband now."

"Lucky me." His eyes settled on her breasts, the rosy peaks of her nipples plain as day beneath the thin fabric. "I, uh… I wasn't certain if you wished me to come to you tonight, or the other way 'round. The bed in my room is a bit larger, I believe, but I understand if you prefer yours."

"No, yours," Rachael replied without hesitation. "I prefer your room."

The thought of invading his masculine domain sent a thrill through her. She knew nothing about men's rooms and men's things. She'd never been allowed into her former husband's chambers. Here was her chance to sample something new and forbidden. To forge an intimacy with Avery that she had never shared with anyone. Her heart rejoiced that he had offered her the choice.

Not that there was anything especially masculine about his room at the moment, nor much that reflected him. It had been furnished and arranged by her staff, like any other bedroom in the house. It only happened to adjoin hers.

"Excellent. Shall I carry you across the threshold to display my gallantry?" His eyes twinkled. "Or throw you over my shoulder like a barbarian?"

She frowned at him. He couldn't be serious. She was as tall as many men, and she was a curvy woman, not a lanky one. She was too heavy to be picked up.

When he scooped her into his arms she let out a squeal of surprise. Her nightgown slid up past her knees, and she felt an irrational burst of shyness. He cradled her against his chest and planted a kiss on her brow.

"Gallantry, I think," he said. A wicked glint sparkled in his eye. "We shall save the barbarism for the bed."

A rush of heat spread throughout her body, followed by a quiver low in her abdomen. A few words from him and she was aching with desire.

He carried her into his room and lowered her down onto his bed. He stood above her for a moment, looking her over with unmistakable admiration. His expression lacked the smug possessiveness of her first husband. Rather than assuming she was nothing less than he deserved, Avery seemed almost stunned to be here with her.

He unfastened and discarded his dressing gown, and she was startled to find he was stark naked underneath. Her eyes widened and her lips parted as she studied the contours of his body. He was fully aroused. She longed to slide her fingers along the trail of dark hairs that ran down his abdomen. She yearned to kiss his neck and suck on his earlobe. She wanted to feel the muscles of his arms and his thighs against her.

Old worries clashed with her desires. That nagging voice scolded her, telling her not to stare, not to think about touching him and tasting him.

To hell with that.

She was New Rachael now, with a husband of her own choosing, whom she wanted not for his title or his money, nor even for his poetry and romanticism. She wanted the man himself, his body, in a very basic and carnal way. And she refused to believe it was wrong of her.

Avery sat on the bed next to her, and she wrapped her arms around him, dragging him close. He leaned in for a kiss, gentle as always, waiting for her response. She ran her tongue across his lips, hoping he would do the same. He didn't disappoint. He devoured her, ravishing her mouth with tongue and lips. She tilted her head for more, letting the fire of the kiss spread across her body.

Rachael's hands began to wander, up his back, across his shoulders, and onto his chest. Hard where she was soft. Solid, strong. Excitement raced up her arms and down her spine. He did nothing to stop her, nothing to direct her. Her mind whirled with this strange freedom to explore. Did he like it? Was she doing it right?

He mimicked her motions, until his large palms came down to cup her breasts through the thin cotton of her nightgown.

He tweaked her nipples, drawing them taut against the fabric. Rachael sighed, her worries evaporating beneath the pleasure of his touch. Each squeeze and caress sent a new tremor of delight across her skin.

Avery broke their kiss so he could tug her nightgown up over her head. She lifted her arms and it slid away, leaving her skin bare against his. Her skin flushed as he gazed at her and resumed his caresses, now with nothing to separate them.

His mouth dropped to her bosom and his tongue lapped against one hard, pink peak. Another sigh escaped her lips, and she arched her back to bring him closer. He alternated between her breasts, letting his fingers pleasure one while his lips were on the other. Rachael tried to answer with her own hands, tangling her fingers in the hairs of his chest and rubbing his small, hard nipples.

Together, they sank down onto the bed, mouths coming together again in a deep, greedy kiss. Rachael clung to his shoulders, her legs spreading.

"More," she gasped.

A hand slid between her legs. His fingers parted her folds and stroked her delicate flesh, finding her hot and slick.

"Please." The word came out on a throaty whisper. "I'm ready for you, Avery. Make me your wife in body as well as name."

His finger found her sensitive nub and stroked it, drawing it tight, provoking a gasp of pleasure from deep in her throat.

"Ah, my Rachael. I'm ready for you, also." He paused to circle her nipple with his tongue. "I have spent days dreaming about feeling you writhe beneath me and hearing you moan my name." He repeated the motion on the opposite breast, his fingers still running teasing strokes across her clit. "It has been agony to wait, but that will make the pleasure all the greater."

Rachael moaned. Her hands clutched at him, not knowing what to do other than hang on as he continued his leisurely exploration. Learning her. Worshiping her.

"Rachael." Her name was harsher now, almost strangled, but still he held himself back, rubbing his shaft along her thigh and slipping first one, then a second finger inside of her.

Gasps and groans poured from her lips—strange pleading noises she had never made before. It had never been like this, not when her first husband had caused her to climax, nor when she had been left unsatisfied and forced to finish things herself. She wouldn't deny having enjoyed those experiences, but this was more. Better. She had never felt such anticipation, such urgent desperation. It was agony. It was beautiful.

The tension inside of her swelled to a level she hadn't thought possible. She thrust her hips at him, aching to pull him inside of her and end the crazed desire that was tearing her apart.

"Please, Avery," she moaned. "Please. I need you."

He growled in satisfaction and plunged into her. He was thick and hard and so very right, just as she had hoped. His strokes began like his kisses, with agonizing slowness. Rachael rocked and clawed at him, begging him to move faster. The room spun as he picked up the pace. He was moaning her name now, in a voice so ragged it sent chills down her spine.

She could feel the climax, hovering so close, just out of reach. Avery moved deeper inside of her, his thrusts coming fast and hard.

"Rachael, I can't..."

"Yes." It was the only word she could form. "Yes."

She clenched around him, breaking apart, the orgasm raging though her. Her body tightened, twisted, bent, then finally uncoiled. With a final lunge, Avery convulsed atop her, shuddering as he spent himself. She sank into the bed, breathless, feeling as if she had melted into a puddle.

Avery rolled over and lay next to her, sweat dampening his brow, chest heaving. His hand wandered up her thigh and settled on her hip. He drew her to him and held her there, his arm embracing, but not confining. Rachael lay motionless, too stunned and satisfied for anything else. She expected him to ask her to return to her room, or to carry her there, but within minutes he was asleep.

She watched him in the dim light, his body still, his expression peaceful. She could hear the soft exhalation of his breath, slow and steady. A curly lock of dark hair had fallen across his brow. With one finger she brushed it back into place, her fingertip skimming over his skin in the softest of caresses. This felt more intimate than their intercourse. She had never slept with a man before. Laying there, in his bed, in his arms, caused an unexpected giddiness inside her. The rapture of her climax had faded into contentment, but it was peppered with odd little bubbles of joy as she snuggled with her husband. She wondered, perhaps, if he might expect her to leave on her own, but she remained as she was. She dared not move and break the spell.

Her eyes drifted closed and she welcomed the oblivion of sleep, happy to let everything fade away but the warmth of Avery's body.

XV

A Rocky Start

RACHAEL'S EYES FLUTTERED OPEN. She flinched, startled to find her husband in bed beside her. He was here. He hadn't left her or sent her away. She snuggled back down into the pillow with a happy sigh.

Her wedding night had been so surprising it almost felt like a dream. It had been beyond everything she'd expected, beyond even what she'd hoped for. Their marriage would be a good one. She wouldn't complain if he wanted her to sleep beside him on other occasions.

Her movements woke him, and he smiled at her, then gathered her in his arms for a kiss. They were both still naked, and the kisses swiftly led them to other things. Their lovemaking was relaxed this morning, his touch soft and soothing. It still left her moaning in pleasure, her body wracked with spasms of ecstasy.

When he rose, she lay in bed and watched him wash up and shave, another new experience for her. She had missed out on many things, she decided, due to Fasching's aloofness. He had given her a comfortable home and left plenty of funds at her disposal, but he'd shown her little affection. Once, she had thought his possessiveness meant he loved her, but she'd come to realize he had seen her as a prize. She was something to show off—the prettiest girl in the room.

Avery was free with his affections. He smiled at her often, and didn't reserve his kisses for the bedroom. She wondered, though, if he, too, felt he had won a great prize in her.

They took a small breakfast together before she adjourned to her room for a long, hot bath. By the time she was clean and dressed for the day, it was nearing luncheon. They were scheduled to leave on their wedding trip directly after the meal.

The traveling dress she had chosen was red with black accents, and matched her driving goggles. Rachael didn't anticipate driving a carriage, assuming they would be traveling by train, but she brought the goggles along anyhow. Perhaps she would have an opportunity to teach Avery to drive. Knowing nothing about the trip, it was best to be prepared.

She fussed with her trunks, making sure every item was arranged just so. Where were they going? Why hadn't he told her? The happiness of the morning faded, replaced with a growing irritation. She grumbled and complained over stupid, silly details. A bit of fluff here, a tiny crease, there. None of it eased her frustration. Avery had planned the entire wedding trip without her, and she wanted nothing better than to scream at him until every cell in his body could feel just how unhappy she was to have been left out.

Rachael clenched her teeth in frustration. She couldn't do that to him. He had done nothing that wasn't within his rights as a husband, and she had to accept that. Avery might not be a domineering sort of man, but he was organized and businesslike, and he probably hadn't thought twice about making arrangements alone. Or perhaps he really did intend it to be a surprise. That would be in keeping with his romantic nature. She liked that idea best, so she clung to it. She would simply tell him she wasn't a fan of surprises, and it would never happen again.

Her gaze dropped to the new ring on her left hand. The

silver band was styled with an intricate knot pattern, like she'd seen in old monuments and manuscripts, and accented with small rubies. She loved it, and it had been a surprise. She couldn't claim to dislike all surprises. Still, given the choice, she would opt for knowing ahead of time.

Steeling herself to tell him just that, Rachael headed downstairs, but Avery was neither in the study nor the library. Puzzled, she sought out her butler.

"Jenkins, would you happen to know where my husband has gotten to?"

"Indeed, madam. He left this morning to take care of a few matters of business before your departure."

"And he hasn't yet returned?"

"I'm afraid not."

That concerned her. He had been at ease yesterday, and she had thought everything settled. This morning when they parted he had been smiling and relaxed. What could have come up between then and now?

"When he arrives, would you be so good as to let him know I'm waiting in the dining room?"

"Of course, madam."

"Thank you."

He gave her a polite nod as she left. She liked him. He was dependable. Rachael had never paid much attention to her servants until she had taken up residence here. In her previous homes, other people had always hired the help, paid them, and handled all other aspects of their employment. They had simply been there, ready to follow her orders, and she hadn't thought beyond that.

Selecting her own staff for this house had been an unpleasant chore, and she hadn't done it well. She had been forced to dismiss several people during the first six months for reasons ranging from theft to simple incompetence. The house remained understaffed for its size, but her remaining employees were all efficient and good at what they did.

She swallowed an unladylike curse.

When she and Avery consolidated their households, she would need to let most of her staff go. The thought dismayed her. She had grown fond of this house and the people who ran it. It was the one thing outside her wardrobe that truly felt like her own, and she would have to leave it all behind when she moved in with him.

Feeling irritated with life in general and her husband in specific, Rachael fetched the book of his poems and sat down to read in the dining room while her employees prepared for luncheon around her. With luck, the book would remind her of why she liked Avery in the first place. It also might annoy him to find her reading it again, which was precisely what he deserved.

A full fifteen minutes after the meal was ready, Avery hurried into the room, apologizing for his tardiness. He didn't even glance at her book. His brow was creased with worry, and sadness lurked in his green eyes. Rachael's irritation dissolved in an instant.

"Avery, what's wrong?"

He pulled up a chair beside her. "Let's eat first. I'm famished."

Rachael stewed and tried not to fidget while the food was served and they began the meal. With each minute that ticked by, her concern grew. His expression wavered between fury and despair, and his fingers clenched so tightly on his fork that she thought he might bend the silver.

He had eaten more than half of his chicken before he spoke. "Hunstable has been arrested and charged with the murder of the digger."

Rachael nearly dropped her knife. "What? No. I can't believe it."

"I don't believe it, either, but it has happened. He is a photographer. He has a vast array of chemicals and potions at his disposal."

"What sort of proof is that? Having chemicals makes one a poisoner? Nonsense. Didn't he have an alibi?"

"Not enough of one, apparently. The men work hard and sleep soundly. I doubt anyone could say he wasn't up sometime during the night."

"He's not a murderer. I'm certain of it. He would never have the nerve to do the deed. I thought he might burst into tears over my viewing of the pictures."

"He *was* in tears this morning. I went to see him before they took him back to Ipswich. That's why I was so long returning. The poor boy is a wreck, and the most I could do was offer him the name of a good lawyer." He put his head in his hands. "I don't know what to do. I feel terrible I haven't done more to further the investigation. You found our only clue, but this is all that has come of it."

Rachael scooted her chair closer and put a hand on his shoulder. "Don't blame yourself. The police have found nothing and choose to cast the blame on the most convenient target rather than work harder. It's a travesty of justice and in no way a reflection on you. Perhaps a word with someone above Inspector Galby?"

Avery nodded. "Purcell is on it. I hope he is able to help. I feel terrible, leaving when this is happening."

"You couldn't have known."

He sighed. "I will keep in touch while we are away. If things become bad enough that I must return and cut the trip short, I promise I will make it up to you with another holiday at another time. Anywhere you choose."

Something of Rachael's former irritation resurfaced. "Why didn't you allow me to choose in the first place?"

"I didn't think about it," he mumbled, not making eye contact. The man was a terrible liar.

She pushed her chair back and crossed her arms beneath her breasts. It was a most inelegant posture, but one that displayed her exasperation to the fullest. "Where are we going, Avery?"

"To the coast."

She rolled her eyes to the ceiling. "There is quite a lot of coast. We live on an island, you know."

"Near Weymouth," he clarified. "To begin with."

Rachael regarded him with suspicion. "'Near,' you say? But not in? And what after? I don't like surprises, Avery. I should like to know our itinerary."

He rubbed his temple as if he had a headache. "Must we talk of this now? I've had a terrible morning."

"Not so terrible as poor Lord Hunstable! As for talking of it now, when else? We leave this afternoon. Don't we have a train to catch?"

"We do. My trunks are on their way to the station. I will give your staff the directions. I assume you are packed?"

"Yes, although I don't know what good it will do. You could be taking me to Iceland, for all I know, and I wouldn't have anything suitable."

He winced at her snide tone. "It will only be a few days," he muttered.

"Pardon?"

He shoved himself away from the table. "Excuse me, I no longer have much appetite."

Rachael stared after him for a moment, then turned and picked a bit at her food. She was no longer hungry, either. She was livid.

XVI

Silence is Galling

$\mathcal{A}$VERY DID HIS BEST TO APOLOGIZE. Rachael ignored him. Every time he tried to speak, she fussed with her skirts, or repinned her hat, or just happened to be fanning herself vigorously. By the time they were seated side-by-side on the train—where she could hear him, regardless of any fidgeting—he had stopped trying. He didn't know what to say, in any case. She was furious with him, and he hadn't even explained where they were headed and why. He could only imagine how she might react to that news. He was already somewhat afraid she would strike him with her fan.

He glanced in her direction, and she opened the fan to hide her face. The train car was a comfortable temperature. She couldn't pretend to have need of it.

He closed his eyes and let his head fall back against the seat. If only he could go back and begin the day all over again. It had begun so beautifully—waking beside her, making love, lingering in bed. Somewhere it had all gone horribly wrong. The time he'd meant to spend preparing his explanation—and ensuring he had a gift to go with it—had instead been spent in a gaol, attempting to comfort his hysterical student. His dour mood had spilled over into their lunchtime conversation. He had answered her questions poorly and walked out when he should have begged her pardon. Now he'd lost his chance.

For more than an hour, he stared at the seat in front of him, while Rachael looked out the window, fanning herself now and again. She remained resolute in her decision not to speak to him, though he knew she must be near to bursting with scathing remarks. The silence grated on him. He would much rather she yelled at him.

"The dining car seemed respectable," he said, hoping his tone sounded conciliatory. "Would you care to go for tea?"

"No."

"Rachael…"

She snapped her fan open between them, and this time didn't even pretend to fan herself.

Avery gritted his teeth. He had no one to blame but himself for his current predicament.

"I apologize for upsetting you," he began, talking through the red lace barrier. "It was never my intent. I had meant to give you a full explanation of my plans for this trip, but the circumstances of this morning prevented it."

Her fan remained motionless.

"Would you do me the courtesy of hearing it now?"

"You are free to speak, regardless of my opinion on the matter. Do as you like."

That was more like the Rachael he was accustomed to. Her words were disdainful, but he preferred that to no words at all.

"It will do me no good to speak if you won't listen."

She had no answer for that, so he forged ahead. Sitting this close, she could ignore him all she wanted, but she couldn't prevent herself hearing him.

"Two weeks ago I received a letter from a Miss Annie Pelham in Seawell, near Weymouth. She is a distant relative of mine, from a branch of the family I knew nothing of, prior to this. She is also a collector of local folktales. From what she tells me, I believe she may have information that could lead me to a cure for my condition."

Rachael's fan dropped just enough to see her eyes. There was some interest there, though tempered by suspicion.

"I have studied for seventeen years with this end in mind. It's not an opportunity I can afford to pass up. I had to postpone my visit until after our wedding, but I couldn't delay further. We will visit Miss Pelham's home for a few days, and she and I will share knowledge of family history. I'm hopeful it will provide the answers I need.

"I'm sorry to have to interfere with our wedding trip, but you must know what this could mean for my life—for *our* life. I did my best to make the remainder of the holiday exactly what it should be. We will tour several seaside towns, making a leisurely journey to Dover. From there we can travel to the continent for two full weeks and do anything you desire."

Her fan rose again, hiding any clue to her feelings. Avery sought desperately for some way to soothe her. Before he had sorted out his thoughts, she closed her fan and laid it across her lap.

"I'm not a great lover of the seaside," she informed him. "It is pretty enough for a day, or perhaps two, but once one has walked the beach and viewed the sunset there is nothing more to do. I also find the ocean has a certain smell I don't think especially pleasant."

Her tone was conversational, but the rebuke couldn't have been more clear. She wouldn't be forgiving him any time soon.

He rose from his seat. "I should like to have some tea and a bite to eat. Would you like to accompany me to the dining car?"

"No, thank you."

Her refusal was expected, but he felt some measure of relief that it was now more than a single word.

"Would you like me to bring you anything?"

She hesitated before answering. "Tea would be welcome,

thank you. Also, a piece of fruit or bread with jam. I would like a bit of something sweet."

"Very good. I will return before long."

Avery considered ignoring his own hunger and returning at once with her repast, but he decided it would appear that he was trying too hard. She would dismiss it as an attempt to mollify her. With no better option, he sat alone with his food, partaking faster than usual so as not to keep her waiting overlong. He brought her two slices of bread with different flavors of jam, and a pot of tea, which he held on his lap while she dined. A few other passengers gave him disapproving glances, but he was far more concerned with making amends with his wife than with proper social conduct on a train full of strangers.

Rachael's hostility began to diminish. He didn't know whether it was the explanation or his attention to her needs that helped, but she no longer glared at him or hid behind her fan. She did, however, remain uncomfortably silent for the duration of the journey.

· · · ◯◯▧ · · ·

Their itinerary was appalling. Rachael had no desire to spend time in Weymouth or any other seaside town. She had even less desire to spend her honeymoon sitting on her duff while her husband chatted with another woman.

The one thing that pleased her was knowing the reasoning behind the plans. She did want him to find a cure. She didn't see why he had to do it immediately. He'd been studying for years. Surely another month of waiting wouldn't be so unbearable.

Unfortunately, there was nothing to be done but to go along with it. She had expressed her displeasure by ignoring him, though it didn't appear to have affected him greatly. He didn't look any unhappier than he had at noon. He'd neither snapped at her nor reprimanded her for her rude behavior.

She'd begun to wonder if he ever grew angry about anything. Perhaps there was something to his claim to lack of emotion.

He must have felt something, deep down. He was full of passion. She had seen it in his heated gaze, and felt it in his eager caresses. Outside the bedroom, however, he seemed anxious to suppress it. Most likely it interfered with his work. His research demanded logical thinking and strict organization. Outbursts of emotion would be of no help.

If only it wasn't his emotional side that captivated her.

There was no train to the village where this Miss Pelham lived, but a rented steam car awaited them at the station. Mr. Bellamy had again proved himself a master of preparation. A pair of porters loaded their things into the vehicle, and Rachael took her place in the driver's seat.

Bringing her goggles had been a brilliant decision. They would go very well with her dress today. If she continued driving with such frequency, she would have to consider purchasing additional pairs to match with other dresses.

Even at the crowded station she hadn't gone unnoticed, and she smiled at the many eyes watching her. The chatter from onlookers pleased her. They were scandalized by something as simple as a woman driving. This car wasn't as nice as the vehicle they had used in Ipswich, but it was functional, and she showed off her skills by steering through the crowd with ease.

The drive to Seawell in the fine weather improved her mood. This car had a canopy to shade from the sun, but it didn't block the cool ocean breeze. The road was well-kept and unpitted. Rachael took it at a good pace, putting them at their destination ahead of schedule.

The moment they entered the village, her good cheer evaporated. The tiny settlement was shabbier than she had expected. Weather-beaten structures, rising no more than two stories, lined packed dirt streets. As many animals as people roamed the roads, and the steam car was such a novelty that townsfolk came outside to stare as it rumbled by.

A worn sign proclaiming, "Seawell Inn," dangled from one of the rickety buildings. It looked to be nothing but a bar with a room or two upstairs. Rachael imagined it filled with ruffians and prostitutes. She might duck inside for a glimpse of such a revolting place, but staying there, even simply for a meal, was out of the question.

Avery had directions and a map and he steered her through the poorly marked streets without error. Rachael pulled up to the address they had been given, stopped the car, and damped the engine. She hopped down, not waiting for Avery to walk around and help her out, and strode over to stand in front of the house. Hands on her hips, she glared at it.

"This is unacceptable."

She'd thought Isobel's home small. Compared to this building, it was a palace. This cottage, if one could even call it that, looked no bigger than her carriage house. It didn't even have a full second story. If there were rooms beneath the roof, they would have low, sloping walls. She couldn't imagine how the residents could house guests in any capacity, or even how they could maintain a reasonable standard of living.

Avery at least had the good sense to look properly horrified as well.

"Perhaps we could return to the inn?" he offered. It sounded like a plea. He'd seen the inn as well as she had. Remaining here would be a wiser choice.

Rachael turned her harsh gaze on him. "Perhaps we could return to London!"

They were prevented from further argument when the door to the house opened, and its occupant came out, alerted by the noise of their arrival.

The young woman had the same dark hair and piercing green eyes as Avery. She wore a plain, gray dress that Rachael's maid would have rejected. She staggered to a halt when she saw Rachael and Avery.

"Miss Pelham?" Avery inquired.

The woman rushed toward them and curtsied, her eyes still wide with surprise. "Yes. Annie Pelham, at your service, sir and madam."

Avery nodded his head in return. "Avery Cantrell. I'm pleased to make your acquaintance. Please allow me to introduce my wife, Lady Rachael Cantrell."

Miss Pelham curtsied again, even lower. "My lady, it's an honor to meet you. I assure you, we will do all we can to make your stay here a comfortable one."

The woman looked sufficiently intimidated, so Rachael gave her a smile and thanked her. This hovel would be their home for the next several days. Her husband had made an impulsive and idiotic decision, but she would persevere with grace and prove to everyone she was a lady in more than name. She would despise every minute of it.

XVII

Progress

AVERY FLIPPED OPEN HIS WATCH to check the time. Half-past ten. Rachael would be abed by now, if not asleep. He hadn't seen her since their arrival except at dinner. She'd taken her paper and pens and shut herself up in their room to rest. He assumed she had passed the time detailing all the horrors of her situation in a letter to her cousin.

Miss Pelham had shown them to the largest bedroom in the house. Avery assumed it belonged to her parents, Mr. and Mrs. Pelham, and the guilt at displacing their hosts gnawed at him. At the same time, he couldn't very well put Rachael anywhere else. The tiny dwelling only had one other bedchamber. He wondered if all three of its residents would crowd inside, or if they would use mats in the attic. He couldn't imagine what Miss Pelham had been thinking, inviting him to stay here. He ought to have confessed his rank to her ahead of time. Clearly, she hadn't realized how vast the disparity in their circumstances was. Avery hadn't realized how spartan her lifestyle was. Her father was a shopkeeper, yes, but he was noted to be an important man in the village. Avery hated to think what the residences of unimportant men must be like.

He adjusted his spectacles and went back to his notebook. The flickering candlelight hurt his eyes. Bloody hell, these people didn't even have a proper lamp. Apparently the recent surge in low-cost potions hadn't yet reached this part of the country. Perhaps he could convince Rachael to drive into Weymouth and buy a portable lamp—and to fuel it for him, since he didn't dare do that himself.

He tried his best to ignore the flickering while he reviewed his notes. The hours he had spent talking with Annie Pelham had been worth the journey. She was a fascinating woman and the two different versions she had given him of her family legends had filled important holes in Avery's understanding of his history. He thought he finally had the full story of what happened all those centuries ago—though some of the details had been lost or muddled by time.

"I'd like to go over your tales one more time, to be certain I haven't missed anything of import," he said.

Miss Pelham's head bobbed in agreement. She had a quiet, but energetic way about her, and Avery found her easy to converse with.

"I know our ancestor to have been an important man. I have heard terms such as 'king,' 'prince,' and 'earl,' though I doubt any of those terms accurately reflect the reality of the situation. They are simply modern attempts to explain his position of power and influence. His disagreement was with a woman of similar status."

"The 'priestess' or 'queen,'" Miss Pelham agreed.

"And 'witch' and 'healer,' as well, which suggest magical abilities. She possessed knowledge of potions. He did not.

"Next point: the nature of their disagreement. Similarly confused. You say he insulted her by treating her as an inferior?"

"That is the tale my family told. The other version I have since heard says they were lovers who had had a falling out." Even in the candlelight, he could see her pink complexion. "That wasn't appropriate to discuss with a young girl."

Avery nodded. In the version he had heard from his own grandparents, the two were rival leaders who had been at war. His ancestor had defeated her through dishonorable means, and she had demanded vengeance. Which would have been justified but for the innocent future generations who had since suffered.

"Whatever the reason for her furor," Avery said, "the woman cursed him and all males of his line. Which leads to me."

"Incredibly enough," Miss Pelham replied. "With such a dangerous condition, I'm amazed the family didn't die out within a generation or two."

"Perhaps that was the goal. Not merely death, but the knowledge that his family line would be wiped out. The ultimate revenge. I expect it would have worked, were our ancestors not so prolific. Given enough sons, one ought to make it to manhood. Our true fortune lies in the centuries when potions weren't in use in Britain. That allowed the family to grow. They also grew foolish, however, and we nearly lost the story of the curse.

"When I learned about you, I turned to genealogical research to piece together our family tree. There were many Cantrells in the seventeenth century, chiefly living in London. Something near a quarter of the family died in the 1665 plague, some of them by drinking the strange new medicines said to contain true magic."

She nodded. "The potions resurgence."

"Just so. By 1700, ninety percent of the Cantrell males were dead. The story of the curse began to spread again, but my branch of the family never learned the details of the curse itself. There was some sense of it being a poison, but no more. This is why your tale is so vital to me."

He scanned the page in his notebook where he had copied down Miss Pelham's version, word-for-word as she had recited it.

"I should like to read this back to you. Please tell me if anything is incorrect:

"And when it came time for the feast, she made him gifts of mead and honeyed bread. But, woe! It was the false honey, the thick nectar of the ryeweed flower, which could be rendered by those of skill into the finest remedies or the most potent toxins. He ate of the bread and fell to the floor, as one dead.

"He woke within the hour, seeming his old self, but scarred with a curse, for now the smallest taste of false honey would be to him as the deadliest poison.

"In the years that followed, he begat sons, and they, too, suffered the curse. He watched them die, one after the other, until, heartbroken with grief, he joined them, leaving only the youngest behind."

The tale may have been hundreds of years old, but it rang terribly true to Avery's ears. He had seen both his father and his grandfather die from accidental potion ingestion. His uncle had died drinking an antidote he had been convinced would undo the curse. Avery's kinship with the ancient warrior-king spanned time. They suffered together.

"That is exactly as I recited it," Miss Pelham assured him. "Some of the words have varied in the retellings, but none of the important ones."

"False honey?" Avery asked. "That phrase has never altered?"

It was an epithet he had encountered in more than one old text. He understood it to be their term for serum.

"Never."

"And it was always said to be nectar?"

"Correct."

"Strange. My recent readings on modern potions have indicated that serum can be extracted from roots and stems, and with our newest techniques, directly from the soil. Your tale suggests it is nectar, but I have never heard of such a thing."

She shrugged. "I have no familiarity with potions. We have never used them in Seawell."

"It doesn't resemble either nectar or honey. It is thick, like molasses, and reddish in color. Perhaps this ryeweed flower has molasses-like nectar?"

"I have no idea. I've never heard of such a flower outside of this particular tale."

"But that is the name in the story? It has never changed?"

"Not to my knowledge."

"Damn. I beg your pardon, Miss Pelham. I feel I am so close and yet so far. Whatever that flower is, I need to find it. If its nectar could be used to make the curse, it could be used to make an antidote."

He closed his notebook and rose from his seat. The candle was burning low and his eyes were aching.

"We will talk again in the morning. I should like to take down as many details as you can give me of your family history, and any further tales you can remember. Every scrap of information could help me in this."

"I will do all I can."

"Thank you." He offered his hand, and she shook it.

"You are most welcome."

"Goodnight, Miss Pelham." He rushed off to his room, hoping to find Rachael still awake. Progress. He had made true progress. He wanted her to know this visit had been worth the trouble.

He found her sound asleep, curled up on the far side of the bed. It wasn't a large bed, and it was impossible to join her without touching her. Avery hoped she would relax into his arms, as she had on their wedding night, but when he pressed against her she only scrunched up tighter. Disappointed, he brushed her cheek with a soft kiss and turned away. He would speak with her in the the morning. He would make things right between them.

XVIII

An Abrupt End

*I*SOBEL,

You must beg my pardon for the shakiness of my hand and the hastiness of my scrawl. I apprised you last night of the intolerable situation in which I find myself (outdoor latrines, no lights, &c.), but my circumstances now are worse. So much terribly worse. I am so aggrieved that I'm not certain my words will make any sense. I may even cry, and you know that isn't like me. I haven't cried since those few terrifying days after I learned the truth about my first husband.

I will be returning to London. You are still there, so I may arrive and see you in person before this letter reaches you. There may be no sense in writing it, but I am desperate for some release of my emotions, and I can't shriek and smash things. My behavior has already gone beyond the pale.

But I must explain. I told you that ~~Avery~~ Mr. Cantrell was with Miss Pelham all evening. He came to bed after I was asleep and this morning when I came down to breakfast, he was at the dining table (the only table) with Miss Pelham and a mess of papers. He hardly *looked up to acknowledge me. I grabbed a piece of fruit and went out walking. The town entirely lacks things to do, so that was my morning. Walking. Thinking. Dodging smelly animals and unwashed fishermen. Peeking into dilapidated taverns just for <u>something</u> to do. I didn't return until half-past noon…*

Rachael stepped through the doorway of the Pelham's hovel at almost exactly half-past noon to find her husband lunching without her. He hardly spared her a glance before turning back to his notebooks.

"Ah, Rachael, there you are." He gnawed on a crust of bread, his mouth turned down in thought. "We were just having lunch. Where on earth have you been?"

Rachael bit her lip. Didn't she merit, "I was so worried," or at least an angry scowl?

"Out."

"Out," he repeated, a look of puzzlement crossing his face. "Yes, out."

He dismissed the issue with a shrug. "Well, no matter. You're here now. Come. Sit. I have exciting news."

We are leaving immediately for Paris? Or Italy and the Roman ruins? Perhaps the pyramids.

Rachael swished over to the table, but didn't sit. "Yes? Do tell."

He smiled at her at last. "Miss Pelham's tales have given me a vital clue. I have engaged her assistance in the search for a flower that may hold the key to my cure. We will begin immediately, interviewing local botanical experts and combing the area during our days in Weymouth. If I haven't found anything by our departure date, then I will return to this part of the country once our wedding trip is concluded. You are, of course, welcome to join me for any portion of the search, but please don't feel obligated. Miss Pelham's assistance will be sufficient."

"Oh, I'm sure it will," Rachael snorted. "And while you go traipsing about the countryside with another woman, I will spend my honeymoon lounging about alone at the seaside, soothing my delicate nerves with the healthful air. After which, I will feel so refreshed that I will be fortified for the strenuous work of sitting at home and knitting."

His complexion paled, and he sprang from his seat. "Rachael..."

"Oh, no need to concern yourself with me. I'm only your wife, after all."

I was so sarcastic, Isobel. You wouldn't believe it. This is what comes of spending too much time with the Ainsworths and Miss Reynolds with her suffragist club. I can't control it. It comes spewing from my mouth before I can stop it. What sort of wife says such things to her husband? I thought he would be furious...

Avery reached for her. "I do concern myself with you. Very much. That is why..."

"Very much?" Rachael interrupted, not caring about the rudeness. "Really? Very? Obviously not as much as you concern yourself with *her*! You haven't said two words to me since we arrived here. You didn't even wonder where I was when I was gone *all morning*! Excuse me if I don't think your concern of much magnitude."

His green eyes flashed, and his fingers clenched. "I was attempting to explain," he growled. "I'm trying to take your feelings into account."

Rachael's hands landed on her hips and she met his angry expression with a glare of her own. "It's a little late for that! Maybe you should have thought about that, oh, *before* you dragged me here against my will and all good sense. But no. You care only for your research. You care nothing—nothing!—for my feelings."

By then I was screaming, Isobel, truly screaming, right there in front of everyone. But, honestly, how could it not be in front of everyone, when the entire house is the size of a closet? ~~Av~~ Mr. Cantrell must take some bit of the blame. I had been so ill-used, and I simply couldn't tolerate it any longer. But, oh, I'm such a wreck of a wife! Why will I never learn? He must despise me.

My apologies for the smudge. I'm so torn between anger and dismay that my hands are trembling...

Avery took a step forward, looming over her. "That is entirely untrue!"

Rachael stood her ground. "Oh, is it? You couldn't even be bothered to find out what I like!" Her shout rang from the walls. "You might have asked me if I enjoyed the seaside. You might have told me you had made an important discovery and wanted to come here as soon as possible. You might have considered that, as your wife, I would have been glad to help you with an important task, and would have worked with you to plan our wedding trip accordingly!

"But, no. I'm just an inconvenience. Something to be planned around. You would have preferred it if I'd just stayed at home while you ran off to do all this work on your own. Well, fine. Go ahead and do it, you inconsiderate lout!"

He gaped at her.

"I'm leaving with the steam car in the morning and taking the first train back to London. Don't try to stop me."

Avery backed away, no longer meeting her eyes. A heavy silence settled over the small dwelling. Uncomfortable seconds ticked by before he looked up again and cleared his throat. When he spoke, his voice was shockingly calm. "You are welcome to do as you please. Do you wish me to accompany you back to town, or would you prefer to return on your own?"

"I don't give a damn." She spun on her heel and stormed

into the bedroom, slamming the door so hard the entire cottage rattled.

I promise that I tell you true, cousin. Perfect composure, from a man whose wife had insulted him, screamed at him, even used sarcasm and foul language. I'm still reeling from it.

I'm afraid I have been very wrong regarding him. He was never enamored of me. It's clear he cares nothing for me at all. I was no more than a convenience necessary for him to acquire his inheritance. His romantical nature is buried deeper than I had believed.

On one point, I will not waver. He does possess a passionate heart. It is simply not devoted to me. Miss Pelham, with her pitiable state of life and her miracle cure, is certain to connect with that side of him.

I am devastated.

I had truly believed we would be happy.

I'm sorry for the splotches. I assure you, I'm not crying. I will be perfectly well. I will remain at home where I am comfortable, and Mr. Cantrell may do as he pleases. I will be a dutiful wife and respect his privacy, and it won't matter a whit that he doesn't and will never love me. I will be satisfied knowing he is a much better man than my first husband. He is a man, however, and it seems that makes him unsuitable for me, or me unsuitable for him, I don't know which. Either way, I am a failure as a wife, but I will continue to try my best.

Your unhappy cousin,
Rachael

Despite Rachael's stated indifference, Avery had no intention of letting her return home alone. He had already mucked things up enough. He wouldn't add irresponsible husband to his list of mistakes. One didn't abandon one's traveling companion, and one didn't leave a lady to travel unescorted.

Rachael was neither as silent nor as hostile as she had been on the previous train ride. While she didn't make conversation, she answered him if he spoke to her, and even accompanied him to the dining car for a late breakfast.

He hefted the teapot. "Would you like some tea, dear?"

"Yes, I would. Thank you."

She accepted the cup and sipped in silence.

"Toast? Jam?"

"No, thank you. I'm quite content."

Avery slathered marmalade on his own toast, trying not to scowl. The eerie calm in her voice set his teeth on edge. He watched her slice her egg into dainty bits, torn between the desire to apologize and the fear of upsetting the fragile peace between them.

"I do hope you are enjoying your own repast," she said.

"The breakfast is very good, thank you."

"I'm so glad."

His jaw clenched. She was nothing of the kind.

As the journey continued, Rachael maintained a polite serenity of manner befitting a finishing school instructor. Every other word was a "please" or "thank you," and she exhibited not the slightest hint of sass or sarcasm. She was the epitome of refinement. Avery preferred the angry snap of her fan.

He abandoned any further attempt at conversation and tried to sleep. He hadn't dared to share the bedroom last night and provoke her further. Most of the night he'd spent awake, his thoughts bouncing back and forth between his plans to identify and locate the ryeweed flower and his plans to win back Rachael's affection. A few hours dozing in a chair had given him nothing but a crick in the neck.

He saw Rachael all the way to her townhouse, then went to his office to speak with Bellamy and squeeze in a few hours of work before the day was done. He had yet to think of any way to make his wife stop hating him, but at least he could make progress on his other problem.

He found his secretary in the office, scribbling away with the ridiculous color-changing ink Avery had told him not to use. The young man jumped when he saw Avery, and his cheeks flushed. He hurriedly put away the pen and paper, looking flustered at having been caught.

"Mr. Cantrell, sir." He rose from his seat. "I hadn't thought to see you for a full month. I hope nothing too terrible has brought you home so prematurely."

"My wife was unhappy with the trip as I had planned it. She wished to return home. I will let her make new plans once she has had time to recover. If you could cancel any remaining tickets, hotel stays, and the like, I would appreciate it."

Bellamy nodded. He was intelligent enough not to comment.

"In the meantime, let me share what I have learned from Miss Pelham."

He gave Bellamy a summary of his findings and handed over his notes. "The next step, as I see it, is to determine what sort of flower supplied this 'false honey' they used. It seems to me they didn't use the same techniques we use when mixing potions. If we can replicate their ingredients, it will give us insight into the poison. We can consult potions experts and doctors as necessary. It's common to use poisons to make antidotes. A cure is possible."

The secretary nodded. "There's a depiction of a flower on that belt buckle Professor Purcell found. Also, I believe we have one or two painted onto scraps of pottery from that era."

"Yes, we do. I will look over our collection and see if I can learn anything more. Flowers are common decorations, unfortunately, but we might find something to help."

"We know more than we did before your visit. You are getting closer."

He nodded. Every step was an improvement. Tonight he would review some of the descriptions of potions in old texts.

"Has anything come up these last few days?" he asked. "Any word on Hunstable?"

"He is in the gaol in Ipswich, and will await trial there. He has an excellent lawyer, but is concerned about the cost. His father is stingy with his allowance and currently out of the country."

"I'll pay the man's fees if necessary," Avery snarled. The entire situation made him furious.

"Professor Purcell thinks all will be well. He has returned to Ipswich, staying at your usual hotel. You can reach him there at least these next few weeks. He'll keep an eye on both the dig and Hunstable."

"I suppose that's the best we can do. There have been no further signs of trouble at the dig site?"

"None that have reached me. Purcell appears calm and says the men are back working on their usual schedule. He didn't say what they think of the situation with the photographer."

"As long as Purcell has the situation in hand and the boy won't be wrongfully convicted, it seems there is little for me to do."

Avery pulled several books and pages of notes from the shelves. He stacked them atop two boxes overflowing with photographs of the pieces in the University collection.

"You may return to your work. I will take these things home to look them over. My wife has a very fine study—paneled walls, a large, sturdy desk, comfortable chairs, plenty of bookshelves. I intend to put it to good use. There is a smaller study in the house, as well. Near the size of this office. I thought perhaps you might make use of it. I meant to show you during the wedding breakfast, but couldn't locate you. You should pay a visit and give me your opinion."

"I've seen it."

Avery was surprised. "Have you?"

"Yes, sir. I was at the house just yesterday. Lady and Miss Stillwell are staying there, as you know. I, uh, have been helping them become acquainted with the city."

"You are playing tour guide?"

His cheeks turned pink. "They are infrequent visitors to town. Lady Cantrell recommended they consult me for assistance."

"Ah. I suppose I ought to have warned her you are a busy man."

"It's no trouble, sir," he said hurriedly. "I assure you. I'm happy to be of help."

Bellamy's blush deepened, and Avery had a sudden suspicion regarding the purpose of the magic ink.

"Good. I want Rachael's relatives to have all their needs attended. Feel free to continue on in that role, as long as it's not a bother to you."

"Oh, no! It certainly isn't."

"I'll leave you to it, then." He picked up his boxes and papers and turned to leave.

"Mr. Cantrell, sir, before you go…"

"Yes, Sebastian?"

"You will have to go in for an interview, sir. I told them you were away on your honeymoon. Since your plans have changed, you should let them know at once that you are in town, so you don't look as if you were lying to hide something."

The hairs on the back of Avery's neck tingled. This couldn't be good. "An interview with whom?"

"With the police, sir."

XIX

In the News

$\mathcal{R}$ACHAEL WALKED CIRCLES around her study, following the pattern in the carpet as Isobel read the letter over twice through.

"Gracious," Isobel said at last. "I'm glad you decided not to post this. I don't think your telling me this now, after so much time to calm yourself, would have had the same effect as reading your feelings from right at that very moment."

Rachael nodded, a sense of apprehension tugging at her. She'd been terribly upset when she had written that letter. She couldn't remember precisely what she'd written. At best, she would come across as overwrought and incomprehensible.

"I'm feeling much better now," she assured her cousin, though "much" was rather an exaggeration.

"I'm glad to hear it. It sounds as if your experience was not a pleasant one."

Isobel always had such a genteel, understated way of expressing things. "No, it wasn't."

"Have you made up with Mr. Cantrell?"

"I'm no longer shouting at him, if that's what you mean," Rachael answered. "I have been most polite. He will have nothing to complain of."

"I see."

"I don't wish to speak of it any longer. What's done is done."

Honestly, Rachael didn't want to even think of it. Too much time dwelling on the subject made her need to blink more often than usual, and caused a slight tremor in her lower lip.

"Tell me what you have been doing," Rachael said. "Are you enjoying your visit?"

"Yes, very much. We have been all over the city, toured the museum, had some lovely walks in the park. It has been exceptionally pleasant."

Isobel's cheeks were flushed, and her eyes sparkled. She was having a grand time. Knowing that buoyed Rachael's spirits.

"Have you received any invitations to balls or other parties?"

"Oh, no. I don't think I will be going to any such things."

"Nonsense. I won't have you miss out on all the social opportunities available during the Season. Didn't I tell you Mr. Bellamy could help you make arrangements?"

"Yes, you did, and he has been most kind, answering our questions and showing us about town."

"But he hasn't procured a single invitation?"

Isobel turned away, walking to the window and looking out at the street beyond. "I don't need any invitations, Rachael. I promise you, I'm quite happy without attending any parties."

"You won't find a husband sitting at home or taking walks in the park. But never fear. Now that I'm in town again, I will take you out to circulate in good society. You won't need to rely on my letters for all your gossip. You can witness it yourself."

"Oh!" Isobel spun around. "Speaking of gossip, Rachael, I have some for you."

"You do? Have you heard of some new scandal?"

"Not a scandal, but news that concerns you."

Rachael reeled. "Me? What news could you have heard

that concerns me? Especially since you haven't been moving about in society."

"I don't need to have gone to a party to hear this news. Everyone is talking of it—the servants, the shopkeepers. One can hardly go outside without encountering some mention."

Rachael's eyebrows arched in surprise. Isobel wasn't prone to exaggeration. The news must truly be everywhere.

"Tell me, then, before someone else does."

"The police have undertaken an investigation of the events at Lady Ellerby's charity ball," Isobel announced. "It has been proven that one of the desserts was tainted with a poison."

"Good heavens!" Rachael had put the party entirely out of her mind, but now all her earlier fears resurfaced. "No one has died, have they? I thought everyone had recovered?"

"Yes, everyone is in good health, now. The motives of the poisoner are unclear. Why sicken a handful of people at such an event? It has done nothing to disrupt her charity. In fact, there has been so much publicity surrounding it that donations have risen."

Rachael began to pace again, her steps brisk, thoughts churning in her mind. "Well, that is a motive right there. Someone from the charity could have poisoned the food to cause a furor, thereby increasing public interest."

Isobel rushed to match Rachael's rapid steps. "It seems to me there are far more sensible ways to increase interest than poisoning people. One could hold a concert, write letters to important persons, pass out flyers on the street, put an advertisement in the newspaper…"

"Fake a book of Anglo-Saxon poetry," Rachael supplied.

"Oh!" Isobel put a hand to her mouth. "I forgot that your Mr. Cantrell had such an odd way of trying to garner attention."

"Don't be alarmed. I don't suspect him of poisoning these people. It is disconcerting, however, that I have twice had encounters with poisonings since meeting him."

"It's only a coincidence."

"That's what I told myself the night of the ball."

The study door creaked. Rachael spun to see who had opened it. Her servants all knew to knock before entering.

Much to her surprise, her husband stood in the doorway, his arms loaded with boxes and papers. He looked equally surprised to see her.

"My apologies," he said. "I hadn't realized you were in here. I was told you ladies were engaged in private conversation, and I assumed you would be in the drawing room."

"The study is better for a private conversation. It has thicker walls and a door that locks, if need be."

"Ah." He was flustered.

She felt the same. "May I ask why you are here?" Rachael hoped the question didn't sound impertinent. She didn't wish to begin another argument, but she was genuinely puzzled.

He frowned at her. "Where else should I be?"

"I had thought you intended to go home."

His frown drew tighter, his lovely lips pinching into a thin line. "This *is* my home."

Rachael's mouth opened in surprise, and she immediately clamped it shut. What could she say to that? They were married. He had every right to be here. What she didn't understand was *why* he wished to be here, instead of at his own residence.

"Did you intend to use this study all evening?" he asked. "I can take my work to the smaller one, if so."

"No. I only stepped in here to have a private word with Isobel. I do most of my own writing at the small desk in the library. It belonged to my mother, once." She was babbling. His presence had rattled her.

"Ah. Would you mind, then, if I conducted my work here? It's a very fine room and a handsome desk. I was hopeful I might be able to spend many of my working hours here instead of at the University."

Rachael remained puzzled. Was something wrong with his own house?

"I don't mind," she replied, more primly than she had intended. "You are free to use any of the rooms in this house, naturally."

"You must excuse me," Isobel spoke up. "I will leave you to talk in private." She moved toward the door.

"Oh, no, don't leave on my account, cousin," Rachael exclaimed. "You couldn't be a bother."

"No, no. You are newlyweds. You don't need a third party hanging about. Besides, Mama will be wondering where I have gotten to. She wished to plan tomorrow's outings."

Isobel curtsied and dashed off, leaving Rachael to face her husband alone.

They stared at one another for a moment, until Cantrell at last trudged to the desk to deposit his pile of work things. The number of boxes and papers dismayed her. He was fixated on the information Miss Pelham had given him.

Determined to be neither angry nor jealous, she seized on the only other topic of conversation she could think up.

"So, Mr. Cantrell, have you heard the latest news regarding Lady Ellerby's ball?"

He glowered. He had heard, it seemed, and didn't like it any more than she did.

"I liked it better when you called me Avery," he growled.

It took her a moment to process his words. "Oh, but that is so very informal," she dissembled. How could she tell him that Avery was the non-existent man she had been so certain was falling in love with her? If she called him by that name, it would only tempt her to sink back into her delusion.

"Informal?" he echoed. "What are you about with this nonsense? Dammit, woman, you started using my first name almost the day we met!"

"Yes, but I was a scandalous widow then. Now I'm a wife, and I must conduct myself in a refined and respectable manner."

"If I had wanted refined and respectable I would have married that fluffy pink chit!"

"No, no. I told you, Miss Helmsley is too flirtatious for her own good. I have no doubt the poor man who marries her will someday find himself a cuckold."

"Perhaps she, too, will turn herself around entirely upon her marriage and be thereafter 'refined and respectable.'"

The sarcasm in his tone stung. Rachael knew she would never be as proper as she pretended. Her tongue was too loose, and she loved to create a spectacle. Cantrell's rebuke implied he didn't want her to be proper, but she didn't see how that could be. What man wanted an improper wife?

He collected himself. "It occurs to me," he began, his tone even, "that I never answered your question. Yes, I did hear the news. It has been established the illness was caused by poison."

"So I was told. It seems my suspicions were correct."

"Sadly, yes. Bellamy tells me the police are conducting interviews with everyone who attended the event. We ought to be prepared to give a statement."

Rachael pulled a face. "Ugh. What a nuisance!"

"Indeed." He sounded serious, but she caught a twinkle in his eye. Was he amused by her complaint or was he laughing at her?

"Do you think it a coincidence? That there have been two poisonings since I met you?"

"I certainly hope so!" Avery exclaimed.

"It makes me nervous," she admitted. "It's simply too strange. Still, I can see no connection between the two incidents. You are the only link."

"If someone means me harm, they are grossly incompetent. It wouldn't be difficult to poison me."

"What if they don't mean you harm directly, but are trying to scare you, or perhaps make you appear to be the culprit?"

He put a hand to his temple. "Please. You are making *me* nervous now. I beg you to let the matter drop. I must believe the two events to be entirely unrelated."

Rachael rushed toward him and laid a hand on his arm.

"I'm sorry. It's only my overactive imagination. I didn't mean to make you fear for your life."

He covered her hand with his own. His emerald eyes locked with hers, and she felt a ripple of anticipation run through her. This was the first intimate touch they had shared in days.

"I don't fear for my life." He moved her hand to his chest and wound his other arm around her. "I fear for yours."

"Avery," she gasped.

She meant to say something reassuring, but he kissed her, and she forgot everything but his soft lips and the sweep of his tongue against her own. The warm, wet deliciousness of his mouth melted her insides. Her fingers clenched on his shirt. Her free hand dropped to his backside, urging him closer. Their bodies melded together.

Avery kissed down over her lower lip and along her jaw until he nuzzled her neck. Her skin tingled where he sucked her delicate flesh. She thought it likely to leave a love mark. She wondered what she might wear tomorrow to best show it off.

"Ah, Rachael," he murmured. "Will you forgive me now?"

She didn't know what she was forgiving him for, but she would have agreed to just about anything to prevent him from stopping. They backed into the desk, knocking papers to the floor. His hands went to her bosom. His mouth moved up her neck until his lips captured her earlobe. She could have stood in his arms for hours, relishing the way he made her shiver.

"Your bedroom, or mine?" he whispered.

"Yours. Always yours."

XX

Two Heads are Better

*W*ORK BE DAMNED. Avery abandoned his scattered notes and photos and scurried upstairs with Rachael, doing his best to avoid manhandling her in front of the servants or her relatives. He wasn't entirely successful. Her lady's maid spied him groping her as he fumbled with the bedroom door. The girl giggled and scampered off, no doubt to spread the gossip throughout the household.

He didn't care. What did it matter if everyone knew he was enthralled with his bride? He wasn't ashamed of it.

He stripped the clothing off of her, grumbling at the buttons and laces. It was all much easier when these things happened after everyone was in their nightclothes. With Rachael's help, it didn't take more than a few minutes, but it felt like an eternity. Damn, was he eager to have his hands on her bare skin.

Her hair smelled of flowers. He yanked her pins out and let her tresses tumble over his fingers. Whatever rinse she used left her hair smooth and shiny. He played with it as he kissed her. The strands were long enough that they fell to just cover her nipples. It was a mouthwatering tease, and it made his heart pound and his body tremble. She was more than merely beautiful. She was overwhelming. It rendered him powerless.

He urged her toward the bed, aching with need for her. He wanted to fling himself atop her and ride her until the madness inside him subsided. He couldn't. He needed to put her first. He needed her to tremble and cry out with delight. He needed to be absolutely certain she had forgiven all his mistakes. She would see he *did* care for her and her feelings.

He nudged her legs apart, kissing along the inside of her thighs until he reached her wet core. He slipped a finger inside her, stroking as his tongue flicked over her taut clit.

"Avery," she gasped. "What are you… Oh. Oh, Lord that's good."

His fingers and lips kept up a steady rhythm, caressing her until she pleaded with him for release. Her throaty voice moaning his name was the most erotic thing he had ever heard. Climbing atop her, he surged in and out until her shuddering climax destroyed the last vestiges of his control and he lost himself in her embrace, spilling all he had into her tight, slick passage. He was defeated, undone by her irresistible charms. It left him filled with satisfaction. He would let her vanquish him any day.

Avery fell asleep inside of her. He awakened sometime later, wet and sticky and still entangled. He slipped from the bed, washed up, and checked the time. It was early enough to have a late dinner and leaf through some of the photographs before bed.

Rachael lay propped on one elbow, watching him. She stretched, giving him a full view of all her luxurious curves. He almost returned to bed, but for the rumbling in his stomach that was loud enough to make her laugh.

"Are you hungry?"

He moved toward the bed, trying not to trip over her discarded petticoats. He let his eyes rake over her and licked his lips. "Ravenous." He wanted her more than he wanted food.

She sat up. "So am I. Let's have dinner. We can return to bed again after, if you would like."

"I ought to work after dinner," he sighed.

"Oh." Her mouth turned down. She pulled the bedsheet around herself, hiding her body, looking away.

It killed his mood. The slightest mention of his work caused her to withdraw. They couldn't live this way.

"I could use some assistance, if you would like to help," he offered. "I have boxes of photos to sort through, and you have sharp eyes."

She clutched the sheet to her chest, regarding him with suspicion.

"It's entirely up to you, of course," he continued, desperate to make some connection with her on this subject. "My work is very important to me, as you know. If at all possible, I would like you to be a part of it."

Her eyes narrowed even further. "Why?"

"Why wouldn't I want my wife to know what I do every day?" Perhaps he would sound more convincing were he not fully naked and standing among a pile of her lacy underthings.

"Because it's none of my business?"

"I disagree."

The expression on her face made him wonder if she thought him completely mad. "You are a very odd sort of man, Avery Cantrell."

"And you are an odd sort of woman, Rachael Cantrell. I hope it makes us a good match."

She continued to frown at him and didn't reply, but moments later she dropped the sheet and climbed out of bed. She hopped over her crumpled clothing in one graceful bound. Her hair swirled and her breasts bounced. Avery's mouth watered. She gave him a coy smile, then disappeared into her own room. The connecting door swung closed with a gentle click.

He took two steps toward the door before he was able to stop himself. There was work to be done, and he wanted to involve her in it. His stomach made another noise of protest. Also, he was damned hungry.

· · · � · · ·

Rachael expected him to follow her after her obvious flirtations. There had been a heated glint in his eyes, and he'd suffered a cockstand throughout the entire conversation. She was baffled, then, when the door remained stubbornly closed. Had she been too shameless? She couldn't understand the man at all.

She dressed in her favorite nightgown, the plain cotton one that was so soft it felt like silk sliding against her skin. Her eastern-style dressing gown went over it, tied snuggly at the waist. She brushed out her hair, but left it down. She had liked the way Avery played with it.

Bother. She was thinking of him as Avery again. It was much too easy to be swayed by the thrills his body offered her. As a lover, he was both passionate and considerate. If they could spend all their time in bed they would have a perfect marriage. Outside of bed, things were considerably more difficult. She couldn't figure out what he did and didn't like. Everything she did seemed to be wrong.

She wandered downstairs. Avery had arranged to have their dinner brought into the study so that they might eat and work at the same time. Her servants were most accommodating. They all seemed to like him.

She settled herself into the cosiest chair in the room and picked at her food, taking small, delicate bites, the way she had been taught as a young girl. She was famished, but she never wolfed down food like a barbarian.

Avery didn't seem to possess such restraint. He shoveled his dinner into his mouth haphazardly, hardly looking at his fork. He didn't even appear to care what he was eating, so long as it was sustenance. His spectacles were perched on his nose, his attention focused on the papers atop his desk.

"You look very scholarly in your spectacles," Rachael observed. "Do you wear them when you lecture?"

He glanced up. "No. I memorize my talks so there is no need to squint at notes."

"You should wear the spectacles. It would give you a very distinguished, professorial air."

"I would wear them all the time were it not such a fashion *faux pas*. Society already regards me as dull. I don't need them to think me old and feeble as well."

"Bah. You look neither old nor feeble. That is nonsense. You should wear them out in public and begin a new fashion trend."

"I hardly have the influence in society to set trends of any sort."

"Perhaps not. But I do. Next time we go out together I will draw everyone's attention and then make comments to the ladies about your eyewear. Perhaps I will wear the ensemble I wore to Lady Ellerby's ball. It didn't get the notice it deserved, what with the poisoning and all."

His eyes dropped to his papers. "I'm still waiting for you to wear the grain sack tied with twine," he remarked. Though he wasn't looking at her, he couldn't disguise his smile.

"I wish to be noticed for being bold and beautiful, not for looking like a street urchin," she snapped.

He didn't look up, but kept sorting documents. "You wouldn't look an urchin. More like a castaway. The fair maiden…"

"Matron," she corrected.

"Lost at sea, washed up on a remote island, forced to make do with what little remains of her ship."

"You are ridiculous," she scolded.

"Stalked by ferocious beasts," he continued. "Ravished by a barbarian warlord."

"Does the barbarian warlord wear spectacles? I won't be ravished by him otherwise. I don't trust men with keen eyesight. They are all murderers or spies."

Avery laughed. The throaty rumble of it made her feel

warm inside—not the tingly sensual heat his kisses brought on, but a happy, comforting sensation.

"He doesn't wear spectacles," Avery said, "but she notices his frequent squinting and brings him a pair from her collection of odds and ends washed ashore from the wreckage of her ship. He considers it the greatest of all love tokens and carries her away to be his wife."

"Hopefully at that point she no longer has to wear the grain sack?"

"No. From then on she is simply naked. Or covered in animal skins if it's cold. They are barbarians, after all."

"That's the silliest story I've ever heard." She tried to sound disdainful, but a smile was tugging at the corners of her mouth, and she felt laughter welling up inside of her.

"Then I suppose I shall not write an epic ballad based upon it."

The laugh burst out, ringing from the paneled walls.

Avery grinned at her. "Unless you would like me to? You are fond of my poetry."

"Yes. As a matter of fact, I believe the poem you wrote entitled *To a Fair Maiden* would fit well with that story of yours. Let me see if I can remember it. It begins with her admirer talking of all her great assets: silken hair, white skin, eyes as blue as the sky. And then…" She faked a frown, but it was disrupted by a giggle. "Then he speaks of her strong arms for plowing, and he praises her for still having all her teeth!"

"Ah, yes. I do remember that one."

"That's not all!" she said. "He finishes by spending three lines gushing about her child-bearing hips. It's most shockingly barbarian. It's exactly the sort of thing your squinting, naked warlord would compose."

"Yes, well, you see, it is only by the hand of fate that I am here, where I can be clothed and bespectacled, and not on a remote island, waiting for a fair maiden to wash up on my shore."

She set her empty dinner tray aside and rose from her seat. She approached the desk and stared him down, hands on her hips. It was difficult to scowl effectively while teasing him, but the posture of annoyance came easily.

"So. Am I to understand that you chose me for my teeth and my hips?"

"For your hips, absolutely. I love the way they look when you stand just as you are now, with your hands upon them. As for the teeth… Truly it is your whole mouth that captivates me. It has a lovely shape and a sweet taste, but mostly I enjoy the words that come out of it."

"You must be addled, for I say many horrid things."

"Do you? I don't remember anything so terrible. Though there *was* some shouting of late. I don't recall the specific words. I was too busy admiring the color in your cheeks, the spark in your eyes, and most especially your heaving bosom."

"Well," she sniffed, "I suppose I shall have to shout at you more often if you like it so."

He laughed again. She could have listened to that sound all night. She had never had more fun flirting.

Avery pushed a box of photos across the desk to her. "Come, darling, help me sort these. I will recite barbarian poetry for you while we are looking."

She flipped through the top few images. "What do you hope to find in here?"

"Flowers. Set aside anything with a flower. I'm trying to track down the ryeweed plant from Miss Pelham's story."

"Miss Pelham," Rachael muttered, losing much of her good mood. "She has plowing arms and child-bearing hips."

"That may be, but she doesn't get to bear my children. Only you have that honor."

"I'm not having more than one child," Rachael asserted.

Avery looked surprised for a moment, then shrugged. "One is enough."

His agreement gave her a feeling of deep satisfaction. She

picked up the box of photos and, lacking anyplace else to work, began to spread them across the floor. Avery brought along the other box and did likewise.

They must have looked ridiculous, lying on the carpet shuffling pictures around, but it didn't take long for Rachael to begin enjoying the work. She liked having a task that required more from her than smiling and looking pretty. She liked the nearness of her husband. She loved that he was true to his word and recited poems as they worked.

They worked together, consulting one another when a tiny detail in a photo wasn't entirely clear. They both grew excited with every flower found, and they talked and laughed about random things, such as why there were sixteen photos of one old belt buckle—which was neither as fine nor as interesting as the intricate gold one Purcell had unearthed.

At length, Rachael found herself yawning. Her eyelids drooped. "Do you have the time?" she asked.

Avery, who hadn't dressed in his nightclothes, sat up and consulted his watch. "Quarter past one."

"Goodness! I had no idea we had taken so long." She yawned again. The carpet wasn't so terribly uncomfortable, and her bedroom was two floors up. It seemed very far away just now. Her eyelids fluttered. "Perhaps I will rest here a moment," she murmured.

Avery's hands slid beneath her, and he picked her up and carried her from the room. "I will not let my wife sleep on the study floor. It would be unforgivably negligent."

"Uh-huh." Her head fell against his chest. She would sleep in his arms. He was warm and cozy.

"Your own bed, this time?" he queried.

Never. She would sleep where he slept. "Always yours."

She wasn't certain if he heard her mumbled words, and she fell asleep before she could repeat them. When she woke the next morning, however, he was there at her side, and she was happy.

XXI

Poetic Sensibilities

$\mathcal{A}$VERY'S SMILE RAN FROM EAR TO EAR. The memory of
the night before played in his mind, threatening to cause an
ungentlemanly bout of raucous laughter. He had expected the
work to be less monotonous with Rachael's help. What he had
gotten instead was an evening of fun. *Fun!*

It was the most peculiar sensation. He didn't do things for
fun. He had no time for fun, and couldn't even recall the last
time he had thought of something in that way.

The book.

That damned book. It *had* been fun writing his collection
of warrior love poems. He had scribbled with a smile on
his face, laughing as he translated, picturing a fierce, proud
fighter laid low by love. He had scorned that memory, buried
it beneath his anger and dismay, until Rachael forced it to the
surface. She was slowly, but surely, undoing his resentment
toward the book. If he didn't watch himself, she would turn
him into a bloody bard.

He paced the study, scanning her books. Names jumped
out at him: Longfellow, Browning, Shelley, Tennyson. All his
favorites. Poems he'd studied, line by line. Ballads he could
recite from memory.

Who was he kidding? She wasn't changing him, only discovering him. Avery had always had a penchant for verse. In his schoolboy days he'd composed odes praising the girls he admired and written mocking rhymes about the teachers he disliked. Most of his former lovers were of an intellectual bent—women with "progressive" sexual morals who frequented the University and held feminist lectures. He had gifted them with sonnets instead of jewels.

No work of his was more personal than his warrior poems. Years of research had gone into their crafting. His imaginings of his ancestors came to life in the words. His joys had flowed freely, and his sorrows also. The pangs of the curse, the longing to be whole, the loneliness of his existence—all of that was reflected in the thirty-eight poems in two languages that made up his magnum opus.

No wonder he had hated it, when that baring of his soul had brought him nothing but giggles and gossip. Until Rachael. The book had brought him Rachael, and now he was beginning to love it again, merely because she loved it.

And I love her.

Avery staggered to a stop, stunned and alarmed by his own unspoken confession.

"I love her," he whispered, the words gushing forth from some deep recess of his heart.

It wasn't possible. He couldn't fall in love. He was unemotional. Years of funneling all of his passion into his research had relegated any sentimental feelings to a dark corner of his soul. Somehow, Rachael had found that part of him and was dragging it inexorably into the sunlight.

The fair maiden of his poems paled before her. Rachael was exciting, frustrating, fascinating. She made him swear and made him laugh. She was a wild creature, made all of wit and passion, caged by the strictures of society, lashing out against her prison with tooth and claw. He wanted to find the key and release her. It would be a beautiful thing, to see her running free. He would compose epics in her honor.

"Bloody hell," he muttered.

His emotions were spiraling out of control. He poured himself a measure of cognac from Rachael's well-stocked liquor cabinet, then downed the entire glass, ignoring the fact that it was not yet ten in the morning.

His incomparable wife chose that moment to swish into the room, dressed to the nines in a scarlet traveling dress with gold trim. A gold purse was tied at her hip, a matching fan dangled from her wrist, and she wore fingerless driving gloves of delicate gold lace. Rubies set into real gold decorated her ears and throat. A highway robber would take one look at her and drool in anticipation. That man would be better off keeping his distance. She would run him down with her steam car and then complain that someone ought to do something about the bumps in the road.

"You are going somewhere?" Avery asked.

Her eyes landed on the empty glass in his hand, but she didn't comment on it. "I thought we might go for a drive in your car. Look for your mystery flower?"

Avery set down the glass and picked up the stack of photos that contained flowers. After discarding those that were obviously roses or other well-known types, they had a dozen images remaining. A few Avery believed dated to a later period than concerned him. He would verify that before discarding them. Several others were too indistinct and would require a look at the original artifacts. He could swing by the University and do that this morning.

"What would you say to a journey back to Ipswich?" he asked.

Her brows drew together. "To what end?"

"We have a small collection there, along with catalogs of all the findings from the digs. Purcell is highly systematic and saves everything. That's why we have so many photographs. I would like to look over things there, much as we have done here."

"We will stay in the same hotel as before? I liked the girl there. It would save me having to bring my maid along."

"Yes. Do you want your own room?"

"I wouldn't use it. I enjoy sharing your bed."

A grin spread across his face. "I had noticed."

A blush tinted her cheeks. She had odd little bouts of shyness, suggesting that certain aspects of their marriage were new to her. Avery didn't mind. All of marriage was new to him. He'd never been in love before, either. He'd wandered into a foreign land, entirely unprepared. He couldn't say she didn't make his life interesting.

"After Ipswich, would you be willing to travel a bit farther north? Dashell does his research in and around Norwich, and I would like to make an attempt to view his collection."

"You're willing to talk to your rival? Do you think he has information that could help you?"

"It's possible. He will have dug up more artifacts in the months since Purcell last pestered him for information. His methods are less rigid than ours, so the records are often not of much use."

Rachael nodded. "Ah. Perhaps you made a comment to that effect in the past and he felt insulted. That could explain his hostility."

"I couldn't care less what the man felt, at this point. I would as soon forget he even exists. He is connected to my research, however, so I must deal with him."

"So, you intend to travel to Norwich and confront him?"

"I'm not looking for confrontation, only knowledge. I will make it clear I harbor no ill will and am open to reconciliation. It's up to him to respond in kind. If he won't..." Avery shrugged. "I don't need to speak with the man, only look over his findings."

"I will go with you when you speak to him. He will be less likely to behave badly in the presence of a lady."

"Thank you, darling. Both for understanding and for agreeing to accompany me."

"Where do we go after Norwich?"

"I haven't the foggiest. Once we identify the damned flower—pardon my language—we'll have to find where it grows, take samples and hand them off to apothecaries and potions makers for testing. I imagine it will take weeks at the least. I will likely spend them pacing back and forth anxiously."

"Perhaps we could take a tour of the continent during that time?" she suggested, a hopeful look in her eyes.

He stepped toward her, opening his arms. She accepted the embrace, resting lightly against him so as not to crush her dress. He ran a hand down her back in long, slow strokes.

"Yes. Wherever you wish to go. You will have your wedding trip, my love." She stiffened at the endearment, but his fingers continued their soothing caress until she relaxed once more. "May we leave today? For Ipswich, then further to Norwich?"

"I don't know why you are asking my permission. It's your research, and you are my husband. I'm sworn to obey you."

He stepped back and looked into her eyes. "I don't think obedience comes naturally to you."

Her gaze dropped to the floor. "I do try."

"Rachael, look at me."

Her eyes lifted immediately, obedient to his request, and he felt a tightening in his gut. He wished he had phrased the request differently.

"I don't know what twisted things the men in your past have told you, but I am not they. I don't want your blind obedience. I want your honest opinion. I want your true feelings. And, for God's sake, say something if I do anything stupid! I'd rather you point out my foolishness than hear the words 'inconsiderate lout' again."

Her hands went to her hips, that posture of annoyance he so enjoyed. Her internal fire sparked in her eyes.

"It seems you do remember what I said that day. Last night you said you couldn't recall my words."

"Ah, well, my memory comes and goes. It's only natural for one as old and feeble as myself." He adjusted his spectacles to emphasize his point.

She rolled her eyes at him. It was a delightfully ill-mannered gesture. Words in praise of those bright, coppery eyes danced through his mind. He could write pages about her. He had turned lunatic.

"I will ask to have our trunks packed and the carriage readied," Rachael said. "We needn't bother waiting on a train. The roads are fine, and there are stops along the way where we can replenish our water and fuel."

"You don't mind driving for hours? My man Thomas handles the car well. We could bring him along, if you prefer."

She waved a hand in dismissal. "I intend to make it clear to everyone that steam cars are for both sexes. Lady drivers will be all the rage next summer, mark my word. Do you know the good shops in Ipswich? I need to purchase additional pairs of goggles. Not *all* my driving dresses are red, you know."

He shook his head in wonderment. She was remarkable.

"I need an hour or so at the University to check the artifacts in these photos and gather materials for our journey," he told her. "Will you be ready to set off by noon?"

"Of course."

"Excellent. Thank you."

"I shall begin preparations."

She turned to leave, but he caught her arm. "One last question. Will you be terribly upset if I write to Miss Pelham and ask her to meet us in Norwich? Our abrupt departure meant that I didn't have the opportunity to thoroughly discuss..."

"You may write to whomever you please," she sniffed and flounced out the door.

"That would be a 'yes,'" he sighed. He would send a note regardless. Miss Pelham had more stories of ancient magic he needed to analyze.

In the meantime, he would do his damnedest to convince Rachael that she alone held his heart.

XXII

Enemy Action

"I T OCCURS TO ME, DARLING, that we have spoken little of our histories, outside my curse and your late husband. It would be nice if we could share some other aspects of our past. Family, perhaps?"

What *was* he on about? They'd been on the road for an hour, and much to Rachael's puzzlement, Avery had spent the entire time attempting to engage her in cheerful discourse. He talked of anything and everything but work, which made her think he was deliberately avoiding the subject. His eagerness to please disconcerted her. Though, considering her semi-public tirade at the Pelham home, she could understand why he wanted to keep her happy.

Her father would have called in her manners coach after such an episode. Her childhood outbursts had led to weeks with hours of extra lessons each day. He had wasted his money. The additional tutelage had done nothing to improve her.

"You already know about my father," she replied.

He coughed awkwardly. "Er, yes. That mess with the Imperial Potions Company. Unpleasant."

"He was a selfish fool," she sneered. "I get many of my bad qualities from him."

"No need to dwell on that," Avery said hurriedly. "I was thinking of your girlhood. You clearly had a fine education. Was your mother responsible for that?"

"I couldn't say. She died when I was small, and I remember nothing of her. I resemble her, I've been told." She turned the tables on him. "What about you? What was your mother like?"

"I can scarcely remember. She walked out on us when I was not quite seven."

Rachael gasped.

"My father had hidden the curse from her, and when she learned of it she was justifiably horrified. She sued my father for divorce, citing his deceit. Soon after, she remarried and started a new family, whom I have never met. I try, now and then, to make their acquaintance, but am always rebuffed. My father's mistake haunted him ever after, but I don't blame him. I, too, suffer the curse, and understand his predicament."

Rachael nearly called Avery's mother a terrible name, but the pain in his eyes made her drop the subject altogether. She regretted having ever asked. They had both had lonely, solitary childhoods. There was nothing more to say.

"You are comfortable, still, with the driving?" he asked. "We can stop whenever you wish to stretch your legs."

"I am perfectly well, thank you."

"Good, good." They sat in silence for a few minutes, before he continued, "Those clouds in the distance are growing large and dark, don't you think? Do you wish to seek shelter in the event of rain, or should I hold an umbrella over you while you drive?"

Rachael rolled her eyes behind her goggles. "Don't fuss, Avery. It won't rain."

"Perhaps. We will stop for tea, of course. I wouldn't wish you to become hungry."

"I have no intention of skipping mealtime."

"I do think those clouds are quite dark, and the wind is picking up. I have my cloak if you grow chilly."

Rachael gritted her teeth. He was behaving a perfect gentleman, determined to see that she was comfortable and that her desires were given first priority. Why, then, did she find it so annoying? Her answers to his queries grew shorter and and tetchier as the ride continued, until he stopped talking altogether.

The rain he predicted did come, not long after teatime, during the last leg of their journey, though it was no more than a light mist and did nothing to hinder to her driving. She pulled a handkerchief from her purse, to wipe her goggles if any drops spattered them, but otherwise ignored the weather. With her hat firmly in place, even her hair wouldn't suffer.

Avery fretted. He tried to shelter them with the umbrella, but the vaporous drops swirled in the wind and blew in from all sides. Rachael waved the umbrella away, and he closed it reluctantly. He fidgeted in his seat, finally blurting, "We can stop at any of these farms. They won't turn us away."

She sighed. "It's only a sprinkle. The sky is clearer in the distance. It won't last long."

"You're certain? I don't wish you to be uncomfortably damp, or to have your clothing ruined, or…"

Rachael snapped. "Stop coddling me!"

He jumped. "My apologies. I hadn't meant to."

"For heaven's sake, Avery, I agreed to this journey. I chose the method of travel. I'm not going to throw a fit over it!"

Yet, here she was, screaming at him again. They had traveled so nicely together before their marriage. Why couldn't it be like that?

"I'm very sorry."

He fell silent and looked away. She heard him muttering, but couldn't make out the words over the noise of the wind and the wheels. The remainder of the journey dragged on, quiet and awkward.

Rachael enjoyed the stunned look on the face of the hotel doorman when she drove up. She stopped the car and waited for Avery to walk around and help her down. A porter rushed to unload their trunks. The hotel had a dedicated driver to park all the vehicles, and he gave her a wide smile.

"A fine vehicle, my lady," he said with a tip of his hat.

"She is," Rachael agreed. "Take care with her." She handed the man a coin and he bowed.

Avery ushered her inside, where he once again began to fuss over her.

"How are you, darling? Can I get you anything? Do you need to change for dinner? Or do you prefer to rest in the room? I can request food to be brought up."

He was nervous. That was it. Now that her attention wasn't on the road and her goggles were off, she could read the worry in his eyes. He expected something to go wrong.

"What's the trouble? You are anxious. I told you, I'm not going to throw a fit. We are at a fine hotel. We will have good food and service. I know why we are here, where we are going next, and what to expect."

His eyes darted around the room, looking for something. "Not entirely."

"What do you mean?"

"Annie Pelham might be here already."

"What?"

"I sent her a telegram directly after leaving you this morning. Her father sent me a reply within the hour. She followed us to London because of our unfinished work. She will meet us here instead of in Norwich. Depending on train schedules, she could be here already. I'm sorry. I know you dislike her."

Rachael didn't know enough about the woman to dislike her. She honestly didn't give two figs about her except for the worry of losing her husband's affection. Avery and Miss Pelham shared a passion and Rachael feared she couldn't compete with that. And yet... last night had been so lovely, and she had felt so connected to him.

This morning he had called her "my love." It had rattled her. It was one of those endearments men tossed about without meaning it, trying to soothe or entice their women. Her first husband had used it often, and he'd never loved her. They were only words. She tried to put it out of her mind.

She laid a hand on his arm, in what she hoped was a soothing manner. "I should like to dress for dinner. Will you assist me, or shall I send for that maid?"

Avery leaned close. "I'm happy to assist you," he whispered, "but if I take this dress off of you I don't think I will want you to put another one on."

The husky timbre of his voice sent a tingle down her spine. "There will be plenty of time for that after dinner. There is nothing else to do here, after all, though I should like to jot a quick letter to Isobel first."

"A very quick letter," he teased, leading her toward the stairs.

They had one of the larger rooms in the hotel, and the efficient porters had their trunks waiting when they arrived. Rachael wasted no time selecting a dress for the evening—all black with little trimmings, and conservative, by her standards. It wasn't a night for showing off.

It took much longer to change than it ought to have, partly because there was considerable groping and kissing, but mostly because Avery was a poor substitute for a lady's maid. He fumbled with buttons and strings, he didn't know the best ways to get items on and off, and he mussed her hair badly enough that she needed to repin it. By the time Rachael looked presentable, she was dreadfully hungry.

She hadn't noticed anything amiss during her preparations, but the moment she opened the door she heard a ruckus from the rooms below. She glanced at her husband.

"What is all that noise?"

"I don't know. I would expect a din if this were a tavern, but in a respectable hotel it's peculiar."

"Whatever it is, I hope it doesn't interfere with our dinner. I'm hungry enough as it is."

Down on the ground floor everyone was talking at once. Servants rushed about sporting worry-creased faces. Rachael couldn't make out what was happening, but the source of the chaos looked to be the dining room. Which didn't bode well for her meal.

They had taken no more than two steps into the room, when Mr. Purcell came running at them.

"Cantrell, you are here! You didn't witness the unfortunate event, I hope?"

"I did not. What has happened?"

"A man has died. Keeled over right in the middle of the room, I hear."

Rachael froze. The hairs on her arms stood on end. "Another poisoning?"

"Goodness, no!" Purcell cried. "Whyever would you think that? Bad heart, everyone is saying. He was an elderly gent. A sad event, but not a suspicious one. Several ladies witnessed it, I'm sorry to say, and fainted. I arrived but a few minutes ago, in time to see them carry the poor fellow out. The distraught ladies are still being attended to."

"Is there anything I can do to help?" Avery asked.

"I was told to keep calm and reassure the other guests, particularly any ladies who might be overcome at the news. Mrs. Cantrell, allow me to escort you to another room. Do you need to sit down?"

He reached to take her arm, and she yanked it away.

"Land's sake!" she exclaimed, betraying her past with the Americanism. "We females are not near so fragile as you men seem to think. I don't know who these ridiculous fainting women are, but I assure you, sir, I will not be one of them."

"Indeed," Avery agreed. "You will recall, Robert, that my wife is possessed of a very strong constitution."

Something behind Rachael caused his eyes to open wider.

A grin spread across his face. Rachael turned to see what had caught his attention. Her heart sank. Standing in the hall in a sad, gray dress, clutching a bag to her chest and looking adorably bewildered, was Miss Annie Pelham. She was the very picture of a damsel in distress, and any true gentleman would be moved by it. Judging by Avery's reaction, he was enamored of her.

Rachael felt a sudden urge to fake a swoon. Perhaps she ought to have been more receptive to his attempts to dote on her. She was rarely in distress. If any man were to come to her rescue, it would mean the situation was grave indeed. As troubling, perhaps, as yet another dead body? She shuddered.

Avery clapped his friend on the shoulder. "Purcell, my good man, here is a young lady in need of your assistance." He nudged both Rachael and Purcell out the door in Miss Pelham's direction.

Miss Pelham spied them and rushed over. "Oh, Mr. Cantrell!" she exclaimed, in a manner much too familiar for Rachael's liking.

Avery was still talking to Purcell. "You have heard, of course, about my recent conversations with a folklorist. Here she is now, come to continue our work. Please, allow me to introduce Miss Annie Pelham. Miss Pelham, it's good to see you again. This is my colleague, Professor Robert Purcell. Robert, the turmoil looks to have caused Miss Pelham some unease. As you have familiarity with this hotel, and my wife and I are not yet settled, perhaps you would be good enough to see to her welfare?"

Purcell bowed to Miss Pelham. "A pleasure to meet you. Are you well? Is there anything you have need of? A chair? A restorative drink? May I take your bag?"

Miss Pelham was overwhelmed by all the attention. "Oh! Yes! That is, I am well. Thank you." She didn't relax her grip on the bag.

"I'm so sorry for the clamor. An elderly man has passed on,

I'm afraid, and the shock of it all has been too much for some. I assure you all is now well."

"Oh!" Miss Pelham squeaked. Rachael wished she would stop. It grated on the ears. "I hadn't realized. I thought perhaps it was always so busy. This hotel, you see, is so grand. I have never stayed in so fine a place in the whole of my life. I… I am quite at a loss."

"Never fear," Purcell insisted. "You will have all your needs attended. Please, allow me to take your bag and fetch you a drink. You must be weary from your travels?"

"Er… yes."

She relinquished the bag at last, and Purcell took her arm with a grip that indicated he thought she might topple over were he not supporting her.

Avery put an arm around Rachael's waist. She flinched, not expecting his touch. His other hand seized her arm, just above the elbow, all but holding her up.

"I told you, Avery, I'm not going to faint."

She shook her arm, but he held firm.

"Are you certain? You had professed to be very hungry, and all the excitement has put off our dinner. You may begin to feel weak from the lack of food."

He shifted to bring his body tight to hers. She squirmed in an attempt to relax his grip, but all the movement did was rub their bodies one against the other and send a frisson of arousal through her.

"I want to find out more about this man who died," he whispered. "Will you play my distraught wife while I investigate?"

She answered by sagging against him. He staggered at the unexpected weight shift. "What about your Miss Pelham?" she hissed.

"Purcell has a tender heart for young ladies in need. He can't help but rush to protect them. He will see that she is comfortably settled here. And if you please, do not call her 'my' Miss Pelham. Stop fretting that she will steal me away. I am yours, Rachael."

She hoped it was true. He certainly liked her body. She had his name and a ring on her finger. Was it enough? She must remember to control herself better. She couldn't continue to shout at him. Two years of independence had ruined her. She'd forgotten how difficult it could all be.

Avery led her back into the dining room, steering around people who mostly seemed to be moving in the opposite direction. Hurrying while in his grasp proved awkward. Rachael stumbled several times. He didn't let her fall, fortunately, and it promoted the fiction that she was in need of support.

In the center of the room, a man with a medical kit knelt beside a prone woman. Avery headed straight at him. Rachael did her best to go limp while remaining standing. She couldn't make her complexion pallid without powder. It didn't help that merely being in Avery's arms made her feel warm and flushed. She hoped it would be taken as a symptom of illness.

"Are you a physician?" Avery blurted, though it was plain for anyone to see that he was. "My wife is ailing."

The man glanced up. "She is standing on her own two feet. Sit her down and give her a cool drink." He turned away and held a stethoscope to the fainted woman's chest.

"I beg your pardon," Avery persisted. "Can't you see how red her cheeks have become? She is unwell."

"She is simply overheated," the physician replied without looking up. "A chair and a cool drink."

"I don't think you understand. She was seated very near to the dead man yesterday. If some external factor caused his demise she could be at risk! Did you examine him? Are you certain of the cause of his death?"

He sounded rather hysterical, Rachael thought with pride. He played his part well. She let her head loll onto his chest to add to the effect. She inhaled his spicy scent and had to bite her lip to stop from smiling.

The physician frowned down at the unconscious woman and put a hand to her brow. A moment later he looked up at a pale, pudgy man who stood nearby. "This is your wife, sir?"

"Yes." He trembled. "Can't you revive her? Have you no smelling salts?"

"I think it best we don't try to wake her just yet. She hasn't merely fainted, she is ill. Her pulse is quick and she is burning with fever. We should move her to a bed or a sofa and send to the nearest chemist for a healing potion."

"Was she near to the dead man?" Avery fretted. "Are the symptoms similar? Is anyone else ill?"

"Someone get him out of here," the physician growled.

A man in hotel livery tried to steer Avery away, muttering placating words. It wouldn't do at all. They needed answers. This woman's illness was no coincidence. The poisoner was back at work.

Rachael felt her husband's grip slacken. She did the only sensible thing and fainted.

Avery dropped to his knees at once. He bent over Rachael, who lay crumpled in an elegant swirl of black fabric. Even her fainting was graceful.

"Rachael, darling!" he cried. Playing the part of panic-stricken husband was oddly enjoyable. He patted her cheek in the manner he had seen others do when trying to revive someone from a faint. When she didn't stir, he pressed his forehead to hers.

"Excellently done, my dear," he murmured. His lips skimmed across hers in the briefest of kisses.

Most of the attention was still upon the ill woman. Avery eavesdropped on the chatter and pretended to fuss over Rachael. She remained still, but he could tell from the occasional twitching of her mouth that she was suppressing the urge to giggle.

The physician had, in fact, examined the dead man, and believed the cause of death to be failure of the heart. His new patient had brought an uncertainty to that diagnosis.

"I don't know what the man's symptoms were," he told the woman's husband. "I didn't examine him until he was beyond help. I was told by witnesses only that he had collapsed, very suddenly."

"My wife's collapse was sudden," the husband wailed. "Please, you must do more for her. You cannot leave her here to die!"

He was in a genuine panic. Avery laid his head on Rachael's chest and squeezed her, flooded with relief that her condition was feigned. He could only imagine what the other man must be going through.

"A man has been sent after a healing potion, and I will remain at her side," the physician assured him. "I take the utmost care with all my patients. Fetch a few able-bodied servants. She will rest more comfortably if we move her to a sofa."

"Yes, yes! I will do so at once." He dashed off, looking relieved to be of use.

The physician turned to Avery. "Does your wife need medical attention? Have you been unable to revive her?"

Avery sat up. He didn't need to pull the man away from his true duties. "She isn't feverish."

Rachael stirred and fluttered her long, lovely eyelashes. Avery took up her hand and patted it in encouragement.

"There, darling. You are well. It was only the heat. No, do not try to sit up."

She sighed theatrically.

Avery looked at the physician with what he hoped was an anxious expression. "That man who died, and this woman… You don't think it was something contagious, do you?"

"I don't know of any contagious diseases that would cause a man to drop dead where moments before he had shown no symptoms. This woman, too, was seemingly healthy, her husband says, before her faint." He bent over her with the stethoscope once more. "I don't think her heart is failing. The health potion will revive her."

Her husband came running back into the room, accompanied by two of the same porters who had taken Rachael and Avery's trunks earlier. It ended Avery's chance to speak with the physician, but he had learned enough. Poison, yet again.

The man who had tried before to take him from the room reappeared, with a glass in each hand. He knelt at Rachael's other side.

"I brought water, sir, and brandy."

Avery helped Rachael sit up. A scowl flashed across her features. She had tired of playing helpless. He handed her the glass of water, and she downed it quickly. Her eyes flicked to the glass of brandy. Avery took it from the man and passed it to her. She deserved a good drink after her quick thinking and convincing performance.

"Sip it slowly," he instructed. Her eyes narrowed at him and he almost laughed.

He thanked and dismissed the servant while she sipped. The ill woman had been carried off, and the hubbub had died down. He gave Rachael a hand up, giving as little assistance as possible so as not to annoy her further. She tossed back the rest of the brandy. It must have been strong, because her mouth twisted.

"That was very reviving," she declared. She scanned the room. "We aren't going to get any dinner here tonight. I shall request to have something sent up to our room. I'm famished."

Avery had never known anyone who could compose himself—or herself—as quickly as Rachael did. He was still in shock from the ordeal, and here she was, standing tall and taking charge. Perhaps fleeing a murderous husband made other crises seem meager by comparison. Whatever the reason, he admired her fortitude.

She ordered dinner to be sent to their rooms, giving strict instructions that all food should be freshly made and that all cooking equipment and dishes must be thoroughly cleansed with soap and water. With a man dead and others ill, no one batted an eye. Avery used his personal silver, regardless.

As they were eating, Rachael remarked, "I'm thinking that I should have my own set of silver for traveling and dinner parties. I can have it specially made, and if I drop hints that I took the idea from the Marchioness of Effield, then word will spread. It could be the new done thing, and no one will ever look at you askance again."

Avery froze with his fork halfway to his mouth. For a moment he couldn't speak. When at last he did, his words were thick with emotion. "That is very thoughtful of you, my love."

He held her gaze for several seconds before she glanced away.

"Is it?" She feigned nonchalance. "I assure you, I was only thinking of myself. I can't be going out in public with so eccentric a husband."

He didn't need the furtive look in her eyes or the hitch in her voice to know she was lying. An eccentric husband suited her perfectly. She would revel in the attention, and sneer at anyone who disparaged him. Her offer had been entirely for his benefit.

He was done for. He had thought he loved her that morning. That feeling was no more than a paltry fondness when measured against the unquenchable devotion that now devastated him. He couldn't fathom the depths to which he might sink on the morrow.

He needed her to love him. He longed for it, with heart and with soul, down to his very bones. The intensity of the desire overwhelmed him. He would do anything, give anything, to have her feel what he felt.

"Avery? Are you quite all right?"

His fork still hovered in midair. He lowered it to the plate, his appetite all but lost.

"Yes, I'm well. My apologies. I was lost in thought. It is… shocking to consider that I might go out in public as any normal man. It would be most welcome. If you could do that for me, Rachael…"

He choked up before he could finish. He grabbed for his glass of wine and drank it half down before he felt composed enough to even look at his wife.

The instant he did, he knew he had to do more to cool his passions. She stared at him, a smile of pleasure and surprise on her face. A rosy tint colored her cheeks, and her golden-brown eyes were soft and full of affection. It gave him hope that she could and would love him someday.

He grasped for something to do or say to wrest control from his mad emotions. If he did nothing, he was certain to either fling himself bodily across the table to kiss her or burst into tears. Neither option was the slightest bit acceptable for a gentleman. He had no desire to ruin her dress or his suit by scattering their dinner everywhere, and he hadn't cried since his father's funeral twenty years ago.

He could think of only one solution.

"When our dinner is finished, I would like to call on Annie Pelham and take down more of her tales."

Rachael's smile didn't change. "Certainly. I will accompany you."

He poured himself more wine. At this rate he would close out the evening blisteringly drunk. It didn't seem a bad idea.

XXIII

An Overture of Friendship

"**M**ISS PELHAM? Might I offer you some of this excellent brandy?"

Rachael and Avery had offered up their sitting area for the evening's folklore discussions, and she was determined to be a perfect hostess. If this work was necessary to finding Avery's cure, then that was that, and best to get it over with as soon as possible.

Miss Pelham flinched. "Oh, no, thank you. Such spirits are best left to the gentlemen."

Rachael filled a snifter for herself. "The gentlemen can share. But what can I get for you? Coffee? Tea?"

"Oh, neither, thank you. They make me jittery of an evening."

Rachael's already false smile pulled tighter. She might need something stronger than brandy to put up with this all night. "I will send for some lemonade."

"Thank you."

With her hostess duties attended to, Rachael turned her focus to her husband. He'd been in a peculiar mood all day, and it had only grown worse since dinner. He'd settled himself onto the sofa, with a notebook and his own snifter of brandy. A dazed look lingered in his emerald eyes. She'd never intended to stun him with her suggestion of buying silver. The thought had simply come to her that she might be able to ease some of his troubles in that way. It seemed a natural sort of thing for a wife to want for her husband. He'd reacted as if she'd offered him the crown jewels.

Miss Pelham had taken the seat beside Avery, so Rachael positioned her own chair as near to the sofa as she could without looking ridiculously possessive. A small table separated her from her husband, but she set her drink beside his, and just so happened to reach for it whenever he picked up his own glass. Each time their hands brushed, he twitched. He would smile at her for a second, then quickly look down at either his notes or his drink.

The old folktales were disappointingly dull. Purcell and Avery listened attentively and asked questions, but Rachael had to fall back on her old habit of faking enthusiasm. Her ears pricked up whenever she heard the words "flower" or "potion," but most of the conversation she simply tuned out. She passed the time observing her companions.

Miss Pelham perched irritatingly close to Avery, clutching her lemonade and fluttering her dark lashes. Rachael was determined to give her a fair appraisal tonight, since they had never truly spent any time together.

Annie Pelham was a pretty girl, with the vivid green Cantrell eyes. Rachael wouldn't have guessed her to be even distantly related to Avery except for those eyes. Her looks were dulled by her terrible dresses and schoolmistress hairstyle, but in a proper gown, with just a touch of cosmetics, she would turn heads. She had an attractive innocence about her that men like Purcell were drawn to.

The professor was watching her even now, Rachael noted with some amusement. He had made a point of asking after her health and comfort while escorting her here. Avery was correct. He liked a damsel in distress.

Miss Pelham rarely looked anywhere but at Avery. She did seem overly attached to him, but Rachael noted no flirtations, and Miss Pelham didn't touch her lips or her hair, as she might have done given a romantic inclination. In truth, the woman sounded starved for conversation. It was only logical, given her meager home life. There wasn't much to do or speak of in her village. It explained her occupation as a folklorist. She had traveled much, apparently, across the south and west of the country, collecting her stories. In her position, Rachael, too, would have jumped at an excuse to go somewhere else and talk to someone new.

Miss Pelham did glance at Rachael now and then, which was inevitable, given her proximity to Avery. Each time Miss Pelham's mouth turned downward, without fail, no matter Rachael's expression.

Rachael frowned into her brandy, struggling to keep her annoyance bottled up.

Well, I don't like you, either, but at least I'm trying!

She abandoned her assessment of the other woman to fret over her husband, who had poured himself yet another drink. His own researchings had taken place primarily in the north and the east, and it was clear there were elements of Miss Pelham's stories that complimented his work. Even so, he struggled to concentrate on his notes and rarely met the eyes of the others. Was it this new poisoning that so distracted him? Even the most optimistic of people couldn't claim that three such incidents were mere coincidence.

A sense of relief fell over the entire party when Miss Pelham at last ran out of legends to relate. Avery and Purcell asked a few questions, but those, too, quickly dwindled. Rachael resumed the role of hostess and rose from her seat to begin the goodbyes.

Avery rose slowly, then shook Miss Pelham's hand in a distracted manner. "Thank you for your time. This information will contribute to my work." He blinked at his own vapid statement. "Er, yes. Excellent contributions. Naturally."

"Indeed," Purcell added. "Our talk has been most enlightening. Do you require an escort back to your room this evening?"

"I would be most happy to walk you there, Miss Pelham," Rachael jumped in, determined to make strides toward amiability. "An unmarried woman such as yourself ought to have a female companion at this time of night. These hotels are filled with strange men, you know."

"An excellent notion, Lady Cantrell," Purcell agreed. "Shall we all walk together?"

Rachael had to suppress a scowl. She wanted a moment with Miss Pelham alone. "Please, don't trouble yourself, Mr. Purcell. We shall talk of women's things, you know, and I shouldn't like to burden you with such frivolities."

"Of course. Good evening to you both." He bowed and left the room.

Rachael took Annie Pelham by the arm. "Come, dear. Allow me to walk you to your room."

Miss Pelham's eyes flashed in anger, but she made a polite adieu to Avery. The moment they were in the hall, she yanked her arm free and openly glared at Rachael.

"I don't know what you mean by this, but I have no desire to speak to you of 'frivolities' or of anything at all."

"A fine way to treat a woman who has done nothing but attempt an overture of friendship," Rachael sneered. The hostile retort came out before she could stop it. The woman was maddening.

"Friendship? Ha!"

"Civil acquaintanceship, then?" Rachael suggested, regaining composure. "It's a simple fact that we are obliged to spend time in one another's company. We did not get off to a good start. I would like to amend that."

"Forgive me if I don't believe that to be your true motive."

"I will not. You have no cause to be rude to me. I hosted

you in my room this evening and saw to your comfort. I don't expect to be repaid with unjustified accusations."

"You have no interest in our work. You were only there to spy on us."

"I don't spy on people in my own chambers. That's absurd."

"I saw how you watched us all. You are jealous of your husband's attentions to me."

"I am not." She *had been* jealous. The day's events, however, had entirely revised her conclusions on the matter.

Miss Pelham only rolled her eyes and picked up her pace. Rachael easily matched the speed with her long strides.

"I don't know what you want, Miss Pelham, with your pretension to modesty and innocence, but you should know that if it is anything beyond academic discussion you will be sorely disappointed." A sudden, mad thought that perhaps Miss Pelham had some connection to the poisonings flashed through Rachael's mind. Could she, perhaps, see Avery as a rival, the way Professor Dashell did?

"I pretend to nothing!"

"Oh? Because you seem a different girl than the helpless, squeaking thing who first entered the hotel."

"How dare you!"

"I don't doubt you felt some apprehension upon your arrival. The hotel was in chaos, and it is undoubtedly far beyond anything you have ever experienced…"

"You arrogant bitch," Miss Pelham snarled. She stabbed at her door with the room key. "You think you're so much better than the rest of us. I'm surprised you would stoop to walk the halls with the likes of me."

The lock turned, and the door swung open. Rachael grabbed hold of it to prevent it being closed in her face.

"I will have you know that one of my great friends used to be no more than a Parisian barmaid. Do you know how she proved her worthiness? By *behaving* my equal. Not by sniveling and accusing others of mistreating her. She gave me her kindness when I had done nothing to earn it. Now I will attempt to do the same. Have a good night, Miss Pelham. I harbor no ill will toward you, and I hope that our next conversation will be cordial and that we can put all this unpleasantness behind us." She nodded to the other woman and stepped away from the door. "Please excuse me, my husband will be waiting for me."

"You don't deserve him."

"That is likely true. He seems fond of me, regardless." She spun on her heel and strode off. The door slammed behind her.

Frustrated, Rachael stomped through the halls to her own room. Owing to the late hour and the earlier uproar, there was no one else to see her behaving indecorously. Her mind whirled as she walked. Was it possible that Miss Pelham was the poisoner? How much did she know of Avery's work? She could have learned of him through other folklorists, or even through Dashell.

And was she truly shy and modest, or were tonight's angry words more her true self? Rachael put on false faces so often she wouldn't have been surprised if Miss Pelham did, too. Or maybe the woman had merely snapped. They were all under stress these days.

The moment Rachael reached her room, concern for her husband supplanted any other worries. She found him sprawled on the sofa, stripped down to his shirtsleeves, drinking brandy straight from the bottle. She stared down at him, too worried to scold him. He stared back, a dreamy smile on his face, his gaze fixed on her eyes. After a time, he shook himself out of it. He sat up and thunked the bottle down onto the table.

"Hasn't made a damned bit of difference!"

"Avery, what is wrong with you?"

"Nothing, m'dear." He stood. "Just thirsty tonight. Might be a touch intoxicated." His words were slurred, and he swayed when he walked to her. His arms slipped around her waist. "Ah, my Rachael. How did I win you? No, don't tell me. My damnable poetry." He kissed her neck. "You smell lovely."

He smelled like spice and too much alcohol. She slipped from his arms and poured him a cup of coffee from the lukewarm pot.

"Avery, you need to go to bed. Here, have some coffee."

He sipped at it. "Vile. I preferred the brandy, tho' didn't work 'tall."

"Didn't work for what purpose?"

"Supposed to dull the senses. Make it all stop in here." He put a hand flat to his chest. "Damned useless. Think I'm stuck with it."

Rachael regarded him with hands on hips. "Stuck with what? Your heart?"

A lopsided grin split his face. "Precisely, darlin'. Had it locked away, and then you came 'round and set it free. This coffee is bloody terrible." He set down the cup and took her by the arm. "Come to bed. I'll write you some love poems."

She walked with him to the bed, but when he moved to lay down, she stepped aside. "You rest. I'll ring for the maid."

Rachael ducked behind the privacy screen and sat at the dressing table. She removed her jewelry, brushed and braided her hair, then picked up her pen and paper.

Dear Isobel,

It may take a very long letter indeed to cover all the strange happenings of the day. I will begin with the good news. Avery is in love with me. It appears to have come as something of a shock to him. He is currently lying in our bed, drunkenly spouting verse. Some of the rhymes are terribly vulgar. For example, he said only now, "I'll gaze into your sparkling eyes and lay between your creamy thighs." I cannot be horrified because I am giggling too much.

I am torn between waiting until he falls asleep or answering his amorous summons—

"Rachael, love, are you not yet ready for bed?" he called. "I'm running out of rhymes."

She glanced up from her writing. "I haven't even summoned the maid. I suggest you go to sleep, and we will talk in the morning." She couldn't summon anyone while he was in this state, in any case.

"I'll be damned hungover in the morning. Beg pardon, I oughtn't keep saying 'damn' in front of a lady."

"I will only be a few more moments."

She turned back to her letter. Within minutes, he was snoring. She rang for the maid and finished preparing for bed, then slipped underneath the sheets beside him. He was still snoring, so she jostled him until he rolled over and fell quiet. Ridiculous man. So terrified of his own passionate nature that he'd drunk himself silly.

Rachael snuggled him, not caring that he reeked of brandy. He loved her. The mad passion she had been craving was within reach. A ripple of anxiety raced through her. She couldn't lose this. And that meant keeping control of her temper and her mouth.

XXIV

Long Gone

Avery's head throbbed with the pain of a thousand invisible knives. Hangovers were worse, it seemed, when one was old and feeble. Or perhaps he'd only forgotten. He'd never been one to get drunk often, and it had been many years since the last time he'd felt like this. He fully deserved it, so he forced himself out of bed when Rachael rose and did his best to look presentable. His spectacles lessened the headache somewhat, so he wore them to breakfast. Fashion be damned.

"You look most distinguished this morning, darling."

Her tone was gentle and sweet, without the least sarcasm or reference to his shameful behavior. She was playing the dutiful wife again, attending to his needs with graceful poise. She even poured him what little was left of the brandy as a hair-of-the-dog remedy. He wished she would scold him.

He spied Miss Pelham in the dining room, and thought to invite her to sit with them, but she turned bright red and scurried away before he could even greet her.

"What has gotten into her?" he wondered.

Rachael's brow crinkled. "I don't know. She is acting shy again this morning."

"She is always shy, but not so much that she should run away."

"She wasn't shy last night."

"She was talkative enough when we were discussing work, that is true."

"No. After that."

Avery didn't recall seeing her after that. He'd been only moderately drunk when she had left their room. He'd never been so intoxicated he wouldn't remember anything. "When you walked her to her room?"

Rachael nodded.

"Why? What happened?"

They took their seats and she gave him a word-by-word rundown of her argument with Miss Pelham from the night before. She had a good memory for detail and an engaging way of relating events. He could see why her cousin enjoyed her letters. He wondered if she might let him read some of them.

"She has certainly taken a dislike to you," he mused. "Though I believe you feel much the same about her?"

"I did try! My intent was to have a civil conversation. But she slammed the door in my face, and now she runs and hides. What is she afraid of? Or what is she hiding? Perhaps I should leave you and see if she will approach you alone. Though I'm loathe to do that, in case she is the poisoner."

"You can't be serious. She was in Seawell when all but this last incident occurred."

"As far as we know. I doubt it's her. Still, she's connected to your work, and we have reached the point where everything is suspicious."

Avery unrolled his silver and speared a bite of meat from his specially cleaned plate. An abundance of caution did have certain benefits.

"We will seek her out later today, after I have completed my review of Purcell's artifacts. We can put your suspicions to rest."

"Yes, darling. I'm sure you are correct. Would you like some more coffee?"

He didn't know which was worse, the hangover or her deferential behavior.

"Please."

After breakfast he spent several hours poring over Purcell's local folklore collection. It exacerbated his headache and gained him nothing. His luncheon consisted of coffee. He hadn't the stomach for anything else.

In the afternoon he walked to the gaol to check on Hunstable. The photographer seemed resigned to his situation when Avery arrived, but by the end of the visit he was in tears again. Avery stormed back to the hotel, itching to punch someone.

He reached the hotel in time for tea, and hurried up to his room, hoping to catch Rachael there. He found her sitting on the sofa, a needle and thread in her hand, stitching pearls onto a pair of driving goggles. An array of packages surrounded her.

"This pair was lacking," she informed him. "It looks more elegant now, don't you think?"

He frowned at the goggles. "You've been out shopping?"

"Naturally. I couldn't very well sit here all day." She peered at her work, her lips curling. "I may have to have this redone when we return home. I'm not the best with a needle. I couldn't wait, however, as these goggles match the dress I intend to wear when we set out for Norwich."

"You went shopping?" Avery repeated, still not quite believing it. "By yourself?"

"Yes, of course. I was unforgivably short on driving accessories. I now have appropriate hats, goggles, and gloves."

"But…" Avery's heart constricted. "Rachael, there is a mad poisoner running around somewhere! What if something had happened? I would've had no idea where to find you!"

The fear surged through him, much as the anger had done. Rachael had demolished what little control he'd had over his emotions. He had thought himself more disciplined, but in truth he had only hidden himself away to avoid situations that might trigger strong feelings. Now circumstances dictated he could no longer hide, and he didn't know what to do. Drinking obviously didn't work. Looking at Rachael made everything worse.

She tossed her work aside and sprang to her feet. She rushed to him and gathered him in her arms. "I didn't think of it that way. I never meant to frighten you. Next time I will let you know my plans."

Avery held her close, feeling her warmth, breathing her scent. Her hair smelled of citrus today. He loved that she hadn't apologized for going out. Even more, he loved that she had made no promises not to go out again, or even to take someone with her. His bold, brave Rachael would not be deterred from her usual activities.

He dropped his mouth to hers in a soft, lingering kiss, letting himself savor every moment of it—the gentle press of her lips, the insistence of her tongue as she sought for more. She was his ambrosia, and he drank deeply of her.

It was a disappointment to end the kiss, but they couldn't spare the time to go to bed in the middle of the afternoon. Business here needed to be wrapped up so they could depart for Norwich first thing in the morning. They drew apart and took themselves downstairs for tea.

"Where do you think she might have gone?" Rachael asked, slowly stirring milk into her tea.

Avery blinked, wondering if he'd missed half a conversation.. "Pardon?"

"Miss Pelham. This room is packed with guests, but she isn't here. She can have no business in town save for ours. She doesn't have the money for a shopping trip. Where could she possibly be?"

Avery set down his teacup, frowning in puzzlement. "I can't imagine. Purcell will be at the dig site today, but he is unlikely to take a woman with him. Shall we call on her when we finish here?"

"Yes, let's."

Shortly thereafter, Rachael led the way to Miss Pelham's room. She rapped upon the door and stepped back. They didn't have a long wait before the door swung open.

A man in a suit finer than Avery's blinked at Rachael in confusion. "You aren't my valet."

"Obviously not!" Rachael retorted.

The man grinned, his eyes traveling over her body, settling on the neckline that was far lower than most ladies wore during the day.

"However," he leered, "I would not be averse to you helping me undress."

Avery would never dream of telling Rachael to choose clothing that did not display her assets, but he couldn't deny it infuriated him when men took it as an excuse to treat her inappropriately.

The roving eyes never bothered her, but the words did. She stepped up to the man and placed a hand on his chest, the way she might have done were she accepting his offer. She shoved him hard enough that he toppled backward into the room, then she yanked the door closed. The walls rattled.

She straightened her gloves. "Miss Pelham appears to have checked out."

Avery felt a surge of pride in her, tempered with a mild disappointment he hadn't had a chance to flay the man for his insolent tongue. He had several choice insults in mind.

"Why on earth did you decide to remarry?" he wondered. "You have no need of me or of anyone. You are the most independent and capable woman I know."

She sniffed. "You don't know my friends. I shall keep you away from them, and from Isobel, too, lest you discover how superior they all are and decide to leave me."

"I won't leave you for anything," he vowed. "You are the finest woman on earth."

A rueful smile played on her lips. "You flatter very prettily. Let's return to business. I must go out again to purchase fuel for the car before dinner, and pack up my new things as well. The mystery of Miss Pelham will have to wait." She paused. "You don't think she could be the poisoner now, do you?"

"I don't, but something is amiss. She had expressed interest in seeing the photographs and aiding in the search for the ryeweed flower. It's puzzling that she would instead pack up and leave."

"Puzzling and worrying. I do hope she's not mixed up in this business. Would you like to come with me to purchase the fuel, or do you have other matters to attend to?"

Avery hated to leave her, but he did have to review the documents he'd borrowed from the collection. He bade her goodbye with a kiss and a promise to find her in time for dinner.

Even without her by his side, her presence lingered. Thoughts of her swirled through his brain as he worked. Making love with her later that evening was exquisite. Holding her afterward was beauteous and torturous. He couldn't sleep. Whatever she might say, he didn't believe that anyone, anywhere, could compare to her. He toyed with the idea of declaring his love in a more open fashion. Would she withdraw, though? She, too, had declared herself to be unimpassioned. He didn't believe it for a moment. Coaxing the emotions out of her, however, could be problematic, especially while he struggled with it himself. A slow, easy course was imperative. The wait would be excruciating.

XXV

A Disordered Mind

*T*HEY SET OUT EARLY the next morning for Norwich. Rachael's black and pearl goggles complemented her beaded ebony dress. A riding hat with a pointed brim and trailing black ribbons completed the outfit. The more people who saw her, the more likely he thought her prediction about lady drivers would come true. She made sitting behind the wheel of a car look splendidly stylish.

The drive to Norwich was shorter than the drive to Ipswich, and a thousand times more pleasant. Avery jotted verses in his notebook and let Rachael do most of the talking. He asked her about her friends, and despite her earlier comment that she ought to keep him away from them, she launched into detailed descriptions of both their fine qualities and their oddities.

He enjoyed the sound of her voice. The writing was likewise soothing. He wrote of the landscape, the villages, even the steam cars bouncing down the road in the opposite direction. Most of what he wrote was rubbish, but giving himself over to the scratch of the pencil and the rhythm of the words calmed his emotions. It seemed he had found a coping mechanism.

Avery had been to Norwich only once, five or six years

prior, but little had changed, and he found his way to Dashell's office without difficulty. The front door was unlocked, and he led Rachael past the small museum space to the office proper. The door stood wide open. Inside, a harried-looking man knelt in front of a bookshelf, pulling papers and books down, frowning at them, then sorting them into piles. Avery cleared his throat and the man glanced up.

"May I help you?"

"Avery Cantrell," he introduced himself. The man looked at him blankly, so he continued, "Head of the Department of Anglo-Saxon History and Literature, University College London. I'm here to speak with Professor Dashell."

The man stared at him. "You haven't heard?"

A feeling of foreboding washed over Avery. "What has happened?"

"He's dead, isn't he?" Rachael blurted from behind him. "Damnation!"

The man gaped. Another chap who had never heard a woman swear. "Y-yes," he sputtered. "Only yesterday. I'm sorry. I was given to understand that everyone with an appointment had been contacted."

Rachael swished into the room and looked around. "How did he die? Has there been an investigation?"

"No! Why should there be?"

She shook her head and circled the desk. "What is this package?"

"I don't know. Please, don't touch anything. Perhaps if you come back tomorrow we can arrange for you to speak with one of our researchers."

Rachael ignored him. She pulled off her driving gloves and swapped them for a fingered pair from her purse. She picked through the mess on the desk, lingering on the unwrapped package in the center. She lifted an open tin and frowned at it.

"This was from the package? What was in this?"

"I have no idea!" the man cried. "Please, madam, there is

important information and precious artifacts everywhere. You must leave."

Rachael tugged her gloves from her fingers, turning them inside out. She turned to Avery. "Aerosolized poison."

Avery's brow furrowed. "What is that? I've never heard such a term."

"Never? Don't you read novels?"

"Certainly not. I have no time for such nonsense."

Her hands went to her hips. "Really, Avery. How do you expect to comport yourself properly in public when you cannot discuss ordinary subjects? You must at least read the most popular of the novels so that you have something to say. You needn't read them all the way through. A basic knowledge can get you through most conversations."

He frowned at her, his jaw tight. "The poison?"

"What? Oh, yes." She let her hands fall to her sides. "Aerosolized poisons appear often in dramatic mysteries. A substance is placed in a sealed container, and when the victim opens it, they breathe in the toxic vapors and die."

"That is fine for a novel, but is it even possible?"

Rachael waved a hand. "I have no idea. I will ask Elle about it when we return home. She ought to know that sort of thing. But it makes no difference. The empty tin could have held a little chocolate bonbon. He eats it and dies. Simple. Whatever it was, something in that tin delivered poison."

"Do you see any markings on the package?"

"The address of the office only. Nothing to reveal the sender. It's printed in precise, square letters, all capital. It could have been written by anyone."

"Damn. We'll have to search the room for more clues. If only Dashell weren't so bloody disorganized," Avery grumbled. "He digs—dug—for treasure and notoriety, not research. He was an insult to the profession."

"Don't speak so negatively of the man. We don't want anyone to think you killed him."

"That is idiotic. I needed his help. Why would I have made things more difficult for myself?"

"I don't think you killed him, Avery dear. Though I wish I knew who did. I don't believe any of these poisonings coincidental, but I fail to see a motive connecting them. I see no purpose behind any of the events, except this last. Dashell's death I suspect to be an attempt to thwart your progress. Why, though, I can't imagine. What benefit would anyone get by preventing you finding a cure?"

"Excuse me," Dashell's assistant interrupted. "This is all highly inappropriate, and I must ask you..."

"We are searching this room," Avery commanded. "Either you go back to your work and leave us in peace, or I call the police."

"Uh... Fine. Look around all you like," the young man muttered. He picked up a stack of papers and plopped down in a chair to shuffle through them, eyeing Avery and Rachael suspiciously.

"I see no reason anyone would wish to stop me from finding a cure," Avery said to Rachael, drumming his gloved fingers on the desk. "It could hasten my death, but if someone desired that, they would poison me, not others. I have no enemies I know of, and I have no heirs who might want my money. Cantrell men die much too quickly to have ever risked an entail on the estate that could bankrupt wives or daughters. Per my will, all my property would pass to you. Should I suspect you of wanting to off me?"

"Absolutely," she replied. "I am the most incompetent murderess in the history of humanity."

He grinned at her. "I love it when you are sarcastic."

She blinked. "Do you? That's peculiar. My father employed a manners coach for years in an attempt to teach it out of me."

"He was a fool," Avery said.

"We are both agreed on that point. I'm afraid I didn't reap a single benefit from the lessons."

"If the lessons did nothing, it's because you didn't need them in the first place. Your manners are impeccable."

She peered at him from beneath narrowed brows, her mouth twisted in a frown of suspicion. Always underestimating herself.

"Why don't you start looking through the papers?" Avery suggested. "Your eyesight is better. I will concentrate on the artifacts.

She nodded and grabbed a thick stack, continuing her speculation as she worked. "So. We have no motive. We have a variety of locations. Near and in Ipswich: clearly the same person. Dashell's package could have come from anywhere. What of the London poisoning? The poisoner must have traveled between the two cities. But for what purpose? Why would anyone come to town to sicken guests at a party?"

Avery tossed aside a useless bit of broken pottery. "Why sicken guests at all? I have yet to understand what purpose that incident served. Not that anything in this bloody mess makes sense."

"We need to stop thinking of what we don't know and think about what we *do* know. We know who was poisoned, and where and when. We know that the poisonings are connected to your field of research. Our criminal has access to poisons or has the means to make them. Our criminal spends time both in Ipswich and in London. Our criminal knows what you are doing, or at least where you are going. How many people knew of our plan to visit Dashell?"

Avery froze. The box he'd been holding clattered to the floor. "Good Lord. Purcell was in London."

Rachael's hand went to her mouth to stifle her gasp. Dashell's assistant stopped pretending to work and stared at Avery with morbid curiosity.

"He and Hunstable had come into town for the lecture," Avery explained, the pieces falling into place in his mind. "I told him I would spread the word at Lady Ellerby's party. I even considered inviting him along."

"He was on-site at the dig," Rachael continued. "He was at the hotel in Ipswich. He knew to the day when we were planning to speak with Dashell. You are correct. He is our murderer!"

Avery's stomach churned. He covered his face with his hand. "For God's sake, why?" he cried.

Rachael leapt to embrace him. "Oh, darling, I'm so sorry. I know he is your friend."

"No longer. Perhaps not ever." He kissed her brow. "I can't comprehend what would drive a seemingly sensible man to such things." He trembled again, and she stroked him with gentle hands. "I am appalled… and heartsick."

"I know nothing I say can soothe you," she whispered, "but I am here."

His arms tightened around her. "Thank you." She was his rock. She would get him through this. "Now we must work. We must find proof. And my cure." He glanced at Dashell's assistant. The young man shuffled off into a corner, busying himself with an untidy stack of books. Smart enough to mind his own business. Good.

Avery spent the next hour swearing under his breath at the disaster of an office. Only Rachael's presence prevented a full-blown tirade or a complete meltdown. Her assistance searching through the documents and photos was invaluable. She worked tirelessly. She comforted him with kisses. She kept him sane.

He turned toward the wreckage that was the remaining bookcase. Books and papers jutted out at strange angles. Battered boxes had been wedged in wherever space could be made. Avery wanted nothing better than to get out of here. The office was twice the size of his own and held less than half as much useful information. He tried not to curse Dashell. The poor bastard deserved at least a bit of courtesy after being poisoned.

Rachael grasped his arm. "Look here first, darling." She held a single photograph. "This image is the most interesting, I think, though it is blurred somewhat. The photographer didn't have the skill of young Lord Hunstable."

He took the photo from her hand and peered at it. He blinked in disbelief and pulled off his spectacles. He wiped them until they were spotless, then looked again at the photo, angling it to get the best light.

"Christ Almighty!" he swore. "Do you know what this is?"

"A fragment of old tapestry, it appears. It looks to have something to do with potions, and there is that flower in the corner, though it is more than half cut off and damaged."

He nodded. The piece was in poor condition, a common problem for bits of fabric and paper. They didn't survive well, as gold and ceramics did. He had experience with such things, however, and could pick out words and symbols others wouldn't recognize.

"I think it shows the entire process of making a potion. I need to look at the actual artifact." Avery's heart pounded. Here was his cure. How long had Dashell had the damned thing? "You there!" he shouted at the assistant. "Where can I find this artifact?"

The man looked up from his sorting. He begrudgingly stumbled to his feet, brushing dust from his clothing. He gave the photo a cursory glance and shrugged.

"You haven't seen it yet? I imagine it must be in one of those boxes." He gestured at the as-yet-untouched shelves. "Such a ragged old thing wouldn't be in the museum display."

Avery wanted to throttle the brat. His every hope in life a "ragged old thing"? These people had no respect for research, no understanding of how precious every scrap and nail and broken bit could be. He scowled and spun away, his face red with anger, his hands shaking with anticipation. He yanked box after box from the shelves, tearing through them like a madman. Rachael knelt beside him, gently examining the things he cast aside.

At the bottom of the third box he tried, he found several scraps of decaying tapestry. He lifted one out, unfolding it with as much care as his trembling fingers could manage. It wasn't the fragment from the photo, but looked to be another part of the same tapestry. The figure at the bottom of the piece was badly worn, but Avery recognized the prone pose as an indication of one dead.

"Clear the desk," he instructed.

With a single sweep of her arm, Rachael flung the contents of the desk to the floor. Dashell's assistant let out a cry, but a sharp look from both the Cantrells silenced him. Avery spread the tapestry out and went back for the next piece.

The box held six fragments in all, and though significant chunks were missing, what remained of the tapestry brought tears to his eyes. It was his story, lovingly crafted centuries ago with beautiful thread and a skilled hand. Here was the warrior-king, seeming dead by poison, then revived and ousting the witch-queen. A later section depicted him weeping over the body of a dead child, a medicinal vial on the ground nearby.

Avery had to bit his lip to keep from sobbing aloud. Salty droplets dripped from his cheeks, splashing on the desktop. His wife's arms encircled his waist, and her head dropped onto his shoulder, offering affection and comfort.

"Lord, Rachael," he gasped. "It's true. The whole bloody thing is true." A part of him had always feared the curse was just nonsense, that his condition was truly no more than an allergy, as Rachael had first called it. Now here was the tale, laid out before him—physical proof that someone, sometime long ago, had thought it important enough to have commissioned a work of art depicting the legendary events.

"Where is the piece from the photo?" Rachael wondered.

Avery pointed. "It should go here. It must be in the last box."

He rummaged through the box, dumping most of the contents on the floor. He found several more photos of portions of the tapestry and two more small pieces of the artifact itself. He added them to the scene spread across the desk. Neither was the piece depicting the making of the poison.

"This is incomplete," he said to the assistant. "Where else would I find more?"

The man shook his head. "There is nowhere else to look. You've been through everything."

Avery thrust the photo at him. "There is another piece somewhere!"

The assistant spread his hands helplessly. "I'm sorry. If you didn't find it in any of the boxes here, then it's nowhere to be found." The look of fury on Avery's face must have scared him, because he hurriedly added, "Unless…"

"Unless what!"

"U-unless it was borrowed. Professor Purcell borrowed a few unimportant artifacts. Er, well, Professor Dashell believed them unimportant. I didn't see what they were, I only heard of it."

"When was this?" Avery demanded.

"Oh… a year ago, perhaps? Maybe more? You see why I can't remember exactly what might have been discussed? I was only a student."

Avery nodded, reining in his anger. There was nothing more to be learned here, and the young man wasn't at fault for the troubles. He began to collect the bits of tapestry, stashing them in the smallest box he could find.

"I'm taking these, along with this photograph. Don't expect them back."

The assistant gave his mute assent, and within minutes Avery and Rachael were out the door, Avery clutching the precious artifacts to his chest.

"A year!" he exploded. "He had my cure a year ago, the bastard!"

Rachael placed a hand on his shoulder. "We have the photo. We will make do with that and report Purcell to the authorities." Her hand slid down to his chest, her other arm coming around his back in a fierce embrace. "We will get you your cure, darling, I promise. I swear I will not rest until you have found it."

Avery felt tears sting his eyes again. Despite the frustrations, despite Purcell's betrayal, he had more, now, than ever. His vague hope had blossomed into the promise of a normal life and a future with his beloved Rachael.

XXVI

A Heart of Silver

$\mathcal{R}$ACHAEL SAW AVERY SETTLED COMFORTABLY in their suite with his artifacts, then went out shopping. Unpleasantness was more palatable when her body was moving and her mind was distracted. She had never been a sit-and-do-nothing sort of woman. The shops were no more interesting than those in Ipswich, but she found a silversmith and bought herself a single table setting. It wasn't as nice as what she had in mind, but it would do until she could have a set custom-made.

Upon her return, she found her husband lounging on the sofa, sipping brandy and reading a novel. For a moment she feared he must have drunk himself silly again, but he stood when she entered and greeted her in a clear and sober voice.

"Darling." He kissed her cheek.

"You are reading one of my books?"

He shrugged. "I needed a distraction, so I thought to take your advice." He glanced back at the book he had left on the sofa. "It's not as bad as I had feared." The corners of his mouth twitched. "It's better than reading my own poetry. Why do you insist upon carrying that book everywhere you go?"

She gave him a broad smile. "I like to have a reminder of why I married you."

He nodded. "A wise decision, given the circumstances. I imagine you must experience frequent regrets, especially now you know I had a mad poisoner for a friend."

Rachael fixed him with an offended stare. "I had a mad poisoner for a *husband*. I understand. And I have no regrets about us. Never."

He regarded her in silence for a moment. "Neither do I," he said at last. He sighed. "I have spent much of the afternoon puzzling over things, and I have gotten nowhere. I can't conceive of any reason Purcell would poison anyone. I have known him for a dozen years, and have never seen any dislike of his fellow man. On the contrary, he has always been one to help. You've seen yourself the way he comes to the aid of any troubled ladies."

"He has never exhibited odd behaviors?"

"None that I saw. I thought him a man who wished to preserve life, not destroy it. Especially after what happened to the woman he loved."

Rachael's curiosity was piqued. Purcell once had a lady love? "Oh? Do tell. This sounds interesting." She picked up the silver she had purchased and carried it into the bedroom to the washbasin. "Please, continue. I'm listening."

"He was in love with a young woman and intended to ask for her hand. This was a few years after I first met him— nine, ten years ago now. Amelia Landry, her name was, and he was utterly devoted to her. Talked about her all the time. Unfortunately for him, things didn't work out. He was too upset about it to be entirely clear, but I gather that either she had already accepted another man's proposal, or her parents had arranged a marriage. He lost out to another man in any event. He was devastated, but determined to remain a friend to her. Some months later, to everyone's shock and horror, she took her own life."

Rachael started. The knife she was scrubbing slipped from her grasp and splashed into the washbasin. "Maybe he killed her!"

"No. He was in London, near fifty miles from her when it happened. She threw herself from the belltower of her local church. I have no idea why. I don't know if he knew of any possible reason. He grieved as expected under those circumstances. If he feigned it, he is greater than any actor I have ever seen."

Rachael set the knife aside to dry and moved on to the fork. She heard Avery wander into the bedroom, but she didn't glance back.

"After the young woman's death, Purcell became devoted to charities, especially those that helped poor or distressed women. He also took up the task of assisting any young lady who looked like she might need the slightest bit of help. I believed it to be his way of coping. He was trying to ensure, perhaps, that such a tragedy as Miss Landry's did not occur again."

"And somewhere in the intervening years he became mad," Rachael suggested. "Perhaps he learned of other women meeting sad ends and decided it was hopeless? If he spent any time working with charities, he would see there are many tragedies in the city every day. I have a friend who purchases far too many clothes and must then donate enormous quantities. She tries to give all her dresses to centers for reformed prostitutes, and she is always bringing back stories of the horrors of the streets."

"I have no idea what might have triggered it. I have seen no noticeable changes in him over the years. I've searched my brain for any clue, but can remember nothing that might have led... What *are* you doing over there?"

Rachael set her fork beside the knife and looked over her shoulder at him. "Washing my new silver to remove any traces of potions. Don't fear, I will have a new bowl brought in and the soap and water replaced."

Avery hugged her from behind. "Lord, Rachael, I love you so much."

The emotion in his voice staggered her. She had told Isobel Avery loved her, and believed it to be true, but his spoken words, in all their intensity and sincerity, cut straight to her heart. This was the passion she had hoped for. He was brimming with it. It alarmed her—she wasn't certain her indifferent nature could handle it—but it inflamed her desire.

She also wasn't entirely certain how she had coaxed it out of him. He thought her beautiful, of course, and enjoyed their physical intimacies, but his strongest reactions seemed to be to odd, entirely unromantic things, such as silverware.

Avery cradled her to his chest, his strong arms enfolding her. His head fell against hers, and he pressed a kiss into her hair. Rachael relaxed into his embrace, a sigh escaping her lips. His fingers went to the buttons that ran down the front of her bodice.

The first button came undone easily, but the second took several tries and a frustrated grunt. "Damnation," he muttered when the third slipped from his grip entirely.

"Shall I ring for a maid?" Rachael teased.

He pried the top of the dress open, peeling it away from her body to allow him to kiss the back of her neck. A shiver ran the length of her.

"No," he answered. "I prefer to practice. I hope to improve my technique."

His fingers swept across her breasts and down her belly, buttons popping one by one, a slow, steady caress that mimicked the path of his lips down her spine. He tossed the bodice aside and began the process again with her corset cover. His every movement was deliberate, every touch lingering. At the rate he was progressing, it would take half an hour to undress her.

Except he wasn't undressing her. He was making love to her. He had turned the entire process into an intimate sport, and he had already defeated her. Heat suffused her skin. Her nipples stiffened. Her loins stirred, growing warm and wet.

Avery struggled with the corset lacings, but it allowed his

mouth ample time to explore. He made a new love mark on her neck and sucked on her earlobe in a way that sent electrifying tingles down her back and out her arms. By the time the corset hit the floor, she felt like jelly in his arms.

Large, warm hands massaged her breasts. His tongue and lips continued their assault on the delicate skin of her neck and shoulders. Rachael hovered in some strange limbo, torn between wanting him to continue forever, and wanting him in bed, immediately.

Her overskirt slithered from her hips. He grasped her waist and lifted her away from it, setting her down nearer the bed, and turning her to face him.

She had seen desire in his eyes plenty of times, but now when she looked into those emerald depths she recognized something more. Devotion. She remembered the look well from her unmarried days. She'd learned to pick out the boys who wore that expression because they would do things for her. She sent them on errands, fetching food and drink, bringing her flowers, running to the shop to pick up a parcel. She pitted them against one another and laughed if they fought, and she never once turned down a gift, though she had more spending money than any of them. Lord, but she had been horrible. For the first time she felt a twinge of guilt for her behavior. She swore never to take advantage of Avery in such fashion.

The red and white striped petticoat that had peeked out tantalizingly from beneath the black skirt was the next thing to fall. Once again, Avery picked her up and set her away from it. She was leaving a trail of garments from the washstand to the bed.

Rachael could easily have shed the last of her layers in seconds, but Avery was having such fun, and was now planting teasing kisses at the corners of her mouth. She decided he could take as long as he pleased.

The single disappointment was that he remained fully dressed. Rachael reached for his tie, undoing the fashionable knot she had done up for him that morning. She had to work the buttons of his waistcoat by feel alone, unable to see while kissing him. She relished the excuse to run her hands up and down his torso.

Stripped down to nothing but her stockings and unmentionables, she was easy prey for Avery's busy hands. His fingers traversed her curves, roaming both over and under the thin fabric. He paused just long enough for her to pull off his waistcoat and shirt. The moment he was freed from the garments, his hand plunged between her legs. They were now no more than two steps from the bed. His fingers glided over her and into her.

Her own fingers fumbled with his trouser buttons, her hands brushing against the thrust of his erection. Even through the layers of clothing it sent a thrill of desire through her. He did crazy things to her insides. She managed to get the trousers open, and pried them down over his hips and backside.

Avery, she had learned, favored simple drawstring drawers, and not the full-body suits she had seen in the gentlemen's adverts that she probably wasn't supposed to be peeking at. She hooked a finger through one loop of the string and froze. She longed to touch him the way he touched her, but years of advice to the contrary left her paralyzed with indecision.

Before her first marriage, her aunt, the Countess of Rothbury, had sat her down and given her strict instructions on proper bedroom decorum. A lady, Rachael had been told, was never to be assertive in intimate situations. If her husband wanted a forward woman, he would hire a professional. Rachael had never cared when Fasching had done just that, or even when he had borrowed another man's wife. The lessons had served her well until now, but Avery was so different from any man she had known.

He continued to stroke her, and her legs began to tremble. The urge to have him clouded her thoughts. Only one piece of advice echoed in her mind. "Ladies take, whores give." She didn't want him seeking elsewhere for his pleasure. The very thought of him lying with any other woman sparked a raging fury inside of her. He belonged to her alone. Ladies take. She gave a yank and his drawers came undone. She stared at the evidence of his desire. Her fingers curled around him. She wanted him, and she was going to take him.

She felt wicked stroking him, but that only added to her excitement. He thrust against her hand, and she squeezed tighter and stroked faster.

"God, Rachael," he groaned. He pulled his hand from her drawers and stripped the garment from her body so quickly she thought he might rip it. She was left only in her stockings, and he stared at her, his eyes wide, his breathing ragged. Rachael had to amend her earlier assessment. Perhaps she could win this contest after all.

She lifted her left hand to his chest, pushing him toward the bed. He went easily, pulling her down on top of him, his pleasurable moans smothered beneath her kisses. He grasped her hips and shifted her until she was fully straddling him. Her hand dropped away from his shaft, and he entered her, at the same time sliding a hand back between her legs. She quivered and let out a moan of her own.

Their bodies danced as one. Pleasure raged through her. Sitting atop him, she could squirm and rock and position him just how she liked. Her nails dug into his shoulders. She swayed in time with his thrusting. They clutched one another, gasping and convulsing as they succumbed to the ecstasy.

When the spasms subsided, she sighed and snuggled into the crook of his arm. He kissed her brow and stroked her hair. They would call it a draw.

"I love you, Rachael," he said once more, his voice sleepy and filled with happiness.

She felt a tear prick her eye. She blinked it away and pretended it was no more than a stray eyelash.

XXVII

Relatively Helpful

"**A**ND NOW YOU SEE WHY I couldn't put all this into a letter."

Isobel paced across the study beside Rachael, the two cousins identical in stride and demeanor, though there was no resemblance between them but in the shape of the mouth and the color of their eyes.

"It would have taken five letters, or more, and it sounds as though you had no time for any writing at all," Isobel agreed. "Gracious, Rachael! More poisoning! I can hardly believe it." Her voice dropped lower. "And do you truly believe Professor Purcell to be behind such wickedness?"

Rachael nodded. "Avery is reporting our suspicions to the police today, both here in town and by telegram to Ipswich. He also intends to consult with some botanists about the mysterious ryeweed flower. Last night we compared the photo of the missing tapestry piece with other depictions of flowers we have seen, and chose the most likely matches. Anyhow, he will be busy all day, and I have nothing to do but wait upon his findings, so you must keep me occupied, dearest, else I will be sick with worry for him. It's hard to let him out of my sight, knowing his friend is a madman."

Isobel gave her a smile. "I will do my best." She paused. "You love him, don't you?"

The question startled Rachael, and she almost stumbled. "Don't be silly, Isobel. I don't love anyone. Except you, of course, and Aunt and Uncle, and perhaps the Ainsworths..." She trailed off before she might think of anyone else to add to the list. "I don't love any of you as greatly as you love me. I have a very hard heart, you know."

"Yes, very." Rachael couldn't tell from Isobel's tone whether she meant the words or not.

"I'm fond of my husband, and that will suffice. It will also make it much easier to bear should he ever fall out of love with me."

"Is that so? I recall you struggling with the mere thought that he might not fall in love in the first place. 'Devastated,' I believe is the word you used. Or am I misremembering your letter?"

"I was tired and upset when I wrote that," Rachael sniffed. "I assure you it didn't last."

"Of course."

Rachael was certain Isobel was secretly laughing at her, so she steered the topic to a more palatable one. "So. How have you been keeping busy these past few days? Have you received any invitations? You were out last night when we arrived."

"Yes!" Isobel's eyes lit up. "I was at the opera. Oh, Rachael, it was so lovely!"

Rachael grinned, thrilled to see her cousin sounding so happy. She wouldn't be rushing to leave London now, and Rachael's plot to get her a husband could move forward.

"Which opera was playing?"

Isobel's face scrunched up in a frown. "I don't remember. I was dazzled by everything, and you know I don't speak Italian. It was a sad story, but so beautiful. I wore the dress from your wedding and felt like a princess! The music and the costumes were everything I had hoped, and we had such a wonderful view. Mr. Bellamy was so kind, and arranged for us to sit in the box that Mr. Cantrell prefers. I'm sorry you and he could not be there to join us."

"Another time we shall. He is a great devotee of the arts, you know, being a poet himself. Now, what about invitations? It's time you mingled a bit more."

"There were one or two, I believe, but you know I don't enjoy parties, Rachael."

"That doesn't matter. You only need to attend enough to find a husband. I will wear boring dresses so I don't cause any distraction."

"Oh, but Rachael, I don't need parties to find a husband."

Her words carried a strange certainty. Rachael raised her eyebrows and regarded her cousin for several silent seconds. "You have someone in mind," she accused.

Isobel blushed. It was confession enough. Rachael tried to think who might have caught her attention. What eligible men had been at the wedding?

"Well. Perhaps we can arrange to go to a party where this gentleman of yours will be in attendance."

She shook her head. "No. He… Oh, you will never approve!" she blurted and ran from the room.

Rachael could only stare after her in shock. She couldn't imagine sweet, conservative Isobel setting her sights on any inappropriate man. She puzzled over it for a few minutes, then decided to put the matter aside for the day. She would find Isobel and they would go out for a walk in the park and some shopping.

Her plans were disrupted when her husband walked into the room.

"Rachael. I was told I might find you here." He glanced around. "Are you sure you are willing to let me take over this room? You seem to be here often."

Hope bubbled inside of her. He was enamored of her study. Perhaps she could remain in her home after all.

She hid her emotions and fixed him with a frown. "Why do you talk as if you intend to move into this house? You continue to spend time here, but shouldn't we begin moving my things to your residence with due haste?"

Avery's frown matched hers. "This house is nicer. I'd rather live here. Unless you object?"

"Certainly not! I love my home. I worked very hard to make it just as I liked."

"Then I will do my best not to disturb it. But as for this room?"

"It's yours. Do with it what you like." She beamed at him. She was almost willing to let him redecorate her bedroom, she was so happy. "Don't expect me to keep out, however, as I find it a very nice size for walking about and thinking, and it's the best place for confidential conversations."

He chuckled. "You may enter anytime you wish. If I have private business I will shut the door so you know to knock, but I find it unlikely I will ever encounter a matter that I wish to keep from you."

Rachael found herself only mildly surprised by his declaration. The man was so eccentric that if he did something entirely normal would it come as a shock to her.

"You have returned very quickly," she observed. "I thought you would be busy all day."

"I made my report to the police. I was wondering if you might like to join me for the visit to the botanist?"

"Yes, I would, but I had plans to go out with Isobel." She threw up her hands. "Though I'm not certain she wants to go anymore. There is some man she admires, and when I tried to question her about it, she ran off. She thinks I will disapprove of him."

To her surprise, Avery laughed. "If the man is who I suspect he is, I will vouch for him."

"What? Who?"

He shook his head. "It's only a guess. I will leave it to her to tell you."

"Hmph."

"I suggest you invite her to join us. We can consult the botanist, and then I will escort you shopping or wherever else you wish to go. If we need to see a second botanist, or if the meeting runs too long, you and your cousin can leave and I will finish up."

"I like that plan. I will see if I can track her down and promise not to bring up her husband search—for a time."

Finding her didn't take long. Isobel was in her room, and she apologized for her behavior with such vigor that Rachael interrupted rather rudely just to make her stop talking. She invited her cousin to join in on the errand, and the two women headed down the stairs to meet Avery and make their departure. Isobel was a curious sort of woman, and Rachael tried to answer all her questions about their findings up to that point.

"Here, Avery has the photos, if you'd like to take a look," she said. "The image from the missing piece of tapestry is blurred, but we think it matches some of the other flower depictions we have found. What do you say?"

Isobel peered at the photographs. "Oh, this is a corncockle!"

Rachael and Avery shared a surprised look. "A corncockle?" Rachael wondered. "What's that?"

"It's a weed," Isobel explained. "A very pretty one, with lovely pink-purple flowers, but a weed nonetheless. It's not uncommon in fields of wheat."

"Or rye?" Avery inquired.

"Yes. It's a nuisance because the seeds are poisonous and can cause stomach troubles if too many become mixed in with someone's grain."

Rachael again met her husband's gaze. "Poison. From a grain weed. It fits."

He nodded. His eyes were wide with excitement. "Miss

Stillwell, how sure are you that the flower in this image is a corncockle?"

"I know it is," she declared. "I love to pick wildflowers, and I have seen these many times. You can see clearly there the shape of the petals and those distinctive black streaks. The artist of this piece even shows the hairs on the stem. It is unmistakable."

Rachael gave her cousin a proud smile, then turned to her husband. "Well. I suppose we don't need to visit the botanist after all. Darling, we must make plans to find the flower now. I don't think we will come across any here in the city. How do we find a farmer who will let us prowl through his grain in search of weeds?"

"I am Baron Wilwood," Avery declared. "I have farms aplenty, and I suspect some are in sufficient disrepair to house weeds by the thousands. What would you say to a weekend at Wilwood House? No, a week. Make it a party. Who is your friend who knows potions?"

"Elle Ainsworth. You met her. She was my other bridesmaid."

"Invite her. Invite others, if you like. Miss Stillwell, you must come along, and your mother too. If your father can take time from his work, he is welcome to meet us there. We will send him a telegram. I'll have Bellamy start on the arrangements at once. Rachael, love, give me a list of anyone you wish to invite, but don't make it too great a list, as the house is not especially impressive."

His laughter rang with joy as he picked Rachael up off the floor and spun her around in a full circle. He kissed her before setting her back down. "Ah, darling, we have done it! We have found the flower! Soon I will have a cure and then I will be rid of these absurdities that plague our life. I can be a proper husband at last."

Rachael made an effort at a smile, but her lips were tight. His last words had struck a nerve. She didn't want a proper husband. She liked him the way he was.

"I'm glad for you," she said, though she feared even that was a lie. "Isobel, shall we go out? If we are to have a party, you must have some new clothes. We will visit Madame Leroy. She will have some ready-mades that can be altered quickly, and we will place an order for a custom ball gown. I'm determined to take you to an event or two before you return home."

Isobel sighed. "Very well. I will enjoy the new clothing, at least." Her brows twitched. "As long as you are paying, that is."

Rachael laughed and linked arms with her cousin. "It's the least I can do."

XXVIII

Wilwood House

"LIGHTER COLOR DRAPERY HERE." Rachael scribbled in her notebook. "And new wallpaper."

Avery nodded, willing to accept whatever changes she wished to make to his estate. The house was in unexpectedly good condition. He hadn't visited in over twenty years, back in the days when the barony still belonged to his father, but the minimal staff had done a masterful job keeping the residence from decaying. Now, with the contingent of servants from his London house, the place was bustling.

Rachael seemed pleased, though he found her copious notes a trifle alarming. She had expensive taste. The thought of spending so much made him wince, even with Aunt Eugenie's money set aside for that very purpose.

In the three days since his arrival, Avery had spoken with nearly all of his tenants. Each one greeted him with good cheer, welcomed him to the neighborhood, and congratulated him on his marriage. Now that he had a wife, it seemed they all believed he would take up residence here and restore the estate to its former glory. Avery had no intention of living permanently at Wilwood House, but seeing that Rachael admired it made him reconsider his plans to sell the property as soon as possible.

The grounds were a wreck. Neither Avery nor his father had ever employed a garden staff, and the lone groundskeeper had spent the decades drinking and fishing. The house looked to rise up from the midst of a tangled wilderness. Fallen gazebos and crumbled fountains dotted the landscape, their ruin a faint echo of past beauty. The path to the carriage house was pitted and overgrown, and even with Rachael's precise steering, they had been badly jostled driving in. Repairs were already underway.

The sound of an approaching steam car drew their attention to the open window, and they looked out in time to spy Henry Ainsworth racing a handsome steam car down the dilapidated road. He drove with reckless enthusiasm, dodging workers and bouncing over ruts, despite his small daughter and pregnant wife. Rachael rushed to the front door to greet them.

Avery trailed after her just in time to see Bellamy drive up with the Stillwell ladies. Moments later, Rachael's suffragist friend Mary Reynolds arrived on horseback, attired in rational dress clothing, carrying everything she needed for the week in a pair of saddlebags. Before Avery knew what was happening, the group had dragged him off on an expedition, tromping about the unkempt grounds like jungle explorers.

Parties, it so happened, were far more enjoyable in his own home. Avery ate his dinner that evening from safely clean plates, using the same silver as anyone else. Rachael was happy, the guests were content, and tomorrow he would hunt down his flower. When the meal had concluded, he headed for the drawing room with a smile on his face and a spring in his step.

He struck up a conversation with Rachael's uncle, Sir William Stillwell, a learned and cheerful man. The topic of Avery's work soon came up, and he reveled in the chance to discuss the matter with someone who showed true interest. Rachael's relatives hadn't much money, but they were good people, and he was happy to have them as family.

"My daughter and Mr. Bellamy appear to make a formidable team," Sir William observed, eyeing the nearby card players. "They have crushed Lady Stillwell and Miss Reynolds in three straight hands."

Avery's gaze settled on his secretary. He had been watching Isobel and Sebastian since their arrival, but had yet to spy any blushes or furtive looks to further his suspicions about them.

"They do seem well-suited as partners."

"Lady Stillwell tells me he is quite mad in love with Isobel," Sir William said softly. "He seems a good man."

"The best," Avery confirmed.

"I'm glad to hear it. I would like to see her as happy as I see my niece now."

Avery's eyes turned automatically to Rachael. He'd been trying not to stare at her, because watching her with Henry Ainsworth threatened to ruin his good mood. The two were alone together at a writing desk, sitting unnecessarily close, discussing potential renovations to the Wilwood gardens. She did look happy. Her cheeks were rosy, her eyes bright. Broad smiles dimpled her cheeks.

If only her happiness weren't because of *him*. Avery couldn't stop regarding Ainsworth with suspicion. Rachael was much attached to him, and there was a decided intimacy to their relationship, despite the man's infatuation with his own wife.

Rachael pointed at something Ainsworth had sketched in his notebook, leaning over the table as she did so.

"What's that?" she asked. The movement gave Ainsworth a perfect view of her cleavage, and he didn't even pretend not to look. Avery clenched his teeth and tried to resume his conversation with Sir William.

"The ruins of an old hothouse," Ainsworth answered. "We didn't walk that far, but I saw it in the distance. I intend to go back to investigate tomorrow. It looked like something out of a gothic novel."

"Perhaps it's haunted," Rachael enthused.

Henry whispered something Avery couldn't hear. Rachael giggled. Damn the man and his flirtations. Their conversation moved to the crumbled fountains and Rachael's thoughts on replacing them. Ainsworth flipped pages and sketched things for her. She continued to laugh at much of what he said, especially the things he kept too low for others to hear. Avery thought he caught a reference to naked goddesses.

It came as a great relief when Lady Stillwell decided to retire for the night and begged her husband to take her place among the card players. Freed from his conversation, Avery walked over to Elle Ainsworth. He hoped to coax her away from her book and cozy chair long enough to drag her scoundrel of a husband from Rachael's side.

She looked up when he approached. "Mr. Cantrell. This is a lovely house. Thank you for inviting us. I hope you are having a pleasant evening?"

"Not particularly. Your husband is flirting outrageously with my wife."

To his surprise, she only laughed. "It's harmless."

"Harmless? It looks anything but." It looked like Rachael was in love with the bastard.

"That's the nature of their relationship," Elle explained. "They flirt because they can. They both know it's safe."

"What do you mean by that?"

"If Henry flirted with anyone else, she might think he meant something by it. Rachael understands exactly where the boundaries are and will expect nothing more and nothing less. She is safe. It works the same in reverse."

"He doesn't look at her like a man who wants nothing more," Avery snarled.

Elle laughed again. "He is a young, vigorous man, Mr. Cantrell, and she is beautiful. Naturally, he has wicked thoughts in his head now and again. I assure you, he is not stupid enough to act upon them. There's no point in being jealous. It would be unfair of me to scold him for admiring a pretty woman when I just as often admire the handsome men I meet."

Avery grunted in a half-hearted agreement.

Mrs. Ainsworth set the book aside and rose from her seat. "If you'd like to stop him, you need only to take my arm and walk about with me talking in confidential tones. If it goes on for more than a few minutes, he will develop a burning need to know what we are about."

"I will make *him* jealous, then?"

"Doubtful. He will have been watching you. He knows why you are here talking with me. But he's dreadfully curious, and if I seem to find you an interesting companion, he will want to know why. Jealousy will only come if he concludes that I find you more interesting than I find him."

"Does that happen often?"

"That he comes to that conclusion? Occasionally. That I find someone more interesting? Never."

Avery decided to test out her theory and offered his arm for a stroll. "I understand from Rachael that you are an expert at potions."

"I am. And I understand from her that you have a life-threatening allergy to them."

Avery's teeth clenched at the word "allergy," but he nodded. "I prefer to term it a 'condition.'"

"I have never heard of any such thing before. I hope you don't mind, but I have all sorts of questions for you. This has plagued you since birth? Do you know anyone else like yourself? Do you have any understanding of the root cause? Is it fatal only if you ingest the potion?"

Avery reeled from the barrage of queries. She called her husband "dreadfully curious"? Apparently they were birds of the same feather.

"Everyone else I knew like me was a relation of mine, and they are all dead now. I'm still working to understand the cause as part of my search into the cure. And, no, it's not only ingestion. I can die from just a touch of any potion—any contact with the skin."

"That's incredible!" she declared. "Terrible for you, I imagine, but from a scientific perspective, it's most intriguing. It is hereditary?"

"Passed father to son. Daughters don't seem to inherit it, but the family tends toward male offspring."

"Interesting. You are a most fascinating man, Mr. Cantrell."

"As fascinating as your husband?" he joked. He liked this woman, odd as she was.

She grinned. "Not quite."

"I'm hoping to find a cure. Would you be willing to help?"

"I would love to. Let me know what I can do."

"I'm going out tomorrow to walk through cornfields, looking for a flower from an ancient recipe I have unearthed. As the stories tell it, the nectar was used to make potions."

She frowned in thought. "Serum extracted from the nectar, perhaps? I've never heard of such a thing, but I would love to experiment with it. May I join you on your expedition?"

"I was hoping you would."

The pair had wandered up behind Rachael and Ainsworth, and Avery peered over his wife's shoulder at the design for a new fountain. A near-naked goddess stood atop a rock, pouring out a jug of water which ran in elegant rivulets down to a glassy pool. The goddess looked nothing like Rachael, thankfully. Avery glanced at his companion, slim even during her pregnancy, with gently curving hips and plump, round breasts. The drawing differed from her enough not to be overtly scandalous, but only just. Avery swallowed a chuckle.

"Interesting design," he commented blandly.

Ainsworth turned in his seat. "Cantrell. I didn't realize you were there."

Elle and Rachael both snorted in disbelief.

"She doesn't quite look the Grecian style, Henry," his wife observed. She, too, looked as if she might laugh.

He shrugged, but there was a bit of pink, now, in his cheeks. "Rachael declined to model for the sketch." Rachael smacked him on the arm with her fan. "Never fear. The sculptor will be able to convince her to pose. These artists have a knack for that sort of thing."

Avery decided the man was intentionally baiting him, so he said, "I came to tell you, Ainsworth, that I intend to borrow your wife tomorrow."

"For some nefarious purpose, no doubt."

"A search for a flower with potential use in potions," Elle replied.

"I will be going along also," Rachael added. "And Isobel, too. I might ask Mary to join us, as she loves to run about in the out-of-doors in her bloomers."

"A ridiculous fashion," Ainsworth commented.

Avery nodded. "We are agreed on that."

"I don't see why women can't simply wear men's clothing if their skirts are inconvenient," Henry continued. "Any reasonable tailor could make adjustments in the fit, and it would look much better than those silly puffy things and the ugly frocks that are so often worn with them."

Avery's brow creased and he frowned. Perhaps they weren't in such agreement as he'd thought. "You can't be serious. You wouldn't want anyone to see your wife in such a costume, would you?"

"Why not? How else can she ride a bicycle?"

Avery glanced at Rachael. The thought of her atop one of those mad toys was not an appealing one. The way she loved to drive, however, made him suspect she would enjoy it. "I hear there are new styles in development that will increase safety. Perhaps then we can consider the matter of women's riding clothes."

"Henry will be most disappointed if bicycles become safer," Elle teased. "The potential for violent death is his favorite part of riding. I should like a safer design, however. Then I would feel better about riding with the children."

"I will buy you one as soon as they have a reliable model," her husband promised. "In the meantime, you will simply have to continue to scandalize proper gentlemen—such as our host—with your trouser-wearing ways."

"Do you think trousers would draw more or less attention than my more daring gowns?" Rachael wondered, her face twisting in the same thoughtful expression she used when pondering a new clue. Avery had a sudden curiosity about what she might look like in such an outfit.

Ainsworth leaned in and whispered something in Rachael's ear. Her eyes grew large, and she clapped her hand to her mouth. She shook her head. "I couldn't do that."

He grinned at her. "I think you would enjoy it."

Her eyes flicked briefly to Avery and she shook her head again. "I know better than to listen to your wild ideas."

Henry shrugged. "Suit yourself. The offer stands." He closed his notebook and rose, offering her a hand up. "Rachael, it's been a pleasure, as usual." He bowed over her hand, then turned to his wife. "Elle, love, are you ready to turn in for the night?"

She linked her arm with his. "I am. Goodnight to you both. We shall see you at breakfast."

Rachael kissed each of them on the cheek and bid them goodnight.

"Let me know if you change your mind," Ainsworth said, his eyes twinkling mischievously.

"Ha!" Rachael scoffed, but she laughed as her friends departed.

"What was that all about?" Avery asked. He hoped he didn't sound as resentful as he felt.

"Oh, nothing. Henry is a tease. He thinks he can incite a reaction from me. It is much like having a brother, I imagine."

"His flirtations weren't very brotherly."

"Except he means nothing by them but to make me laugh."

Avery sighed. "You don't really want a naked goddess dumping water for a fountain, do you?"

"I thought it nice. Very classical."

"I don't relish the idea of hiring a sculptor. Ainsworth is correct. Any artist will want you to model for him. You would make a perfect Aphrodite."

"Nonsense. What tradesman would be so brazen as to try to seduce his employer's wife? It could be the ruin of his career. He would either have some image in his head already or hire an actress to model."

"In that case I see no point in having such a statue. It would be entirely unrealistic to have a goddess who cannot compare to your beauty."

"Don't be silly, Avery. I am blessed in my looks, but I'm not so remarkable as all that. The world possesses other pretty women."

"Not in my eyes."

She kissed his cheek. "Perhaps you need new spectacles, darling."

He scowled, but was mercifully saved from making a foolish retort by Isobel's approach. The final card game had ended, and the players were ready to follow those who had already taken themselves off to bed. The two cousins stepped aside and walked about the room, speaking in whispers. Rachael's eyes were shining, her smile broad. Her laughter rang through the room. Avery wished he could make her laugh as easily as her friends did.

He stopped Bellamy at the door. "May I have a word?"

"Of course. What can I do for you?"

Avery kept his eyes on Rachael and Isobel. The women were far enough away that he wouldn't be heard if he kept his voice down.

"How can I woo my wife, Sebastian?" he pleaded. "I need her to love me."

Bellamy looked surprised. "She doesn't already? Why did she marry you?"

"She finds me attractive and she loves my damned poetry."

The secretary chuckled. "Then take her to bed and write her a sonnet. It's too bad you can't use my magic ink. Try perfumed stationery, instead. Send flowers with your love notes."

"Perfume and flowers?" Avery scoffed. "I will look a fool!"

"They are traditional gifts of courtship," Bellamy countered.

"She will have received hundreds of such gifts from lovesick boys who hoped to win her. I can't be lumped in with the fops she has rejected."

"Write her, Avery. Tell her how you feel. If she admires your words, then use them. The flowers are only to add a dash of romance."

"Fine. A poem. I can do that. I've been scribbling nonsense for days. I have half a sonnet written, but only one line is useable. I've thrown a dozen others into the fire. I will lie awake all night thinking on it. What else? How do I make her happy? She is so at ease tonight, so full of joy. How can I give her that?"

"Ask her friends. They will offer you better advice than I. I can claim no expertise, as I have been in love with exactly one woman in the whole of my life."

"Yes, how is that working out for you?"

Bellamy's cheeks reddened. "I believe she is fond of me. She has responded to my letters with pleasure."

"Glad to hear it. I wish you the best of luck."

"Thank you. I wish you the same. Truly, I think you are needlessly worried."

Avery disagreed. He muttered some words of thanks and bid his friend goodnight. Not bothering to wait for Rachael, he stomped up the stairs to his bedroom, grumbling to himself. He was going to be up half the night working on this stupid poem. He had one good line. Why couldn't he think up a damned rhyme?

XXIX

A Beauteous Flower

"YOU ARE CERTAIN YOU DON'T WISH to join us, Aunt?" Rachael asked as they descended the front steps, arm-in-arm. "We would be happy to have you."

The entire party had tromped out-of-doors, gathering on the drive in anticipation of Avery's excursion to find the corncockle. Rachael couldn't quite understand everyone's eagerness. Though it *was* a fine day, she supposed, with the sun shining and a pleasant, gentle breeze.

"Oh, no, no," Lady Stillwell insisted. "Your uncle and I are much determined to have a private drive in the country. We haven't had a romantic day to ourselves in some time, you know."

"In that case, I won't press you further."

Lady Stillwell smiled. "It will give you young ladies a chance to spend time on your own and chat about young people things. Also, Lord Wilwood has been so gracious as to allow us the use of his steam car, and I can't turn down that offer!"

She is my *car,* Rachael thought in irritation, though she knew in truth the vehicle belonged to Avery and she had no right to claim it. She had grown fond of the speedy carriage and had dubbed her "Annabelle."

"She is a fine car, if you treat her well," Rachael replied. "Don't let the water level drop too low, because her motor likes power, and tell Uncle to go easy on the throttle. She accelerates faster than you might expect."

"You sound as though you have become quite the expert, Niece!"

"I'm trying to set the fashion for lady drivers."

"I don't doubt you will succeed. Isobel has spoken of learning to drive more than once."

"I will teach her. I would like to pass on my knowledge, and I don't particularly wish to teach my husband, as I would prefer not to share the driving with him."

Her aunt chuckled. "Most men, I think, would be hesitant to let their wife take on that role, but Lord Wilwood seems a unique sort of man."

"He is. I'm finding it suits me."

Rachael walked her aunt to the carriage house and chatted a few moments with her uncle regarding the car before rejoining the remainder of the party. Unlike Rachael, whose blue and cream striped dress was best fitted for afternoon visits and taking tea, the other women had chosen plain, simple garments for their trek. Rachael didn't own anything that could be considered either plain or simple. She hoped Avery intended to bring something to sit on, because she had no desire to spoil her outfit.

Her husband was in a sour mood that morning. It wasn't unusual for him to be groggy upon waking, but most days he perked up with a bit of food and drink. Today he had glowered all throughout breakfast and she had yet to see him smile. There were dark circles under his eyes, suggesting he hadn't slept well. Rachael hoped he wasn't feeling ill. He hadn't come to her bedchamber last night. It was the first time they had slept apart since their fight at Miss Pelham's house, which now seemed an age ago. She'd lain awake for hours worrying, but she hadn't dared to invade his privacy.

"Bellamy, I'm relying on you to see that Mr. Ainsworth is suitably entertained while the ladies and I are away on our outing," Avery instructed his secretary. "Perhaps you might go out fishing. The pond is the one portion of the grounds not neglected."

"I find fishing insufferably boring," Henry replied casually. Avery glared at him. Rachael couldn't understand his hostility. He had no cause to be jealous. Henry was utterly devoted to Elle.

"No matter," Henry continued, "Hannah and I will find some way to keep occupied." He tossed his daughter into the air. The little girl squealed in delight and begged him to do it again. She would grow up wild, no doubt.

Rachael wanted to protest that Henry and Bellamy should both join the party of flower hunters, but she couldn't defy her husband in public. Had they been alone, she would have argued with him. She was confident now he would hear her out, even if he disagreed, but they hadn't had a moment alone since their guests had arrived. Why hadn't he come to her last night? She kicked at a stone in irritation, and it skittered across the drive. If anyone noticed the unladylike behavior, they didn't comment. She would never improve herself in such indulgent company.

Avery and the ladies set out on the long walk past the tangled grounds to the nearest farm. Rachael had imagined this journey would be like a walk in a grassy park, but discovered instead that it was as filthy as walking the city streets. Every step kicked up dust from the road. Fortunately, she had her skirts tied up to keep them from dragging. She suspected they would become terribly soiled even so. She would need to give specific instructions to Avery's people on how to properly clean the garments. Or perhaps she would simply wait until they returned home and let her own servants handle it.

Rachael's long stride made her a good walker, so she soon relaxed and began to enjoy the outing, regardless of the dust.

She chatted with her friends and watched her husband, whose ill humor faded as they drew nearer to the cornfields.

"I spoke with several farmers the other day," Avery said, the first words he had uttered since their departure. "They are happy to have us pick as many weeds as we please."

He turned from the road to walk between two green and leafy rows. Rachael lifted her skirts higher and followed. She had no idea what plants were growing around her. She saw no recognizable fruits or vegetables. As a lifelong city dweller, her entire knowledge of country life consisted of drives from city to city and her visits to Isobel. Even her "country home" in New York had been no more than a large house with a bit of land just outside the city, and she had never spent much time there. She tried to remember if she had ever been on a farm before, but couldn't recall a single instance when she had done anything but pass by on a road.

Now that she had a true country estate, she thought she might try to learn something more about it. She couldn't picture herself or Avery living at Wilwood for any length of time, but she liked the idea of holding long country parties with her friends. The house was only a two hour drive from London when the roads were in good condition. Coming out for a weekend here and there would be easy, and pleasant if she brought company. She was astonished Avery hadn't visited for two full decades. His entire life had been devoted to his research. She wondered what he might do now that a cure was imminent.

Isobel, who often wandered the farms near her house when the village grew boring, took the lead, chatting with Mary about crops and horses and other outdoor sorts of things that Rachael had zero interest in. Rachael fell into step beside Elle.

"I've never been on a proper farm," her friend marvelled. "I've ridden through the country and walked about in forests and fields, even visited serum sources. I can identify herbs with my eyes closed. These ordinary food crops are a mystery, though. What do you suppose all this is?" She gestured at the planted rows about them.

"I have no idea," Rachael answered honestly, pleased to find her usually knowledgeable friend as ignorant as she was. "Perhaps they need special farm visitation days for city girls such as us to acquaint ourselves with the origins of our foodstuffs."

Elle's eyes lit up. "I love that idea! I shall take my children on such trips when they're old enough to understand."

"One more thing to add to their training regimen? You will have the most well-rounded children in the history of forever."

"I doubt that."

"I imagine my own child will be haughty, ill-informed, and naive, but she will be beautiful and wealthy, so she will never lack for suitors."

"She may well carry herself with an air of superiority," Avery stated flatly, startling Rachael, who hadn't realized he was listening, "but she will never be ignorant."

"Oh!" Rachael blurted, fearing she may have offended him. "You will see that she has a first-rate education, naturally."

"That's not what I meant."

"Perhaps she will take after you and be scholarly."

"Nor that."

"Then I can't imagine what you might mean. Anyhow, it was no more than a joke. You know I am often sarcastic. I will try to be less so."

Except her words hadn't been sarcastic. She fully expected to have a child extremely like herself. Such thoughts were probably terribly conceited. She felt a sudden pity for the future governess of this conceited, sarcastic, theoretical child. Herself, she was certain to be an indifferent, neglectful parent.

Rachael hated to dwell on her own shortcomings, so she picked up the pace and forged ahead into the field of a taller crop that might be the cornfield they were looking for.

"Oh, look, I think we've arrived," she declared, cutting

off whatever Avery was about to say and leaving him and Elle behind.

"Rachael…" she heard him call, but she ignored it. He would say something about her sarcasm not bothering him, because he was a sweet man and readily forgave all her mistakes. It was understandable. He was newly in love.

None of the wheat was so tall as to be over her head, but it was high enough in places to obstruct her view, and Rachael felt as if she were wandering through someone's elaborate hedge maze.

Mary and Isobel had wandered away in one direction, so Rachael turned the opposite way, thinking to cover as much ground as possible. If they were going to search for this flower, they might as well be systematic about it. And the faster they found it, the sooner they could leave this field where the plants kept snagging on her skirts.

She bent to untangle herself and froze. There, not two feet away, was her mystery flower, the purple petals standing out in stark contrast to the green-gold stalks of the grain. She squatted for a better look.

"Avery!" she cried. "Avery, darling, I have found it!" She plucked the blossom and raced back the way she had come, nearly crashing into her husband as he rounded the end of the row. She thrust the flower at him. "Look! Isobel was correct. It's just like in the images."

He staggered backward a step, then reached out a careful hand and took the flower from her. He examined it for a moment, keeping it at arm's length, then passed it on to Elle.

"I agree," he said. "It looks correct. I think I will let you ladies do the picking. If the nectar is what we expect, I don't want to risk getting any on myself."

Another cry from further off told them Isobel and Mary had had similar success. The trio rushed off to join them. Avery had brought along a spade in the picnic basket, and the group dug up at least a dozen specimens for study. Rachael picked her own bunch of flowers, tying them up with one of her hair ribbons into a pretty little bouquet.

With their bounty harvested, the group left the cornfields for a grassy meadow. Avery hadn't brought a blanket. The other ladies plopped themselves down without a second thought, but Rachael wandered about, looking for a place that wasn't too terribly dirty and pretending she was only enjoying the view.

Isobel, who knew well Rachael's dislike of sitting on the ground, made a casual-seeming comment that she hoped the grass wouldn't stain anyone's clothing.

A stricken expression crossed Avery's face. He shrugged out of his jacket and spread it on the ground for Rachael to sit on.

"I'm sorry, love. I'm not practiced at planning for picnics. I promise I will do better next time."

Rachael nearly retorted that she would prefer never to have a "next time," but caught herself and babbled some insincere assurance that she was perfectly fine. This was Avery's special outing to find his cure, and she was determined to behave herself for his sake.

He had transformed entirely from the sullen, silent man who had left the house. Now he smiled and chatted amiably— primarily with Elle—about the flowers and their potential. Every part of the flower, it seemed, was destined to be studied. The nectar was discussed at length—its color, its thickness, its scent. Rachael sniffed at her own bouquet, and caught a whiff of spice, but nothing that struck her as extraordinary. There was talk of dissecting the other parts of the plant and steeping them as one would tea. Elle even talked about the smell of the dirt near where the plants grew. She had filled several bottles with various samples and stashed them in her bag.

Rachael listened with interest at first, but as the conversation moved into the more technical aspects of potion making, she grew bored. She ate her lunch in dainty bites and tried instead to join Isobel and Mary's conversation about horses.

"Annabelle would give you as smooth a ride as any horse," she said, attempting to make some contribution.

Mary frowned at her. "What sort of creature is Annabelle?"

"She's not a creature. She's my steam car."

Mary and Isobel shared a puzzled look. "You named your car?"

"Why wouldn't I? Ships are always named. It stands to reason that cars should be as well."

"It seems rather funny, Rachael," Isobel said, "to name a machine. Horses have their own personalities. Each one is unique and you can come to know their likes and dislikes, just like a person."

"Exactly," Mary added. "This is why it takes an experienced rider to handle an unfamiliar horse. The two of you must get to know one another at a moment's notice."

"Well, each car is unique, too," Rachael argued. "They all have quirks, and you must handle each one differently to take full advantage of its abilities. Annabelle is vastly different from the cars we have borrowed at other times."

Her friends looked unconvinced, and she let the matter drop with a sigh.

Rachael's mood grew steadily worse. Lumps of sticks or rocks jabbed into her rear, even through the layers of fabric. Avery's jacket wasn't large enough for sitting on, causing her to repeatedly set her hands down in the dirty, itchy grass. She ate so slowly that the meat pie, which had come so carefully wrapped, grew completely cold.

Worst of all, she fretted that the cure, which now seemed inevitable, might transform her husband into an ordinary man and he would cease to be the Avery she had married. His peculiarities were what drew her to him. Would she stop caring for him? Would he lose his love for her and turn his affections on an ordinary woman?

Conversing when in a bad mood was impossible. All she

could do was sit and listen and feel wretched. She didn't even have the appetite to finish her food.

A large, wet droplet splatted on her arm. Startled, she looked up. The sky in front of her was blue and the sun shone brightly. She hoped a bird hadn't done its business on her dress. A second drop splashed in her lap, then a third.

"Goodness, it's raining!" Isobel exclaimed.

Rachael whirled around. A large, dark cloud loomed behind the picnickers. Distant thunder rumbled. More fat raindrops fell and the sunshine began to fade.

Her companions sprang to their feet, tossing everything back into the basket and gathering their collection of corncockles. Avery gave Rachael a hand up and picked up his jacket, brushing the grass away before donning it.

"I'm sorry to cut our picnic short. We should return at once before we get too wet."

The words were no sooner out of his mouth than the sky opened up. Rachael stood rooted to the spot, stunned by the suddenness of the storm. The rain came down in a torrent, ruining her hat, plastering her hair to her neck, and soaking through the layers of her clothing down to her drawers.

Her frustrations boiled over.

"Oh, I detest picnics!" She stomped her foot like a spoiled child, threw her bouquet of ryeweed to the ground, and stormed off in the direction of the house, not caring whether anyone was following.

XXX

A Little Help From My Friends

$\mathcal{S}$ERVANTS RUSHED TO HELP the soggy party that stood dripping all over the hall floor. Towels and blankets were fetched with due haste, and hot drinks ordered to be sent up to bedrooms. Rachael was nowhere to be seen. Avery assumed she had stomped up to her bedroom without waiting for assistance. He would leave her be. He didn't need to compound his latest mistake by bothering her while she recovered. She was embarrassed, he suspected, by her outburst. She worked so hard to conduct herself in a refined manner, no matter the circumstances. Too hard, he thought. It made things all the worse when she snapped. He didn't know how to convince her she needn't pretend for him.

Bellamy ran into the hall, looking flustered. "Mr. Cantrell, sir, I'm so sorry. One moment we were in the library discussing books, and the next he had just disappeared! I hope he didn't bother you too terribly."

Avery blinked at him in confusion. "Pardon?"

"Who did what, then?" Henry Ainsworth inquired, wandering in, his little girl once again in his arms. Avery had never seen a man do so much child-minding. Both father and daughter were dressed in clean, dry clothes, but their wet hair suggested that they, too, had been caught in the rain. Ainsworth walked straight to his wife's side. "Are you well? That was a horrendous storm."

"Didn't you go out to join the picnickers?" Bellamy insisted.

"Certainly not. It was much more satisfying to follow from a distance and watch them surreptitiously. Having a noisy toddler along was an enjoyable challenge."

"Henry, do be nice," Elle chided.

"I see no purpose in lying about it. If Cantrell doesn't like me when I'm honest, he will never like me at all. Come upstairs and change. You are shivering."

"That man is insufferable," Avery growled the moment the Ainsworths were out of the room.

"I rather like him."

Avery and Bellamy turned together to gape at Isobel.

"He has been a great friend to Rachael these last years, when she had few others she could turn to. He is strange, yes, and stubborn and sarcastic, but then, so is Rachael, and I love her very well as she is."

Avery continued to stare at her for several moments. "So do I," he replied at last. He offered his arm. "Miss Stillwell, please allow me to escort you to your room. I don't wish to leave you standing here, cold and wet."

Her gaze lingered on Bellamy for a moment, then she looked up at Avery and nodded. "Thank you."

"You know Rachael better than anyone, don't you?" he asked once they were alone.

"I expect so."

"There are things about her I still don't understand. If she hates picnics, why didn't she tell me? I would have made different arrangements."

Isobel looked thoughtful. "Did you ask her?"

"No. It didn't occur to me. I simply told her I intended to go on the outing to find the flower and we would make a picnic of it."

"Is that how you phrased it?"

"Something similar. I can't recall. Why didn't she say something?"

"You are her husband. If you told her you both would be going on a picnic, she would obey you, regardless of her thoughts on the matter."

"It wasn't an order! I wouldn't do that to her."

Isobel sighed and stopped walking, putting her hands on her hips in a posture much like her cousin. "Mr. Cantrell, you are accustomed to being in charge, and you have a manner of requesting things that causes people to jump to make them so. You stated your plan as a fact, and Rachael took it as such. You didn't ask for her feelings, so she didn't offer them. She would say it's not her place to question you."

He scowled. He had heard Rachael make remarks to that effect too many times. "What did that bastard of a husband do to her?" he demanded. "She must have put it in her letters."

Isobel shook her head. "It came well before him. It was my uncle—her father. He had very strict rules of behavior for her, and she took many of them to heart. She wanted dearly to please him. You must understand, Mr. Cantrell, she was a very lonely girl, and hungry for affection."

"She need never starve for love again," he vowed. "She owns my heart."

"She knows that. That's why she tries to please you."

"It doesn't please me when she goes along with my ideas knowing it will make her unhappy. I would never want that! I'm always willing to compromise."

"You should tell her so. If it's any consolation, I believe she knows you value her opinion. She may have questioned your picnic idea, were it not tied to your search for that flower. She knows how important a cure is to you."

Avery nodded. "I will do my best to explain that she is allowed—no, encouraged!—to question any statement I make, no matter how imperative I may sound."

"Good," Isobel agreed. "Keep in mind, however, that even if she wants to assert herself, she may still *feel* obligated to do as you say. Old habits die hard, and you are her husband."

He sighed. "It may have been easier had I never married her. No doubt she would happily tell me off were she only my mistress or my friend." A sudden realization hit him, one that seemed so obvious he felt an idiot for not understanding before. "Well, damn. That's why she loves him."

"Mr. Ainsworth, you mean?" Isobel was nothing if not astute. He could see why Bellamy admired her.

"Yes. She owes him nothing, feels no obligation toward him save that of friendship. He could order her about all day, or ask anything of her, and she would simply laugh and do as she pleased. He is 'safe,' indeed." He bowed to Isobel. "Thank you for the talk, Miss Stillwell. I shall see you at dinner. If you will excuse me, I need to shed these wet clothes and get to work finishing a sonnet and thinking up ways to befriend my wife."

· · · ∞ · · ·

Rachael intended to stay in her room through dinner, claiming illness brought on by the soaking. She didn't want to face Avery after her tantrum. It was bad enough to behave a spoiled brat in front of her friends, who knew what she was. Her husband, though… Rachael longed to be a good wife, to make him proud. Thus far in her marriage all she seemed able to do was to embarrass him by making a spectacle of herself.

She hated being shut up all alone, so she imagined it would be a fitting punishment to confine herself to her room until the next morning. As the day wore on, however, her boredom increased and her misery began to wane. By dinner time, she was hungry and done feeling sorry for herself.

She donned her favorite evening dress. Imported from Paris, it layered complimentary shades of red satin and silk damask with antique lace skirt panels. She loved every bit of it, from the asymmetrical design to the bodice with lacing up the back and the v-shaped neckline. She had already worn it on more than one occasion, and would continue to do so because she looked smashing in it. It was unnecessarily lavish for a dinner party at home, but Rachael didn't care.

Her friends greeted her with smiles in the dining room. No one mentioned the picnic or remarked on her absence during the remainder of the day. Avery did ask if she was feeling better, to which she replied in the affirmative.

Elle was late to dinner. She wandered in after everyone was seated and plunked a small cup of something down in front of her husband.

"Drink that."

Henry tossed the potion back in a single gulp, without bothering to ask what it was.

"Revolting." He grimaced and poured himself some tea. "Poison, I assume? You are finally done with me?"

"A mild intoxicant. Let me know the moment you begin to feel tipsy. Then we will make note of how potent it seems and how long it lasts."

Much progress had been made during the afternoon, Rachael discovered. The ryeweed nectar did, in fact, work as serum for potions, though the potency appeared to vary wildly from flower to flower. Avery had made copious notes while Elle investigated, and he started in on a lengthy and technical explanation of everything they had done.

Rachael glanced at her friend. "Could you summarize for those of us who grow easily bored?"

Elle smiled. "The corncockle looks to have the ability to suck up even trace amounts of serum from the soil. Rather than lingering in roots and stems, the serum gathers in the nectar. I suspect the more serum in the soil the stronger the nectar. I have flowers sitting overnight to test that theory."

"Thank you."

"What I find relevant is that the nectar-serum matches the poison that killed your excavation worker," Henry commented. He ran his finger along the blade of his steak knife, as if contemplating stabbing something with it. "This needs sharpening."

"Don't play with knives while you are intoxicated," Rachael scolded.

He spun the knife in his fingers, tossed it in the air, caught it by the handle and sent it flying across the room, where it skewered an unattractive painting of a pudgy baby angel.

"Why not?"

Elle jotted, *good motor skills, impaired judgement,* in her notebook.

"Is he correct?" Rachael asked Elle. "Is the nectar a match for the poison?"

"Absolutely. I knew it the moment I sniffed the corncockle. Henry, could you please pass along that tray of olives?"

He muttered an oath and shoved the plate across the table with a look of revulsion.

"Well. That is more evidence pointing toward Purcell's guilt, though I suspect the police will be baffled by it."

The arrival of the main course distracted the party from further work-related talk, but the moment dinner ended, the brainy group retired to the drawing room, eager to resume the talk of potions and botany and the science behind Avery's curse.

Rachael preferred to discuss the murder investigation, but only Henry shared that particular desire. He was now unmistakably tipsy. His every other word was an obscenity. Rachael talked at him anyway, because it was better than talking to herself.

"It seems Purcell discovered the tapestry with the story of the curse and the scene depicting the making of the potion something near to a year ago. The poison used the ryeweed/corncockle nectar, which proves he has identified the flower and made potions with it. He must either have some skill himself or have a potion-maker working with him."

"Damned simple to make a mediocre potion," Henry said. "I've done it."

Rachael nodded. "In that case, I will begin with the assumption he is working alone. He is a learned man and very methodical."

"'Sall it takes."

"He's slurring words," Rachael called to Elle. She checked the time and jotted a note. Rachael turned back to Henry. "Now. I have a suspicion the worker at the dig site was an accidental death. That poison bottle was buried in haste. It doesn't fit with Purcell's usual manner. If he had planned the murder, he would have planned for proper disposal of the weapon. I think he must have been experimenting. Here's how I see it happening: He has a potion he wishes to test. He rouses himself early in the morning and waits for a hapless victim to come by. A digger stumbles out of bed to relieve himself, and Purcell convinces the sleep-addled dullard—none of them seemed the brightest of men, mind you—to drink from the vial. Instead of doing what Purcell expected, the potion works as a poison, and the man drops dead. Purcell panics. He decides he must hide the evidence, grabs the closest tool, and buries the bottle. He races back to his tent and pretends to be asleep, with no one the wiser."

"Bloody good story. You should write it up for the newspapers."

"His experiment has failed, but he has gotten away with murder. He is emboldened. He moves to a new phase of experimentation: poisoning large groups. I don't think he means to murder them. He isn't killing to kill. He is conducting research. A multiple murder would bring swarms of investigators. A poisoning where people recover quickly is soon shunted aside for more important matters. He tests one concoction at Lady Ellerby's party, tainting the Apple Charlotte. He poisons something else at the hotel in Ipswich—drink, perhaps? There could be other incidents we didn't hear of. Bad food is not all that uncommon, and perhaps not all of his experimental potions are poisonous."

"Might not be potions 't all."

"Pardon?"

"Sounds 's if he's testing dith…" He coughed. "Distribution methods. Elle, how long'll this last? I've a devil of a headache."

"Not long. Let me know if it wears off gradually or abruptly."

"Distribution," Rachael echoed, considering the idea. "That makes sense. How many people can be poisoned at once? Does it work better in food or in drink? How easy is it to sneak a poison into a dish without being caught? Does it make more sense to spread the poison on the dishes? Yes, one could test all those things with these mass poisonings, and no deaths, save the sensitive old man, because the purpose is to learn. He is preparing for something."

"Preparing for what, do you think?" Avery asked, crossing the room to join the conversation.

Henry nodded at him. "Cantrell. You deign to speak to me?"

Avery ignored him. "Preparing for what?" he repeated.

"A mass poisoning of some sort, clearly," Rachael replied. "He will weigh the number of affected people against the ease of dispersing the poison quickly and without being caught. I'm still baffled by the why of it. He has some goal in mind. He isn't killing at random, or he would have done so already. Is there a specific group of people he wishes to target, and he is preparing to kill them all? And why experiment with the ryeweed, when any potion or poison would do? Why steal the tapestry and keep it from you?"

"He killed Dashell to hamper our progress, so that tapestry must be important to him. My cure must be important."

Rachael gasped. "No! Not the cure. The *curse*. He's going to replicate it! The tapestry shows how to make the curse. And he's not killing because he doesn't want people dead. He wants to make them like you!"

Avery's face went ashen. "Good Lord. I hope you are mistaken, but I fear you are not."

"Rachael, you're brilliant!" Henry exclaimed. "God, do I love your mind. It's the most dazzling part of you, even in your fancy dresses. Who the devil are you dressing up for, anyhow? You know you'll never get in my bed, no matter what you wear. Course, you'd never want to." He leaned closer and spoke in a drunken half-whisper, plenty loud enough for most of the room to hear. "And I don't think your Lord Wilwood needs extra enticing. He'd tup you wearin' any damn thing at all. No complaints, though. You're always a picture of loveliness. Near as nice to look at as my Elle." Henry cast an adoring look in his wife's direction. "Bloody hell, I hope this potion she fed me wears off soon. I can't keep my damned mouth shut."

Avery clapped him on the back, the first friendly gesture Rachael had seen between the two men. "I rather like you this way, Ainsworth. I think I need to sit down and have a drink while I ponder this latest theory. Would you care to join me?"

Henry smiled, but shook his head. "I don't drink. Addles the brain, y'know."

Avery's brows quirked. "Right. Excuse me." He wandered off in search of brandy.

Henry chuckled softly to himself. "I wonder what he would say if he knew I was stone-cold sober before he ever walked over here. It happened the headache was the end of it."

Rachael frowned at him. "Why pretend it wasn't?"

"To make him believe I was honest." He kissed her cheek. "Goodnight, Rachael. I think I'm ready to turn in. I need to give my wife a full rundown on her potion experiment and get her to give me something to take away the headache."

She let him go and joined Avery, who had seated himself on a sofa, a decanter at his side and a snifter in his hand. He didn't hesitate to pour her a glass of brandy, though it wasn't a ladylike evening drink. They sat together in silence, sipping and savoring. The brandy was strong, but smooth. Avery was a knowledgeable consumer.

"I hope you are mistaken," he repeated.

"As do I."

"I believe, however, we must move forward as if you are not. We will relay these latest suspicions to the police. I can send an express first thing in the morning."

"Good. The more we can tell them, the more apt they are to act upon it. If they do their jobs, Purcell will be in custody by the time we return home, and we will have nothing more to worry over."

"I would hope they have already questioned him. I want him behind bars. Then we can see that poor Hunstable is released. I won't press that issue yet. I hate that the boy is suffering, but he is safe enough in prison. I'm concerned he might know something about Purcell's habits that could put him in danger."

Rachael shivered. "How did we come to be mixed up in all this?"

Avery leaned back in his chair and sighed, shaking his head morosely. "I'm cursed."

XXXI

Playing Dress-Up

*R*ACHAEL FOUND A BUNDLE OF CLOTHING sitting atop her dressing table when she arrived at her bedroom. She picked up the accompanying note.

Try it. He will like it. No need to return anything.
-H

"What's that then?" Jenny wondered.

Rachael shoved the clothes beneath the table, kicking them into the far back corner so the maid couldn't get a good look at them. "Oh, nothing. Old rubbish from a friend." She folded the note and dropped it into her jewelry box, because she didn't have a fire at hand where she could burn it. "Come, help me out of this dress."

Rachael unpinned and brushed her hair while Jenny undid her laces. The maid helped her out of the dress and hung it carefully. Rachael thanked her—something she had only begun doing since hiring her own staff—and shooed her from the room. Jenny bobbed a little curtsy and bid her goodnight.

Rachael slipped out of her underthings, tossing them in a pile to be laundered. She had lifted her nightgown to pull it over her head when her curiosity got the better of her. It couldn't hurt to have a bit of fun in the privacy of her own bedroom. She dropped the gown and retrieved the clothing Henry had left her.

The clothes were nothing fancy—a pair of plain black trousers and a white button-down shirt. Her eyes darted all around the room, a nervous check to make sure no one could see her. She chided herself for her ridiculousness and stepped into the trousers. They were too big around the waist, but sat nicely on her hips. The shirt came next. It was a good thing Henry had broad shoulders, because it only just buttoned across her chest. Had he been any smaller, she would have had to sneak one of Avery's shirts instead.

She didn't button the shirt all the way down, opting to tie the tails into a neat knot behind her back. It left her navel exposed, making her feel thrillingly like a courtesan or other wicked woman. The buttons above her bosom remained likewise unfastened, leaving a deep v-neck.

For several minutes she stood by the mirror, twisting, turning, examining herself from all sides. She liked what she saw. The outfit displayed her body nicely, while still covering most of it. Less of her breasts were showing than in most of her dresses, yet she looked equally as scandalous.

Rachael imagined the reaction if she went out dressed this way. The sleeves would have to be slimmed down, because Henry was unfashionably well-muscled. A few other nips and tucks here and there would perfect the fit. She would have the trousers shortened, as well, to display her red ankle boots, then further accessorize with red kid gloves and her felt riding hat. Her mother had left her a cameo pendant that was the perfect size and length for the neckline, and she could match her earrings to her cufflinks. She would be spectacular. She couldn't wait to show off.

The door to Avery's room creaked, and she stifled a cry of surprise. She dove behind her privacy screen, her fingers yanking at the buttons of her shirt. She couldn't let him see her this way. She couldn't behave so shamefully in front of him, no matter what Henry advised.

"Rachael?"

"I'm still undressing," she called, hoping her voice didn't sound panicky. She threw the shirt to the floor and grabbed at the trouser buttons. It was a good thing that undressing Avery had given her familiarity with the fastenings on men's clothing. The bed squeaked. He had sat down to wait for her.

She let out a sigh of relief and composed herself. The trousers dropped to the floor, and she stepped out and kicked them into the corner with the shirt. She would stash them somewhere later.

She stepped out from behind the screen fully naked and smiled at her husband. "Should I put on my nightgown?"

"No. Come sit with me."

She skipped across the room to him. His arms wrapped around her waist, and he pulled her onto his lap.

"Why bother with a nightgown, when I shall have to remove it momentarily?"

"You are a very practical man," she laughed.

"I try," he murmured, his mouth on her neck. One hand moved up to massage her breast. His other slowly traced a line up her spine. It tickled, making her shiver. "I think tonight we will use your bed, if that is acceptable."

"Whatever you desire." She opened his dressing gown and allowed her hands to wander over him. Clearly some of the novelty of *his bed* had worn off, because at the moment what they were doing was far more interesting than where they were doing it.

"Why *do* you prefer my bed?" he asked against her mouth.

"Huh? Oh." She pulled back. "I like the intimacy of being allowed into your personal space."

His lovely lips twisted into a frown. "You may enter my room at any time. There is nothing I need hide from my wife.

I hope I haven't offended you by invading your chambers uninvited?"

"No, of course not! I wouldn't dream of keeping you from my room."

"Nor would I turn you away. We are married. This house is not mine, but ours."

He drew her closer, and they tumbled together onto the bed.

"There is one other reason," she mumbled, trying to finish the thought before his kisses drove her to distraction once more.

"Um?"

"I like to sleep beside you."

"Yes." His mouth was too preoccupied for any further response. She didn't know if he was only acknowledging her, or if he meant that he, too, enjoyed sharing a bed.

"Will you sleep here with me tonight?"

"Mmm."

The sound was positive enough that she allowed her mind and body to relax. Neither of them uttered another word until they were finished and Avery cradled her against his chest, whispering that he loved her.

XXXII

Word From Town

$\mathcal{R}$ACHAEL GLANCED UP FROM her morning tea. Her husband hovered over the breakfast table, a paper clutched in his hand.

"Did you need something, darling?" she asked.

"I hoped to update you on the results of our experimentations, if you can spare a moment?"

"Of course."

He nodded and took the seat beside her. "Thank you. Let me begin with our basic finding. The nectar from the flowers works when used as serum, however it isn't as reliable as we might have hoped. The effects of the potion Mr. Ainsworth drank last night, for instance, should have gradually increased and decreased, with the entire process lasting something on the order of one hour. As you know, that wasn't his experience. It also shouldn't have left him with a headache."

Rachael shrugged. "I consider that a mild consequence for drinking a strange potion without even asking what it might be."

"He appears to have absolute trust in his wife."

"Hmph. I should hope you wouldn't trust me so foolishly. I don't think I am near so reliable. What else have you found?"

"Mrs. Ainsworth sprinkled a growth potion on some seeds

in the conservatory and left them overnight to sprout. Only about fifty percent of the plants responded, and of those, several grew the expected amount, while others grew twice that. We also had Bellamy do some writing with color-changing ink. You can see the results for yourself."

He passed Rachael the paper, and she looked it over. Bellamy had written out an entire page of quotations, most of which were about love. The color of the words changed across the page, purple to blue to green and so on, in the order of a rainbow. When Rachael tilted the paper, the colors would shift. In a few locations, however, the colors remained stagnant, no matter how vigorously one fluttered the sheet. A spot in the center of the page, about three lines long, was a flat, ordinary black.

"Yes, I see. So, potions can be made with your flower, but they are unreliable. What does this mean for your cure?"

His brow furrowed. "I don't know. Mrs. Ainsworth has promised to continue her investigations. I thought we might drive to that farm and collect as many samples as we can before our return to town."

Rachael nodded. "I should think the largest problem with your cure is that there is no way to test it short of asking you to drink it. That sounds terribly dangerous. Even the slightest error in the potion—" She seized his wrist with a grip so tight that her nails dug into his skin. "Avery, promise me you won't try anything unless you are absolutely certain it won't harm you!"

He covered her hand with his own. "I have put a great deal of work into keeping myself alive all these years. I won't throw it away foolishly. You have my word."

His assurance relaxed her somewhat, and she released him. He lifted a hand to greet Isobel as she entered the room.

"Good morning, Miss Stillwell. Please join us. You will like to see this."

She pulled up a chair beside Rachael and accepted the paper, giving Avery a friendly smile.

"Did he write out all those quotations from memory, do you think?" Rachael wondered.

"I suspect so," her husband replied.

"Oh, yes," Isobel agreed absently, her eyes glued to the page, "Sebastian is a very learned man." Her head snapped up, her cheeks flushing as she realized what she had said. "Er… I meant Mr. Bellamy, of course."

"Isobel!" Rachael chided herself for not having seen it sooner. She had never considered the young secretary as a marriageable prospect. He was an employee, after all. From Isobel's perspective, however, he was a kind, intelligent man, and not terribly far beneath her.

"I know. I'm sorry. He's not at all what you hope for me, but he is a good man, and I think he truly loves me, Rachael."

Rachael took her cousin's hand. "You misunderstand me. I'm surprised, not disappointed. If you love him, you should marry him."

Isobel's furtive glance gave lie to her casual tone. "Perhaps. We haven't known one another so very long." She tried to pass the page of quotations back to Avery, but he wouldn't take it.

"Keep it, Miss Stillwell. He meant it for you."

Isobel folded the sheet with care, and tucked it into her bodice when she thought no one was looking. Rachael fought back a snicker. Her cousin was smitten. That was one goal achieved. Isobel would be married before year's end.

Rachael finished up her breakfast and walked with her cousin and husband to the drawing room, where the remainder of the party had gathered to discuss potential indoor activities. She glanced at the window. Rain sheeted down the panes, and a steady patter beat upon the roof. She twitched. If she had to play Charades…

Before she could even voice an opinion, a servant entered with a stack of mail and two newspapers.

"Beg pardon, your lordship," he said to Avery. "The post came just now, and you had requested your letters?"

"Yes, thank you. I've been awaiting word from town."

He took the papers over to a table and leafed through them. "Several of these ought to have been forwarded days ago. This is why I cannot do without Bellamy. No one else is competent." He ripped open one of the letters, scanned it, and swore.

Rachael hurried to his side. "What's wrong?"

"After Miss Pelham's disappearance, I wrote her father, asking if she had returned home. He has responded that she has not."

"That blackguard had better not have murdered her!"

"Murder?" her Aunt Stillwell gasped. "Gracious, Rachael! I should hope you haven't had news of any such horrible thing! What on earth has been going on with you of late?"

"As far as we know, the woman is simply missing," Avery assured her, though his tone was so gruff and his expression so tight it was difficult to feel any consolation.

"It's just like a man to prey on an innocent and unsuspecting female," Miss Reynolds snarled. "It's time we women stood out against such things—learned to defend ourselves! I have taken up the rapier, personally, and I am a fair shot with a revolver."

Rachael found the idea of handling weaponry distasteful, but in the event of an emergency she knew how to gouge eyes and jab knees or elbows into sensitive parts.

"Perhaps we should entertain ourselves with some basic self-protection maneuvers," Mary continued. "I would be happy to show you ladies a thing or two. This room is large enough if we move that sofa."

"I don't think that will be necessary," Avery said stiffly. "I assure you, no one will come to harm in my home."

"But consider, sir, you can't be with even your wife at all times."

Avery scowled. "You may conduct your defense lessons elsewhere. They do not belong in a drawing room. I doubt all the ladies here have interest in such things, and you can't expect Mrs. Ainsworth to participate in her condition."

Elle and Henry shared a look, then burst out laughing.

"Please, return to whatever amusement you had planned," Avery begged. "I will join you as soon as I have looked over the remainder of these letters."

Rachael hovered at her husband's side. Her aunt and uncle tried to suggest some calm activities, but Mary continued on and began demonstrating stances and jabs she considered useful. Henry tried to give her pointers, which caused a terrible row when she interpreted his suggestions as condescension. He gave up and wandered off to play with his daughter. The moment he picked the girl up, she threw her doll across the room and shrieked, "Dammit!" at the top of her tiny lungs.

Avery closed his eyes and rubbed his temple. "No more parties. I'm living in a madhouse."

"Perhaps I ought to have warned you how very eccentric my friends are."

"I don't disapprove of your friends, but perhaps I need them in smaller doses. Or perhaps at a time that isn't so stressful. Help me decipher this letter. I can't make sense of what the boy is trying to say."

He scooted over to the edge of the chair to allow Rachael to perch beside him. He pushed a letter at her that had been sent him by his student, Mr. Beech. She read the first few sentences and then gave him a puzzled look.

"It says only that Purcell hasn't been arrested and has gone missing. That's upsetting, but not difficult to understand."

"Continue on."

She read further. Mr. Beech referred to an enclosed note from the police, which Avery provided.

> *Mr. Purcell was not at home at his flat. Galby reports that neither is he in Ipswich. We have left a summons and will speak with him as soon as practical.*

Rachael scowled. They didn't believe her theory about

Purcell and meant only to appease. She tossed the note aside and returned to the letter.

David Beech had a rambling style of writing that used a great many words to express a thought and often repeated the same point multiple times. He made it abundantly clear he didn't understand the situation with, "ancient curses and potions, or was it curses and ancient potions?" He also went on at length about his worry and bafflement that Professor Purcell seemed to be a murder suspect.

At last she reached the portion of the letter that must have confused Avery, because she found it rather difficult to follow, herself. The boy carried on about "mysterious happenings" with people dying of poisons.

Rachael began to read aloud.

> *At first I thought it a misprint, but later I heard of the death of Mr. Farnsworth (see enclosed newspaper), who was one of those who did <u>not</u> fall ill at Lady Ellerby's party. The notice of his death was most distressing, as it seemed he ingested only his usual tonic. I did not see the word 'poison' anywhere. Another woman, of whom I had never heard, died when she drank a stamina potion at a party to allow her to dance all night without tiring, and it was suspected the potion supplier was at fault. Again, I refer you to the newspaper. The next day (see second newspaper), several more strange deaths were reported, and I am now certain the initial report of the shocking deaths of Miss Hardwick and her father was written up accurately and was not intended to say 'poison' as I had at first believed. I have heard talk that there is a reporter investigating. I will write more when I have heard his conclusions.*

"Goodness. Is there another letter?"

"Not in this pile. If he has more to tell, it hasn't yet reached us."

"Well." Rachael stared down at the letter, letting her eyes rescan the words. "It is chaotic and verbose, but it sounds to me as if people have been dying after drinking potions."

"That's what I was afraid of."

"This Miss Hardwick must have died of a potion, and he thought it meant poison, and he didn't realize until he read about the others. We can read the death notices in the newspapers to confirm."

"Purcell has done it, then. The curse has been replicated. My God." He put his head in his hands. "Who knows how many are infected? Hundreds, thousands could die before anyone understands what's happening."

"We must tell the police at once. They can find the connection between these cases and protect others who might have been victims."

"If they believe us. They are skeptical already. Now we bring up magic flowers and ancient curses? We will sound mad."

"It's better than doing nothing!"

Avery sighed. "I agree."

"And if we can't trust the police to help, then we will need to hunt down Purcell ourselves and stop him before he can curse anyone else."

Her husband's eyes grew wide with fright. "No, Rachael. That's far too dangerous. I will not allow it."

Her eyes locked with his. Innocent people were dying. She knew who the murderer was. She couldn't let him continue to kill. She bit her lip, then took a deep breath. "In that case, I will have to disobey you. I'm sorry." She sprang from the chair and raced out of the room.

XXXIII

The Gift of Verse

"I'M AFRAID THERE IS NOTHING to be done but to prepare to return to the city first thing tomorrow," Avery concluded.

His guests nodded, sympathetic expressions all around. His skin still crawled at having such a large group privy to his secrets. After the many discussions here at Wilwood, however, he'd had no choice but to tell all. It wouldn't do to have anyone speculating or asking questions.

They were odd people—perhaps excepting Sir William and Lady Stillwell—but good people. It had made the talk bearable. Even so, he wished Rachael would have done it instead. She remained stubbornly in her room. He'd sent a message to her to say he wasn't upset, but she clearly didn't believe him.

He would give her the sonnet that afternoon, though he wasn't yet entirely happy with it. Several of the lines he thought very good, but others he considered only adequate. It would have to suffice. He'd spent too much time on it as it was.

He reviewed the poem in his head as the others consoled him over his predicament. He was assured several times of potion-free environments when he came to visit or dine. Elle

Ainsworth reiterated her resolve to keep working toward a cure. Mary Reynolds offered the services of an investigator she knew from her feminist club. Avery took down her address. Mrs. Smith was probably more reliable than the police.

His mind, however, remained fixated on his poetry. Damn, he didn't like the word "against." He would have to alter that line, at least, before he could give it to Rachael.

"...Out of the country."

Avery blinked. "Pardon?"

"I will be working abroad these next few weeks," Ainsworth restated. "Otherwise I would offer my services tracking down your miscreant."

"Oh, uh, thank you." A frown crossed his face. "I don't mean to pry, but what *do* you do to earn a living?"

"Civilian consultant to Her Majesty's armed forces."

"Vague."

"Reconnaissance and retrieval specialist. I draw maps and fetch things." He spoke casually, but his voice was pitched low enough that only Avery could hear. Bloody hell. The man was a spy and a thief. Rachael had probably known this for years.

"Well." The single, huffed syllable sounded like his wife, he thought wryly. "Try not to get yourself killed."

Henry grinned. "Always a priority. My family likes me to return home unscathed, for some reason. But enough about me. We should send someone for Rachael. This party needs some diversion. And more tea."

"I have a sonnet to give her."

"Splendid! You ought to do a reading."

"Miss Stillwell," Avery called out before Ainsworth could make his suggestion loud enough for others to hear. "Won't you suggest an activity before our evening meal?"

The rain had died down, and the party quickly voted for a walk in the gardens to take a bit of fresh air and exercise. Lady Stillwell coaxed Rachael from her room to join in, but to

Avery's dismay, she again assumed the persona of calm, polite, "perfect" wife.

He walked two steps behind her, watching as she picked her way through the weeds and vines, careful not to snag her dress. He slipped a hand into his pocket, toying with the folded paper. Would the sonnet do as he hoped? Would she at last believe in the depth of his affections? He had to try.

In one area with particularly tricky footing, he seized the opportunity to take her arm and help her along. He slowed the pace, and she didn't complain, though he could tell from the look on her face she was annoyed.

When enough of a gap had opened up to speak privately, he took the finished sonnet from his pocket, unfolded the paper, and handed it to her.

"I wrote this for you. I have been fretting over it for some time, but I believe it is as good as it will ever get."

She scanned the page for only a moment. "Would you read it? I should like to hear it in your own voice."

He paused, letting the rest of the party pull further ahead. "Very well." He cleared his throat and recited, not needing to look at the paper.

For Rachael
The fall of your dark tresses, smooth and sleek,
The creamy smooth perfection of your skin,
The rosy blush of color in your cheek,
Your shapely curves, so soft, so feminine.
With but a look my heart is set afire,
Undone before your elegance and grace.
Your golden eyes, they smolder with desire,
And sparkle with a joy that lights your face.
A smile parts your lips, full, red, and fine.
I tremble when they do but speak my name.
That fateful day you pressed them up to mine,
It sparked a love too vehement to tame.

I'm lost to you, my darling. This I swear:
No gem was e'er so precious or so rare.

"Thank you, darling. That was very sweet." She folded the paper and tucked it away. She wore a smile, but it was hardly the passionate response he had hoped for.

"I don't know a better way to express my feelings," he persisted. "I love you. Ardently." He snatched up her hand. "I would do anything for you, Rachael. You need never doubt me."

Her golden eyes gazed sadly up at him. "Oh, Avery," she sighed. "I should never have married you. I knew you had such a passionate soul. I can never match that, and now I will break your poor heart." She brushed away a tear. "I'm so sorry." She picked up her skirts and ran ahead to catch up with the others.

"No. Darling…"

She was wrong. Her emotions ran deep. Over and over he'd seen the way she suppressed them, forced them into submission, until they smashed through her polished shell. He had only to find the key to releasing them. He wouldn't give up until she was free from the anxieties and strictures that prevented her embracing her true nature. She had brought him out of hiding. He swore to return the favor.

He hurried up to her and took her arm again, to escort her as a good husband would.

"That is a lovely hat you have chosen today," he complimented her. "Did you buy it to match the purple driving goggles?"

"Yes." A bit of a smile returned. "You are very observant."

"You are my favorite subject of observation."

She looked wistful, and he wondered what she yearned for. She turned to kiss his cheek and the look disappeared.

"You are a dear man. The very last line of your poem is my favorite. Your words are beautiful."

"They can't do you justice."

She shook her head. "I will do my best to be a good wife to you."

"Be yourself. I want nothing more."

She looked skeptical, but she kissed him again. His resolve intensified. New poetry began to form in his mind. He would woo her until she believed every word he said.

XXXIV

On and Off Road

$\mathcal{R}$ACHAEL STUFFED HER MEN'S CLOTHES down to the bottom of her small travel satchel. Again, she caught herself glancing furtively around. No one was here to see her. No one was here to criticize her. Why was she being so silly? Besides, she was back in her own home. If there was any place she ought to be able to do whatever she wanted, it was here.

She hefted the bag, nodding her approval. It wasn't heavy, and had room for things to be added if necessary. This bag would go where she went. Her trunks could stay at whatever hotel became their temporary residence. They couldn't visit the same Ipswich establishment. They were too familiar there, and Purcell might expect them there. Rachael had no idea whether he knew they had uncovered his crimes, but she planned to operate as if he did.

Satisfied she was prepared for the journey, she knocked on the door connecting her bedroom with Avery's. No reply came. After a few silent seconds, she turned the knob. He had told her she could enter at any time, but she stepped tentatively through the doorway.

"Avery?"

The room was deserted. It had been redecorated during

their absence. The old furniture was gone, replaced with what she could only assume were the furnishings from Avery's house. His possessions gave the room a masculine feel. He liked dark wood with clean lines. Rachael approved of the sturdy, new bed.

The draperies, too, had been swapped out, and now red curtains flanked the window, tied back with braided gold ropes, devoid of any tassels. Shaving supplies and other men's grooming items sat atop the washstand. She touched a few with a hesitant finger. She could smell his shaving soap. It had that spicy tang she would now forever associate with him.

Every passing moment emboldened her. She poked through his books and the papers at his small writing desk. She recognized the letters he had received while at Wilwood, sitting beneath the journal he liked to write in. Her fingers brushed the small book. It was wrong to pry. Everything she had ever been taught told her to leave it be. Still, it called to her. This was his poetry at its rawest. It was a window into his soul. If she were ever to truly understand him, the book would give her the clues she needed.

She flipped it open, turning the pages gingerly, as if the tiniest rustle of paper might announce her transgression to the world. Bits and scraps of poems covered the pages, overflowing into the margins, with words added and crossed out at an alarming rate. His writing was messy—near illegible in some places. The thoughts came too quickly, and his hand struggled to keep pace with his mind. That didn't surprise her. He was so full of ideas, of emotions, of the opinions he kept in check for civility's sake.

Disregarding her own uncivil behavior, Rachael picked up the journal for a better look. Several pages in, two short poems had been written out in a neater hand, finished works pulled from the preceding scribbles. One page further, the chaotic scrawls began again.

The pattern continued. Rachael wanted to hug the book to

her chest, it was so beautiful. This was her husband's essence in written form. His boundless passion streamed onto the paper, where he would scratch and struggle and force the words into meter and structure, giving them at last the organization he so prized.

She didn't care that there was a very silly poem about her eyes, or that there was a long-winded one about rain entitled "A Damned Nuisance." He could have written about dung, and she would have loved it. It was the process that entranced her. In his love of words, she could see his love of life, of beauty, and of her. The sonnet he had given her held a new significance, and she regretted that she hadn't been more grateful for it. Her thanks were rarely more than perfunctory. She was a superior, selfish sort of person.

She closed the book and clutched it to her chest. Tears welled in her eyes. Why, oh, why had she lured this romantic, good-hearted man into such a plight? What would happen to him when she grew old and her beauty faded? There would be nothing left but her sarcasm, her supercilious attitude, and her rampant curiosity.

The door to the hall opened. She jumped, startled, but there was no time before her husband walked in. The moment he saw her, he rushed to her. She tried to turn away, but his long stride prevented any escape.

"Rachael, darling, whatever is the matter?"

He had seen her tears. It was no use hiding. She buried her head against his shoulder and let him hold her.

"Oh, Avery. I'm so very sorry."

"For what? Reading my journal?"

So he had seen that, too. She still held it, now pinned between their two hearts.

"I admit, it's rather embarrassing that you have seen some of the mistakes and drivel contained therein, but it's hardly worth crying over. Please, if anything has upset you, tell me so I might rectify the situation. I assure you, every woman mentioned in those pages is you."

A snorting laugh broke through her sobs. "Obviously!"

He tipped her chin up and kissed her. "That is my incomparable wife. You don't doubt my love?"

"Not at all." She doubted only herself. She couldn't live up to his belief in her.

He dabbed at her cheek with his handkerchief. "Then why the tears?"

"I was overwrought for a moment," she replied, composing herself. "Stress, I'm certain. All this poisoning and murder was bound to cause some worry. I am well now."

He quirked an eyebrow. "You don't become overwrought."

"I told you, it was only momentary."

"I see. Perhaps you would prefer to remain here? In case it happens again? I can interview Hunstable and hunt down Purcell on my own."

"No!" The very idea was horrifying. She wouldn't let Avery go anywhere near that madman alone. "We will go together, or we won't go at all!"

They had already discussed why it wasn't an acceptable option to sit idly by. Avery had grumbled about it the entire drive to London, but had reluctantly agreed. Rachael wouldn't be swayed.

It gave her an amazing sense of freedom, this open defiance of her husband. She could assert herself with no repercussions other than sour looks and growls of disagreement. The knowledge obliterated her old worries. It no longer mattered what her father had said, or how her manners coach had told her to behave. She had no wish to cross her husband, but it wasn't out of fear of punishment, fear of being considered a bad wife, or any other outside factor. Her only concern was for Avery's feelings. She hated to upset him because he was a wonderful, loving man who deserved nothing but respect and kindness.

He gave a curt nod. "Are you ready to be off, then?"

"Yes. I have a small bag in my room. We can leave as soon as I fetch it."

"Fine. May I have my journal, or did you wish to continue reading it?"

She handed it over, her face flushing. "I'm so sorry. My curiosity got the better of me."

"It was bound to happen sooner or later." He gathered the other papers from the desk and his favorite stylographic pen, then followed her into her room to retrieve her satchel. "Here, let me carry that for you." He took the bag despite his other burdens, and they started down the stairs.

"Why do you never become angry with me for my misdeeds?" she wondered, voicing the question that had been nagging at her since they married. The last of her inhibitions had vanished. She thought perhaps she might say anything at all to him. Their future could prove interesting. A smile touched her lips as she thought again of the men's clothes she had packed. She could wear them. It might shock him, but he wouldn't stop her.

"What misdeeds?"

"Screaming at you in front of Miss Pelham and her parents. Throwing a tantrum when it rained on your picnic. Reading your private journal just now. I'm sure I could think up other instances."

"When you scream, I worry. I don't like to see you upset. As for the journal, I told you it was embarrassing, but nothing more."

"It seems you are a strange man who never becomes angry."

"Untrue. When you refuse to speak to me, I become angry. And when you put on that oh-so-polite false persona, I want to scream and smash things like some crazed barbarian."

Rachael blinked. She would never have guessed it might affect him that way. To her the contrived perfection had always provided a shield against criticism and arguments.

"I…" She was at a loss for words. "I suppose every time we disagree I could shout at you instead?" she ventured.

"Thank you. I would prefer that."

Peculiar man. It fit with what she had seen in his journal. He would rather have a passionate row than see her sit stewing in silence, unexpressed emotions roiling inside her. It was a reflection of his own struggles, she surmised. To maintain his gentlemanly demeanor, he needed a constant outlet, whether work, poetry, bedsport, or perhaps the occasional argument.

She continued to mull over his oddities as she donned her outdoor clothing and prepared the carriage for the drive. Her butler had seen to having Annabelle washed and refueled, and she looked in tip-top shape. Rachael expected a journey of approximately four hours. Dinner would be late, but not excessively so.

The weather was fine, and she enjoyed the drive more than any they had shared before. They talked of boring things that married couples ought to talk about: chiefly the arrangements for consolidating their households and restoring Wilwood. Avery had plans laid out for personnel changes, including adding several of his own servants to Rachael's staff and relocating many others to the country on a permanent basis. Few people would be let go. She approved.

She eased off on the throttle to slow Annabelle's speed. Another steam car had been bouncing down the road behind them for some time now, and she had grown tired of it. It was one of those older models—wide and heavy, with a large boiler. It rattled and belched smoke like a train, a veritable monster next to her quiet, efficient machine with its discrete puffs of steam.

Much to Rachael's dismay, the noisy car slowed when she did, rather than passing her. She muttered an unladylike curse, then scolded herself for her increasing use of bad language.

"What's the trouble?" Avery wondered.

"That car behind us. It's noisy and foul, and I hoped to let it go by. I know it's large, but the road is wide here. It should have no difficulty overtaking us." She steered closer to the edge of the road and waved a hand to tell the other driver to pass her.

Avery twisted to watch over his shoulder. "He seems unwilling to comply. Perhaps he doesn't trust his skills as a driver?"

"In that event, he ought to drive much slower," she snapped.

"Or perhaps he is stunned by the beautiful lady driver and wishes to trail after you making puppy-dog eyes." He turned his gaze on her and did his best imitation of a love-sick simpleton.

She narrowed her eyes at him, though he might not be able to tell through the goggles. "I'm not in the mood to appreciate your humor just now."

She slowed the car further, prepared to stop if necessary, and waved at the offensive vehicle again. She punctuated the gesture by squeezing the bulb of the warning horn attached to the dash for such purposes. She had never had need of it before. It let out a horrid squawking sound.

Avery jumped. "Good Lord! Did you run over a flock of geese?"

"You had the awful thing installed," she complained, the ringing in her ears diverting her attention from the man behind her. "Didn't you try it out beforehand? Now we shall have to—"

Annabelle jolted. The smoky, old car had pulled close enough to bump her. Rachael whirled half around in her seat, furious at the damage to her carriage and the danger to her person.

"You bloody bastard!"

She could see the expression on the man's face now. He gave her a smirk as he backed off. She wished she knew an appropriately rude gesture to use as a reply. His engine roared, and the monstrosity lurched forward.

Rachael let out a screech of fright and shoved at the throttle. It was too late. Metal crunched. Her seat slammed into her back, flinging her forward into the steering wheel. Beside her, Avery toppled from his seat, nearly sliding from the vehicle altogether. He yelped in pain and cursed using a word she didn't know the meaning of. Rachael screamed his name and cried for him to hold on as she struggled to maintain control of the car.

Annabelle did her passengers proud. She was dented, but her working parts were undamaged, and she responded well to Rachael's maneuvers. With the throttle fully opened, they rocketed forward, narrowly missing another attempted ramming. Rachael aimed the car straight down the road, counting on her speed and lighter frame to pull away from the behemoth behind. The road sloped upward, adding to that advantage.

Rachael's confidence grew with every yard her car gained on the other. She could outrun him until they reached the safety of a town. The moment they crested the rise, however, all her hopes were dashed. At the bottom of the hill lay another car of the same type, turned sideways to block the road, barring her path. Two men sat inside it, one of them holding a rifle. Terror knifed through her.

"Avery, hold on!" she shouted again, wrenching the wheel so violently that Annabelle's tires squealed in protest. The carriage careened off the road, obliterating the shrubbery bordering on a field of grasses and wildflowers.

Some people outfitted their steam cars for off-road driving, but Annabelle had no such adaptations. She bounced and lurched over the rough terrain. Bits of sticks and rock flew from beneath her tires, ringing off her body and biting into the flesh of her passengers. Rachael clung to the steering wheel, her clenched fingers the only measure preventing her flying from the car. Avery gripped the leather seat, his knuckles white, his feet wide apart for additional bracing. She was terrified for him, but she dared not slow down.

A shot rang out. Rachael let out the most ear-piercing scream she had ever made in her life.

She had grown up around military men. She knew a trained soldier could reload and fire again in seconds. She swerved to make herself a more difficult target. The second shot hit her car even so. The enemies were gaining, their larger tires crashing through the underbrush with ease.

"Trees!" Avery shouted, wasting his breath because Rachael had already spied the wooded area ahead. She kept her head as low as possible and aimed straight at it.

Somehow they reached the treeline still alive, though two more bullets had struck the carriage. Rachael steered them into the forest at top speed, ducking under branches and whizzing past trunks with mere inches to spare. Chunks of decaying matter splattered them, some dry and brittle, others wet and goopy. Birds screeched and small mammals darted away from the crushing wheels.

Behind them, the belches and rattles of the other cars began to diminish. Among the trees, the smaller, more maneuverable vehicle had the advantage. A scream and a crash told Rachael that at least one pursuer had been thwarted. She risked a glance behind. She could hear the other car, but not see it. She veered sharply to the left, hoping Annabelle's quieter ride would let them change course undetected.

She had no such luck. The attackers, anticipating such a move, were undeterred. The trees in front of her began to thin out, and soon they were bouncing once more across an open field. Her eyes swept the landscape, but she saw no place to shelter.

Annabelle began to protest. Hiccups punctuated the hum of her engine, and the puffs of smoke faded to wheezes. She wasn't meant to be driven this way. The water and the fuel would run out sooner than intended, though she was an efficient car.

A vastly more efficient car than her hulking pursuer.

Rachael changed tactics, taking the clearest, easiest path, avoiding ditches, hills, and other obstacles as much as possible. The gunfire had stopped, likely for lack of bullets, but that did little to lessen her fear. The men were sure to have other weapons and wouldn't hesitate to use them. Anyone could kill Avery with even the simplest of potions.

Annabelle sputtered. Rachael eased off the throttle to conserve what little fuel she had left, aiming the car downhill. Behind her, she could hear the choking sounds of a stalling engine.

"Tell me when he stops completely," she shouted at her husband.

He looked back. Not a minute later, he said, "It's done. The car is dead."

Relief flooded Rachael, and she slowed to a comfortable speed. "I think I can get one more mile out of her."

With the throttle eased back, the sputtering died down, though Rachael continued to keep the car pointed downhill wherever possible. At length they came across a stream, and she turned to drive alongside it, hoping it would take them to a road, a town, or at least a farmhouse. Before they saw any signs of civilization, however, Annabelle decided she'd had enough and puffed her last.

XXXV

The Great Outdoors

AVERY SPRANG FROM THE CAR and raced around to help his wife from her seat. Rachael sat with her goggles perched atop her head, staring down at one of the dials on the dashboard, running her fingers over it. She wore a sad smile.

"Nearly two miles," she said proudly. "She is such a good car."

"You are a good driver," he answered, taking her hand as she stepped down. "A remarkable driver. Rachael, that was the most incredible feat of skill I have ever witnessed in my entire life. You are amazing. Astonishing! Brave, clever, determined!" He stopped himself before he could continue on through the entire alphabet. "You are my hero."

"Oh, Avery." She brushed away a tear. "Forget about me. You are hurt!"

"What?" He paused to take stock of himself. His knee was throbbing where he had smashed it against the dash, he suspected other bruises from the flying debris, and he could feel a trickle of blood dribbling down his forehead. He reached up to touch the spot and winced. "It's nothing."

"Ha!" She dug a handkerchief out of her purse and dunked

it in the stream. Her gentle fingers washed his face, then she folded the cloth and pressed it to his wound. "You may need to hold it a while."

She allowed him to take the handkerchief, but instead of doing as she asked, he rinsed the cloth in the stream and used it to tend to her. Little-by-little, he brushed the dirt from her smooth skin, wiping her brow, her nose, the red welt on her cheek where something had struck her. He cleaned her chin and her neck, and then, letting the handkerchief flutter from his grasp, he ran his thumb in a tender caress over her luscious red lips.

"Rachael," he sighed. "My Rachael."

He kissed her then, bypassing his usual gentle beginnings. This was intense, deep, desperate, fraught with the fear of the chase and the relief of the escape. He needed to taste her, to hold her, to know they were real and they were together.

Rachael was the first to pull away. He gazed at her, his head all awhirl, while she bent to retrieve her handkerchief. She pressed it to his brow once again.

"Hold it there until the bleeding stops," she commanded.

She was giving him orders now, and expecting them to be obeyed. Bloody brilliant woman. The more she lost her inhibitions, the more he loved her.

"I have an ointment that has no potion in it. Let me see if there is some in my trunk."

She walked back to the car and began to unfasten the straps that secured her trunk to the side of the vehicle. He was reaching to help brace it in case it toppled off, when she let out a cry of dismay.

"No! Oh, no!" She scrambled to undo the remaining straps.

"What's wrong?" He grabbed one end of the trunk and helped her bring it to the ground. Only when the box hit the dirt did he spy the problem. One corner had been shot clean through with a rifle bullet.

Rachael pried the trunk open and began to paw through

to check for damage. A sad little sob escaped her throat when she found it. The bullet had passed through her red traveling dress and her favorite hat.

"Ohhh," she moaned, falling back onto her rump. "It's all so unfair! Those bloody bastards!" She flung the hat a good ten yards. "Those bloody, rotten, flea-ridden, maggot-eating, wart-faced bastards!"

He liked her creative cursing. "Agreed."

"They ruined my car!" she wailed. "They ruined my clothes! They hurt my husband! I hate them! I hate Robert Purcell! I hate the police! I hate poisons and potions and curses and everything! I hate *everything*!" She collapsed in a heap, sobbing.

Avery knew her well enough by now to know she would recover quickly, once she had cried through the emotions of their ordeal, but he nonetheless sat at her side and drew her into his arms to comfort her.

"Come, now, my love," he soothed, stroking her hair. "You can't possibly hate everything. You don't hate me, I hope? Though I noticed I rank a distant third, behind Annabelle and your wardrobe."

"I don't hate you," she sniffed. "I could *never* hate you. And you're not third. It's only that you were mildly hurt, not ruined."

"Ah, but I *am* ruined. Shattered beyond all hope of repair. You have destroyed me."

"Then I hate myself, too," she huffed. She wiped her eyes with her sleeve, because he had once again abandoned her handkerchief. "We can't stay here. They may come after us."

He helped her to her feet. "I agree. We will have to walk. I promise once we reach a town I will send someone to retrieve the car and all our things. I'll have her repaired for you."

A smile touched Rachael's lips. "Thank you." She surveyed the area and herself. "Well. I can't go on like this."

"Why not? You are a bit dirty, perhaps, but..."

"Because we must walk! For God only knows how long!

The sun is going down. It could be dark before we reach civilization. My skirts will catch and trip me up and slow us down. I must change." She fetched her bag from the back seat of the car. "Help me out of this dress."

"Here? In the open?" He'd never heard a woman make a more shocking suggestion in all his life.

"Do you see anywhere better?"

She had a good point. He began to unfasten buttons, doing his best to shield her between himself and the car. "What do you intend to wear?"

"This." She pulled a man's shirt and trousers from her bag.

"Good Lord. Wherever did you get those?"

"Henry Ainsworth."

Avery grunted. "Please tell me you two were never lovers." He was confident they weren't, but he still envied the long history between them.

Rachael rolled her eyes. "Land's sake, Avery, that man is so innocent he would turn red and run away before my skirts ever got as high as my knees!"

"He doesn't seem to run away from your décolletage."

"Oh, well, everyone has seen *that*," she dismissed. "It's not as if I can hide it, you know." She helped him with the corset strings, then cast the garment aside. "I mean, look, Avery." She hefted her breasts, now clearly visible through her flimsy chemise.

It was the silliest thing she had ever said. How could he *not* look? They way she was standing there, hands on her own bosom, he thought he might ravish her on the spot.

"They are enormous! I may as well display them beautifully, because they will stand out no matter what I do." She stripped off the chemise and pulled on the shirt, buttoning it with mercifully quick fingers. It did little to help. He still wanted to ravish her. "It can be a trial," she continued. "They are very heavy and can get in the way. At times I wish I was tiny like

Isobel." She wriggled out of the last layer of skirts and bent to remove her boots.

"No. You are perfect as you are."

"If perfect means 'nice for fondling,' I suppose."

"Perfect means perfect."

She donned the trousers and buttoned them up. They sat low on her hips and displayed her rear end to great advantage, especially when she bent again to tie up her boots. He hoped she didn't intend to dress this way often. He didn't care for the thought of fighting off hordes of randy suitors. He also feared she might be arrested for indecency, though she was fully covered.

"Well? What do you think?" She held her arms out to display the outfit.

"The clothes are surprisingly…" He nearly said "enticing," but at the last moment moderated it to "flattering."

She smiled. "Thank you. Let me gather a few things and then we must go. I'm concerned those men may renew their chase."

She tied her purse to a belt loop on her trousers and donned her red driving gloves and the hat with the bullet hole. A nightgown went into her bag, along with all of her jewelry and her hairbrush. Avery stuffed his travel shaving kit into the case with his papers and journal. He decided to wear his best pair of spectacles, tucking his spare pair into his pocket in their place. Everything else he could do without for a time. They secured the trunks and began their walk, following the stream.

"I can't believe you are wearing that," he blurted, only a few minutes in. "I can't believe I participated in helping you dress. I must be the worst husband in history."

"You are the best husband," she insisted. "When we find somewhere to stay for the night, I will have to write Isobel. She will be delightfully scandalized. How should I begin? Perhaps, 'Dear Isobel, You won't believe what has happened. I was forced, through unavoidable circumstances, to strip down naked and adopt men's clothing—in the middle of a field! When you have revived yourself, let me explain why.' And then I shall tell her how we came to be here and all about our terrible fright."

"You do have a way with words, my dear."

"Do you think so? It's not like your poetry, of course, but I do love writing. I can't be a novelist, obviously, because novels are much too long, and I would grow bored before I finished. And I have enough enjoyment telling true stories that I haven't felt a great need to make up my own. So I write letters."

"A suitable pastime for a lady of your station."

She grew silent, her lips pursed in thought. She was conjuring up an idea of some sort, and he wondered what it might be. Something that pushed the boundaries of scandal, no doubt. It was time he resigned himself to the fact that his life would never be quiet and uneventful again. So be it. That was the cost for having Rachael, and he would gladly pay it. Better to be in the papers beside her than hidden away with some boring, normal sort of wife.

Their walk alongside the stream was tedious, the footing was uneven, and the sun sank toward the horizon at an alarming pace. Rachael walked stiffly, her arms crossed beneath her breasts to keep them from bouncing. She wore a pinched expression, but she didn't complain.

"I'm miserable," Avery said, hoping his words might encourage her to give voice to her own feelings. "My knee hurts, I fear I may turn an ankle with every step, and my mind has gone numb from the endless fields of… this." He waved his hands at the unknown plant life surrounding them.

"Yes!" A sudden enthusiasm sparkled in Rachael's eyes. "It's growing cold, also, and I think that vulture overhead is waiting for us to die." She gripped his arm. "Avery, we may have to sleep out-of-doors! There are vermin living out here that might *touch* us!" She was growing impassioned and enjoying her tirade. "Do you know how to build a shelter?"

"No."

"How to start a fire?"

"Not without matches and a fireplace."

"How to navigate by the stars?"

"Ah! Yes, that I do know. Theoretically. I read a book."

"We are doomed."

"I suspect so. Are you certain that vulture doesn't want your hat? Between the feathers, the blood-red color, and the bullet hole, it could be misconstrued as a dead grouse."

"Avery!" She laughed, which had been his goal all along. He was getting better at this husband business. "I'm very fond of this hat. I won't give it up without a fight."

"And I won't allow my wife to sleep on the ground, even if it means carrying you all night."

"You won't need to carry me. I'm a very good walker." Her grip tightened on his arm. "Oh, oh, a bridge!"

He shielded his eyes from the sun—his own hat had been thrown off during the car chase—and followed her pointing finger. Sure enough, a small footbridge crossed the stream some quarter-mile off. He could just make out the top rails over the weeds.

They raced ahead, Rachael complaining with great gusto about the sun, the itchiness of the grass, and anything else she could think of. He began to reshape her words into a bar-song style ballad. They remained tired, hungry, and lost, but airing their miseries heartened them.

Beyond the bridge lay an overgrown path, and by the time Avery had hammered out the chorus of his drinking song, it had widened into something a human might consider walking on.

"*So here I will stay, and I'll ne'er go away to the Great Outdoors,*" he sang. "Lord, if we ever make it to a city, I think I will get sloshing drunk and stand on a table teaching the words to everyone."

Rachael succumbed to a fit of the giggles. "You must make great flapping motions with your arms when you mention the vulture."

"You wish me to make a spectacle of myself, my dear?"

"It would make for a most entertaining letter. Isobel would think we had both gone quite mad."

"I think perhaps we have. Too long outdoors, you know. All that fresh air can't be good for a body."

She linked her arm through his. "I agree. We ought never to leave town again."

Their banter carried them down the broadening trail, their spirits buoyed by the likelihood of soon encountering something resembling civilization. Despite the darkness and the late hour, they had renewed hope of a hot meal and a roof over their heads.

It was a full hour after sunset when they spied a structure in the distance. They broke into a run, exhaustion all but forgotten. House or barn, it didn't matter. Somewhere near would be a human who would see them appropriately situated.

Rachael stumbled to a halt twenty yards from the small dwelling. Avery came up alongside her and surveyed the area. Four tiny houses made a neat square where the trail crossed something that could almost be called a road. No barns, shops, or other buildings were within sight. The community—it didn't even rate as a village—was silent and absolutely dark. Not even a single candle shone in a window. Anyone living here was abed, likely asleep. No one would have room to accommodate strangers. He was disheveled and muddy, and his wife was dressed like a man.

Avery didn't mind being thought eccentric, or even downright strange. It was necessary, given his curse. Rude and inappropriate, however, were monikers he had always prided himself on avoiding. He didn't know the unfortunate people who lived here, but he expected they would think both adjectives fully suited to his behavior.

And yet he couldn't allow Rachael to sleep on the ground. He swallowed his pride and pounded on the nearest door.

XXXVI

Crime and Punishment

*T*HE MAN AT THE FIRST HOUSE *turned us away. I was stunned, I must tell you. Imagine, refusing assistance to a peer of the realm in clear distress! Fortunately, the woman who lived in the next house over was not equally boorish, though she seemed greatly put upon. We slept on a threadbare old quilt by the fireplace. On the floor, Isobel! The floor! Even now, I almost can't believe it. I know I never would have slept had I not been so very tired and had Avery to curl up against.*

This morning I awoke with pains in my neck, still feeling hungry and cold. No one had added fuel to the fire the entire night. Our hostess, if one can even call her that, did not provide us any breakfast, but tossed us out at first light. It was appalling. I don't believe I have had anyone treat me so meanly in my life, excepting those bedlamites who attempted to do us in yesterday.

You will be most proud of me, dearest, as I behaved the entire night and this morning in an entirely ladylike fashion. My only questionable behavior was when I plucked several tomatoes from her vegetable garden upon our departure. We were starving, and had been treated most uncivilly, so I don't think it wrong of me.

We were forced to walk, once again, but some way down the road we were able to hail a passing wagon and ride into the city. It was a farm wagon, going to market, full of hay and terribly smelly. I honestly would have preferred to walk, had it not been such a distance to Ipswich.

Again, I behaved with great decorum. I have found a wonderful way to express my displeasures that prevents frustration from building and overwhelming me. I now simply snuggle close to my husband and whisper all my complaints to him. He is most sympathetic and confesses his own unhappiness to me in return. He turns our troubles into silly poems to make me laugh.

I think he must be the best man in the entire world. I don't know how I was so fortunate as to marry him.

I must close this letter, as it has become quite lengthy, and Avery and I have much work still to do. I promise to keep you informed of our progress, and you will forgive me if I do not provide you our exact location. It is a matter of safety to be circumspect in this regard. Give our best to my dear Aunt and your Mr. Bellamy.

Your devoted cousin,
Rachael

Avery posted Rachael's latest letter as an express. He had no doubt she had detailed everything that had happened since leaving London, and the faster word reached Isobel—and through her, Bellamy—the better. He prayed this time someone in law enforcement would take them at their word. The sooner this was ended, the better. With hired thugs lying in wait, their intended visit to interview Hunstable had become a dangerous proposition.

Rachael, naturally, had thought up a plan. Avery hated it. It put her at risk of both scandal and bodily harm. The plan required her to go out on her own, without his protection, and acquiring the necessary clothing would be tricky and illegal.

The worst part was how brilliant the plan was. He wouldn't be able to think up anything better. Purcell would never expect it. Avery gave it a better than even chance of success, provided he could manage his own part in the scheme.

Their rented phaeton bumped down the road away from Ipswich proper. Avery disliked the vehicle. Its over-large wheels didn't give a smooth ride, and the body was a bare minimum of frame and seats. If anyone plowed into them, the entire thing would collapse. The lightweight design was meant for speed, but the reality was the car was no faster than Annabelle. Rachael added additional scathing remarks about the power and handling to the collection of complaints.

"I imagine I would feel less hostile toward this poor car were I not pining the loss of my own vehicle," she sighed.

He patted her arm sympathetically. "I will see that she is repaired for you."

She gave him a quick smile, then turned her gaze back to the road.

Thankfully, it didn't take long to reach their destination. Rachael slowed the car, and it rumbled to a halt beside the quaint village church. It was a small structure, but well built—made from locally sourced stone about two centuries prior. Avery had attended services here many times while visiting the dig site. Guilt began to gnaw at him.

"With the weather being nice, I expect you will find the vicar in the garden between the church and the vicarage." Avery spoke in a low voice. "I don't recall a time I've been here when he hasn't mentioned this hobby of his."

"Good," Rachael replied. "I will distract him."

"I don't doubt that, given your clothing." He didn't mean

to sound disapproving, but something of that tone crept into his words.

"You could have bought me something new to wear, if you dislike my costume so."

"It's not that I dislike it," he clarified. "In fact, I think you look rather wonderful. It's only that I dislike you wearing it when out and about. I'm concerned others may get the wrong idea about you."

She turned up her nose. "I know how to handle overly-familiar men, and I don't care if strangers hereabout think me inappropriate. It won't be for much longer, in any event. I should like to get back to my usual clothing when we finish today's work."

Avery nodded. "Let's get to it, then. I feel horrible already, and I have yet to do anything but plan this crime."

She slipped an arm around him. "All will be well. You are helping to prevent Purcell cursing more innocent people. We can even make a large donation to this church as thanks for the vicar's unwitting assistance."

Avery cringed. "I'll never be able to show my face in this village again."

Rachael released him and put her hands on her hips. "Do we need to swap roles?"

"No," he sighed. "Create your distraction. I won't be long."

She nodded and departed. He waited by the car for only a minute or two before he heard raised voices in the distance. He wandered out past the church and alongside the gardens. The vicar, a quiet, conservative man of middle years, stood among the vegetables, his back to Avery, cowering before Rachael's tirade.

"My good sir, I realize I am no biblical scholar," she ranted, her voice just shy of shouting, "but at no point did Our Dear Lord tell the women, 'You shall not wear trousers.' Am I in the wrong in this? If so, please enlighten me."

Avery caught her eye and nodded.

"Modesty is a virtue," Rachael continued. "Still, I don't see…"

Avery hurried toward the vicarage, his footsteps smothered beneath his wife's resonating voice. The door to the house was closed, but unlocked. He slipped inside.

He stood motionless in the front hall for several moments, listening. The vicarage wasn't large, but it still warranted a housekeeper. She wouldn't live here, he expected, and he didn't hear any indication she might be at work.

"Right, then," he whispered to himself. "Get on with it."

He crept from room to room, wincing at each creak of the floorboards. His insides were twisted with guilt. He'd never stolen anything in his life, never even filched sweets as a boy. Perspiration dampened his brow. He vowed never to agree to this sort of scheme ever again. If only they could spare the time to purchase or borrow what they needed. If only people would be less insistent on asking for explanations, or believed those explanations when he gave them.

"Damn and blast," he muttered. He may as well curse. He was already well on the path to hell.

It couldn't have been more than five minutes from the time he entered the vicarage to the time he exited, but the ordeal left him exhausted. He raced to the car to hide his loot. Not touching the stolen clothes eased his anxiety enough he could walk back to the garden without cringing.

Rachael stood in her familiar pose of irritation, staring down the vicar, who spoke in gentle, though flustered, tones. Avery suspected the man didn't have much experience with assertive women. If it had been a real argument, Rachael would remain unconvinced.

"Darling, there you are!" Avery rushed to his wife's side. The vicar looked at him with a mixture of relief and disapproval.

"Is this your wife? Why did you let her out of the house dressed as she is?"

Better to blame the husband than assume Rachael had her

own mind, it seemed. Dangerous things, thinking women. Avery felt a sudden longing to be back at the University. He could use the company of some of his more progressive colleagues.

"Ah, you see, she is learning to ride a bicycle," he explained. "Her skirts are not practical for such purposes, so she must make do. We had hoped that by consulting with learned men such as yourself we could gather some sound arguments in favor of alternate—but modest—dress for women engaged in sporting activities."

"She looks anything but modest."

Avery feigned bewilderment. "She is covered from neck to ankles. How is that not modest?"

"You can see her entire…" The vicar mimicked Rachael's curves with his hands. "Shape."

"Ah." Avery took Rachael's hand. "I suggest you avoid attending balls, in that case. The women often wear clothing that makes them appear quite *shapely*. We will take our consultations elsewhere. Good day to you."

The vicar turned red. Rachael chewed on her lower lip to prevent herself laughing. Avery drew her close and steered her toward the car.

"I told you those clothes were much too flattering," he whispered. "Every man will be leering or preaching."

"You are doing neither of those things."

"I will be leering when we are alone in our bedroom, don't doubt it."

She grinned. "Well, we *are* still newlyweds. You can't be bored of me yet."

"I will never grow bored of you," he vowed.

Under Rachael's watchful eye, he started up the phaeton's engine, then helped her into the passenger seat. He took the place behind the wheel with no small amount of apprehension. He had been content with his ignorance of steam carriages, but today's activities required him to drive. He wished he had hired a horse-drawn vehicle.

The car lurched forward. He had opened the throttle too quickly. He eased it back, then forward again, doing nothing but bumping them about and causing the engine to emit questionable noises.

"My apologies. It seems I wasn't meant to be a driver."

"Nonsense. You need only relax."

He didn't think that possible.

Steering was easier, to his great relief. Once the car had reached cruising speed, he didn't struggle to handle it. A few miles down the road, he pulled over and practiced stopping. Again, the vehicle shuddered and protested, though somewhat less than during the acceleration.

Avery hopped down from the car and paced a bit, trying to calm himself. Rachael took the stolen clothes from beneath her seat and examined them. No one was in sight, so she began to dress.

"This will do excellently," she praised him, buttoning the black shirt with its clerical collar over the white one she wore. A shapeless frock coat went on next, hiding her body. "I think perhaps I might actually be mistaken for a man."

She had braided her hair into two long plaits and pinned them atop her head. The wide-brimmed hat hid it well, and shaded her face. If she kept her eyes down he thought she might be right. With the anxiety of stealing from the vicar in the past, the next part of Rachael's plan began to eat at him.

"Rachael, I'm terrified. I can't leave you alone to do this. Those men who ran us off the road may be awaiting you. There may be others."

"We discussed this. We can't go together. They expect a man and a woman. You can't go alone, even in disguise. They would be looking for a tall, dark-haired man. They won't expect an average-sized priest, and clergymen visit the gaol often to lend spiritual aid to the prisoners."

She stepped back into the car, taking her seat before he could forget himself and help her. She would accept no further argument, and he could see no better alternative.

"You are a brave woman, my love." His voice caught. "Please, promise me to take utmost care."

She squeezed his hand. "I promise. I want a long life with you, Avery, and no one will take that from me without a fight."

He nodded, not trusting himself to reply. His throat was tight and his hands shaking. He opened the throttle and the car jerked into motion with all the grace of a waltzing elephant. He'd be damned if he drove one of these hellish machines ever again.

The only upside to the driving was that it helped keep his mind distracted from the danger Rachael was walking into. On the city streets, his concentration grew so intense that his fear of crashing almost outweighed his fear of murderous thugs.

He rolled to a stop several blocks shy of the gaol. Rachael hopped from the carriage and nodded to him. He watched her go with an aching heart. In her disguise he couldn't kiss her, or even take her hand for a moment. He couldn't tell her he loved her. He could only pray for her safety and hope everything he had said before had been enough.

Avery drove off, stopping the car near a park where he could wait out the hour until he returned to pick her up. He grabbed for his journal. He needed an outlet before he became too nervous to function. He needed his Rachael back at his side. He needed her arms around him. He needed to hear her voice. He needed her love. The words began to flow.

· · · ◦◦ · · ·

Rachael found Hunstable sitting on the cot in his cell, reading. A stack of books piled a dozen high sat beside the bed. She supposed he had little else to do. He looked well-fed, she was relieved to see. It would have been a shame to damage his pretty face with malnourishment.

His cell was among the nicest the gaol had to offer, meaning it had both a sagging cot and a rickety chair. He had it to himself, however, due to his noble birth and his capable legal counsel. By now, a man of lower class would have been tried, convicted, and sentenced to hard labor, or even hanged. The lawyer Avery had chosen was doing a masterful job dragging things out while he waited for enough evidence to set the young man free.

The bored man who opened the cell hadn't even looked closely enough at her to become suspicious. He unlocked the heavy door, waved her in, and locked it behind her. Hunstable frowned up at her, laying his book aside. She doubted he ever had any visitors besides Avery and the lawyer. His Most Honorable parents were too busy touring the Continent to read their correspondence.

Rachael waited until the gaoler's footsteps faded before speaking.

"Good afternoon, Lord Hunstable." She tipped back the wide-brimmed hat to allow him to see her face.

His mouth dropped open in shock. He emitted a series of unintelligible noises before managing to stammer, "Mrs. Cantrell? Er, Lady Wilwood?"

"Whichever." Rachael pushed the chair close to the bed and perched on the edge, hoping it would support her weight. "I apologize for the shock. Circumstances of late have dictated the necessity of a disguise. I would appreciate it if we could keep our discussion quiet and confidential."

"What has happened?" His frown morphed into a look of hope. "Am I to be released soon?"

"I hope so. This is no place for a gentleman."

He gave a grim nod. "I have at least been able to continue my schoolwork." He gestured at the pile of books.

"Ah." He was rather dedicated to even think of his studies under such circumstances. She could see why Avery called him his best student. "Well." She folded her hands in her lap and looked him directly in the eye. "I believe the best thing you can do to help yourself is to help us track down Professor Purcell."

"He has gone missing?"

Rachael nodded. She withheld the reason behind the disappearance. She didn't know what the boy had been told, and he was already agitated. She wouldn't compound that with news of more murders unless it became a necessity.

"We know he has been in and out of London in recent days, but he hasn't been seen at his apartments. He should be watching over the dig site, yet he is neither there nor at the hotel where he was recently in residence."

"Curious. It's not like him to abandon his work."

"We believe he has another project which has taken his focus away from his usual duties."

Hunstable looked thoughtful. "He has always taken time for personal research. He has never before neglected our excavation, however. Perhaps he has made an important discovery?"

"Given what I know, it appears he has made a breakthrough in his experimentations."

"Oh! Has he replicated an ancient potion, then?"

Rachael felt a rush of excitement. "You *do* know something! Was that his aim, this ancient replica?"

"He never said as much, but he did talk about his belief that they had done things differently in the past. The way he spoke made me think he wanted to discover their techniques. It is only a guess, of course, but you said he was experimenting…"

She nodded. "Avery and I believe he has been running experiments for some time. You have never seen him doing anything of the sort?"

The young man shook his head. "No. He didn't conduct any personal research at our excavation site."

"Nor at the office here in Ipswich?"

"No, no. It's much too small. We use it for storage, chiefly. The professor doesn't like the books and papers to be near the digging. Most of my photographs are there as well. I only send the best of them to Professor Cantrell in London."

Rachael tapped her foot in annoyance. "Where, then, did he conduct this 'personal research' you spoke of? He would require a laboratory in order to replicate potions. One can't hide that sort of thing."

"I, uh…" Hunstable's voice trailed away. He scratched his head, looking perplexed. "Yes. I had not considered…"

"He has a laboratory somewhere. He can't have developed these poi… potions otherwise. He has been conducting these experiments for months, perhaps longer. You know of nowhere he might have done such work?"

The boy again shook his head. Rachael began to fret that perhaps his information might not be useful after all. It was possible that Purcell lay in hiding somewhere in London. The city was plenty big enough for a man to disappear. Any dingy warehouse could be converted into a workshop.

She dismissed that idea, and not only because she hated the thought of a futile search throughout the seamier side of town. What she knew of Purcell suggested he would prefer a more civilized venue. He liked things neat and tidy and proper. He would want a location that was private, but genteel. It had to be in the country. She couldn't imagine him in a dark city room.

"Did you ever know him to visit a house or cottage in the area?"

Hunstable's face lit up. "Oh, indeed! I hadn't thought of it as a research venue, but he often goes to a country home on our days off. Most of the chaps hie off to nearby family, or pop into Ipswich for drinks and entertainment." His face turned pink at the word "entertainment," suggesting the men were seeing prostitutes, not opera. "Professor Purcell prefers not to join us. He is a prim sort of man you know, and he doesn't like strong drink or gaming or…"

Or whores. His cheeks, now very red indeed, spoke the words he wouldn't utter in the presence of a female.

Rachael nodded, her own complexion entirely unaffected. She didn't care what sort of carousing Hunstable got up to on his own time—though given the boy's jittery nature, she didn't think it could be as bad as all that. She also cared nothing for Purcell's opinion on the matter. The man didn't gamble or pay for sex, but that didn't redeem him in the slightest.

"Can you tell me anything more about this house?" she asked, trying to steer the conversation back on course. "The location? The type of residence? Is it his own property?"

"Uh, I don't recall him giving many details. It's somewhere between here and London."

Somewhere? Rachael tried not to scowl. More than eighty miles of road lay between the two cities. Searching the entire area was as hopeless a task as combing the streets of London.

"He praised his steam car often," Hunstable continued, "saying it gave him the chance to visit the residence with regularity. He could reach it from the excavation in under two hours."

Rachael made a quick estimate of the distance. Nearing halfway between the cities, she decided, but closer to Ipswich by at least five miles, if not ten. Purcell's car wasn't as fast as Annabelle, and additional driving time would be needed because the house would be off the main road. That narrowed the search considerably.

"The only other recollection I have about the house is that it belongs to a relation of his, or perhaps a friend who was like family to him? He referred to the man as 'Uncle,' but it wasn't a Purcell. Landsdown or Landon or some such…"

Rachael gasped. "Landry? As in Amelia Landry?" The woman he had loved. The lunatic was using her old house as his poison-making lair? He was beyond mad.

"Yes, Landry," Hunstable confirmed. "I don't know an Amelia, but perhaps she is a cousin? 'My good Uncle Landry' or 'dear Mr. Landry' is what he would say. I believe the gentleman is infirm. The professor always has a sad sort of look when speaking of him. The visits must be uplifting, however. He returns in better cheer than when he leaves. If he has disappeared, perhaps he is there." He frowned. "Or perhaps the gentleman has died at last? That would explain the professor's prolonged absence. I hope that isn't the case. I would feel very sad for him, poor man."

"Poor Landry, perhaps," Rachael snapped. "If he's dead, it's at Purcell's hand." She was tired of hedging the true issue. Sensitive Hunstable sitting unfairly in gaol having feelings of sorrow for the killer who had put him there was too much.

The photographer gasped.

"I'm sorry to shock you, but that is the truth of it," Rachael said. "All evidence points to Purcell as perpetrator of the crime for which you have been arrested, among others. We also suspect he has recently kidnapped a young woman. We hope to find her alive. It's imperative we locate him at once, if she is to be saved."

"Lord help us," Hunstable breathed.

"Once he is in custody, you will be set free. Everything you have told me will help yourself and the others in danger. Please, if there is anything more you can tell me, say it now."

The young man sat for a moment in thoughtful silence. "Only that he spoke of his research as something that would change the world for the better. He never gave specifics, and I thought it exaggeration."

Rachael nodded. That only confirmed her impression of Purcell's madness. She thanked Hunstable for his help, and assured him once again he wouldn't remain here much longer. She took his hand in hers and gave it a squeeze, causing him to blush pink a second time.

"Thank *you*, Mrs. Cantrell. Please convey my thanks to your husband as well. I don't know what I would have done if you hadn't been looking out for me."

She hadn't done anything for him at all, but she accepted his thanks with grace and asked after his schoolwork. He chatted while she nodded politely until the gaoler returned and let her out with the same ambivalence he had shown before.

Rachael checked that her hat hid her face and her coat obscured her figure. She only nodded goodbye to Hunstable, and didn't speak to anyone on the way out. She didn't have a high voice, but it wasn't easy to keep it pitched low enough to pass as a man. After a successful interview, she didn't want to ruin everything by being caught out and tossed into the gaol herself. Her long stride served her well on the streets, and no one gave her much notice.

Avery awaited her at the rendezvous point. She hopped into the car, and he drove away, still struggling to make the phaeton accelerate smoothly. It was clear he hadn't been practicing during her absence.

She whispered that her visit had been a success, but told him no more until they were a safe distance out-of-town. Avery turned down a side road, and when no other cars were in sight, brought them to a bouncing halt. Rachael whipped off her disguise and reclaimed her rightful seat. Avery sighed in relief.

"Now, tell me everything you have learned," he insisted.

Rachael eased the car up to a comfortable speed. "Everything? Well, for starters, darling, you are a horrid driver."

XXXVII

Plan of Attack

$\mathcal{R}$ACHAEL ADJUSTED HER SKIRTS around her before opening the throttle and setting the car into motion. Her new dress—bought off the rack, much to her shame—was better suited for visiting than driving, but it was the best she had been able to do on such short notice. The fit wasn't too terrible, and she liked the materials and colors. It was a deep blue, lightweight cotton with silk accent panels in a shade that bordered on purple. Still, it needed work. The bodice lacing wasn't how she liked, the neckline was too severe, and the hem needed letting out.

"You know the village where Miss Landry lived?" she inquired, sparing Avery a quick glance.

His new suit need tailoring as well, but she thought it would look very fine after alterations. She liked how the maroon waistcoat stood out beneath the charcoal frock coat. With his spectacles on, he looked appropriately professorial.

"I know *of* the village and its general direction, but the area is unfamiliar to me, and I don't know the location of the house itself. The Landrys are gentry and possess some amount of land. They could be miles from the village or nearly inside it. I couldn't say."

"We shall talk to the locals to learn more. If it's miles, we have already established that I am a great walker."

"I will be sure to add that to your fine attributes in the next poem I write," he teased.

Rachael grinned, but quickly sobered, her mind already moving on to the next step. "Once we identify the house, it will be necessary to investigate it. That can't be done in daylight. If Purcell sees us coming, it will ruin everything."

Avery shifted nervously. "I know."

"Good. We will sneak out in the middle of the night to take a look. It sounds rather terrifying, but it can't be as difficult as all that. Elle tells me she has done midnight sneaking many times." Rachael did her best to sound serious, not eager. Beneath her apprehension lurked an excitement about the whole adventure.

"I'm not surprised she has gone out sneaking. She's married to a spy."

"They aren't actually married, you know. I assume it's because she's French and Henry is half Scottish. There's a terrible amount of wildness when you put the two together."

"You have the strangest friends."

"Yes, and I rather like them."

"Indeed. I suppose even Ainsworth has his good points. You shall have to invite them back to Wilwood House for our next party."

Rachael tensed. Not only was he talking of their future, he was offering to be social! Was he feeling well? Perhaps the anxiety of their current situation was too much for him.

"We shall invite them when we unveil my Greek goddess fountain."

Avery grimaced. The tension eased from her shoulders. He was still his usual self.

Rachael paused to wipe a bit of moisture from her goggles. Gray clouds masked the sun, and a light drizzle had begun to fall.

"When you have Annabelle repaired, see that you have one of those retractable roofs installed," she instructed. "These open-topped carriages are all fine and good on a sunny day, but one can't always leave off driving until nicer weather comes along."

Avery opened an umbrella and held it over her. "Pick what you like and I shall pay for it. We have clearly established that I know nothing about cars."

She chuckled and turned the topic of conversation to their honeymoon. If he was in the mood to host parties, it was a perfect time to plot destinations and outings for the wedding trip. As she chattered of shopping and exotic locales, he nodded and agreed. He offered no suggestions himself, nor did he question even her most outrageous ideas.

His coolness began to frazzle her nerves. The closer they came to the place where they had been run off the road, the more apprehensive she became. His indifference made it difficult to distract herself.

"Avery, do you even care about this trip?" she blurted.

"Honestly, no. Not in terms of particulars. I care only that it happens. I'm happy to travel with you anywhere, provided it has quality food, adequate heating, and water closets. If you suggest we sleep in a tent or climb a mountain, I shall have to object."

"Hmph. You know full well I have no interest in either of those things."

"Precisely."

"Well. As long as we attend a performance or two at the Paris Opera House and..."

"Slow up a moment," Avery interrupted.

Rachael eased back on the throttle, peering into the distance. "What's wrong?"

"That car up ahead looks like the ones that chased us before."

She paused to wipe rain from her goggles. In the hazy distance, a dark, hulking vehicle blocked the road ahead.

"I see it. It's difficult to be certain from this distance, but I don't think it wise to take a closer look."

"No. We shall have to turn back."

Rachael made a wide circle and took the car out of sight before slowing once more. "This can't be more than a few miles from where we were run off the road. I hadn't thought to connect our ordeal with the location of the Landry household, but it makes sense. He means to keep us away from his laboratory."

"And it confirms that he is there, or at least that something he deems important is there. We will have to approach the village by another route. I suggest we go cross-country."

Rachael's brows rose. "Cross-country? You, who just said no tents? We can't drive off road. This phaeton is less fit than Annabelle for such a journey, and you saw the difficulty I had driving her."

"We will go on horseback. You can ride, can't you?"

"Er… yes, but…" Rachael's protest died on her lips. She didn't ride well, hadn't ridden at all in many years, and her dress was entirely inappropriate for such sport. Still, the idea was sound. Avery had been willing to steal from a vicar to carry out her secret interview. She could show him a similar courtesy. "But I won't like it," she declared. "Expect no argument, but much complaining."

He beamed at her. "Rachael, you are a treasure. I swear to do my best to make the journey as easy as possible."

They drove a few miles, to another small village, where Avery saw to borrowing a serviceable pair of horses. The rain ebbed, to Rachael's great relief. Carrying an umbrella on horseback seemed ludicrous, and she would need both hands on the reins.

Her slim skirts were absurdly unfit for riding. In order to take her seat, she had to hike the fabric up to her knees. It did show off her lovely blue and white striped stockings, but she would have preferred to give her husband a discreet peek here and there rather than having them on display for any vagabond who happened by.

Avery may not have known cars, but he did know horses,

and the mare Rachael sat upon was calm and responsive. She didn't seem to care in the slightest that her rider was showing an indecent amount of leg and had a bustle jutting out at a ludicrous angle. Avery, too, seemed unfazed by these troubles. He merely grinned at her.

"Your stockings are lovely."

By the end of the ride, Rachael was determined she shouldn't take up riding as a hobby. She much preferred the car or a brisk walk. She was tired, sore, and her legs lacked their usual sturdiness.

They dismounted a short way outside the village so as not to startle everyone with her unconventional appearance, and led the horses the remaining distance. This was the sort of country life that appeared in romantic novels—small buildings, tidy roads, and pretty lasses carrying pretty wildflowers tied up in ribbon. Rachael would have called it "quaint" were she only passing through. As a place to spend the night, it had a less favorable appearance.

They stabled the horses at the inn, and Avery saw about getting a room for the night. Everyone stared at Rachael and her upper-class gown. The innkeeper actually gaped.

"No, no, you must have two rooms," he insisted. "The rooms are small and no fine lady can be expected to spend the night in cramped quarters. I will charge only for the single room."

"Nonsense," Avery replied. "I will gladly pay for both. Your courtesy is much to be commended."

The innkeeper protested again, and Avery began to place money on the counter, restating his arguments. Rachael rolled her eyes and turned away. For goodness' sake, all she had was a tiny bag and she now knew what it was to sleep on a floor! She would make do.

She let the men bicker and turned to a woman carrying a tray of drinks.

"Tea, please?" she asked. "And make it strong. I think I'll need it."

Avery took a seat beside his wife, who sat calmly slicing a sandwich into bite-sized pieces. He was unsure what about her was garnering the most attention: her fancy dress, her use of her personal silver, or her preference for eating her sandwich with a knife and fork. Several questioning looks were cast in his direction, as well. He'd drawn attention while discussing room arrangements, then caused a bigger stir by asking the kitchen staff about the methods used to clean the dishes.

The dining area had several long, shared tables. Rachael and Avery spent several silent minutes sipping their tea before any other guest sat close enough to greet.

"Good evening," Avery said.

"Evening. Welcome to our town."

"Thank you. Please, allow me to introduce my wife, Lady…"

"Pythia Bowles," Rachael interrupted. "How do you do?" She gave the man a polite nod.

"Pleased to meet you, my lady. My name is Jonathan Stropper."

"A pleasure, Mr. Stropper," Avery said, trying to take back the conversation. Rachael's sudden use of a false name had thrown him. Pythia? Where had that come from? He would simply have to play along. He held out his hand. "Eadric Bowles." He countered her Greek name with an Anglo-Saxon one.

Her brow crinkled as she watched them shake hands, a slight frown on her face. She disliked his choice of pseudonym, he guessed, but couldn't complain about it. He disliked hers, too, so they were even.

Stropper's hand was rough, his grip firm. "Traveling the countryside?" he asked.

"Yes, but on a business matter." Avery saw no point in wasting time. He needed information. He bypassed casual chatting for a direct question. "Do you know the house owned by the Landry family?"

Stropper's eyes widened. "Oh, you don't want to be going there, sir. They've been stricken with a plague. Two deaths confirmed this week, and word the entire household may have fallen ill."

Avery and Rachael shared a grim look. The curse had been spread here. The Landrys and their servants may have been the first victims.

"The house is shut up," the man continued. "No one goes in and out except the doctor."

"They have summoned a doctor?"

"Oh, no, same fellow who's been by off and on for years. Close with the family. Quiet man. He comes and goes often these past days—running to London, we think, for medicines—but we're all keeping a distance until we know the plague is gone. He could be a carrier."

"Of course. Just to be clear, this doctor is an average-sized man, sandy hair, brown eyes, well-dressed, very pleasant in manners?"

Stropper blinked. "You know him?"

"He is a colleague of mine. I'm here to assist in the investigation of these deaths and illnesses."

"Well, then! I hope you brought some stronger healing potions. Can't have plague spreading about, and two grieving families in the area is enough. I'd advise you, though, sir, don't take your wife out to that house. You can't be exposing a lady to such a danger, if you'll pardon my presumption."

"I'm aiding in the investigation, myself," Rachael chimed in. "We work together, my husband and I."

"What, a lady physician?" Stropper exclaimed. "I heard there were such things in the city."

Rachael responded only with a condescending smile. Avery wanted to laugh at the thought of her studying medicine and working with patients. It suited neither her temperament nor her fastidious sense of hygiene. Given her circle of friends, however, he wouldn't have been surprised to find she knew a female doctor. It occurred to him that her driving and trouser wearing might cause people to consider her dangerously radical. He would add it to his own list of eccentricities: hates cars, won't eat at parties, has a feminist wife.

Stropper eyed Rachael warily and gave a little shake of the head before turning his gaze back to Avery. To head off any potential arguments about the merits of women in the scientific world, Avery asked whether it was advisable to travel to the house on foot or on horseback, and which street would take them on the most direct path.

Stropper responded with detailed descriptions of the path to the Landry residence, which Avery dutifully jotted in his notebook.

Rachael swiped a tiny jam tart from his plate, replacing it with a little cake sprinkled with crushed pistachios. He gave her a questioning look, but ate it.

"I don't like pistachios," she informed Avery when Stropper moved on to converse with another patron. "Were you terribly looking forward to that jam tart? I suppose I ought to have asked."

He shrugged. "I'm not particular."

"I am," she replied, with a rueful half-smile.

"Quite all right," he assured her. "A choosy woman has chosen me. I must be special."

"Yes. Yes, you are." The smile she bestowed on him was full of affection.

He loved that look. If only she would accompany it by saying she loved him in return. There was nothing he wanted more.

He flinched at the realization. This desperate longing for her love had supplanted even his desire for a cure. He would throw away his years of research, live out all his days as the crazy man who carried his own silver, if that's what it took to capture her heart.

He couldn't say what had triggered this change in him. Perhaps it had been the scare of the car chase, or else the competency and aplomb with which she formulated and executed plans. Maybe it was how she had stopped pretending to be anything other than her true self.

Whatever the cause, Avery craved her love with a fervor that defied reason. He had devoted seventeen years to his research. He would spend the next seventeen years devoted to wooing Rachael, if necessary. He prayed it wouldn't be so long.

"Come, *Eadric*," Rachael said, in the tone he had termed her polite-sarcastic voice. "We ought to be getting to bed. It's been a long day."

What she meant was they needed some sleep if they were to sneak out to the Landry house during the night. Avery's mind agreed, but his body didn't. This insane plan had left him too nervous to consider sleep.

Rachael rose from the dining table, staring down at him, waiting for him to follow. He remained in his seat, ignoring propriety, pulling his journal from inside his coat. He hoped some writing would calm his nerves. He also had scribblings of a new poem he wished to finish.

Her eyes narrowed at him. "Aren't you tired?"

"No. I believe dinner has revived me somewhat. I wish to spend a bit of time working out this verse. Don't let me keep you from your rest. I won't be long."

She eyed him with suspicion. "Very well. I need to write a letter to Isobel, but I believe I will do that up in my own room. You know where to find me."

Avery seized her hand to kiss it before she could walk out of reach. "Good night, dear. I love you."

She said nothing, only looked at him for a long moment before withdrawing her hand and waltzing away in a swirl of blue fabric. He hoped she would sleep. It would be better if at least one of them got some amount of rest. Knowing Rachael, he had his doubts.

XXXVIII

Pythian Revelations

A Ladies' Guide to Enjoying the Countryside
By Mrs. Pythia Bowles

*M*Y DEAR READERS,

For those who wish to venture out of the city, Nature has abundant beauties to offer. In order to fully enjoy them, however, it is necessary to adjust one's habits, as country life and city life are as different beasts as fish and bird. In order to make your time in the outdoors as carefree and relaxing as possible, I offer you these tips…

Rachael reread her article, making a few corrections, then tucked it into her bag. She would get Avery's opinion on it before finding a newspaper to print it. Someone on her mother's side of the family would have the right connections. They would, of course, be scandalized that she was taking up a profession, but no more scandalized than when she had married an American, been widowed under mysterious circumstances, or married for a second time to a notoriously strange man. They would help her out.

She was elated to have found something to do with her life.

The idea had come from her talks with Avery about writing. The things she detailed in her letters were the very sort of tales that society ladies wished to read about. Scandals and gossip, fashion and fads—eager readers were always hungering for interesting tidbits. She had been such a reader for years.

Mrs. Bowles would write not simply the usual gossip, but also advice pieces like the one she had just penned. Pythia was an oracle, after all. Rachael liked the idea of the ancient priestess offering up modern wisdom. This article would be a good beginning. She had another idea in mind for a series of articles making up a guide to a happy marriage. She would reference her husband, Eadric. Avery would scowl and pretend he didn't love it.

Rachael checked the time, wondering if he was still down in the dining room, scribbling in his journal. She had undressed at leisure, neglecting to summon a maid, and her letter to Isobel was lengthy. Writing the article had taken an additional chunk of time. Surely he couldn't still be downstairs.

She rose from her seat at the desk, but the room was too small to allow her to pace. The innkeeper had been correct in his assessment. The bed, only large enough for two if they were intimately cozy, took up most of the space. Pegs on the walls offered the only way to hang clothes. Under ordinary circumstances, she would have found such a chamber inadequate for herself alone. The evening, however, all she wanted was Avery's comforting presence.

Where was he? Surely he would at least stop by to kiss her goodnight? She hoped for even further intimacies. She wanted to be close to him. She would put up with a small bed so they didn't have to sleep apart.

She checked her pocket watch again. Time was crawling. Another few minutes ticked by, until she could stand it no longer. She sprang from the bed, stomped across the hall, and hammered on Avery's door.

For a moment, she worried he might not be there. What

if he were still downstairs writing? She couldn't very well go tromping down there in her nightgown.

She sighed when his door opened. "Oh, good, you are here. Don't go anywhere." She dashed to her room, locked the door, then hurried back to where her dazed husband stood in his own doorway.

"Rachael?" Avery stared at her. He was dressed for bed, and the room was dark behind him. "You're not asleep?"

"Of course I'm not asleep! Did you think I would go off to bed without you? I have been waiting up. You won't even kiss me goodnight?"

He opened his arms. "Darling, of course I will. I didn't wish to disturb you."

Rachael stepped into his embrace and backed him into the room, kicking the door closed behind her. The lamp beside his bed, turned down low, cast dim shadows. "I was only disturbed when you didn't come to me."

He dropped a brief kiss on her mouth. "We should sleep. We have a long night ahead. Will you be more comfortable here?"

"I will be more comfortable once I'm out of this nightgown," she declared. She tugged the offending garment over her head. "I'm too nervous to sleep. Why should I lie awake fretting? I'd rather make love." She tossed the nightgown into the corner. "Don't you agree?"

"We ought to make an attempt to sleep, but, uh…" He couldn't seem to finish the thought. His eyes raked over her, and a smile of appreciation touched his lips. It vanished a moment later, as he struggled to find his words. "It's not that I don't want to…"

Rachael sighed and put her hands on her hips. If he didn't hurry up she was going to grab his nightshirt and start removing it.

He saved her the trouble. "Never mind. I can't resist you naked *and* exasperated."

"Good."

She climbed into the bed and he wasted no time joining her. The kiss he gave her this time was a proper one—deep, wet, hungry. She loved kissing him. Whether a quick peck hello or a long, passionate prelude to physical intimacy, the taste of him always made her body tingle and sent bursts of happiness through her.

"This is a terrible idea," he mumbled against her lips.

She drew back, studying his face in the low light. "You say that about all my ideas."

That was not at all true. He was often quite supportive of her ideas, sometimes even when they disagreed. She liked teasing him, however, and felt she had gotten rather good at it.

"I do," he agreed. "And I'm always wrong."

Rachael laughed. "Ah, my romantic husband. I was right about you from the first." She lay her head on his shoulder and kissed his neck.

"I was wrong about that, too."

He shivered. She had found a ticklish spot. She ran the tip of her tongue across his skin, and he let out a groan. She had never left a love mark on him, and she meant to try tonight. She stopped just shy of biting him, but judging by the pleasurable noises that rumbled from his throat, she didn't think he would have complained.

She moved lower, trailing her kisses down to his chest. His hands roved across her curves, but he made no attempt to wrest control from her. This had been her idea, and she was fully in charge. She shivered from the terrifying thrill of it.

She reached across him and doused the lamp. In full darkness, she would have to rely on her other senses to explore him. Her hands and mouth were eager to take up the task.

Rachael flicked at a small, flat nipple until it hardened into a tight point. She teased it with her tongue and sucked gently. Avery arched into her touch. She was discovering he liked many of the same things she did. She spent time on the other nipple, then began a slow downward path toward his shaft.

She intended to kiss him there. It was not at all ladylike. In fact, she was quite certain it was the sort of thing men did with their whores. Well, she wasn't going to let him have any whores. Not now, not ever. He belonged to her, and her alone, and she was going to do whatever she pleased.

He moaned her name when her tongue swept over the tip of his cock. She tormented him with licks and kisses, reveling in the feel of him writhing beneath her. Heat suffused her body. The taste of him was like a drug. What dull sorts of people needed potions to make them feel this way? She needed only Avery.

"My Avery," she sighed, the words tearing out from somewhere deep inside her. It was half a plea to never leave her, and half assertion she would never let him go.

"Rachael." His fingers tangled in her hair. His hips lifted, begging for more. "God, Rachael."

Her tongue stroked from the very base of his cock all along the length of him, and he answered with a strangled noise. Emboldened, she took him into her mouth, sucking and licking, feeling the clenching of his muscles beneath her.

"Christ, Rachael. This is… You're so…" He pulled away from her, gasping. "I'm going to spend in your mouth if you don't stop."

That didn't sound so terrible, really, and she was highly curious what it might taste like. Perhaps next time. Tonight she wanted him deep inside her. She clambered back up him to kiss his mouth.

"My darling," she murmured. She clung to him, rolling onto her back, pulling him along.

My love.

She didn't say the words, her lips too busy drinking from his, but they echoed in her mind as their bodies joined. Always together.

"Avery. My Avery."

Rachael didn't know if he could understand her mumbles, but he could feel her embrace, could share the spasms of her ecstasy as he surged in and out of her. Her moans, at first full and throaty, tapered off into a slow exhalation, her body riding a wave of pleasure over the crest and settling into a languid happiness.

She snuggled into the crook of his arm, breathing him in, her fingers gliding in lazy strokes across his chest. With her physical desires fully sated, she was left to bask in the warmth of their love.

Love. The word washed over her once again.

There was no denying it. She had fallen in love with Avery Cantrell. She wasn't incapable of love. She was primed for it. Avery had chipped away the ice around her frosty heart, breathing life and warmth into it. With him she had no need to be a "good wife" or a "proper lady," but simply Rachael. His whole-hearted adoration gave her the freedom to be herself, to explore, to let herself *feel* every deep fragment of the emotions she had striven for years to bottle up. And oh, were those feelings grand.

This was her passion. This was what she'd been longing for, without ever quite understanding. His love and hers. Equal. Entwined.

She wanted to make a big production out of telling him. It would make him so terribly happy. She could give him flowers. Or, perhaps a more masculine present would be preferable. A new journal would be good. He had written nearly clear through the old one.

After lying awake for a time, she slipped from the bed, turning the knob on the potion-fueled lamp to give her enough light to see by. Avery slept on.

She picked up his journal from atop the small desk, flipping through to see what he had written since she had last peeked. An entire page had been dedicated to descriptions of her. Some were physical, others behavioral. Several had potential rhymes written in the margins. The word "sarcastic" appeared multiple times. This baffled her. He couldn't *truly* like her caustic wit, could he? A bawdy limerick scrawled on the next page confirmed he did.

> *My lady's relentless sarcasm,*
> *Has caught up my heart in a spasm.*
> *It makes me so love her,*
> *I must lie above her,*
> *And f--- 'til she reaches orgasm.*

Rachael laughed aloud and had to cover her mouth. How could he write such a poem and yet not write out the word itself? His skewed sense of propriety was adorable. She was blushing furiously, herself, already thinking about repeating this night's exercises. She continued on.

The last written page listed terms for speaking, singing, and other forms of vocal communication. At the bottom she found a nearly-finished poem, marked with several changes and corrections, but easily readable. The words rent her heart.

> *A Plea*
> *Speak, my beloved. Sing me a song.*
> *Yell at me, darling. Tell me I'm wrong.*
> *Whisper, my angel, the secrets we keep.*
> *Cry out my name in our bed ere we sleep.*
> *Laugh at my foibles, joke of your own.*
> *Coo at our babe, even after she's grown.*
> *Talk, dearest one, of whatever you please.*
> *Sigh in my arms, breathe the gentlest breeze.*
> *Vow before God to be ever my wife.*
> *Say that you love me, my heart and my life.*

Unlike the naughty limerick, this verse was no joke. He did love her at her sarcastic worst. He loved her even when she screamed or pouted. Pretty and proper or spoiled and stubborn, he loved her. He was suffering thinking she didn't return his love. She could forget the presents and fanfare. She needed to tell him at once. She considered waking him to tell him, but thought he might drift off again and think the whole thing a dream.

Her confession would have to wait until he was fully awake. It might, she rued, even have to be postponed until they had tackled Purcell. She wouldn't risk endangering Avery with too much romantic distraction.

Frustrated at the thought of yet more waiting, Rachael picked up her husband's pen and wrote out a neat line of elegant script in the bottom margin of the page.

My dearest Avery, I love you with all of my heart. Your ever-devoted, Rachael.

It would do for now.

XXXIX

A Midnight Adventure

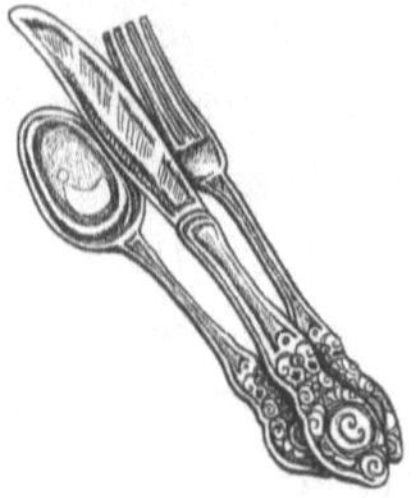

"Avery."

The voice was whispered, but urgent. He clung to a lovely dream. Who would be so unfeeling as to drag him out of it?

"Avery, love, you must wake up."

Rachael? Perhaps she was part of the dream. It was slipping ever more from his grasp. Something jabbed him in the ribs. He forced his eyes open and grunted his displeasure.

"Heavens, you are a sound sleeper."

Ah, yes, that was Rachael, and she looked annoyed. Her nightgown was on and her hair altogether too tidy. He would have to ravish her.

"You must get up. It has grown very late, and if we don't sneak out soon we won't have enough time to investigate the house."

Damn. He wished he had slept through until morning. Spying on his traitorous colleague was the last thing he wanted to do.

It could be the end of it.

If they could find concrete evidence, they could take it to the authorities. All they needed was something as simple as a page of notes, and Purcell was an inveterate record-keeper.

Begrudgingly, Avery crawled from the bed and began to dress himself in the dirt-splattered suit from their involuntary steam car race. He preferred his new clothes, though they weren't yet properly tailored. This ensemble, sadly, was more appropriate for tromping through fields in the dead of night—if such a thing could ever be termed appropriate.

Rachael tied the necktie for him. Her knot wasn't as crisp as if his valet had tied it, but he liked it regardless. He didn't pass up excuses to let her touch him.

Gloves of sturdy leather completed the outfit. They were new and stiff, and he flexed his fingers to break them in a bit. There would no doubt be potions everywhere if Purcell's lab was indeed at the Landry house. Avery wouldn't risk touching anything bare-handed.

They crossed to Rachael's room, where she swiftly donned her own outfit. She buttoned her man's shirt over a simple corset and took a glimpse in the mirror, nodding her approval. She pinned her hat in place, pulled on her gloves, and they set out.

The halls were dark. The small inn shuttered its doors and doused the lights at half-past ten. With no keys, and no knowledge of how to pick a lock, Avery and Rachael were forced to turn to a window to make their exit. They chose a secluded location, near to a corner at the back of the building.

Avery helped Rachael up and over the sill before climbing out himself. He pushed the window all but closed. Rachael wedged a stick into the gap. He smiled and nodded his thanks, though he didn't know how well she could see him. Slivers of moonlight shone through gaps in the clouds. His eyes hadn't yet fully adjusted, but he could see enough to walk.

"I didn't think to bring a lantern," he whispered.

"It would give us away," Rachael replied. "We are better without."

He nodded once more and gestured for her to follow. They slunk through the town, eerie in its silence, taking what Avery hoped was the correct route. At length, they happened upon a battered wooden sign for "Grovesdale Manor." A pitted, dirt path wound uphill, away from town, just wide enough for a single carriage.

"We will follow this for now," he suggested. "If we spot anything suspicious, we can move off the road, and when we approach the house, we should be more circumspect."

"I agree. I'm prepared to run, if necessary." Her brow furrowed. "Though I hope it won't be necessary. It makes one all hot and sweaty."

They lapsed back into silence. Avery flexed his fingers as he walked. The gloves remained stiff. Several minutes in, Rachael began to hum and, eventually, to sing. He recognized his drinking song, though she had improved upon the tune.

"*Oh, it ain't such a pity to be in the city, with the smog and the rats and the whores—*"

"Rachael, dear, you oughtn't sing that."

"Because it's not very ladylike?"

"Because someone might hear us."

"I don't think anyone else is up and about at this time of night. If there are guards, they will be nearer the house."

"Perhaps." He had to admit the silly song helped calm the nerves, much as it had the night they had written it.

"What is smog?" she asked a moment later. "Smoky fog? I don't think it's a real word."

He shrugged. "It is now."

"Hmm."

She returned to humming, continuing on until they spied the house looming in the distance. The structure was ghostly in the streaky moonlight. Sections of brick and glass appeared and disappeared from view, seeming to wink in and out of existence.

"Lord, it looks haunted," Rachael whispered.

"Nonsense. You've read too many novels."

"Miss Landry's ghost may be flittering around, begging

Purcell to help her. It would drive anyone mad, I imagine. Perhaps he thinks he can set her spirit free by cursing people."

Avery gaped at her. "You can't possibly believe in ghosts."

"Well, I don't honestly know," she answered primly. "I've never encountered such a thing. But Purcell might believe. He must have *some* reason. Let's head out in that direction and circle around to the back of the house. If there's a laboratory, it wouldn't be anywhere near the front entrance."

"Good thinking." He decided to drop the matter of ghosts for the moment. "I suggest we try to maintain this distance until we find a good location from which to approach. Perhaps something with bushes or the like to provide cover."

Rachael took his hand. "We shouldn't talk any longer. We'll need a signal. If you see any danger, hoot like an owl."

"Absolutely not," he hissed. "It's bad enough I'm trespassing in the first place. I will not behave like a ninny."

"What do you propose, then?"

"I will continue to hold your hand. If one of us sees anything suspicious, we need only squeeze."

"And if we become separated?"

"I will take pains to ensure that doesn't happen."

She gave a curt nod and strode off. Unable to release her hand, he had no choice but to follow.

The tall grass and wildflowers, pretty by day, made for treacherous footing in the ever-shifting moonlight. Their steps were slow, deliberate, but still they crunched and rustled through the brush. Even beneath the incessant chirping of insects, Avery's every footfall rang in his ears. He shivered, and pretended it was only the night breeze.

Rachael, with her nerves of steel, continued to lead. His grip on her hand was like iron. If anything happened to her because of this, he would never forgive himself. He wished she were safe at home, yet he knew he couldn't do this without her.

An elegant glass and steel conservatory jutted from the southeast corner of Grovesdale Manor. Fashionable gardens surrounded it, providing plenty of places to hide as Rachael and Avery crept nearer. Avery saw no signs the house was guarded, and no lights illuminated the windows. Even the crickets seemed to have calmed. The place was still as death.

Rachael pressed her face to the glass to peer inside. Avery did the same, squinting into the darkness. When the clouds shifted and moonlight at last penetrated the overhead windows, he spied a laboratory bench along the far wall where the conservatory connected with the house. Neatly arranged equipment covered the table, with more on the shelves above.

Rachael gasped.

"What did you see?" he whispered.

"Corncockles. Dozens at least. You?"

"Lab equipment."

A strange burst of excitement ran through him. Their efforts hadn't led them astray. This was unquestionably Purcell's base of operations. The thrill of discovery was tempered by the thought of the next step. They would have to break in.

Rachael was already moving. He hurried after her, anxiety once again pounding through him. If he didn't stay glued to her side, she wouldn't hesitate to run off on her own. Stubborn, remarkable woman. She was his life. If things went sour, he was prepared to kill to protect her.

A strange thought entered his mind.

"Who killed your first husband?" He had a suspicion. For a time he'd thought it must have been Henry Ainsworth, but now he had an alternate theory.

"Why do you ask?" Rachael's tone was wary. She wouldn't betray a friend's confidence.

"I should like to thank her."

Rachael flinched. He had guessed correctly. His arm wrapped around her.

"It's remarkable what we do for those we love," he murmured into her hair. "I will do whatever it takes."

She spun around and kissed him, hard. "So will I."

The kiss stunned him, but he had no time to contemplate its implications or those of her words. Glass tinkled. She had used her elbow to smash out a door panel. She reached through the opening and unlatched the door from the inside. It swung open on well-oiled hinges. Avery took a deep breath and followed his wife into the laboratory.

XL

Discoveries

ᎡACHAEL MADE ONLY A CURSORY EXAMINATION of the many plants in the conservatory. Aside from the numerous corncockles, she spied several common herbs, and plenty of things she didn't recognize. She assumed most of them were intended to be mixed into potions.

She turned her attention to the table of equipment. It contained a microscope, two burners, and a number of vessels and utensils for mixing. They all appeared clean and precisely placed—no less than she would have expected.

Avery lit a lamp sitting on the corner of the bench. Even turned down low, it would ruin their night vision, but they would need the light to read any papers they found. He opened the cabinets above the laboratory bench and angled the lamp to illuminate the insides.

Rachael moved to the desk that stood off to the left, just past the door leading into the house. She tried the wide, center drawer first and found it locked. Annoyed, she yanked on a side drawer. It stuck fast. Only the center drawer sported a keyhole. She would need to get it open to get into any part of the desk. She glanced around for a useful tool. Nothing sat atop the desk except a single leather cup with several pens and pencils.

She returned to the laboratory bench to see what she could find. Avery stood leafing through a large notebook.

"Look at this," he murmured. "He has catalogued everything in these cabinets. All his experimental potions." He ran his finger across the page beneath an entry dated several months earlier. "Basic stamina potion: unsuccessful. Shelf five, number sixteen." He pointed. "Every shelf is labeled to match. Most of the early entries say 'unsuccessful.' He has kept them regardless. Somewhere in here must be his poisons. I don't yet see a pattern to the shelving, so I will have to search the book."

"Keep at it. I'll open his desk and search the papers. Something here will give us evidence enough to convince the police."

Rachael picked up a sturdy apothecary's spoon and a scalpel and took them to the desk. She began with the scalpel, sliding its thin blade into the keyhole. She poked, prodded, jiggled, but the lock didn't budge. When she poked harder, the blade broke off inside.

She tossed the broken scalpel onto the desk. Perhaps brute force would work where finesse had failed. Rachael jammed the handle of the spoon into the lock and felt it shudder. She pushed the spoon deeper, wiggling and twisting. Metal groaned. She pried at the lock, pulling on the drawer with her opposite hand.

The spoon snapped and the drawer flew open at the same moment. Rachael staggered backward. A triumphant grin spread across her face as she regained her footing. It wasn't the most elegant break-in in history, perhaps, but she had succeeded.

When she looked into the drawer, her pleasure grew into elation. The missing piece of tapestry lay inside, its purple corncockle visible even in the shadows. Several other artifacts accompanied it. She would leave those to Avery.

With the center drawer ajar, the others now slid easily open. The top right drawer was packed with letters, standing back-to-back. She pulled one out and held it up to the light.

It was addressed from Mr. Robert Purcell to Miss Amelia Landry.

"Avery, I need more light."

He pointed the lamp toward the desk and jogged to her side. "What have you found?"

"Letters. And your missing tapestry."

He dove at the center drawer, eager to get his hands on the artifacts. Rachael opened the letter and scanned it. It was what she would have expected from a prudish sort of man trying to woo a young woman—friendly and proper, and not particularly interesting. The next letter, Miss Landry's reply, was similar. Rachael flipped through more of their correspondence. Purcell had every letter ordered by date. She wondered if the man still had his baby teeth stored somewhere.

The letters began to change further to the back. Miss Landry's replies became less frequent and more terse. She made references to a Major Breitstone. Purcell's missives at last admitted to his feelings, sounding desperate. Rachael found the entire thing depressing. She skipped to the last letter in the drawer, written by Miss Landry.

It was short, smudged in places with tear stains. "My Dear Robert," it began, the first time she had used Purcell's given name. Rachael's hands shook as she read it.

> *I am sorry to bother you, but I have no one to turn to. How can I have been so deluded? I have been terribly deceived as to Major Breitstone's character. He has deserted me. I am certain, now, he never intended to marry me at all. I do not know what will become of me. I am ruined. I feel you deserve the truth. You have always been a friend to me, and for that I owe you great thanks.*
>
> *Yours in despair,*
> *Amelia Landry*

Rachael blinked back a tear. The poor girl. Seduced and abandoned, she had taken her own life rather than face the world. No wonder Purcell had been devastated. It didn't explain, however, what might have led him to want to curse everyone. She replaced the letter and moved on to the opposite drawer.

It contained only a single field notebook, well-used, with the corners of several pages folded down to mark places of importance. Rachael grimaced. How could such an organized man dog-ear the pages of a book? It was a sign of his madness, no doubt.

The notebook bulged out in places, where other bits of paper or pressed plant specimens had been pasted in. Rachael thumbed through it. This was his working journal, with his analysis of the tapestry fragment and other research relating to the curse. An entire section from an old book had been glued inside. She opened to a page labeled in Purcell's deliberate writing, "Cantrell curse—excerpt from book of folklore, c. 1593."

"Avery," she breathed. She turned to her husband, who was still bent over the frayed tapestry. "Look—"

A noise from inside the house stopped her mid sentence. Avery ran to douse the light. He reached the workbench too late. The door opened. Miss Pelham stood in the entryway, wrapped in a dressing gown, her mouth open in shock.

"You!" she gasped in horror. It wasn't the exclamation of a woman relieved to see her rescuers.

Rachael dropped the notebook. Before Miss Pelham could recover from her surprise, Rachael grabbed her about the waist and clamped a hand over her mouth.

"Outside," Rachael ordered her husband, pushing Miss Pelham toward the garden door before he could utter a word.

XLI

Persuasion

A VERY TURNED OUT THE LIGHT and ran into the garden, still holding the tapestry. He tucked it inside his coat. If they had to flee he wouldn't leave it behind.

Rachael dragged Miss Pelham behind a hedgerow, where they couldn't be seen from the house. Miss Pelham squirmed, but Rachael had the advantage in both height and weight, as well as possessing a significantly more determined temperament.

"I intend to release you," Rachael told Miss Pelham, her voice ringing with authority. "Do not scream or attempt to run, or I shall be forced to seize you once again. It is most unrefined, and I shouldn't like to find it necessary."

Rachael relaxed her grip and took a single step back from the other woman. Miss Pelham jumped away.

"Unrefined?" Her voice squeaked. Avery couldn't determine whether it was from fear or indignation. "Says a woman wearing… that?"

"You aren't one to talk, wandering about in your nightclothes. What are you doing up at this hour?"

"I often wake at night and must walk about before

returning to sleep. I heard a noise and came to investigate. And good thing I did, for I found you in the midst of a crime!"

Avery stepped between the two women. "Miss Pelham, are you well? We were quite worried when you disappeared from the hotel."

Annie Pelham met Avery's questioning gaze with a puzzled frown. "Disappeared? I never disappeared. Robert invited me to aid his research."

"Oh, hell," Rachael swore. "She's fallen in love with her kidnapper!"

"I have not fallen in love with anyone," Miss Pelham replied primly, "and I was not kidnapped. I am here of my own free will."

"You are a willing participant in these murders, then?"

"Certainly not! How dare you make such an accusation? I have done nothing but work to save lives!"

"Save lives? You are spreading poison. Afflicting hundreds with a deadly curse."

"No! We are preventing infection from *dangerous* potions."

Rachael threw up her hands. "For heaven's sake. How can you be so naive? This is impossible. Don't let Miss Pelham run off, Avery, dear. I'm going back for that journal. It will help convince our misguided companion here, as well as the police. Give me a few minutes more to look around, and then we will return to the inn."

She darted around the shrubbery and vanished.

"Rachael—"

Avery wanted to run after her, but he couldn't leave Miss Pelham behind or take her back to the house and risk her alerting other members of the household. He stared in the direction Rachael had gone, though he couldn't see her through the bushes. He would give her ten minutes, no more. If he could wait that long.

"Horrid woman," Miss Pelham sniffed.

Avery's head snapped around. "You are speaking of the love of my life. Kindly refrain from insulting her."

"My apologies."

It was difficult to puzzle out Miss Pelham's expression in the dark, but he didn't think she looked contrite.

He adopted his best professorial manner. "My dear Miss Pelham, this is no time for a civilized individual to be up and about. I should very much like to escort you to a safe and comfortable bed before turning in myself. In order for that to happen, however, we must clear up this misunderstanding between us. You say Purcell has brought you here, uncoerced, in the capacity of an assistant?"

"That is correct."

"I'm sorry to say I have lately seen a great deal of evidence indicating he is responsible for a number of deaths. That has not been your experience?"

"Certainly not. We are doing good work. Saving lives."

Her demeanor was calm without Rachael nearby. Avery spoke just as he had during their previous interviews, hoping she too would fall into old habits.

"May I ask how?"

"Professor Purcell has been developing an inoculation against dangerous potions. You gave him the idea, yourself, sir, with your hereditary intolerance for potions of any kind."

"And how do you contribute to this work, Miss Landry? Are you making potions?"

"I have been employed chiefly with the care and harvesting of herbs. Many you saw in the conservatory, but most of my time has been spent here in the gardens. I also have harvested nectar from the corncockles. I understand the ancient recipe is vital for the inoculate."

He nodded. The moonlight illuminated him. He tried to look thoughtful and unthreatening. "I'm not quite understanding this concept of 'dangerous' potions. Perhaps it's because they are all dangerous to me. Could you explain further?"

"I have very little familiarity with potions myself," she replied. "They are uncommon in my village. It seems, however, a great many people use them without checking their origins. With no system in place to guarantee purity of ingredients or quality of production, people are vulnerable to harmful concoctions. Now that people are digging up serum anywhere and producing cheap potions by the hundreds, the problem has become an epidemic."

"Purcell has told you this?"

"Yes, and the Landrys have confirmed it. They have been such gracious hosts. Dear Mr. Landry is infirm, and his wife spends all her time caring for him. I don't think they ever recovered from the loss of their daughter."

Avery pretended to know nothing of Purcell's past with the Landry family. "Miss Landry died recently?"

"Oh, no. Many years ago."

"Of course, and she was a friend to Professor Purcell? Or relative?"

"A friend, I believe. Poor Amelia was a victim, you see. A bad potion drove her mad and she jumped from the church tower. Fortunately, the professor was able to testify to the true reason behind her fall and save her from a suicide's grave."

"The family must be very grateful."

"Indeed. They have given him this workspace in her memory. He is dedicated to ensuring others do not suffer the same fate."

Avery nodded. He had some understanding, at last, of Purcell's goal.

"Miss Pelham, I was informed that two members of this household met a sad end in recent days. The villagers are calling it a plague."

"A terrible tragedy," she sighed. "The professor tried to warn them, but they insisted on using a suspect hair tonic. I'm afraid the inoculation he had given them failed. But there is hope! He returned from the latest trip to London with excellent news. He believes the last attempt to have been a success. He says hundreds have been protected."

A sick feeling lodged in Avery's stomach. Hundreds, stricken with the same curse that had made his own life hell. This needed to end tonight.

"Miss Pelham, I apologize if what I am to say next upsets you. I am aware you relish the opportunity to go out in the world and do some real good. Unfortunately, my wife was correct that you have been deceived. We have recently learned of a number of deaths in London caused when people drank potions—ordinary potions, some medicinal, from reputable sources and quite safe.

"What Purcell has termed an 'inoculation' is, in fact, a curse. He has fed this concoction to unwitting victims, giving them the same allergy from which I suffer. It's not something I would wish on anyone, even an enemy. It is my firm belief that he wishes to rid the world not of bad potions, but of all potions. He cannot banish serum from the earth, but if he spreads this curse widely enough, potions will become not only useless, but feared. Society will be forced to change, and not for the better. We will lose our medicines and our fuels, just as they are becoming affordable to all. I detest potions, and even I can see the devastation this would bring."

Miss Pelham shook her head. She didn't want to believe him. He couldn't blame her. She came from a village where potions were rare and mysterious things. Purcell could be charming, in a modest manner she would relate to. They were on a first-name basis and that suggested she had feelings of friendship for him, at the least. Disillusionment would be painful.

Her posture betrayed her worries. Her shoulders were hunched, her arms crossed over her chest. Avery couldn't ascertain whether she feared him, or only the truth.

"I'm certain Purcell believes he is in the right," Avery said. "He has a vision for a potionless utopia, and he sees the deaths this curse will cause as a necessary step to achieve that future. I can't say what drove him to this, only that I suspect Miss Landry's death played a role."

Miss Pelham gave a single nod. Not agreement, perhaps, but an acknowledgement of his words. It gave him hope.

"Please, allow me to walk you back to the house," he offered, extending his arm. "I will present you with my evidence, and if you aren't convinced by the time we reach the conservatory, I will speak no more on it. You will be free to remain here, or accompany us, as you like. Come. I'm concerned for Rachael and won't be at ease until we are reunited."

She hesitated. Avery tried not to fidget. He couldn't stand being away from his wife. If Miss Pelham refused to return with him, he would leave her here. He wouldn't wait any longer.

He was ready to turn away when her arms unfolded and she placed a trembling hand on his arm.

"The first trouble was a worker dying at our excavation," he began. This was his last chance to convince her. He would give it his best shot.

XLII

Things Fall Apart

THE WITCH-QUEEN IN HER FURY mixed a tisane of sage, chicory root, and deadly nightshade. The nectar of a single ryeweed flower infused the brew with her foul magick. Slipping it into his wine, she toasted his health, and he drank. After but a single swallow, he choked and collapsed. The Witch-Queen was seized and executed, but her revenge was complete. The Warrior-King woke from his near-death, seeming in good health, not knowing she had reversed him such that all remedies were now to him as poison.

Rachael closed the journal without reading further. The bastard! Not only had he possessed the knowledge of the corncockle, but he'd had a recipe for the curse, and he'd hidden it from Avery. She wanted to punch him right in his priggish face.

Her eyes darted to the cabinets, still open from Avery's investigations. Somewhere on those shelves was the curse potion. The poison that had killed the digger was likely there as well. The tiny vial she had found at the dig site held no more than a quarter of what these larger bottles could hold. Organized Purcell would have saved the rest. Either potion would give the police all the evidence they needed.

She flipped the cabinets closed so as not to bang her head, and pointed the lamp at Purcell's hand-written catalogue. She bypassed the early pages, scanning for dates from this spring or summer. The man had conducted an insane number of experiments. She was up to entry 756, and there were several more pages to examine.

A noise made her jump. She looked toward the door. She had neglected to close it after Miss Pelham had entered. The light from the desk lamp spilled into the hall.

"Annie? Are you working at this time of night?"

Purcell! Rachael snatched up the journal and clutched it to her chest. She could run and take it with her. She flicked off the lamp. She would have a better chance in the dark.

Two large lights flared overhead. They were so bright Rachael squinted. Purcell stood by a switch on the wall, regarding her with an expression of mixed anger and amusement.

"It seems we have an intruder."

"Better that than a murderer."

Purcell's affable features twisted into an ugly scowl. "I knew from the first you would be trouble, you interfering slattern. Cantrell never should have married you."

"Why? You think he wouldn't have found you out without my help? That is flattering, but he is clever enough to have done, though perhaps not as quickly."

Purcell stepped over to the desk, opening one of the lower drawers Rachael hadn't searched. He withdrew a revolver. "Hand over that notebook, Mrs. Cantrell."

Rachael backed toward the garden door, still clinging to the journal. "Don't be a fool. You can't shoot me in cold blood and expect to get away with it."

He aimed the gun at her chest. "Stay where you are," he snarled.

Rachael froze. The man was insane. She couldn't expect him to listen to reason.

"Purcell!"

Her husband's deep voice echoed through the conservatory. Rachael glanced back automatically, feeling a rush of relief at the sight of him striding toward her. Miss Pelham huddled by the door, blocked from Purcell's sight by a clump of foliage. She hugged her arms across her chest, eyes wide, face drained of color.

Rachael's eyes darted back to Purcell in time to see the gun swing toward Avery. Terror coursed through her. He could shoot her husband. He could shoot them both. Was he truly as mad as that?

"Robert, put down the gun," Avery instructed, his voice soft and even, though not without authority. "You don't want to do this."

"No, I don't. But your interference has left me no choice. You have come to disrupt my work. You will have to be silenced for the greater good."

"Greater good? You are murdering people!" Rachael shouted the words, hoping she might wake another member of the household.

"No! I'm saving them! Freeing them from the elixirs of evil that poison their lives!" Purcell waved the gun at her, jerking it up and down to punctuate his words.

"Poison? *You* are the poisoner! First the digger, the man at the hotel, Professor Dashell... how many others?"

"Sacrifices must be made," he intoned. It sounded like a mantra. Rachael imagined him saying it to himself over and over as he worked.

"Sacrifices? Ha!" she scoffed. "Excuses! You're just a common killer."

He stalked toward her, wildly brandishing his weapon. "Shut your mouth, bitch!"

She took another step backward, her hand sliding along the workbench, feeling for anything she might use as a weapon or a shield.

"Rachael," Avery whispered. He had moved close enough she could feel him standing just past her left shoulder. "Run. I will shield you from him."

Rachael would countenance no such thing. She pretended she hadn't heard him. Her hand touched the metal frame of a laboratory burner.

"You've been using these 'evil elixirs' yourself," she persisted. "Dosing people with poisonous potions to test your methods. Do you deny it?"

Purcell said nothing. He steadied the gun with his other hand. Rachael's fingers felt for the switch on the burner.

"Do you? If this is such a good thing you are doing, why haven't you done it to yourself?"

"Sacrifices must be made!" he roared.

Rachael flipped the switch and hurled the burner at Purcell's face. He shrieked and flung up his hands to protect himself from the flames. Avery rushed him, knocking both men to the floor and sending the revolver flying. Avery scrambled after the weapon, grabbed it, and emptied the bullets onto the floor. He threw the unloaded gun out the door, into the dark hall.

Rachael couldn't fault her husband for his dislike of violence, but she wished he had kept the revolver for protection. She reached for the second burner to give herself another weapon, but when she turned the switch, it didn't light. It was empty of potion.

Avery picked himself up, and stared down Purcell, who cradled a burnt hand. "It's over Robert. I won't allow you to harm anyone else."

Purcell growled in rage. He scooped up the burner from where it lay flaming on the ground and spun to open a cabinet. He grabbed a handful of potions and dashed one on the ground at Avery's feet. Avery skittered backwards.

Rachael swung the unlit burner at Purcell, but he hardly

seemed to notice. He kept her at bay with the flame while he threw half a dozen more potions.

"You think these aren't evil?" he screamed. "You think they are 'safe' and 'good'?" More vials shattered against the tiles. Potions ran across the floor. "Why do you shy away from them? Come and stop me, Cantrell, if you are so determined!"

A bottle exploded at Avery's feet, splashing his boots and trousers. He jumped back in fear, tripped, and staggered. His hand shot out to steady himself, but when he spied a cluster of corncockles beside him, he jerked it away. The movement knocked him further off-balance, and he fell into a bed of herbs. Purcell grabbed another handful of potions.

Rachael charged him, prepared to suffer burns to protect her husband. Purcell surprised her by dropping everything in his hands and shoving her roughly away. He was stronger than she expected. She crashed to the floor, yelping in pain. By the time she clambered to her feet, he had already gathered a new armload of potions. He stalked toward Avery, who had only just struggled to his feet.

"You call this good?"

Avery ducked and covered his head as a potion sailed past him and shattered against the window.

"They are evil! Evil!" Each cry was accompanied by another crash. "They killed my Amelia! She never would have loved him! Not without these devil's elixirs!"

Rachael's heart pounded. Purcell had come unhinged. He had Avery backed into a corner. She spun about, desperate to find another weapon. The burners and other tools on the workbench wouldn't slow him for more than a moment. She had all but determined to try tackling him when a wrought iron plant stand caught her eye.

Rachael snatched the pot from atop the stand and shoved it into the trembling arms of Miss Pelham, who stood watching the scene in silent terror. She may have been a timid woman, but she was sensible enough not to drop the plant and alert Purcell to her presence.

Rachael hefted the metal jardiniere. The weight of it shocked her, and she struggled to carry it across the conservatory. She gritted her teeth and willed her arms to hold on. Her Avery was in danger.

"They aren't evil." Avery's voice remained calm. "I could attack you with a stick. It doesn't make trees evil." He ducked again, as a bottle flew perilously close to his head.

"Do you know what this is?" Purcell snarled. He uncorked a bottle. "It's a medicine. It lessens the symptoms of the common cold. If it's a good thing, then drink it!"

Rachael swung the plant stand with all her might. A crack reverberated through the room as the iron bars slammed into Purcell's back and head. He crumpled. Rachael dropped her improvised weapon and ran to her husband. His face was ashen. A yellowish liquid ran down his cheek and neck, soaking through the collar of his shirt.

"No, oh, no," she gasped.

"Rachael..." He staggered. His features contorted in pain.

She caught him and helped him down to the ground, frantically wiping away the potion with her sleeve. She didn't know if it would do any good. He had already begun to wheeze.

"Rachael," he began again.

"It's all right. I will make it right. You will be well." She willed her words to be true, prayed to God that they might be.

Avery grasped her hand. "I'm always well when I'm with you."

Tears welled in her eyes. "You won't die. You can't die. I won't let you!"

"I'm so sorry." His eyes closed.

"No!" A grief unlike any she had ever felt pervaded her. "Don't leave me!"

She couldn't be a widow again. She wasn't meant for a lifetime of veils and black crepe. She needed bright colors and gay parties. She needed to see and be seen. She was not a mourning person—but if she lost him, her devastation would be absolute.

"Avery!" she shouted.

His lids fluttered open again. He grimaced in pain. "Oh, my Rachael," he sighed.

A fierce determination surged through her veins. "You stay alive, do you hear me?" she commanded. "I'm going to fix this. If there's a curse, then there's a cure. I'm going to find it, goddammit!"

She leapt to her feet. He reached for her. "Rachael. Hold me," he gasped.

"Don't you die on me, Avery Cantrell, don't you dare!"

"Please."

She raced to the laboratory bench. "Write me a poem, Avery!" He needed to concentrate on something. She needed to know he was still alive. "Do it!"

He mumbled something.

"I can't hear you!" She grabbed Purcell's potions catalogue. She needed the curse potion. Elle had said that antidotes were often made from poisons.

"Nothing so… great," Avery babbled, "grand, vast… yes, vast."

"Good! Keep going!"

Rachael ran her finger down the page, flipped to the next, began again. She had no idea what she might do once she found the potion. She knew nothing about potion mixing.

"No man, no beast," he wheezed. He coughed, a horrible hacking sound that sent a knife of new fear through Rachael's heart. "No grass, no tree."

She whirled about, looking for the notebook she had dropped during her altercation with Purcell. If anything held a clue to a cure, it was the journal.

"No stream, no river, no lake, no sea." Avery's voice sounded weak, but calmer now.

Rachael found the book and opened it to the first marked page.

"No forest, no desert, no mountain high."

"That is beautiful, darling. Don't give up!" She wiped at the tears that ran down her cheeks and clouded her vision.

She turned pages wildly, hoping something would jump out at her. The book fell open to the place where the story of the Cantrell curse had been pasted in.

"No field, no earth, no cloud, no sky."

Rachael gasped. The story gave her a burst of hope. "She had reversed him," she murmured. If he were truly *reversed*, and all medicines became as poison, then poisons should help, rather than harm. It was a slim chance, but this version of the tale contained the recipe and was the most accurate of any they had encountered. Rachael had neither the time nor knowledge to make her own cure. She could take the chance or watch him die.

"No moon, no sun, neither stars up above."

Rachael scrambled back to the catalogue, turning to the date range for the potion that had poisoned the excavator. The entry read, "Attempt 5: unsuccessful, harmful." She read the number and yanked cabinet doors open.

"Not a one is so vast as my unending love."

An audible sob escaped her lips. She seized the correct potion and a bottle of brandy from a shelf of assorted ingredients.

"Avery! Avery, my love," she cried. She ran to his side.

His eyes were glazed, his cheeks devoid of color. She dropped to her knees and slid an arm beneath him, levering him into a half-sitting position. Her arm, still aching from wielding the jardiniere, protested the additional burden. Avery didn't seem able to help support himself. His breathing had grown shallow, and his eyelids drooped. Rachael used her teeth to pop the cork from the poison and pressed it to his lips.

"Drink."

She tipped the bottle, and he obediently swallowed a mouthful. Tremors wracked her body. The tears she had fought overcame her, and she wept. She didn't know whether she had neutralized the potion, undone his curse, or sealed his fate. She could only wait, and cry.

Rachael unstoppered the brandy and gave him a good, long drink, partly because she was certain the poison had tasted terrible, and partly to wash away any remnants so she might kiss him. She lowered him to the ground and pressed her body to his, one arm tightly around his waist, kissing his cheek and lips, splashing him with her tears.

"My Avery," she murmured. "I love you so. I love you more than anything in this world."

Rachael heard a sob from behind her. Miss Pelham, too, had come out of hiding and was weeping.

Avery sucked in a sharp breath, as if in intense pain, then slowly exhaled. Rachael felt his body relax beneath her. She sat up, terrified this was the end. He blinked a few times, then met her gaze. His eyes had regained some of their customary intensity.

"That was the worst damned brandy I've ever tasted."

"Oh, Avery, darling!" She flung herself back atop him, hugging and kissing him. This time his arms went around her, and he returned her kisses. Her joy lasted only a moment, before he lifted her off of him and sat up.

"My love, we aren't alone," he murmured.

"I don't care. You are no longer dying!"

He took her hand between both of his. "Thanks to you. What did you give me?"

"Poison."

His eyes grew wide. "Perhaps I ought not have asked."

"I will explain all in time."

"In a letter to your cousin, no doubt."

She laughed. It was the most satisfying laugh of her entire life.

"Perhaps I ought not ask this either," he said, his voice sober, "but do you really love me?"

"More than life," she vowed.

"I feared it may have been a fever dream, or that perhaps you said it only to encourage me to fight for life."

"Are you calling me a liar?"

"Er..."

She folded her arms across her chest. "Well, fine. Perhaps I won't love you any longer." She realized after she spoke that he might think her serious. "No! I'm only joking! I will love you forever, I swear it!"

He embraced her once again. "I don't doubt you, Rachael. I only wonder how I got so damned lucky."

"Your luck won't last forever, Cantrell."

Rachael and Avery turned together to see Purcell struggling to rise, a bloody handkerchief clasped to the back of his head.

"I'll send you to hell if it's the last thing I do," he snarled.

Miss Pelham walked over and dropped the flower pot on Purcell's head. The ceramic vessel shattered against his skull, and he went down in a heap of dirt.

"Shut your mouth, you manipulative madman," she commanded.

Rachael smiled up at her. "Miss Pelham—Annie. I wonder if you might assist me in rousing the household and summoning a constable? I don't wish my husband to exert himself until he is fully recovered."

Miss Pelham extended her hand. "It would be my pleasure, Rachael."

Epilogue

"SUCCESS!"

Rachael looked up from her correspondence as her husband burst into their hotel suite, a bottle of brandy and two empty glasses in his hands.

"I have here the very best cognac available to man," Avery announced proudly. "I've ordered three cases shipped home to London. You must try it." He set the glassware on the table and poured each of them a small measure of amber liquid before lowering himself into a chair.

Rachael took a dainty sip of the liquor. "You are determined to spend our entire fortune on spirits, it seems."

"Unless you spend it all on furniture first."

She gave him a wide smile. "I cannot deny the shopping has been excellent. Wilwood House will be grand when the redecoration is complete. We must throw another house party, but this time without picnics. We can hold an unveiling for the Greek goddess fountain. I've found a sculptor who comes highly recommended."

Avery toyed with his drink. "Did he ask you to model?"

"Don't be silly. He has replied to my inquiry saying that his assistant will be a perfect Aphrodite. He calls her *'une donzelle aux formes généreuses.'*"

Avery gestured at Rachael's papers. "Is that what you're about this afternoon, then? Reading lurid letters concerning nude women?"

She faked a frown. "Why do you ask? Do you want to read them?"

"Yes."

"Well, darling, I'm afraid I can't fulfill your wish. All I have here is the latest word from Isobel."

"And how is your cousin?"

"Well, it seems. Exceedingly thrilled about her own upcoming wedding, though she will give me none of the details." Rachael pushed the letter toward Avery. "Nothing! Look at this. Not a single word about flowers, the dress, the guest list. I'm terrified she and Mr. Bellamy mean to elope."

Avery adjusted his spectacles and peered down at the papers. "That would be tragic, indeed."

Rachael huffed. "You're making fun of me."

"But lovingly, my dear, always lovingly." He shuffled the papers, plucking out one of the newspaper clippings Isobel had forwarded. "What are all these?"

"Oh, the latest gossip columns. News and advice for ladies, that sort of thing."

"The Ladies' Guide to a Happy Marriage, by Mrs. Pythia Bowles," Avery read aloud. "You know, I met Mrs. Bowles once. Interesting woman. Her husband Eadric is a bit dull, though."

His laughing smile faded as he became absorbed in the article. Rachael clasped her hands in her lap, her muscles tense, trying not to fidget in the silence. She had Isobel's word that Pythia's columns had been well-received, but to watch someone reading in front of her was a strange and disquieting experience.

"Good God, Rachael," Avery said at last. "You're going to start a riot. This verges on scandalous."

"Why? Because I hint—very subtly, if I do say so—that every wife should do her best to please her husband in the bedroom?"

"No. Because you baldy state that she should expect, even demand, he do the same for her."

"I think it's entirely sensible."

"I agree." He raised his eyebrows and glanced toward the bedroom. "But it's still scandalous."

"Well, you know me. I love to set new trends. Speaking of which, this is the important article." She picked up another newspaper clipping and read a portion of it aloud. "The fashion of carrying specially-made personal silver has officially taken off. In the past week, Colonel Windbourne, Lord and Lady Pinehurst, and Mrs. George Hayward-Bryce have all been seen at the silversmith inspecting their new purchases. It is said that Lady Rachael Cantrell, most well-known for her daring mode of dress, recently acquired monogrammed silver for both herself and her husband while in Paris on her curiously-delayed wedding trip. If the fad has come so far that Parisian tableware is the cutting edge, so to speak, we must own the trend is here to stay."

"Rachael, how can you possibly know what these people are doing? We've been in Europe an entire month now."

The corners of her mouth ticked upward. "Elle's potions shop is directly across from a silversmith. Henry has provided me a list of additional names, if this article doesn't make it the done thing."

Avery's eyes shimmered with love, and he leaned in to press a gentle kiss to her lips. "I can never thank you enough for all you do for me."

"Nonsense. It is merely a paltry attempt to return some measure of your absurdly ardent love. Now, there is a letter here for you from Bellamy, as well. Read it and tell me what he has to say. Does he give better information about the wedding than my cousin does?"

Avery opened the letter and scanned it. "It doesn't appear so. He has news, though. Hunstable is back at school and doing well. He and Miss Pelham will be collaborating on a book using my notes and hers, annotated with photographs."

"Lovely. I will have to read it, though I expect I will find it somewhat boring."

Avery's lips curved. "That's my Rachael. Supportive of all your friends, even when you don't share their interests." He returned to the letter. "Bellamy also makes mention of Purcell. The doctors at the asylum have declared him dangerously unstable and he must remain there indefinitely. His thugs have been convicted and sentenced."

"That is good news."

"There is more. Work continues on producing a cure for those who were drugged with the curse. Every attempt thus far has proven unreliable. The corncockle serum is unstable, at least with our modern methods. Some people have risked drinking potential cures, but nearly half of them have perished."

Rachael nodded. "Elle's last letter said that she is testing methods of purification of the corncockle nectar in order to improve reliability. If anyone can make a true cure someday, she can. Though I can't imagine how she is still working when she could have her baby at any moment."

"She can take her time. I don't mind." Avery fished out the small bottle of poison he now wore around his neck. "In the meantime, I have this. I suppose we may never know whether it cured me entirely or merely counteracted the potion."

"There is no way to know, short of touching a potion."

He shifted his chair close enough to wrap an arm around her waist. "And I swore to you that I would never attempt such a thing. The poison is for emergencies only."

Rachael let her head drop onto his shoulder. "Does it bother you? Not knowing?"

"Not especially. I find I have made peace with myself as I am."

"That's good, because I love you desperately just as you are."

"If, one day, a safe and certain cure can be made, I will likely drink it. But I won't jeopardize a lifetime of happiness with you for the chance to be normal."

"Normal is overrated," Rachael replied.

"It is, love. It very much is." He downed the last of his drink and rose from his seat, taking her hands to help her to her feet. "I know we have some hours yet before we attend the opera this evening, but I'm afraid to inform you that there is a drastic shortage of lady's maids at this hotel and you will have to settle for your fumbling husband's assistance with changing your clothing. It may take a great deal of time, and I think we ought to begin at once."

Rachael wound her arms around his neck. "I can see you are taking Pythia's advice to heart."

"How can I not? She's my new favorite writer." He kissed Rachael soundly, then steered her towards the bedroom. "I have an idea for a truly sensational article once we return to England."

She swiftly did away with his coat and necktie, pressing kisses to his bared throat. "Oh? Do tell."

"Pythia will reveal the true author behind the warrior love poems: her husband Eadric."

Rachael froze with her fingers on his shirt buttons. "You wouldn't! Avery, it can't be terribly difficult for people to discover my true identity. If we attribute the poems to Eadric, you are certain to be revealed someday!"

He continued methodically working the laces of her bodice, as if she were his only care in the world. "If that happens, I'll simply tell the world you were my inspiration."

"But I wasn't."

He lifted his head, meeting her gaze and staring deeply into her eyes. "You are now. And always will be."

Hours later, as they lay tangled together in a contented embrace, he announced, "I've had another idea."

"What is it this time?"

He twisted a strand of her hair around his finger and murmured a long string of guttural sounds that she assumed must be Old English.

"What are you saying, Avery? I don't understand all that Anglo-Saxon chattering. Tell me your idea."

His green eyes danced with laughter. He gave her a quick kiss and a smile of pure happiness. "Volume Two."

The End

Extras

• • • ⟨binoculars⟩ • • •

A Ladies' Guide to Enjoying the Countryside

By Mrs. Pythia Bowles

My Dear Readers,

For those who wish to venture out of the city, Nature has abundant beauties to offer. In order to fully enjoy them, however, it is necessary to adjust one's habits, as country life and city life are as different beasts as fish and bird. In order to make your time in the outdoors as carefree and relaxing as possible, I offer you these tips:

1. *Cars are lovely. Driving slowly on a sunny day allows you to travel from one area to the next while seeing the world all around you. For inclement weather, a canvas roof will keep you and your belongings dry. Stylish goggles are a must.*

2. *Do <u>not</u> pack your usual daily changes of clothing. It sounds shocking that one might spend the entire day in the same dress, but a serviceable traveling outfit will do for most any time of day, and fashion in the country is more relaxed than we are accustomed to. There is not always room for many belongings at quaint country inns, and if you are hiking or picnicking, you will not want your best outfits to become soiled. Add a riding habit if you intend to ride, or an evening dress if you expect to attend a party, but no more.*

3. *The country is just as filthy as the city, only in a different way. Instead of smoke, trash, and unwashed factory workers, there is dust, mud, and unwashed farm workers. Expect to need to bathe and launder clothing as often as usual, or more if you are a frequent picnicker.*

4. *Good manners will go far. You may find yourself feeling out of place away from buildings, people, and the energy of life in town. Do not fret. Let your good breeding guide you. Polite greetings are always appreciated by the locals, and proper courtesies will ease your nerves. If you are uncertain what to say, the weather is <u>always</u> an acceptable topic.*

5. *Take a companion. Whether a friend, relative, or spouse, travel with someone whose company you enjoy. No matter how you may feel about country life, having someone with whom to share your opinions will make any journey more pleasant. Adhere to this rule, even if you follow no other, and you will come away from your adventure a happier person than before.*

Poems

Old English:
     Lýpig, lífbysig.
     Wit áfégaþ, wit áfiehtaþ.
     Sigefæstu samwist.

Literal translation:
     Solitary, struggling for life.
     We join, we fight.
     Victorious matrimony.

Sonnet:

For Rachael
The fall of your dark tresses, smooth and sleek,
The creamy smooth perfection of your skin,
The rosy blush of color in your cheek,
Your shapely curves, so soft, so feminine.
With but a look my heart is set afire,
Undone before your elegance and grace.
Your golden eyes, they smolder with desire,
And sparkle with a joy that lights your face.
A smile parts your lips, full, red, and fine.
I tremble when they do but speak my name.
That fateful day you pressed them up to mine,
It sparked a love too vehement to tame.
I'm lost to you, my darling. This I swear:
No gem was e'er so precious or so rare.

Limerick:

My lady's relentless sarcasm,
Has caught up my heart in a spasm.
It makes me so love her,
I must lie above her,
And f--- 'til she reaches orgasm.

Avery's Plea:

A Plea
Speak, my beloved. Sing me a song.
Yell at me, darling. Tell me I'm wrong.
Whisper, my angel, the secrets we keep.
Cry out my name in our bed ere we sleep.
Laugh at my foibles, joke of your own.
Coo at our babe, even after she's grown.
Talk, dearest one, of whatever you please.
Sigh in my arms, breathe the gentlest breeze.
Vow before God to be ever my wife.
Say that you love me, my heart and my life.

AVERY'S "DYING" WORDS:
    No man, no beast, no grass, no tree,
    No stream, no river, no lake, no sea.
    No forest, no desert, no mountain high,
    No field, no earth, no cloud, no sky.
    No moon, no sun, neither stars up above,
    Not a one is so vast as my unending love.

DRINKING SONG:
    The Great Outdoors (A Drinking Song)

    Intro:
    I have heard people say that a long country stay
    Can be good for the body and mind.
    But if you ever try, you may bloody near die.
    Let me tell you the things that you'll find:

    You can spend many hours admiring flowers
    With their colors so bright and so gay.
    But their blooms make you sneeze, and they're swarming
       with bees
    Who will sting if you don't keep away.

    So you look to the sky watching white clouds roll by,
    Never fearing a tempest might form.
    Then you'll probably drown as the rain hammers down
    When you're caught in a ruddy great storm.

    Chorus:
    Oh...
    It ain't such a pity, to be in the city
    With the smog and the rats and the whores!
    So... here I will stay, and I'll ne'er go away
    To the Great Outdoors!

Some say nature's treasures can bring you such pleasures.
"Go forth and enjoy all its charm!"
That natural beauty is trying to do me
A terrible bodily harm.

All the corncockle weeds with their poisonous seeds
Cause great pains when they mix with your corn.
When the insects begin to leave bites on your skin
You'll be ruing the day you were born.

Chorus

The sun overheats you, the wolves want to eat you,
They howl their ravenous call.
The vulture it loves you. It circles above you,
Awaiting the moment you fall.

There are foxes around, and the snakes on the ground
Lie in hiding to nip at your heel.
And I've heard that somewhere lives a vicious old bear
Who is eager to make you his meal.

Chorus

You can't walk for the roots that entangle your boots
And the hidden rocks smash all your toes.
Half your clothing gets torn when it's caught on a thorn
Why'd you stop just to smell that damned rose?

All the grass makes you itch, and you can't see that ditch,
So you're likely to fall on your face.
Now you're lying in clover and muddy all over.
Ah, the country's a marvelous place!

Chorus

No…
It ain't such a pity to be in the city
With the smog and the rats and the whores.
So… here I will stay, I won't dare go away
To the Great Outdoors!

About the Author

CATHERINE STEIN started reading at age two, when her mother noticed that she could tell the difference between words that started with the same letter. Ever since, she has wandered around with a book in her hand, her backpack, her purse, or even tucked down the back of her pants. A few years after she began to read, she also began to write, spending the majority of her school career writing non-school-related stories in her notebooks. Now she writes sassy, sexy stories set during the Victorian and Edwardian eras and full of action, adventure, magic, and fantastic technologies.

Catherine lives in Michigan with her husband and three rambunctious girls. She can often be found dressed in clothing that was purchased at a Renaissance Festival, drinking copious amounts of tea.

· · · ◦◦◦ · · ·

Visit Catherine online at
www.catsteinbooks.com
and join her VIP mailing list.

Follow her on Twitter @catsteinbooks,
or like her page on Facebook @catsteinbooks.

Also by Catherine Stein

The Earl on the Train

An earl with a problem.
A woman with a plan.
The journey of a lifetime.

How to Seduce a Spy

A barmaid with a rare talent.
A spy on a mission.
A love neither can resist.

Available at your favorite online retailer.

www.catsteinbooks.com

· · · 0🍷0 · · ·

Thank you so much for reading.
If you enjoyed the book and are so inclined, I would love for
you to leave a review. Happy readers make an author's day!

I love hearing from readers,
so feel free to contact me on social media, or email:

catherine@catsteinbooks.com